ANDERS
and the
COMET

Gregory Mackay

ALLEN&UNWIN
SYDNEY · MELBOURNE · AUCKLAND · LONDON

For inventive children

This project has been assisted by the Australia Council for the Arts Children's
Picture Book Illustrators' Initiative, managed by the Australian Society of Authors.

First published in 2015

Copyright © text and illustrations and hand-drawn fonts, Gregory Mackay 2015

Allen & Unwin
83 Alexander Street
Crows Nest NSW 2065
Australia
Phone: (61 2) 8425 0100
Email: info@allenandunwin.com
Web: www.allenandunwin.com

A Cataloguing-in-Publication entry is available
from the National Library of Australia
www.trove.nla.gov.au

ISBN 978 1 76011 115 1

Cover and text design by Gregory Mackay and Sandra Nobes
This book was printed and bound in July 2016 at Griffin Press, Australia.
www.griffinpress.com.au

3 5 7 9 10 8 6 4 2

anderscomics.com

MIX
Paper from
responsible sources
FSC® C009448

The paper in this book is FSC® certified.
FSC® promotes environmentally responsible,
socially beneficial and economically viable
management of the world's forests.

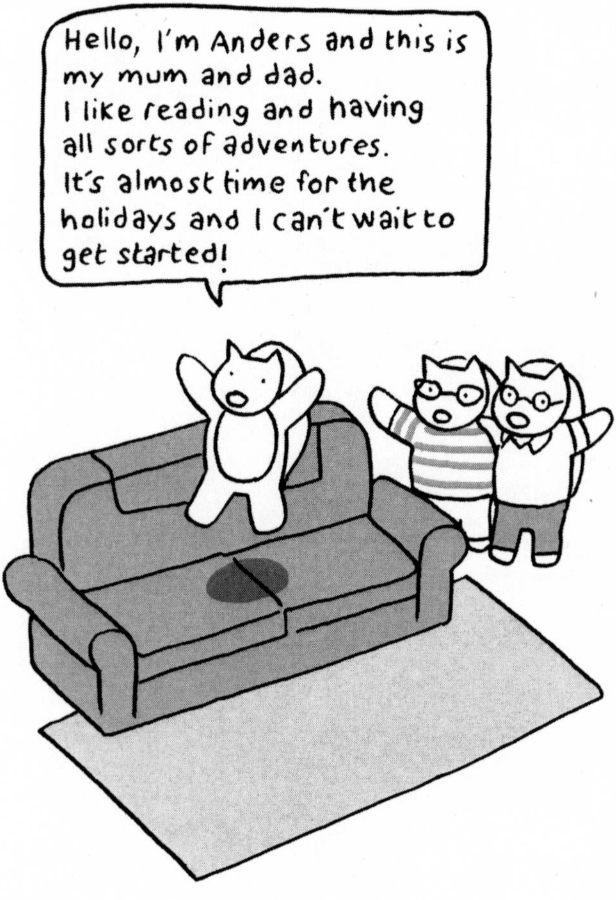
Hello, I'm Anders and this is my mum and dad. I like reading and having all sorts of adventures. It's almost time for the holidays and I can't wait to get started!

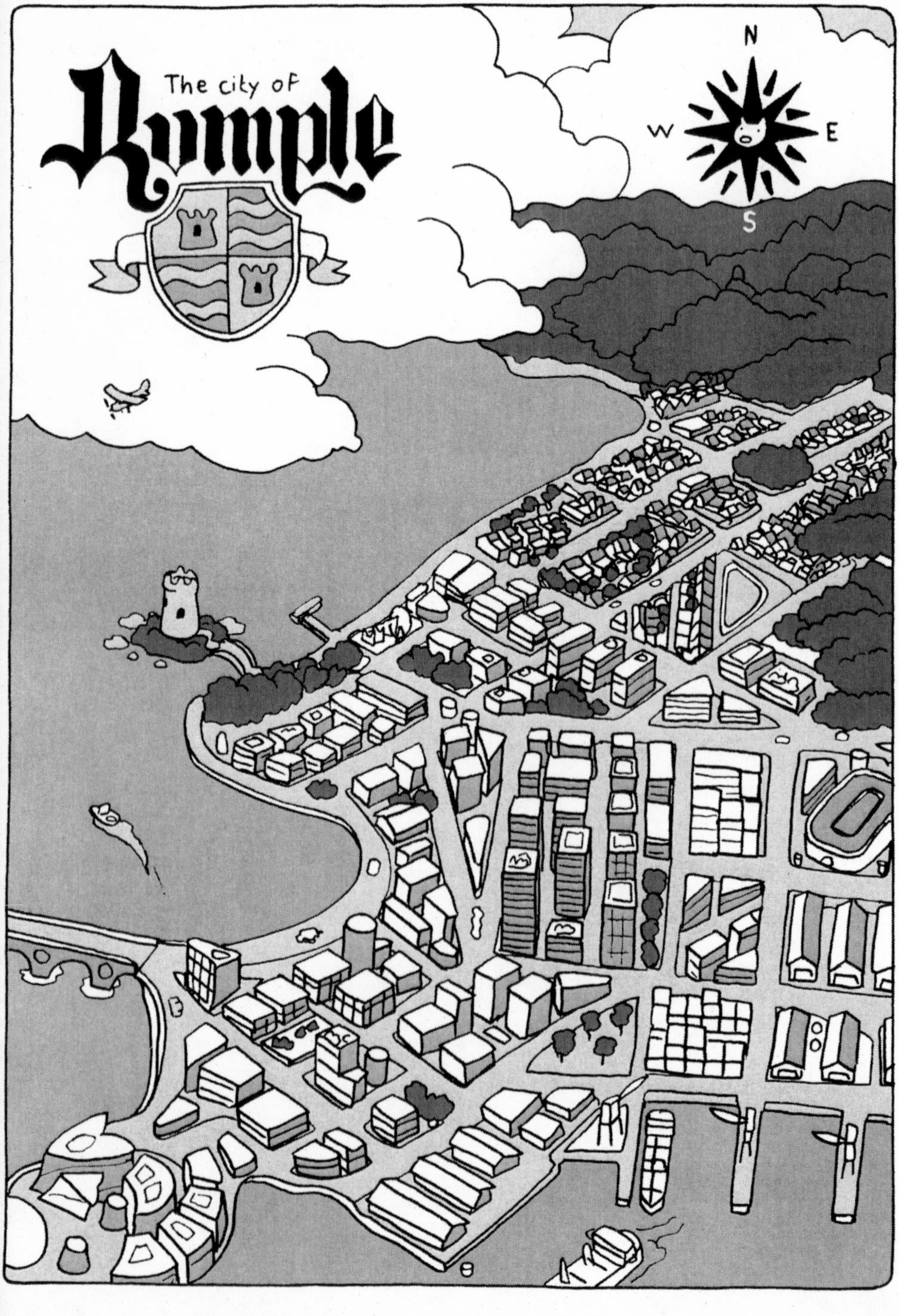
The city of
Rumple
N
W
E
S

Chapter 1

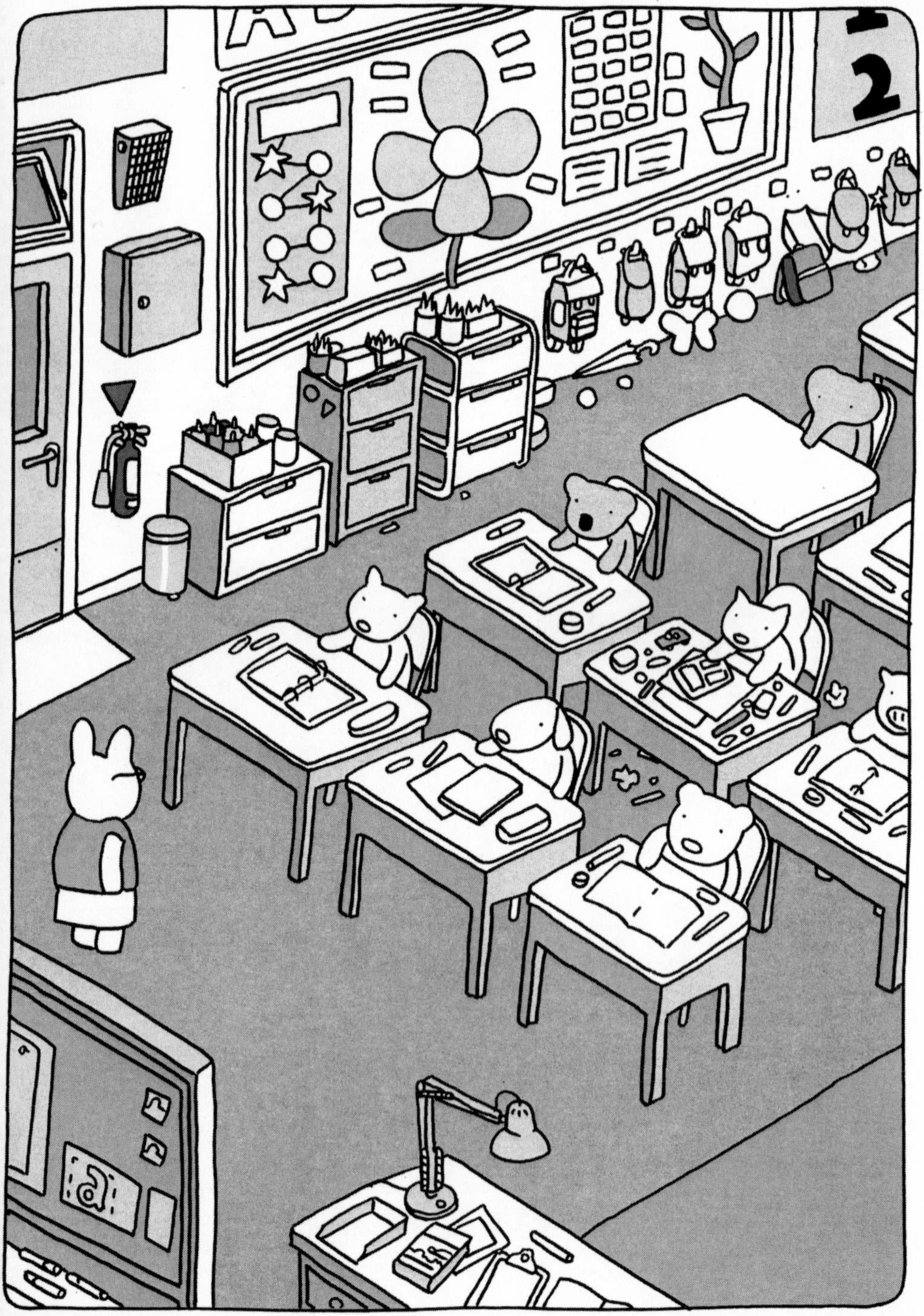
2
a

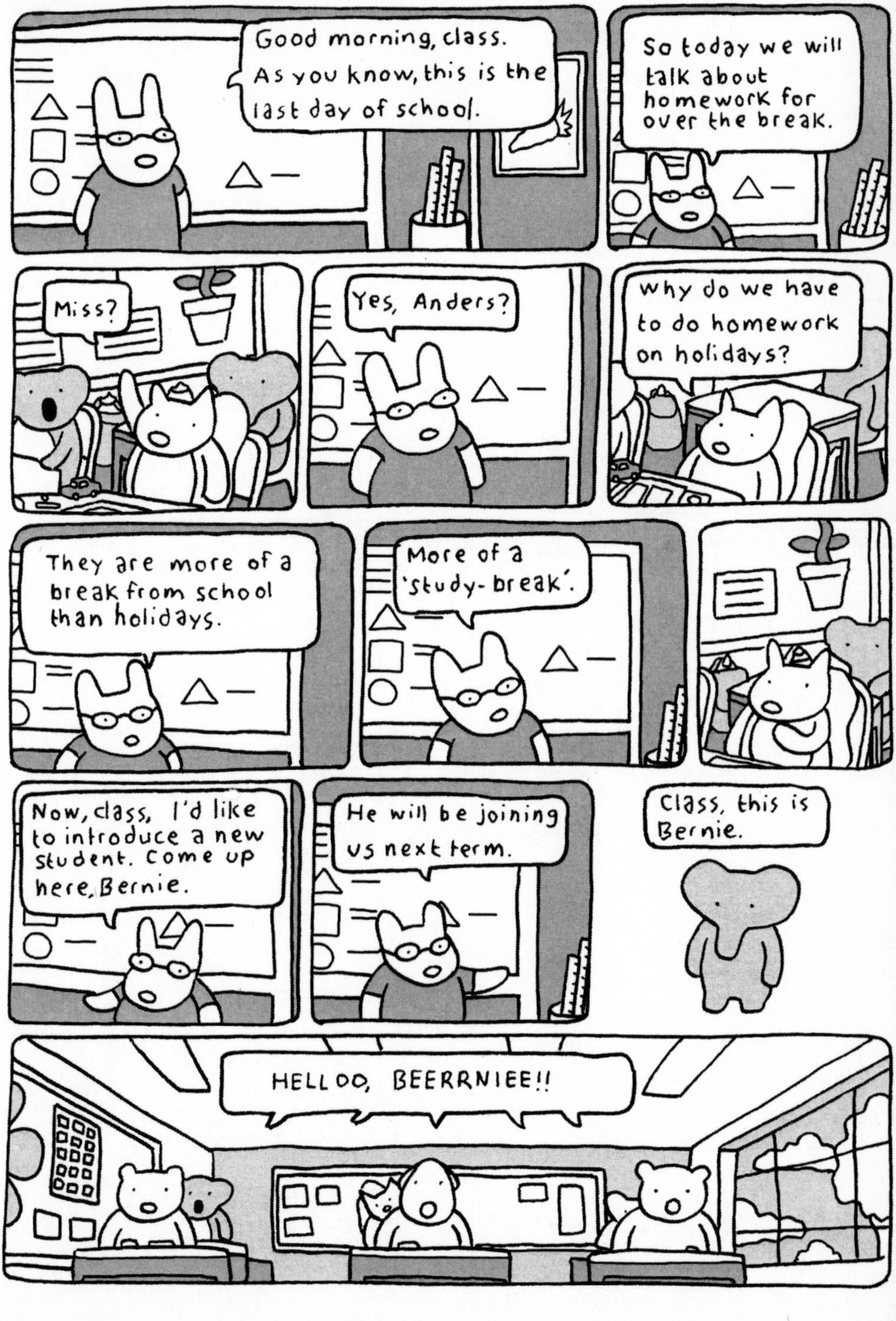
Good morning, class. As you know, this is the last day of school.
So today we will talk about homework for over the break.
Miss?
Yes, Anders?
Why do we have to do homework on holidays?
They are more of a break from school than holidays.
More of a 'study-break'.
Now, class, I'd like to introduce a new student. Come up here, Bernie.
He will be joining us next term.
Class, this is Bernie.
HELLOO, BEERRNIEE!!

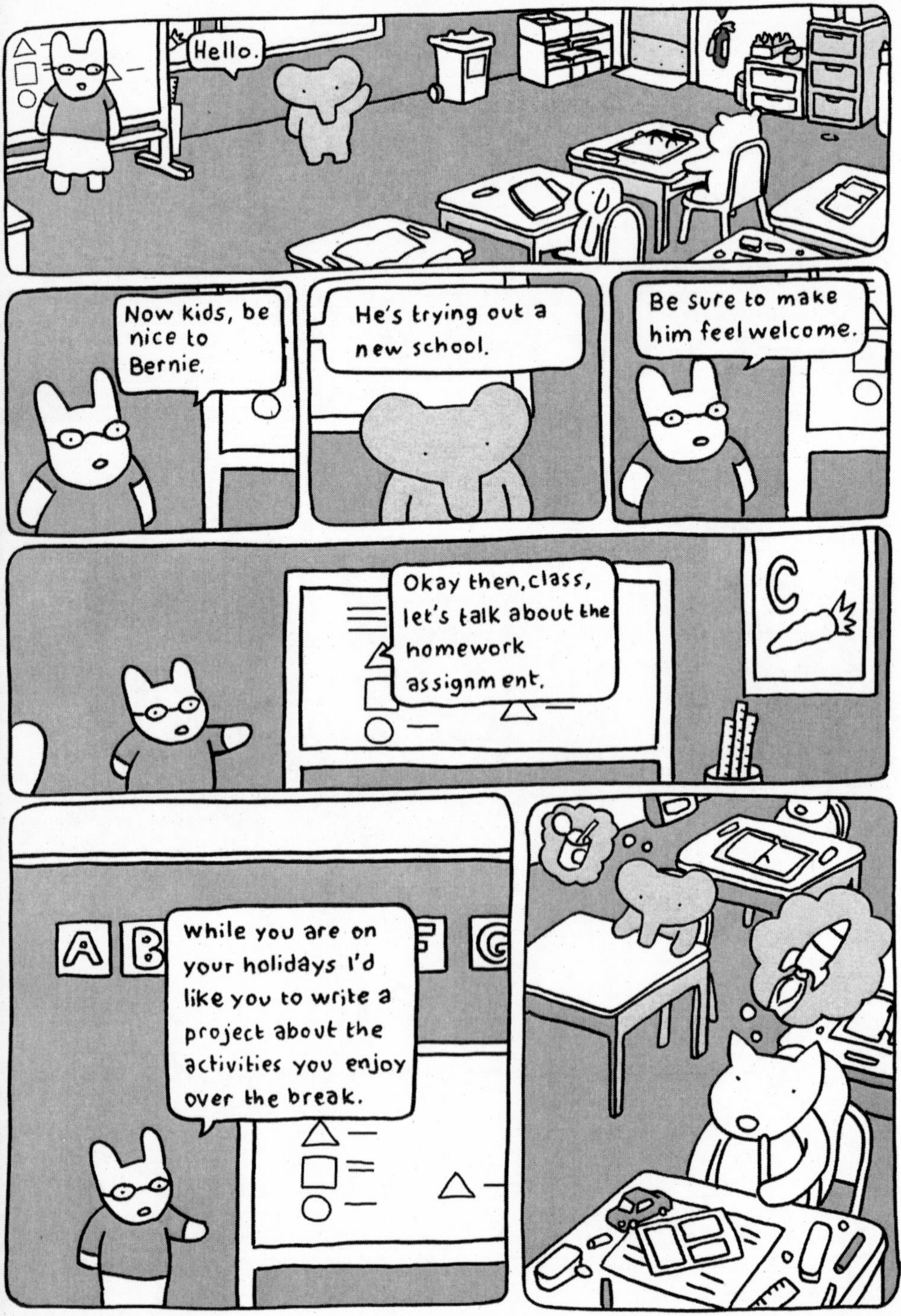
Hello.
Now kids, be nice to Bernie.
He's trying out a new school.
Be sure to make him feel welcome.
Okay then, class, let's talk about the homework assignment.
C
A
B
F
G
While you are on your holidays I'd like you to write a project about the activities you enjoy over the break.

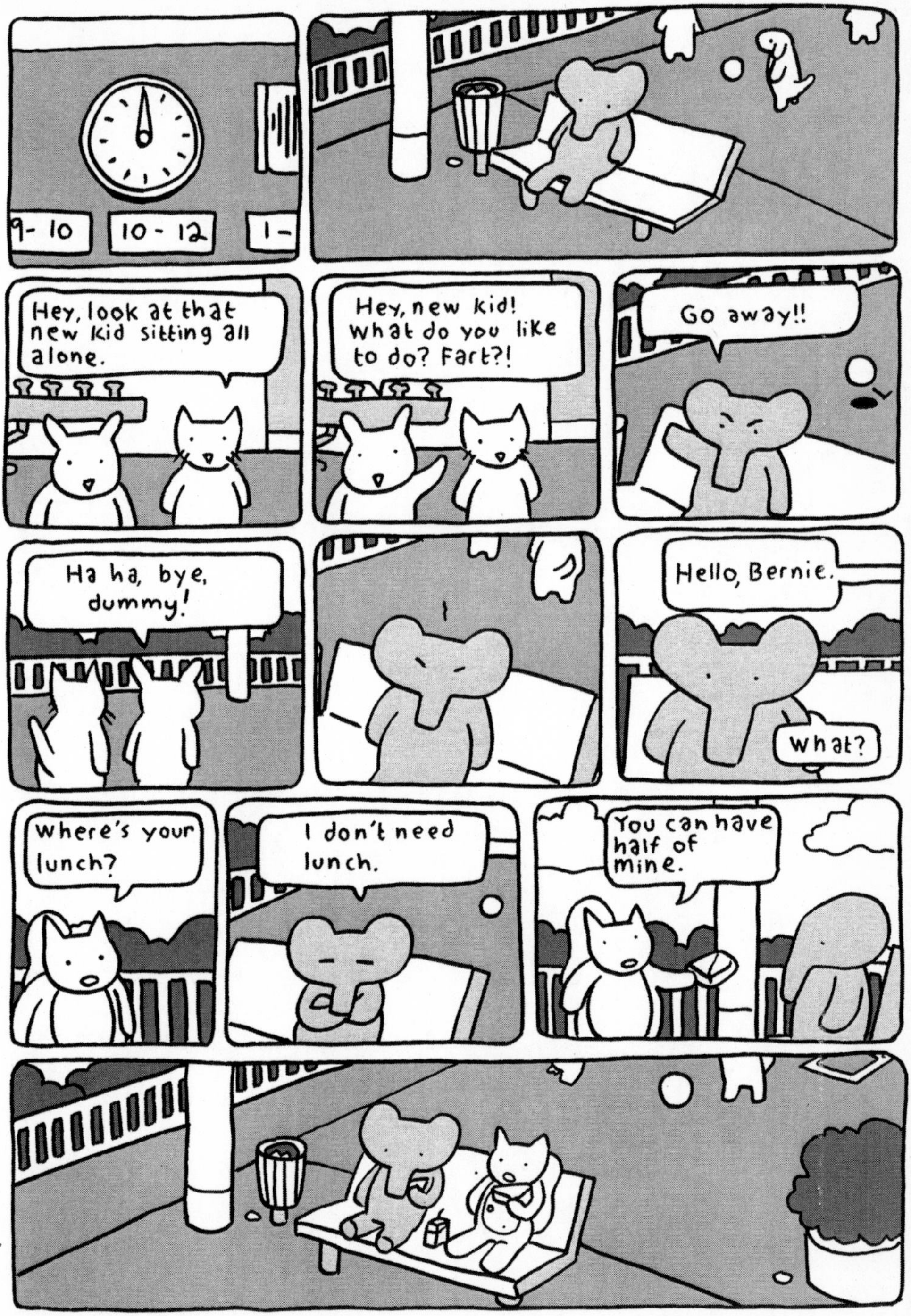
9- 10
10 - 12
1-
Hey, look at that new kid sitting all alone.
Hey, new kid! What do you like to do? Fart?!
Go away!!
Ha ha, bye, dummy!
Hello, Bernie.
What?
Where's your lunch?
I don't need lunch.
You can have half of mine.

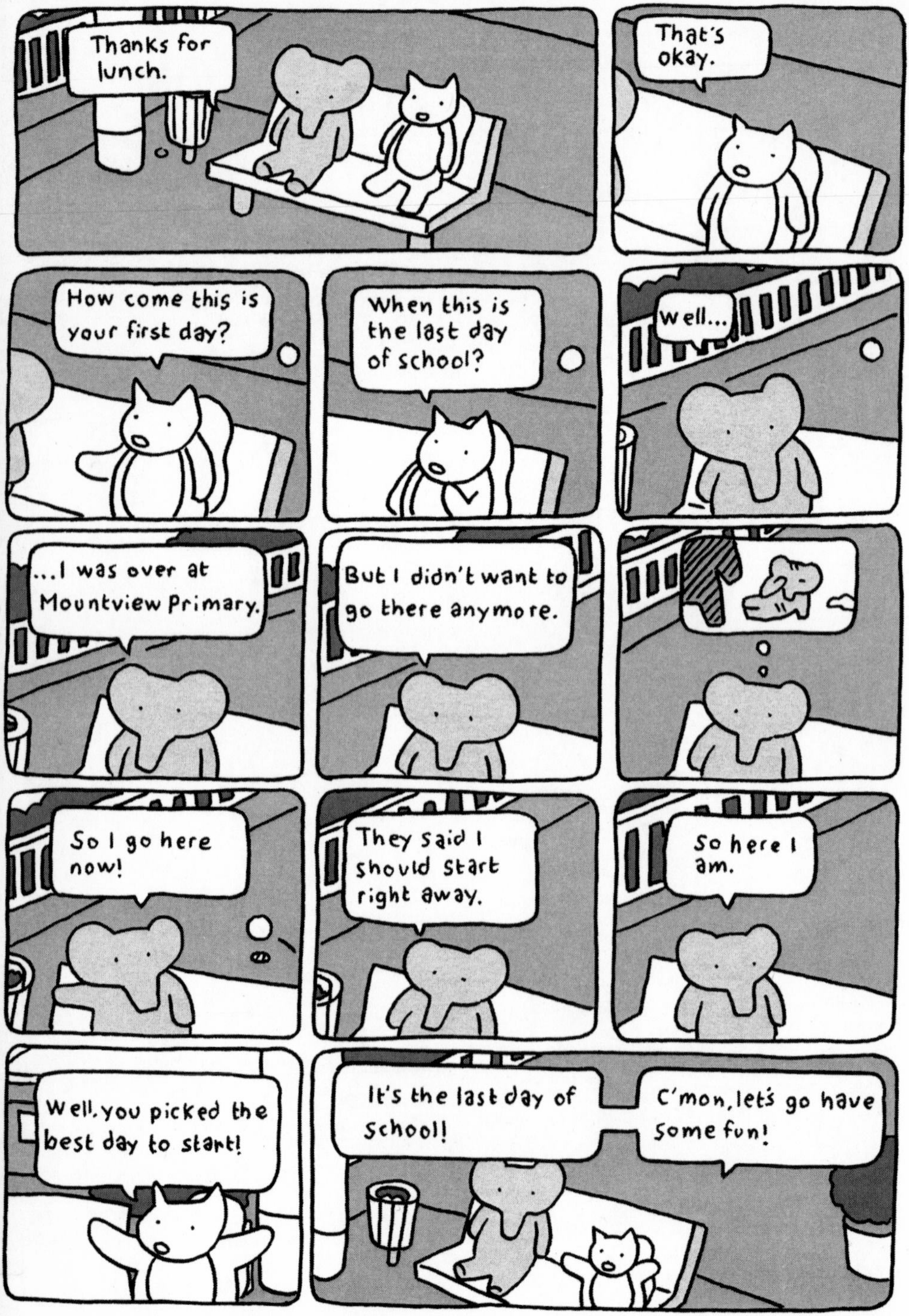
Thanks for lunch.
That's okay.
How come this is your first day?
When this is the last day of school?
Well...
...I was over at Mountview Primary.
But I didn't want to go there anymore.
So I go here now!
They said I should start right away.
So here I am.
Well, you picked the best day to start!
It's the last day of school!
C'mon, let's go have some fun!

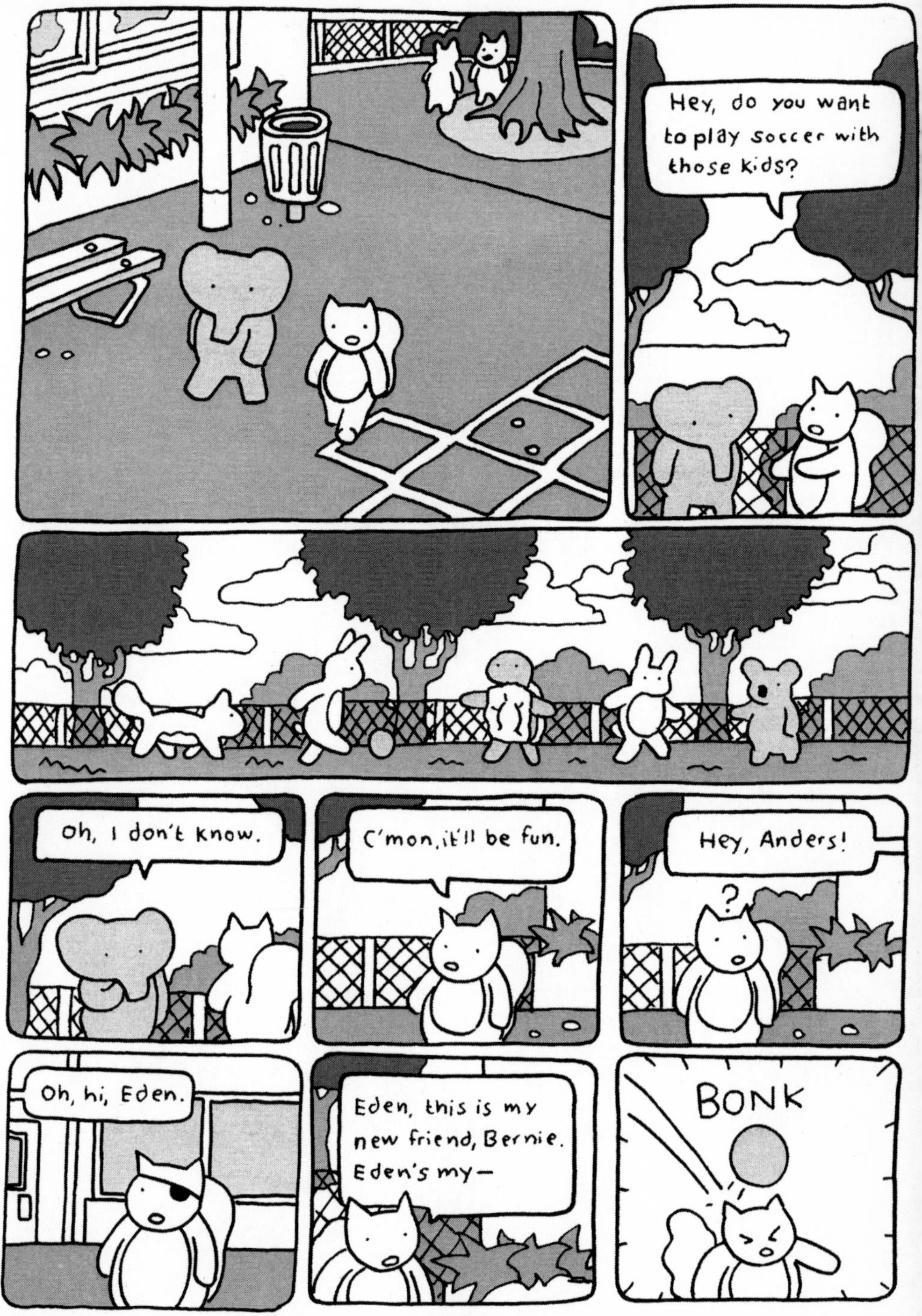
Hey, do you want to play soccer with those kids?
Oh, I don't know.
C'mon, it'll be fun.
Hey, Anders!
?
Oh, hi, Eden.
Eden, this is my new friend, Bernie. Eden's my—
BONK

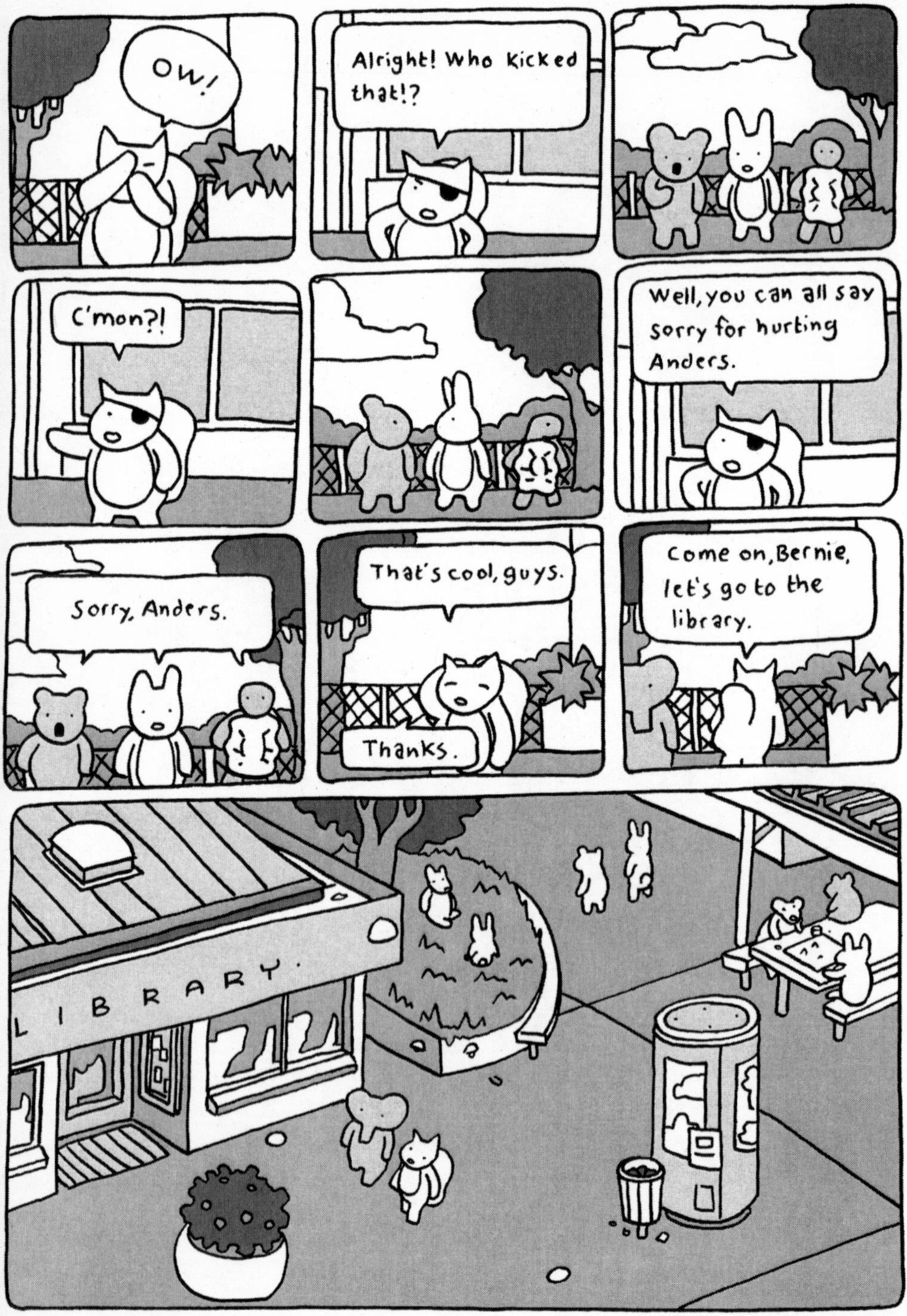
OW!
Alright! Who kicked that!?
C'mon?!
Well, you can all say sorry for hurting Anders.
Sorry, Anders.
That's cool, guys.
Thanks.
Come on, Bernie, let's go to the library.
LIBRARY.

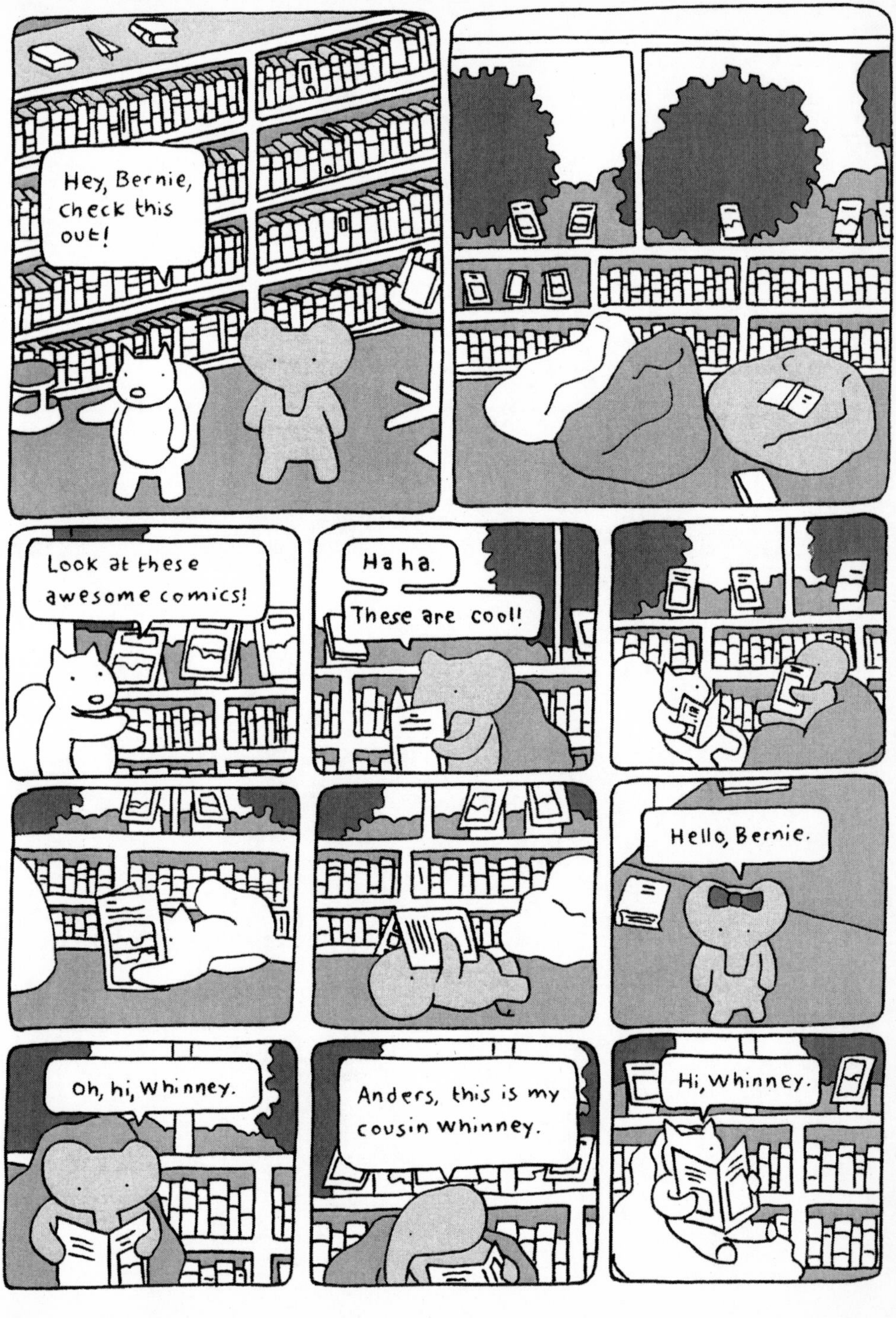
Hey, Bernie, check this out!
Look at these awesome comics!
Ha ha.
These are cool!
Hello, Bernie.
Oh, hi, Whinney.
Anders, this is my cousin Whinney.
Hi, Whinney.

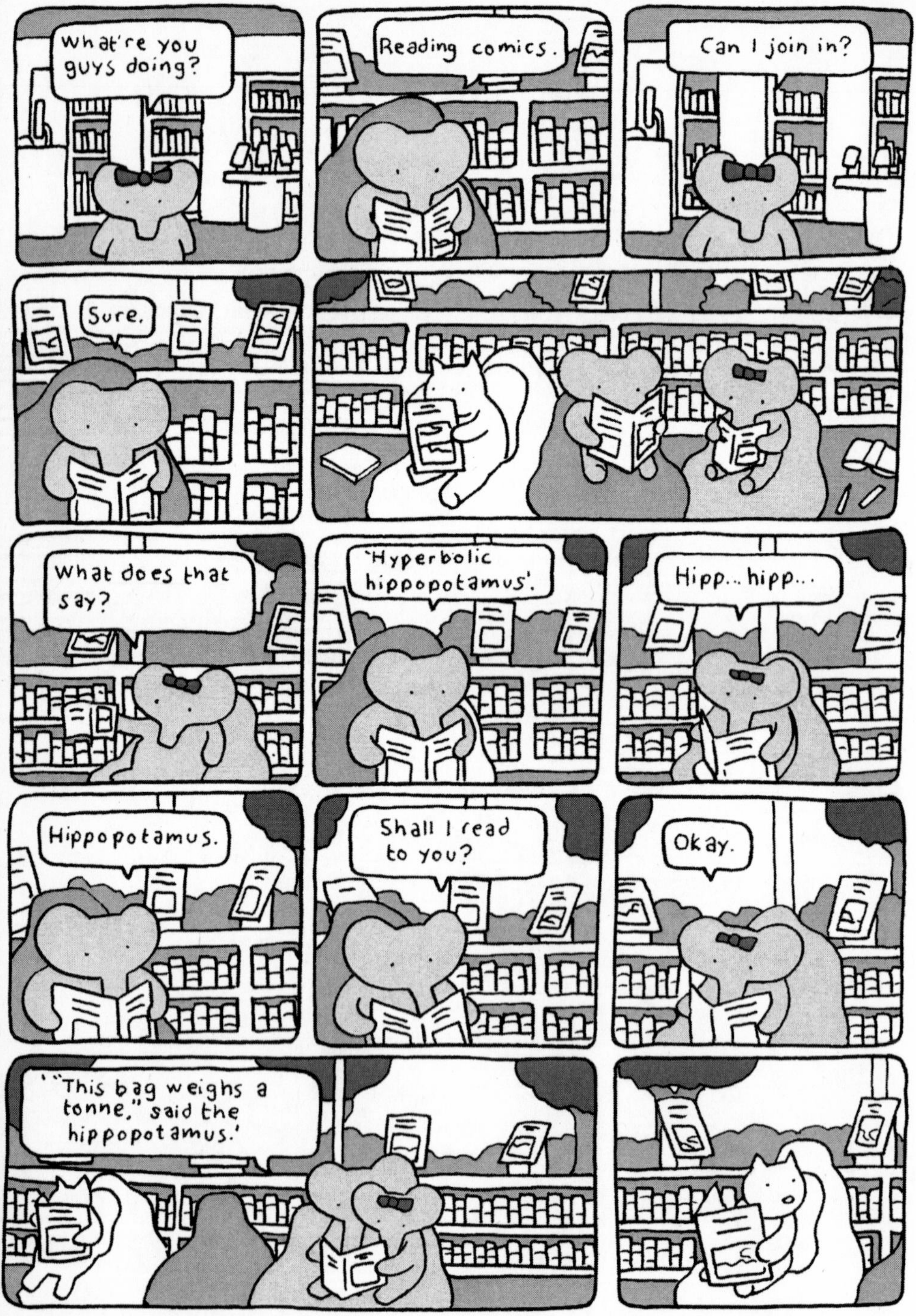
What're you guys doing?
Reading comics.
Can I join in?
Sure.
What does that say?
'Hyperbolic hippopotamus'.
Hipp... hipp...
Hippopotamus.
Shall I read to you?
Okay.
'"This bag weighs a tonne," said the hippopotamus.'

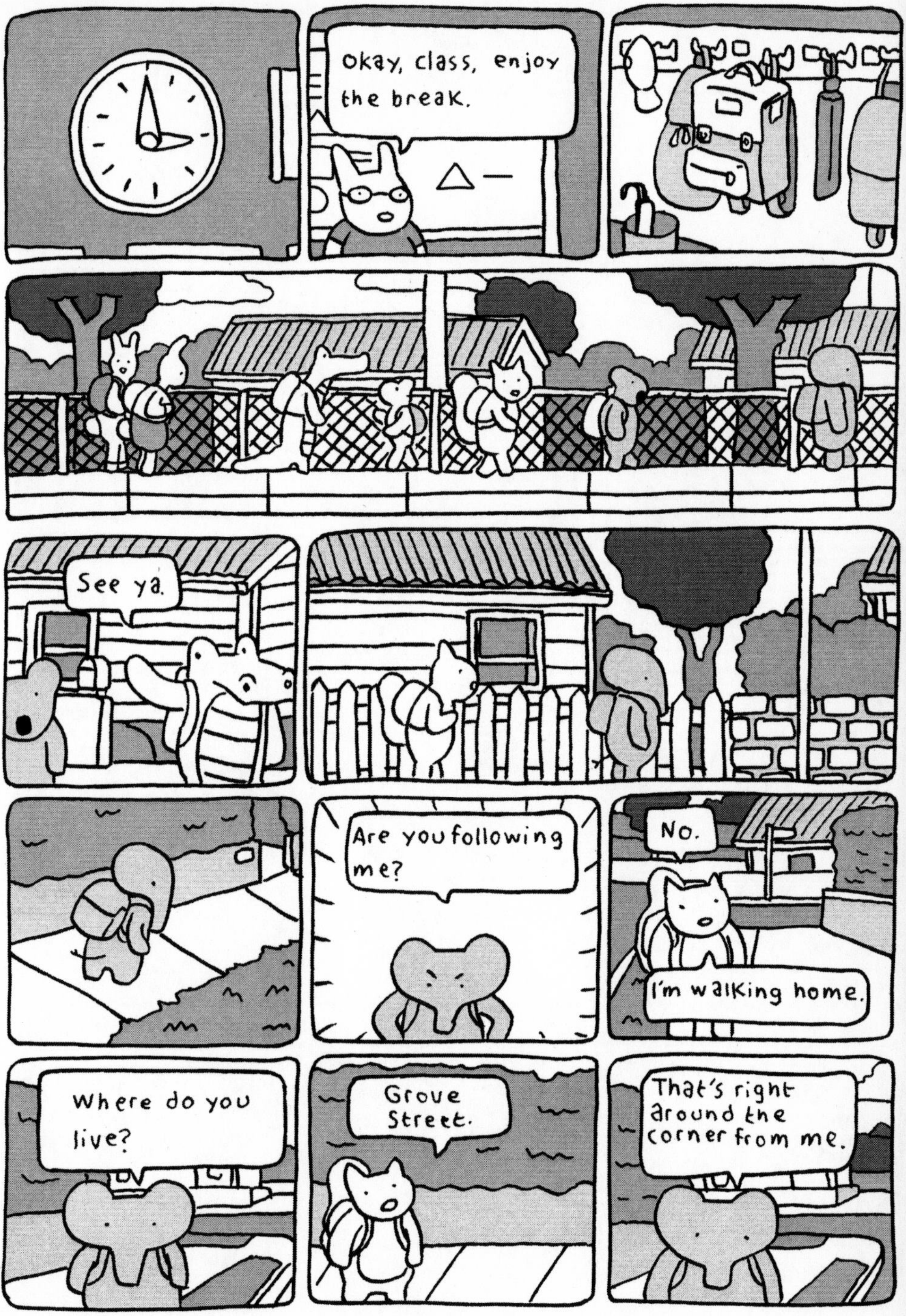
Okay, class, enjoy the break.
See ya.
Are you following me?
No.
I'm walking home.
Where do you live?
Grove Street.
That's right around the corner from me.

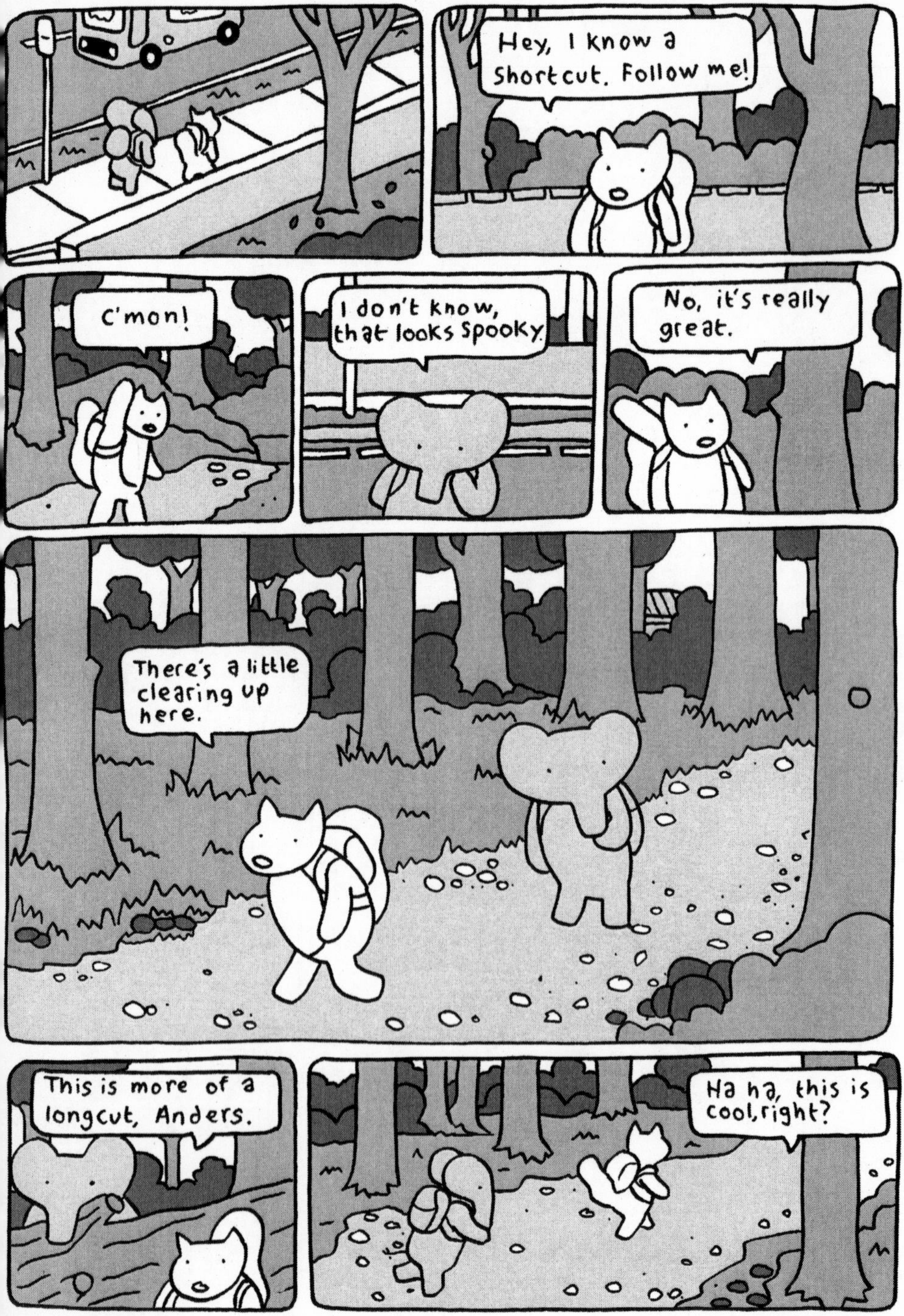
Hey, I know a Shortcut. Follow me!
C'mon!
I don't know, that looks spooky.
No, it's really great.
There's a little clearing up here.
This is more of a longcut, Anders.
Ha ha, this is cool, right?

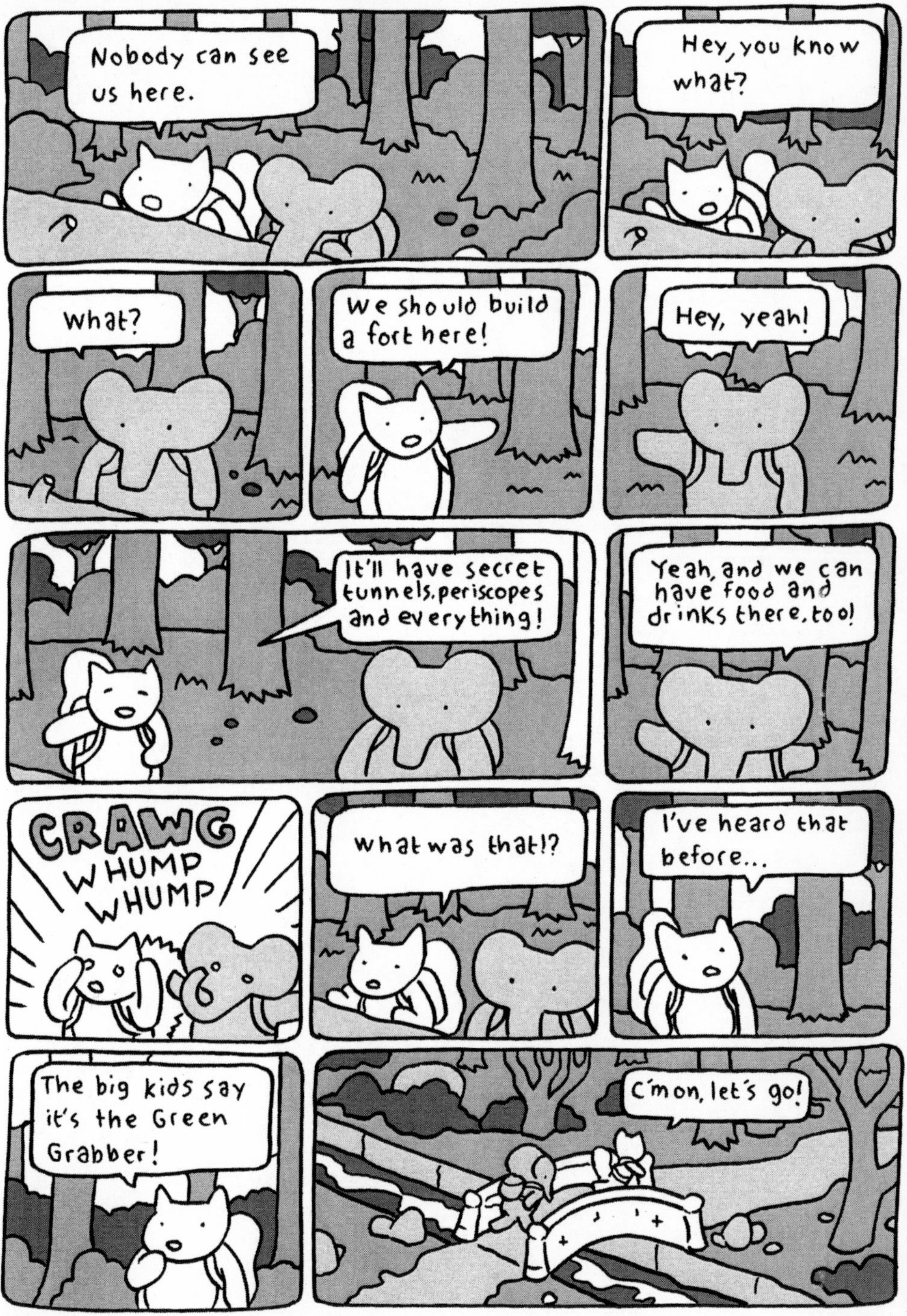
Nobody can see us here.
Hey, you know what?
What?
We should build a fort here!
Hey, yeah!
It'll have secret tunnels, periscopes and everything!
Yeah, and we can have food and drinks there, too!
CRAWG
WHUMP
WHUMP
What was that!?
I've heard that before...
The big kids say it's the Green Grabber!
C'mon, let's go!

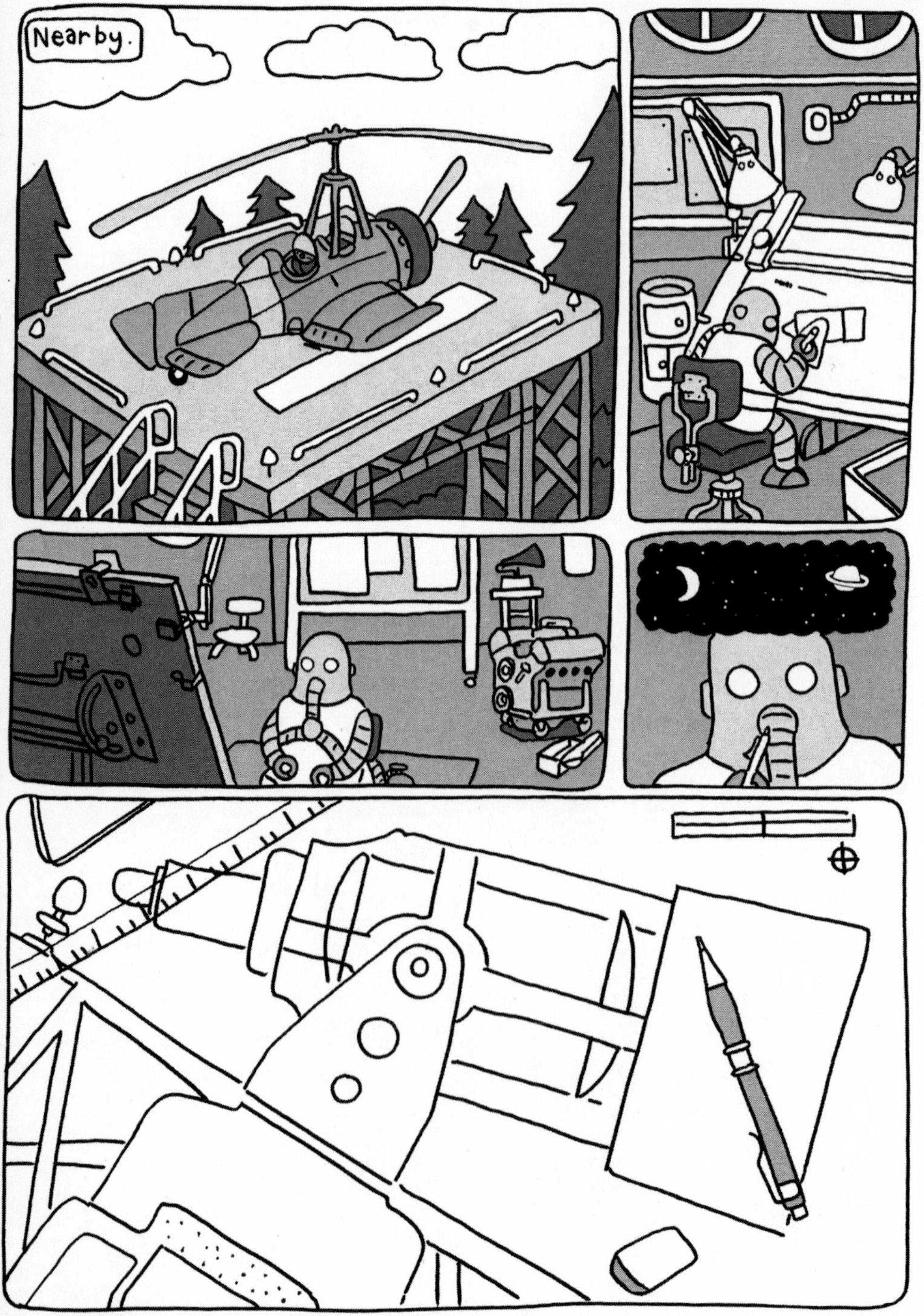
Nearby.

Chapter 2

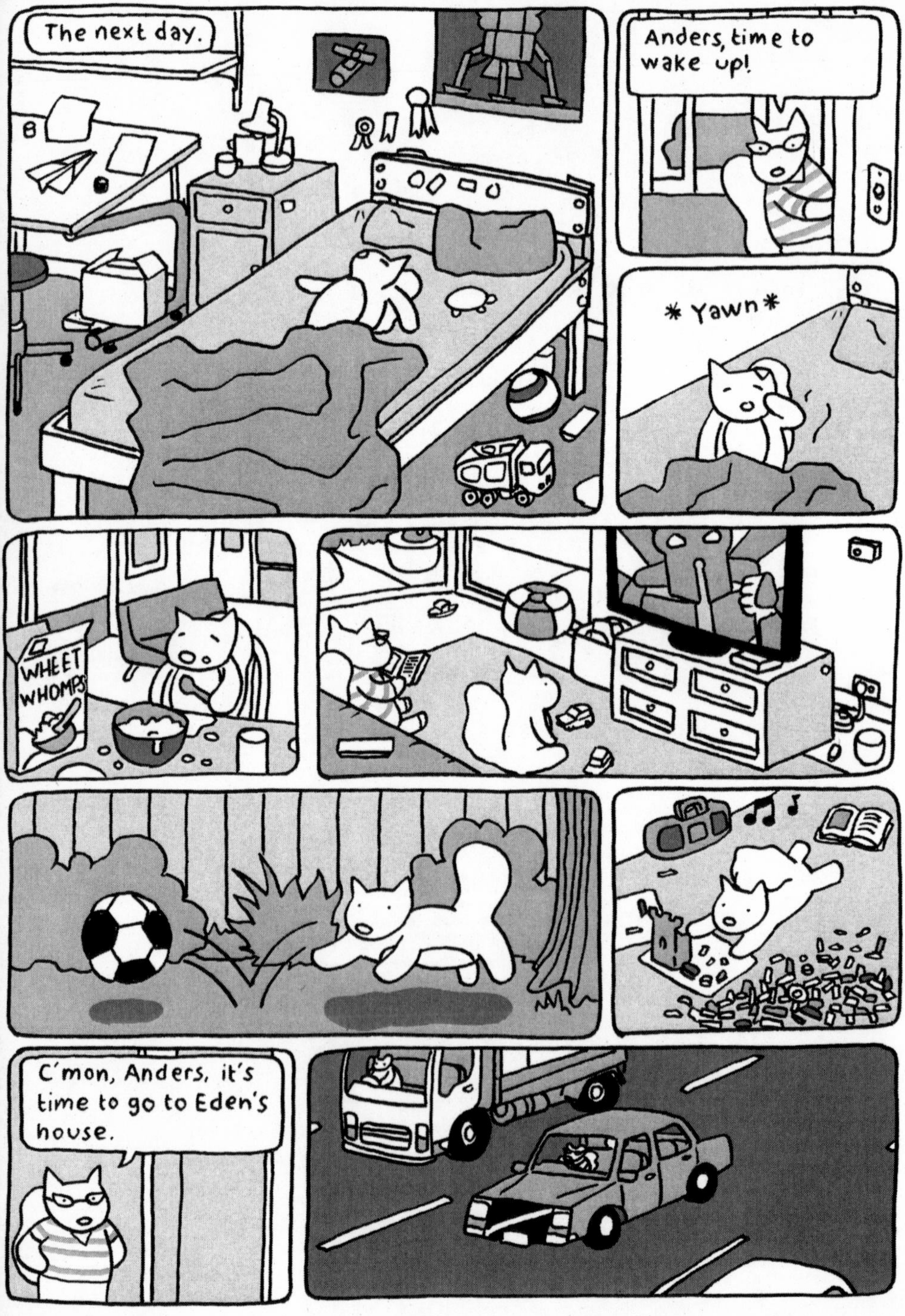
The next day.
Anders, time to wake up!
* Yawn *
WHEET WHOMPS
C'mon, Anders, it's time to go to Eden's house.

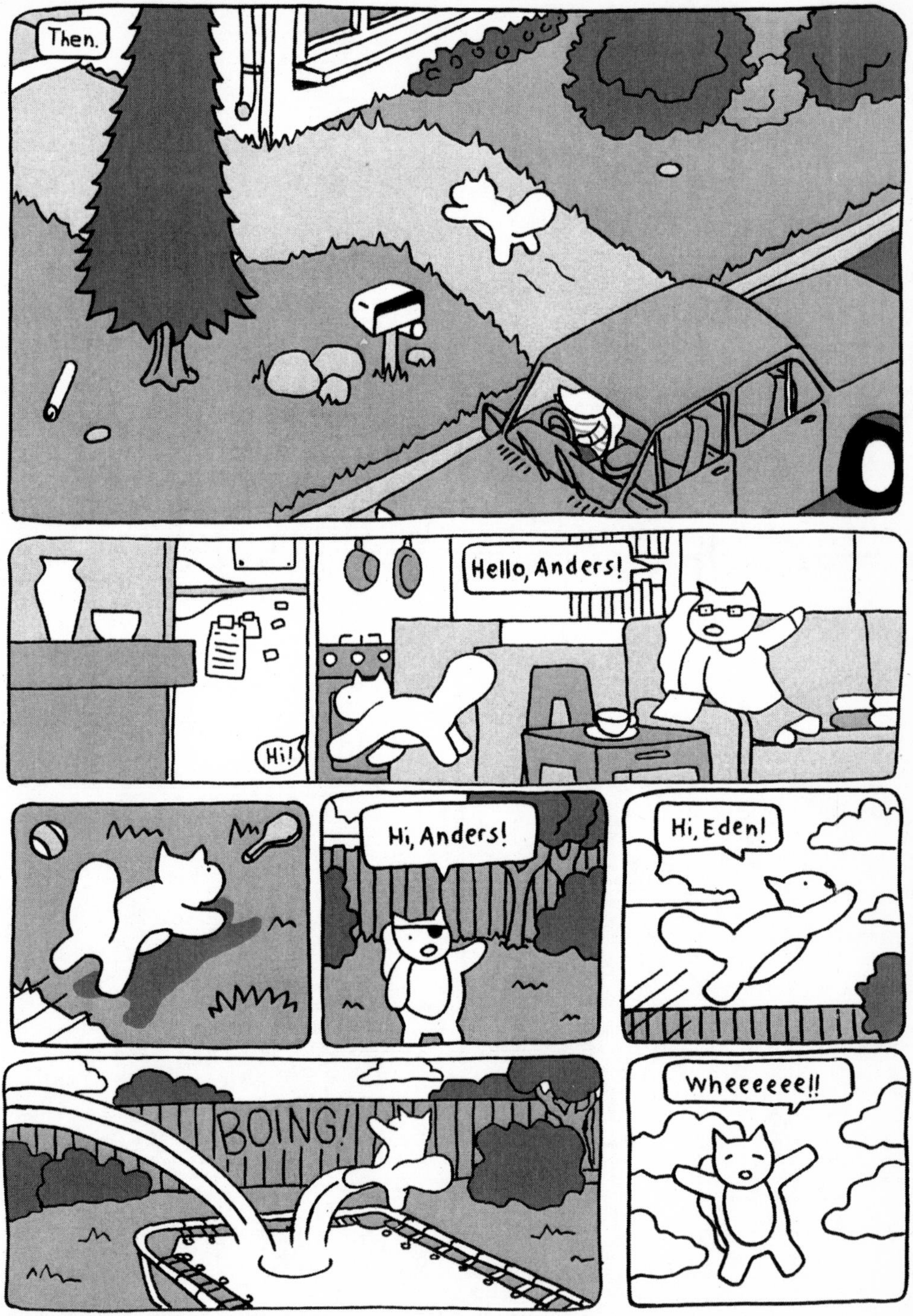
Then.
Hello, Anders!
Hi!
Hi, Anders!
Hi, Eden!
BOING!
Wheeeeee!!

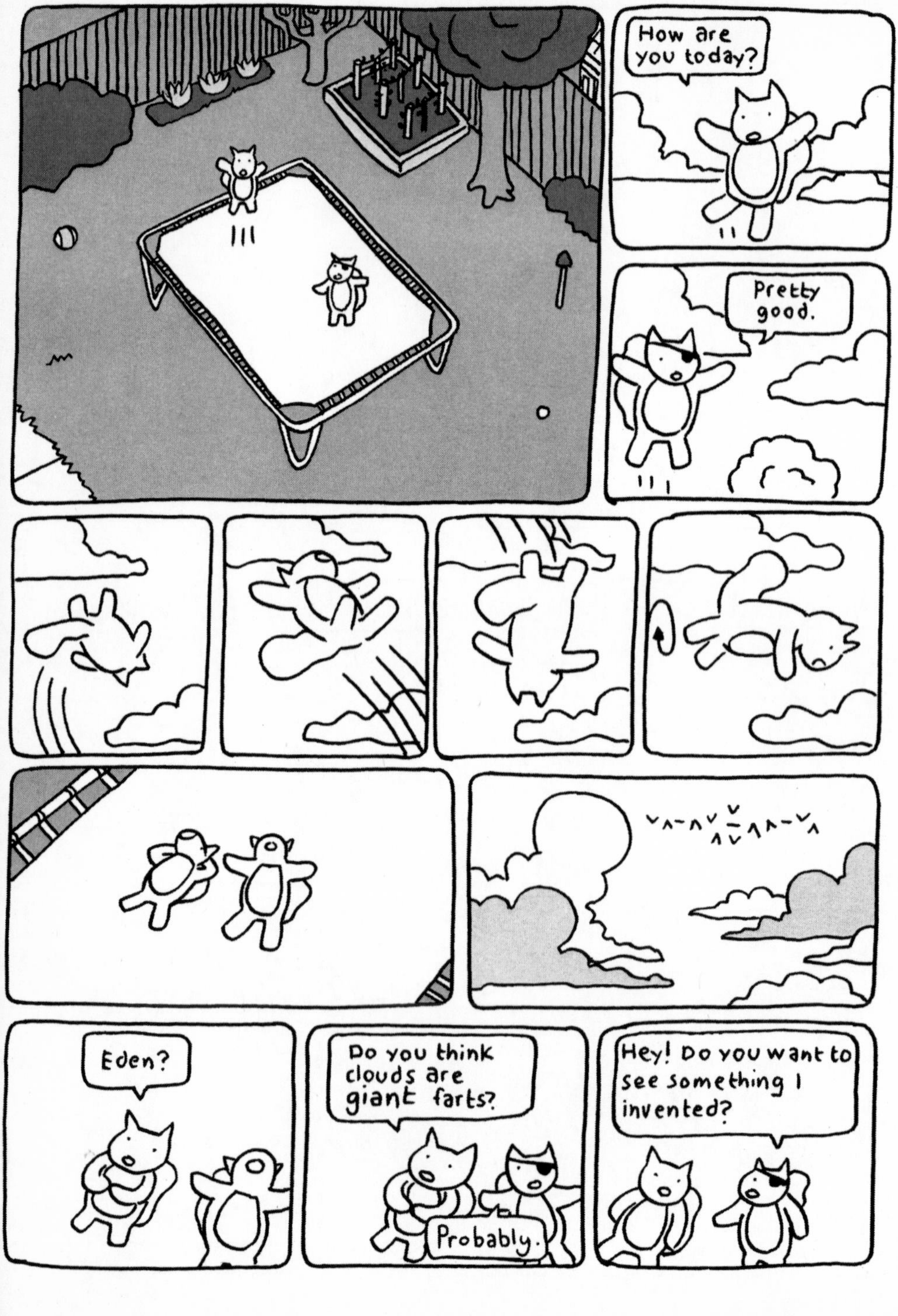

How are you today?
Pretty good.
Eden?
Do you think clouds are giant farts?
Probably.
Hey! Do you want to see something I invented?

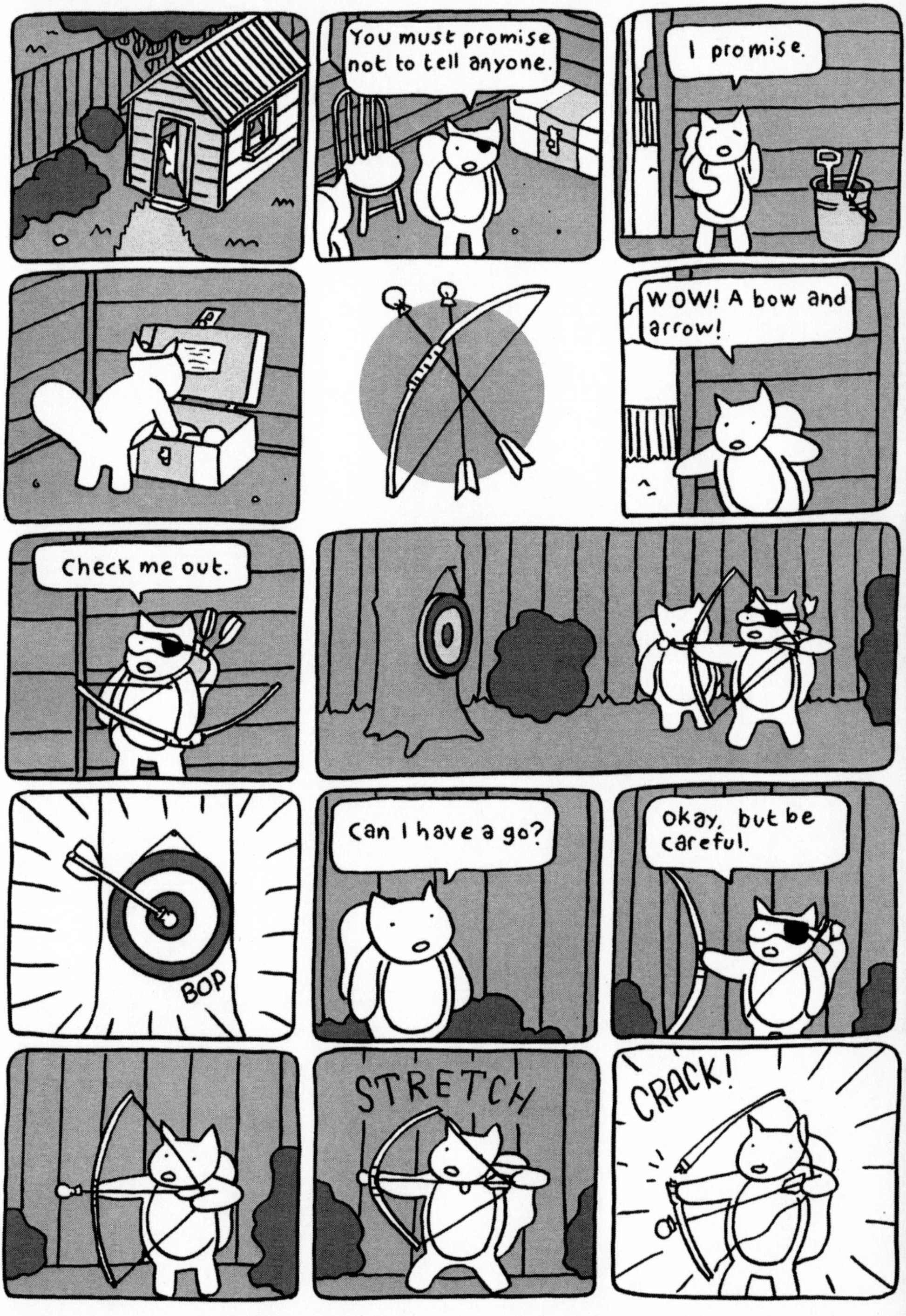
You must promise not to tell anyone.
I promise.
WOW! A bow and arrow!
Check me out.
BOP
Can I have a go?
Okay, but be careful.
STRETCH
CRACK!

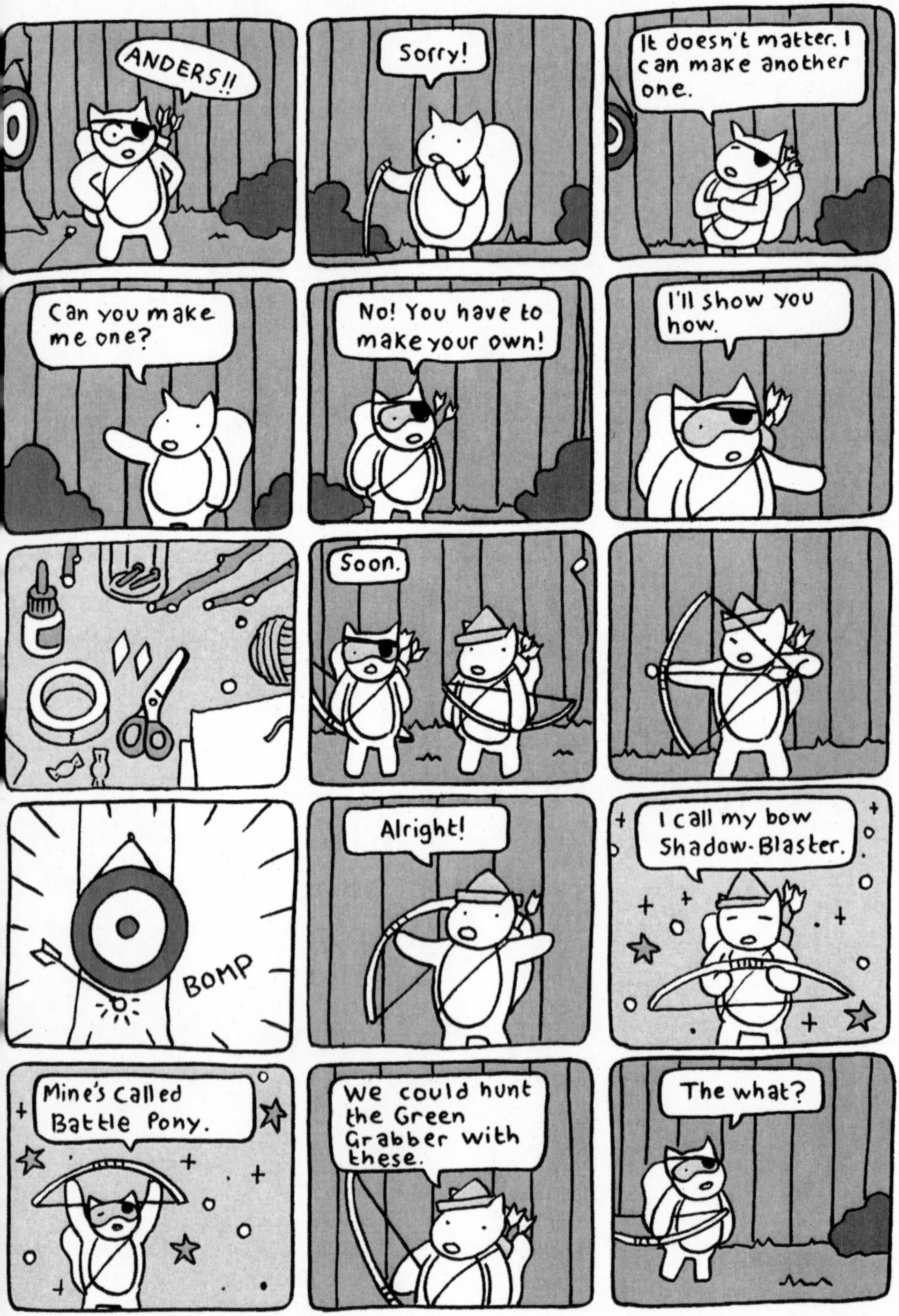
ANDERS!!
Sorry!
It doesn't matter. I can make another one.
Can you make me one?
No! You have to make your own!
I'll show you how.
Soon.
BOMP
Alright!
I call my bow Shadow-Blaster.
Mine's called Battle Pony.
We could hunt the Green Grabber with these.
The what?

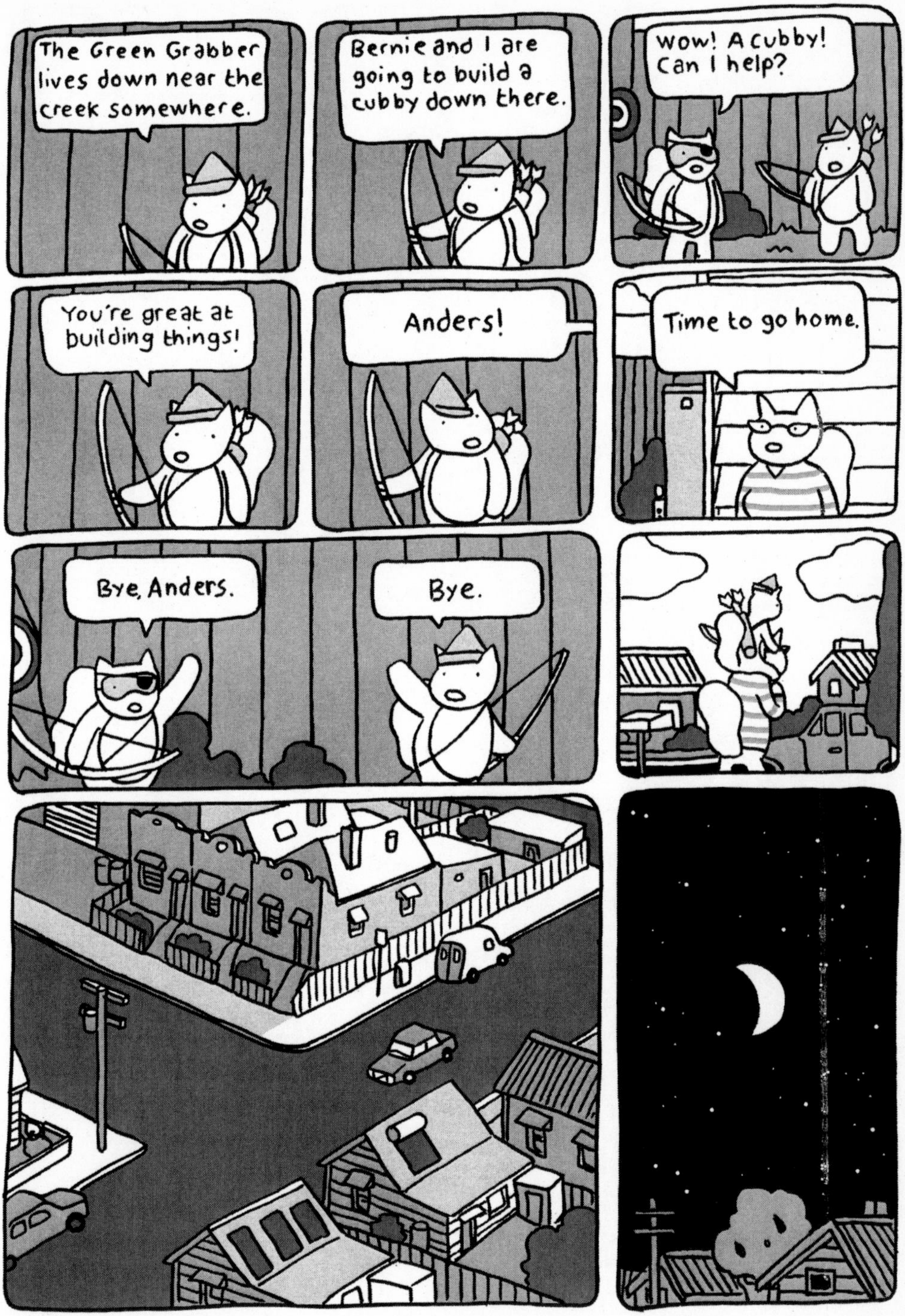
The Green Grabber lives down near the creek somewhere.
Bernie and I are going to build a cubby down there.
Wow! A cubby! Can I help?
You're great at building things!
Anders!
Time to go home.
Bye, Anders.
Bye.

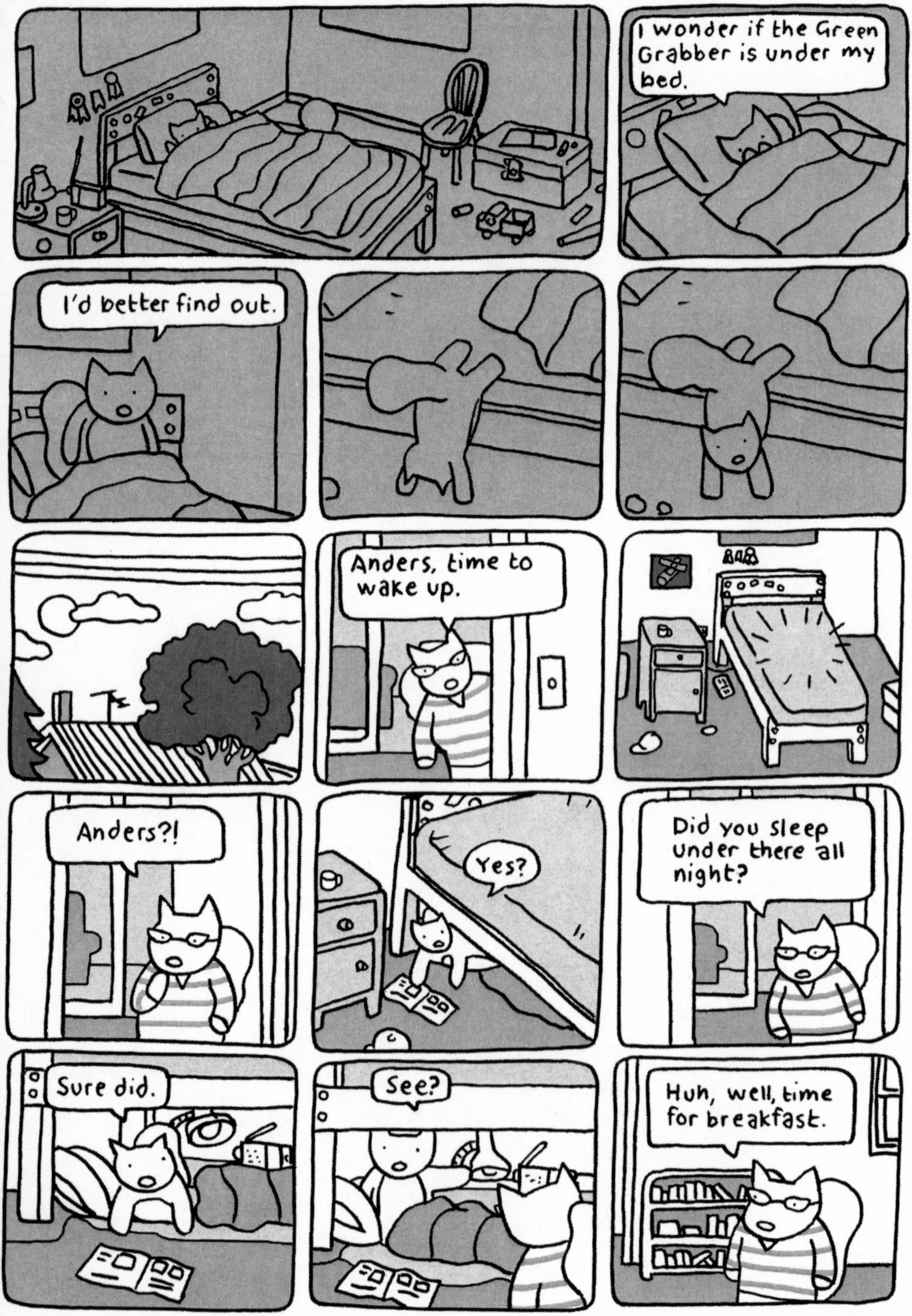
I wonder if the Green Grabber is under my bed.
I'd better find out.
Anders, time to wake up.
Anders?!
Yes?
Did you sleep under there all night?
Sure did.
See?
Huh, well, time for breakfast.

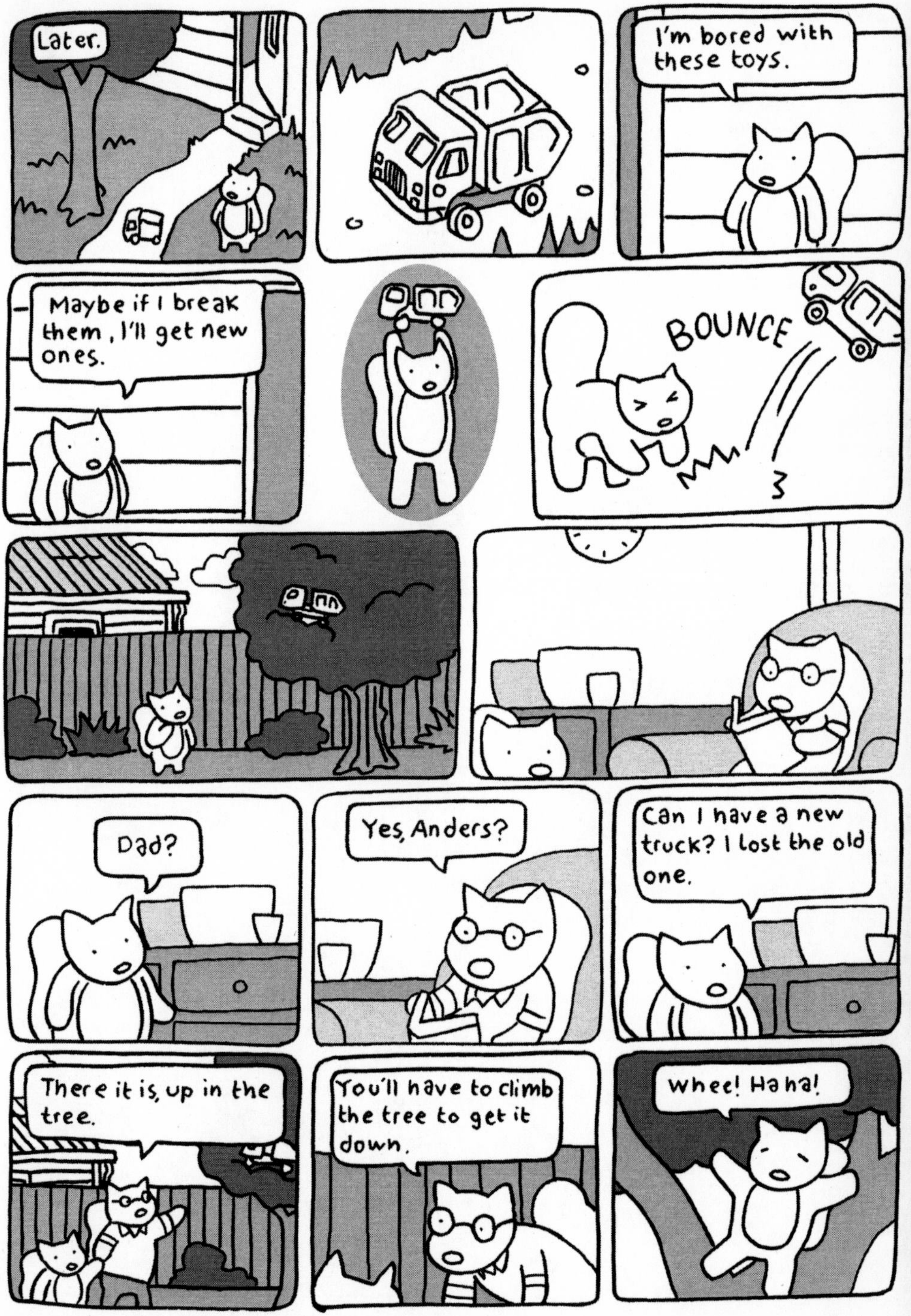
Later.
I'm bored with these toys.
Maybe if I break them, I'll get new ones.
BOUNCE
Dad?
Yes, Anders?
Can I have a new truck? I lost the old one.
There it is, up in the tree.
You'll have to climb the tree to get it down.
Whee! Ha ha!

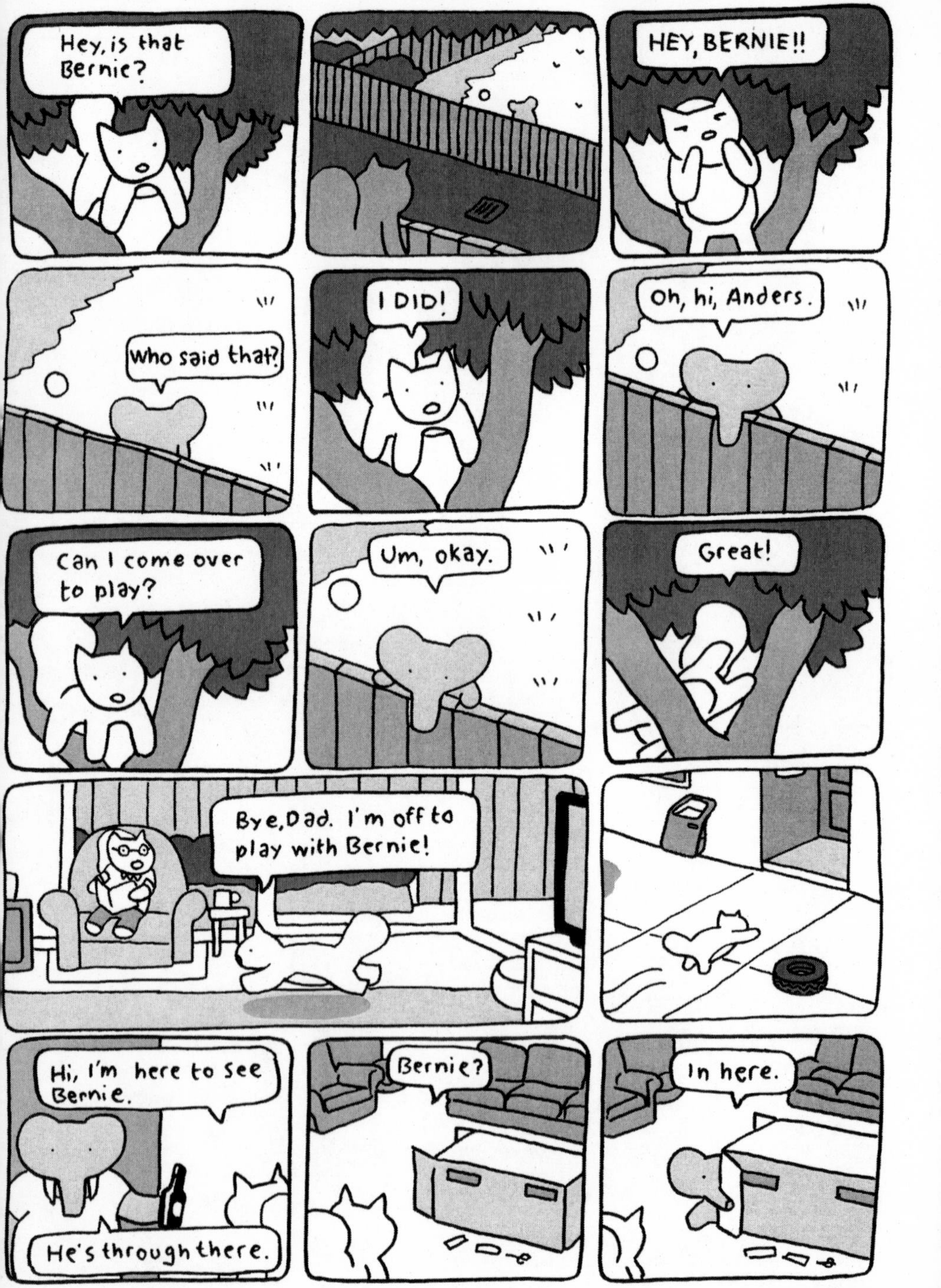
Hey, is that Bernie?
HEY, BERNIE!!
Who said that?
I DID!
Oh, hi, Anders.
Can I come over to play?
Um, okay.
Great!
Bye, Dad. I'm off to play with Bernie!
Hi, I'm here to see Bernie.
He's through there.
Bernie?
In here.

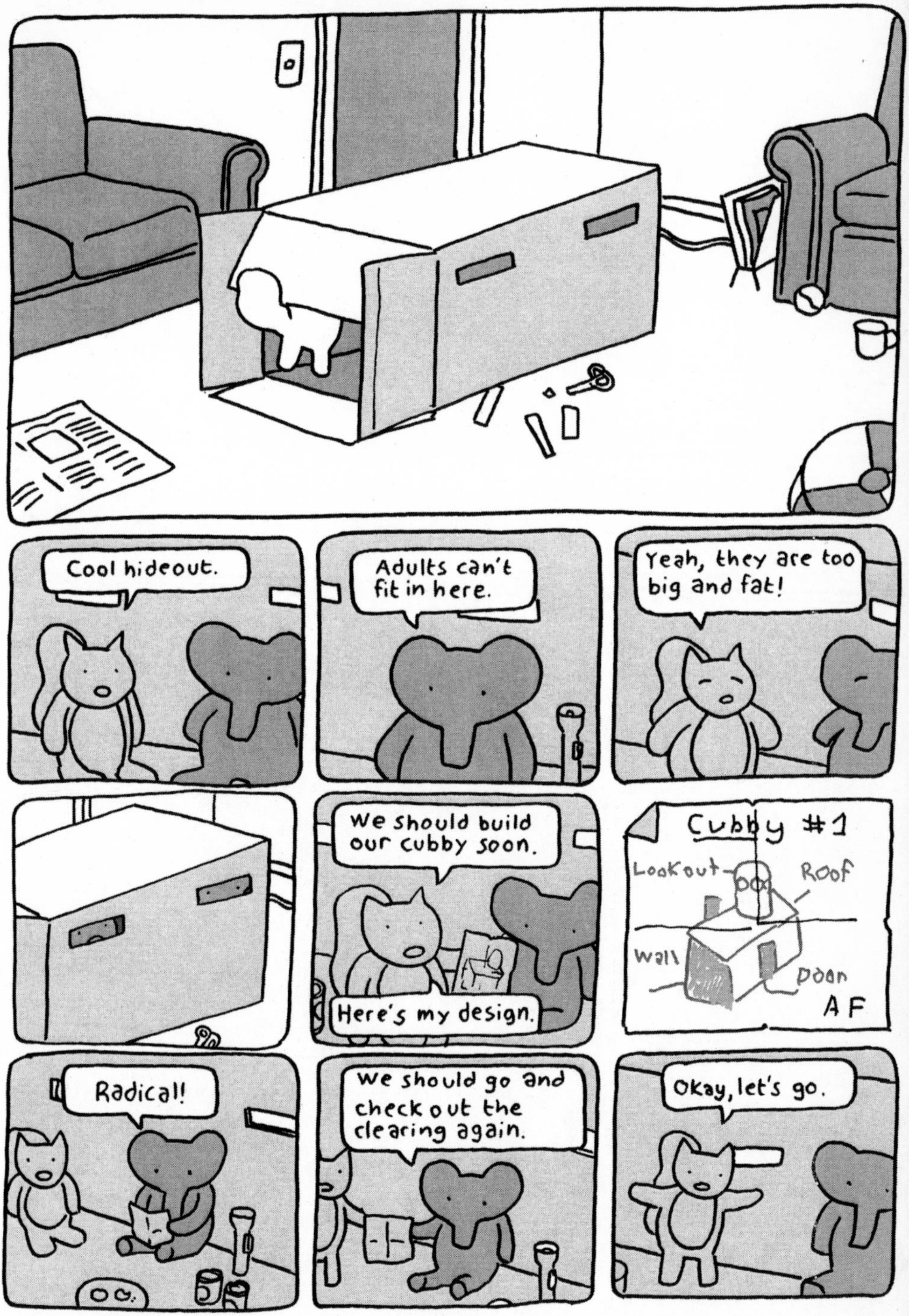
Cool hideout.
Adults can't fit in here.
Yeah, they are too big and fat!
We should build our cubby soon.
Here's my design.
Cubby #1
Lookout
Roof
Wall
Door
AF
Radical!
We should go and check out the clearing again.
Okay, let's go.

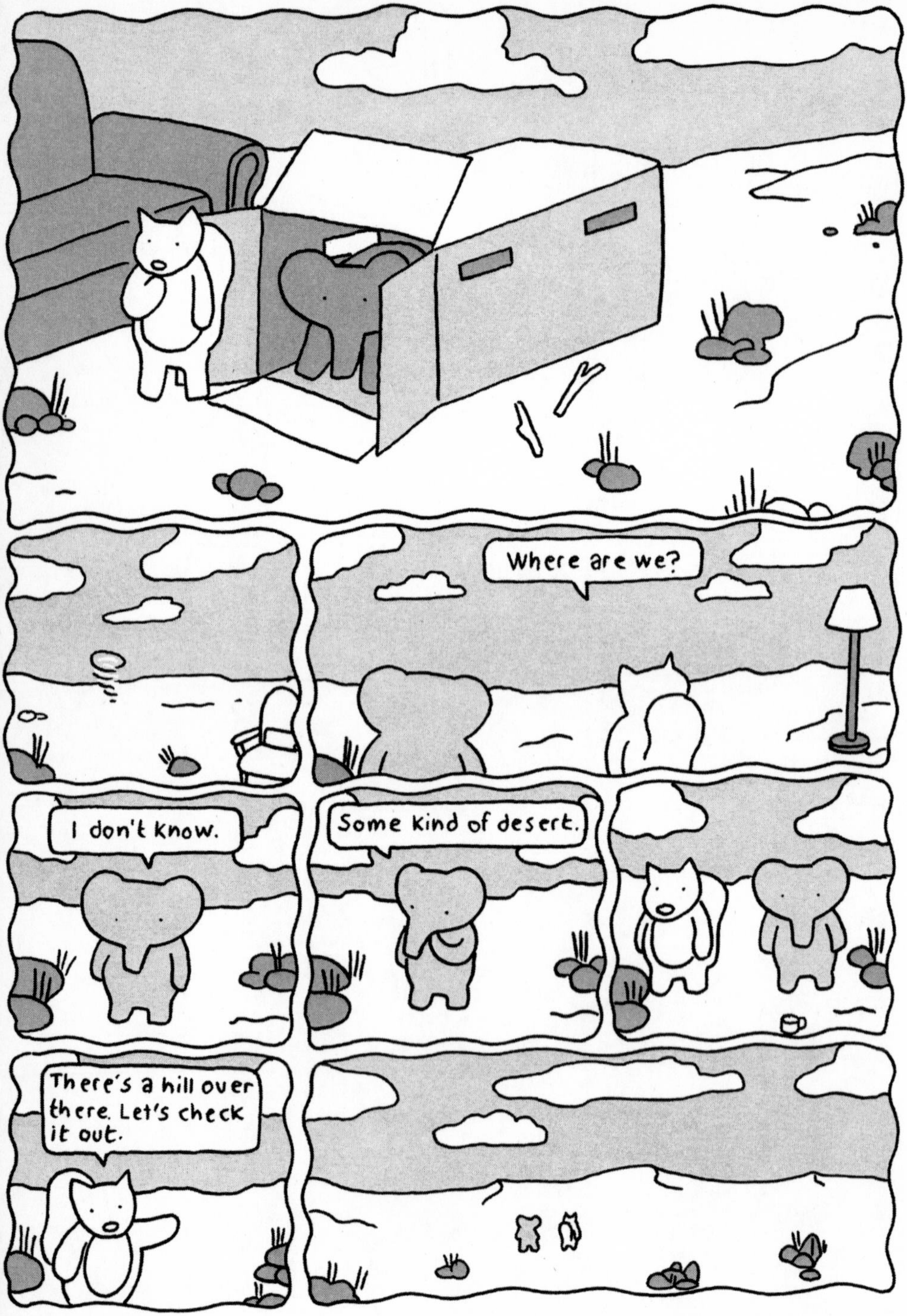
Where are we?
I don't know.
Some kind of desert.
There's a hill over there. Let's check it out.

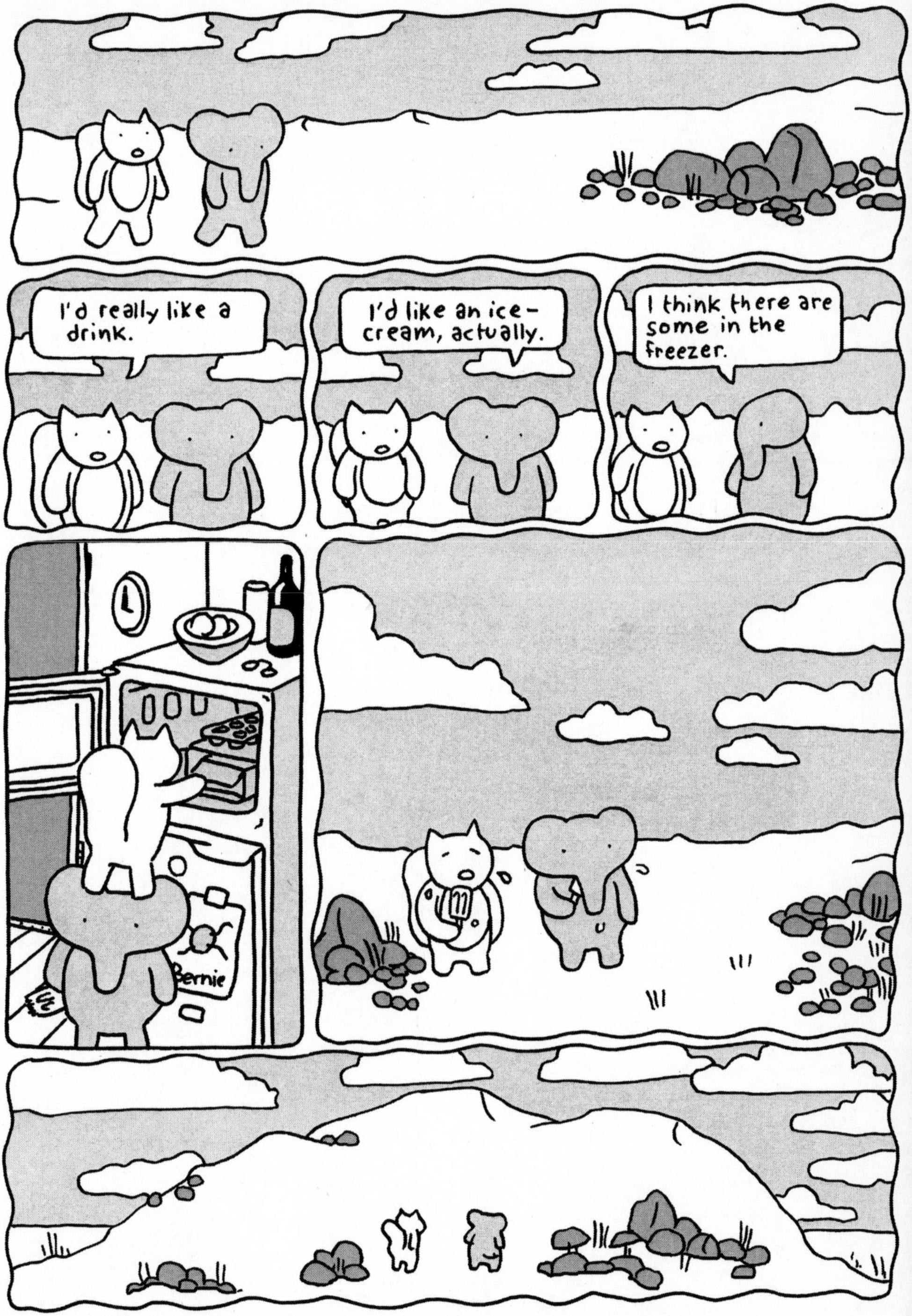
I'd really like a drink.
I'd like an ice-cream, actually.
I think there are some in the freezer.
Bernie

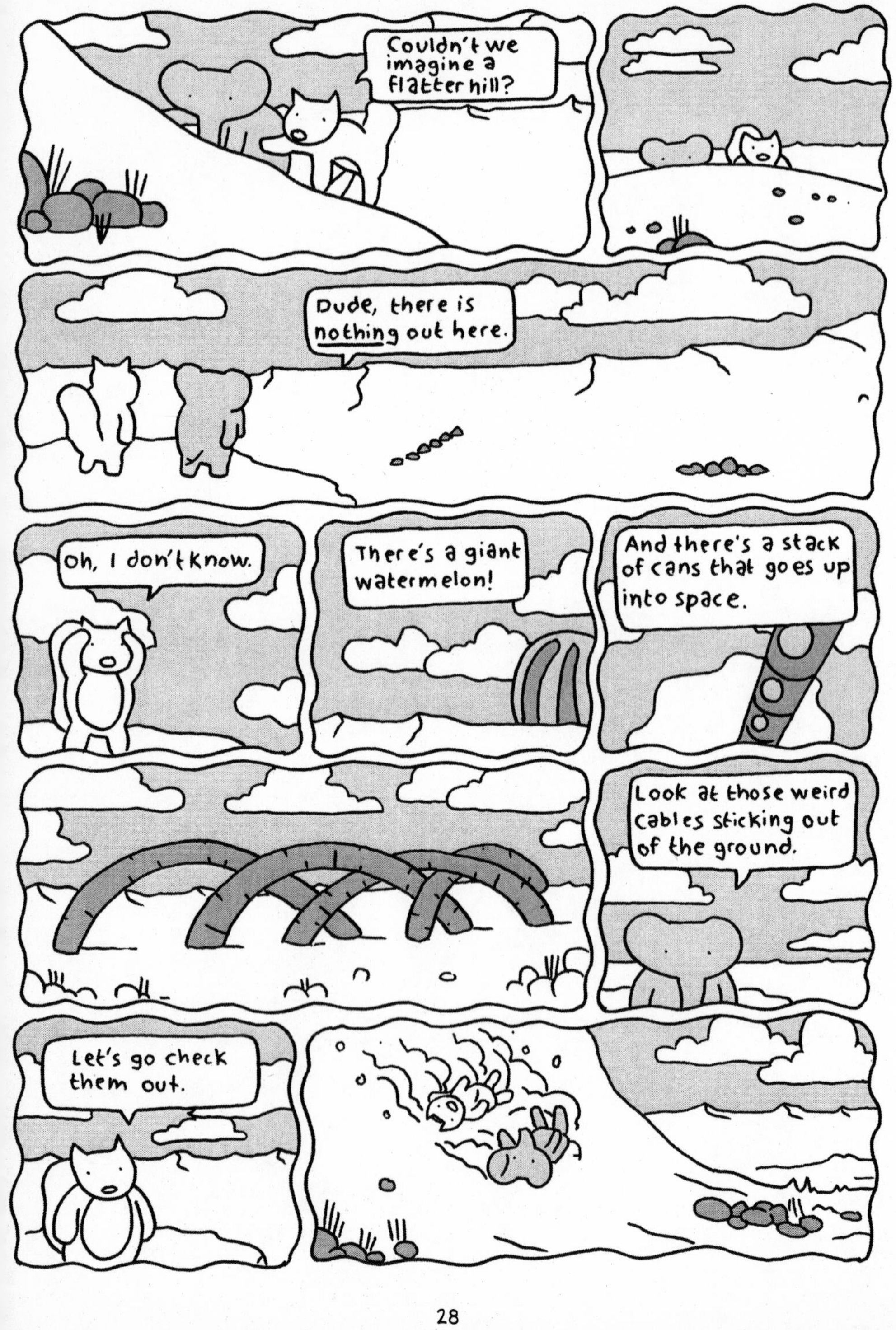
Couldn't we imagine a flatter hill?
Dude, there is nothing out here.
Oh, I don't know.
There's a giant watermelon!
And there's a stack of cans that goes up into space.
Look at those weird cables sticking out of the ground.
Let's go check them out.

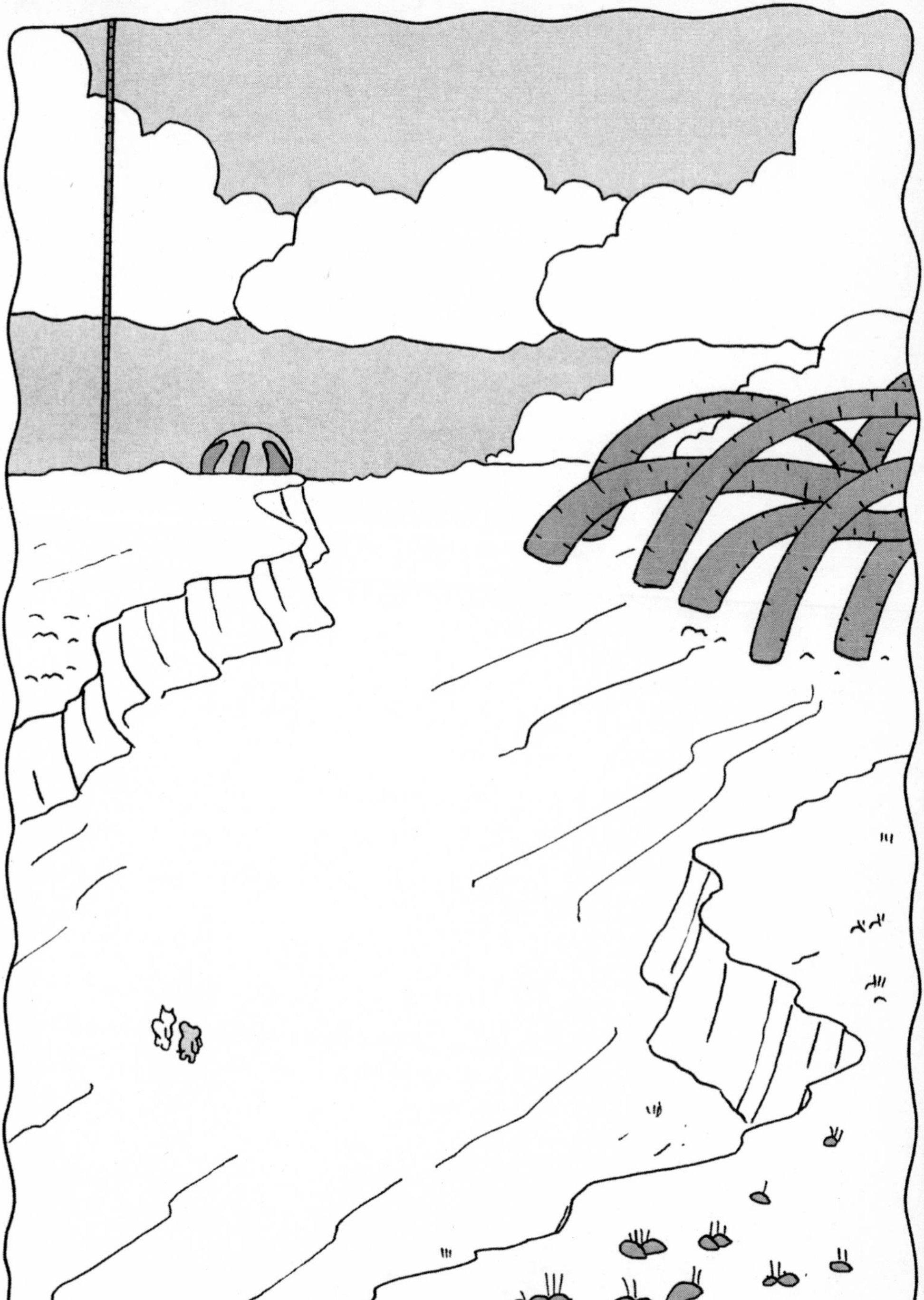

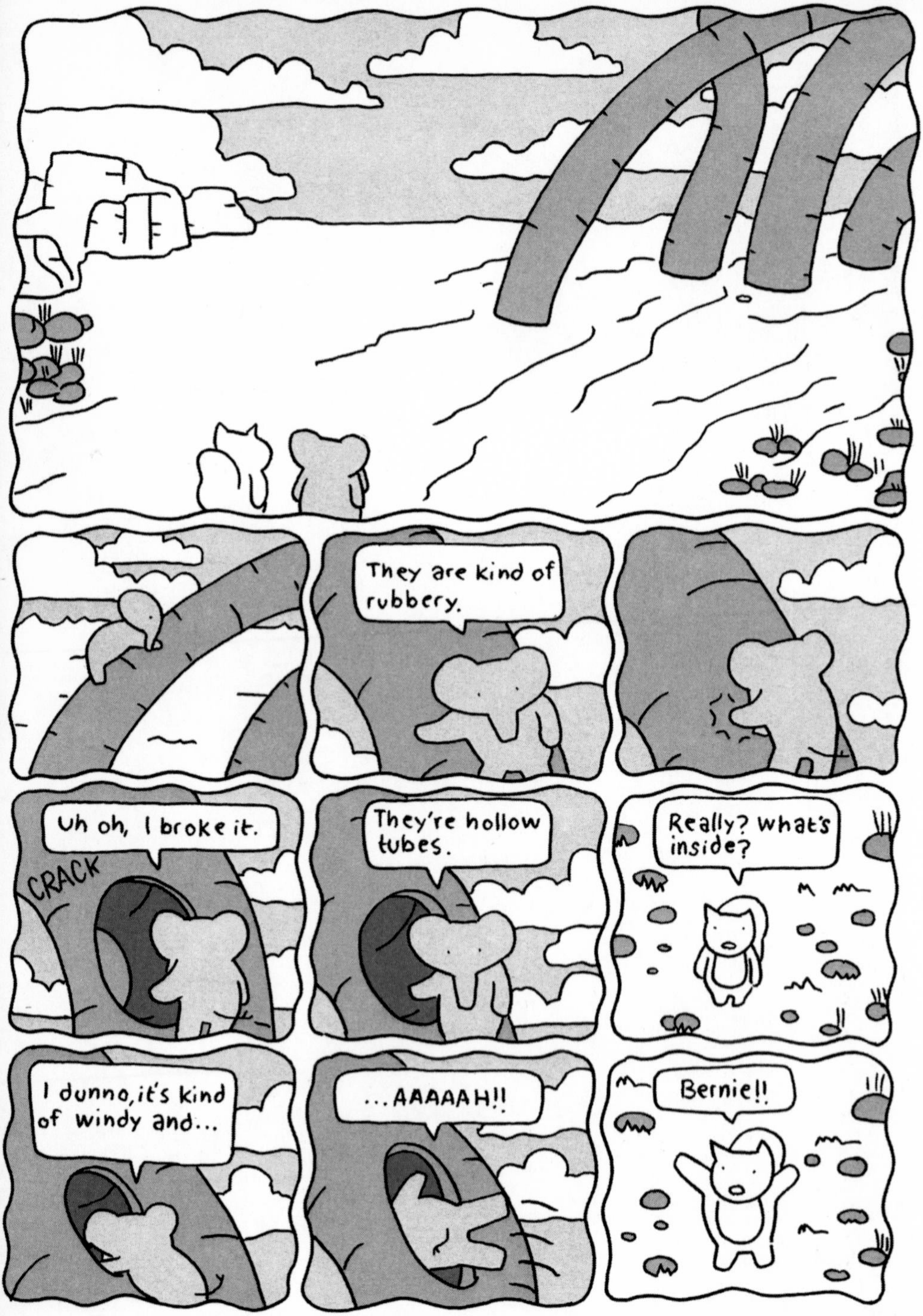
They are kind of rubbery.
Uh oh, I broke it.
CRACK
They're hollow tubes.
Really? What's inside?
I dunno, it's kind of windy and...
...AAAAAH!!
Bernie!!

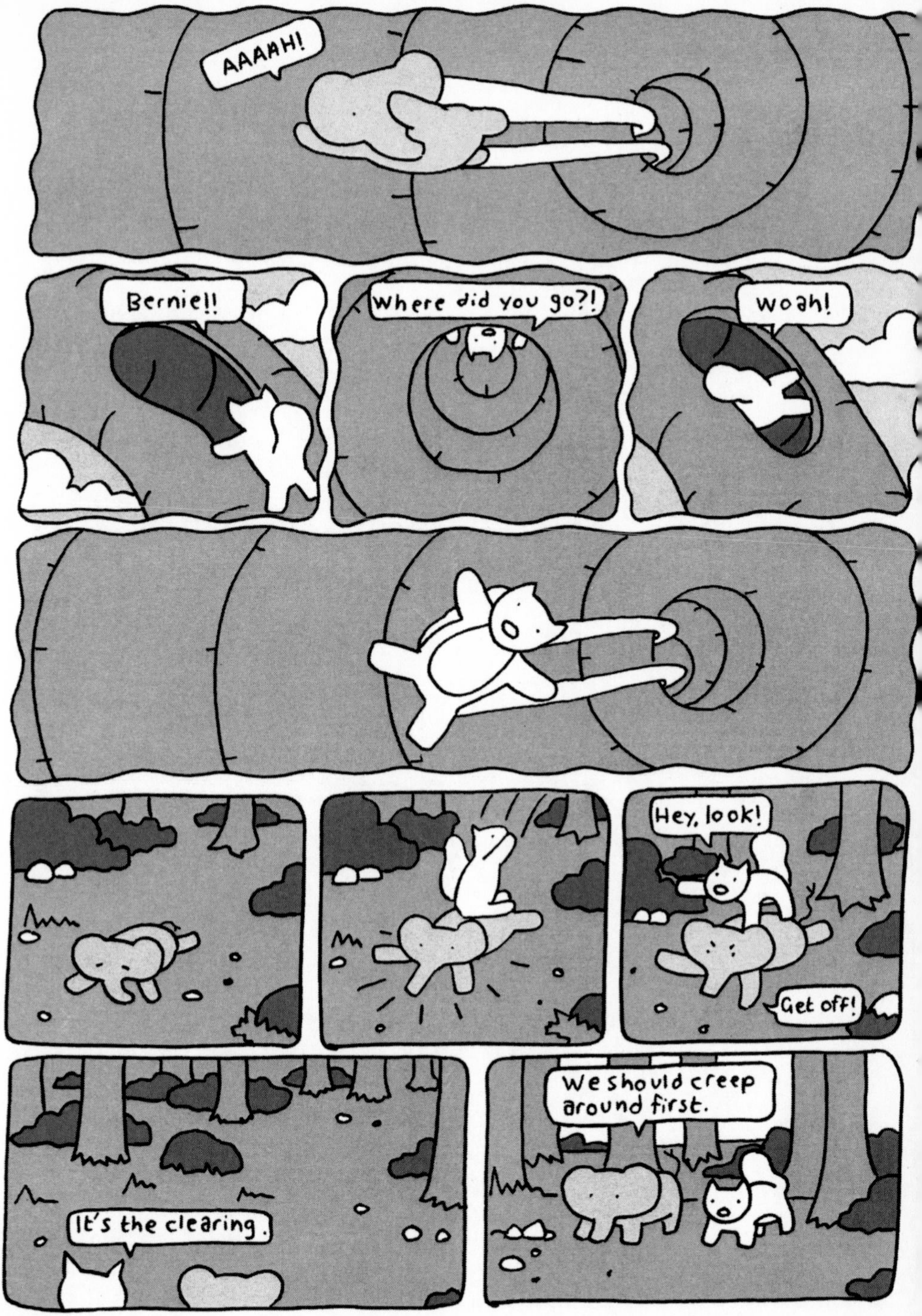
AAAAH!
Bernie!!
Where did you go?!
Woah!
Hey, look!
Get off!
It's the clearing.
We should creep around first.

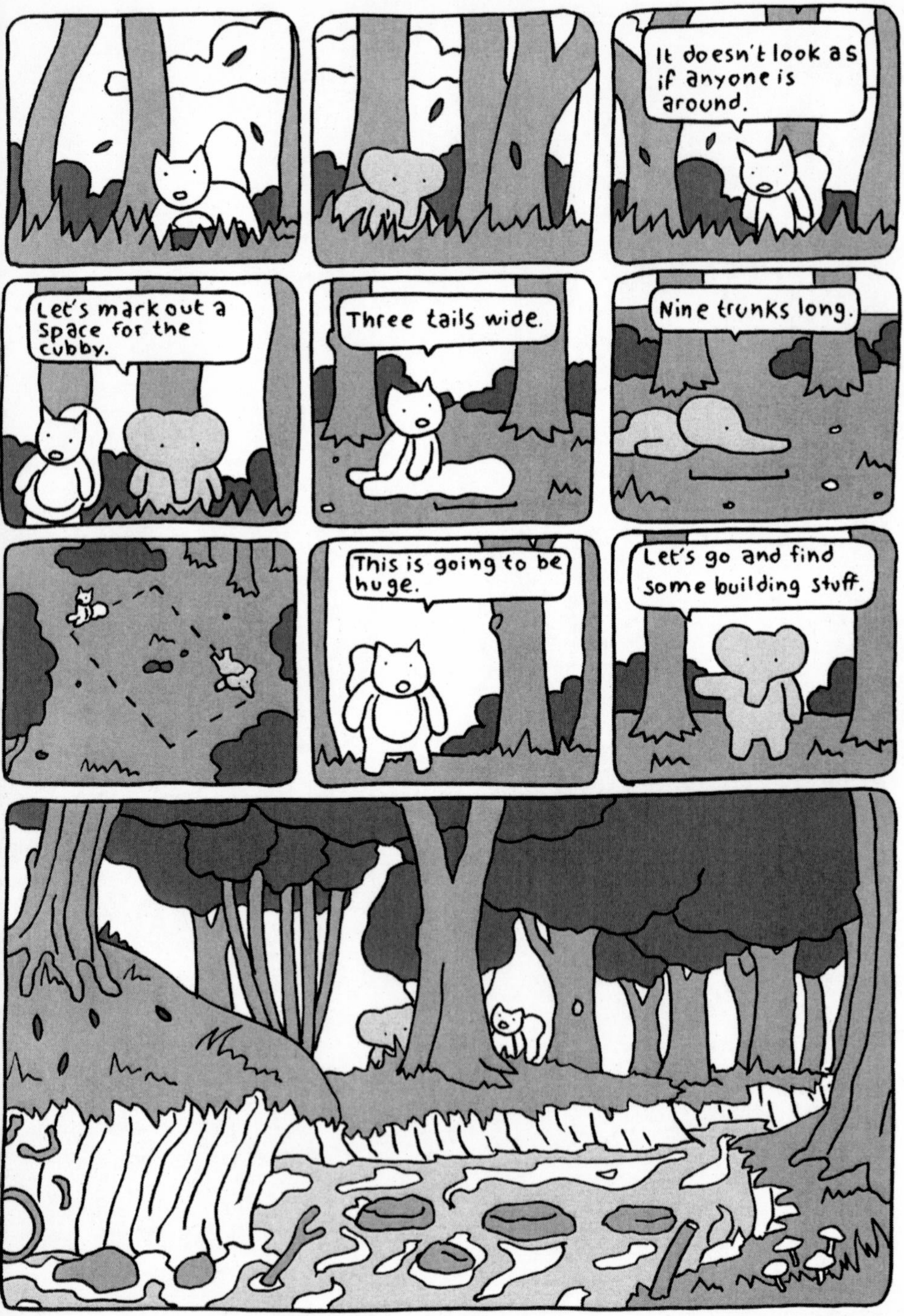
It doesn't look as if anyone is around.
Let's mark out a space for the cubby.
Three tails wide.
Nine trunks long.
This is going to be huge.
Let's go and find some building stuff.

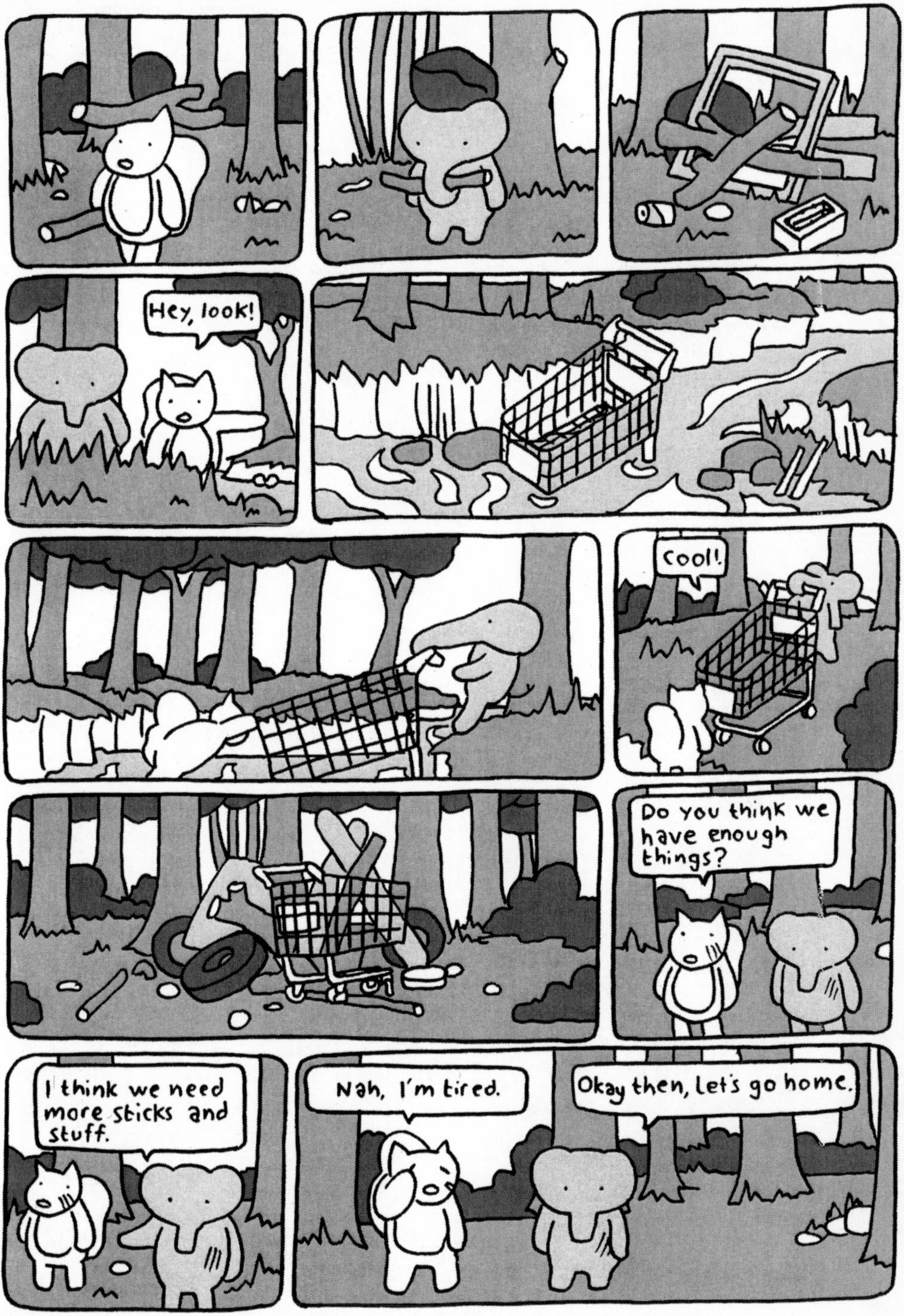
Hey, look!
Cool!
Do you think we have enough things?
I think we need more sticks and stuff.
Nah, I'm tired.
Okay then, let's go home.

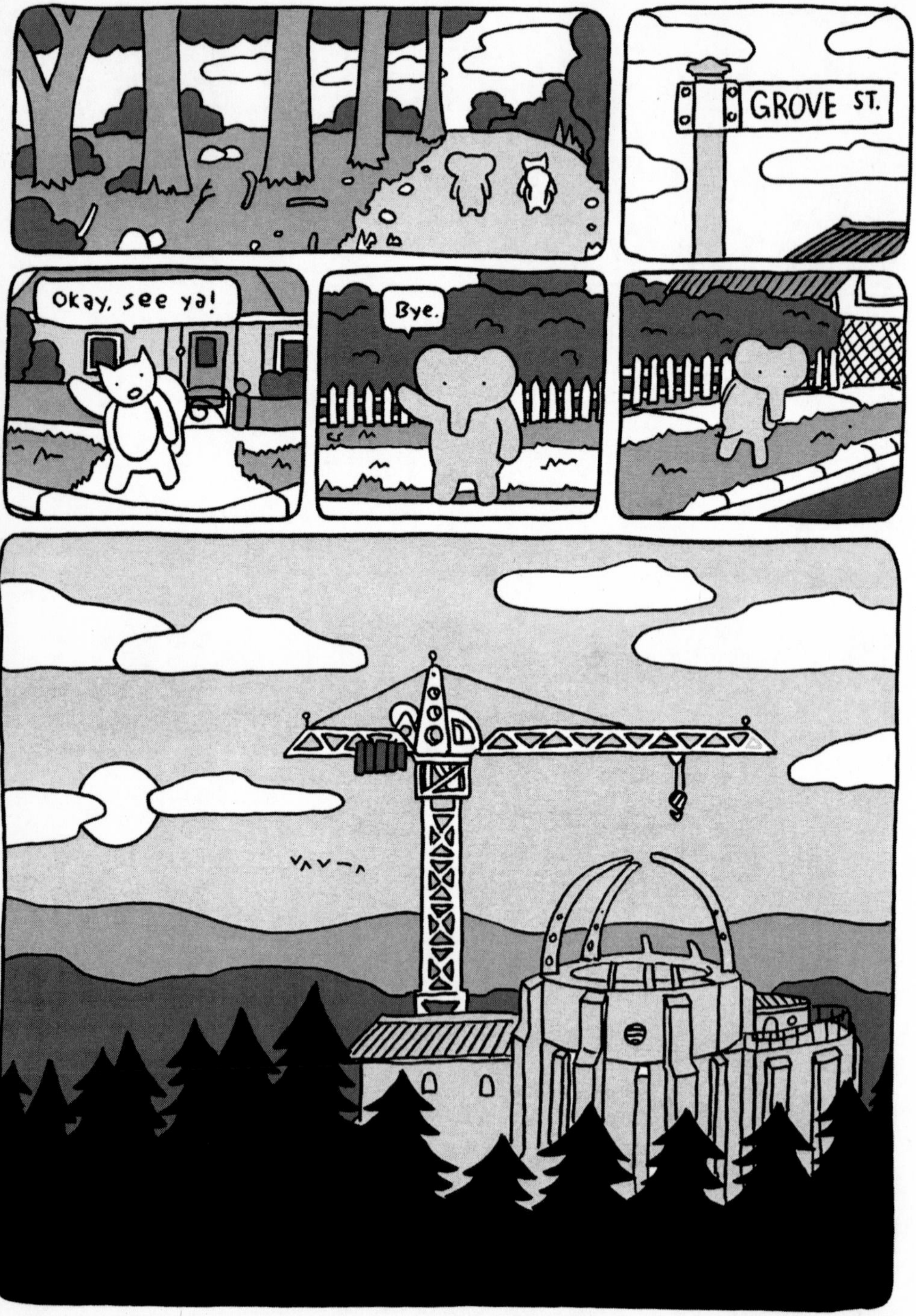
GROVE ST.
Okay, see ya!
Bye.

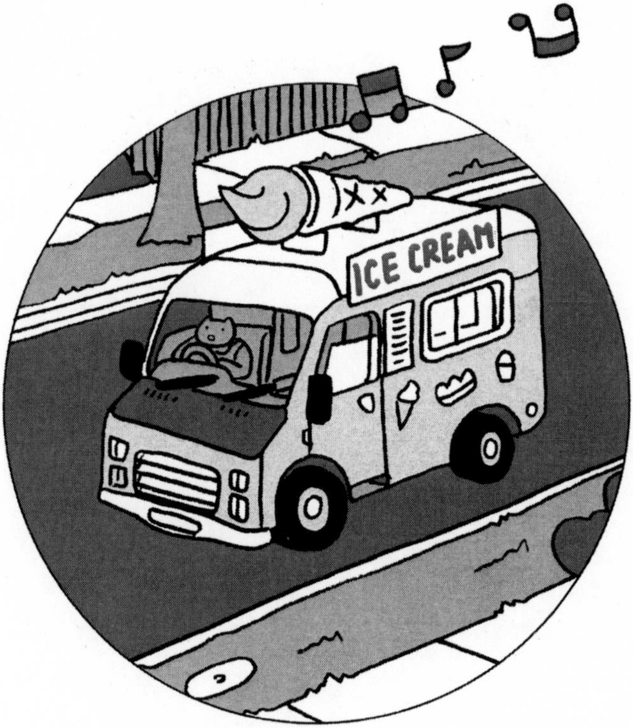
ICE CREAM

Chapter 3

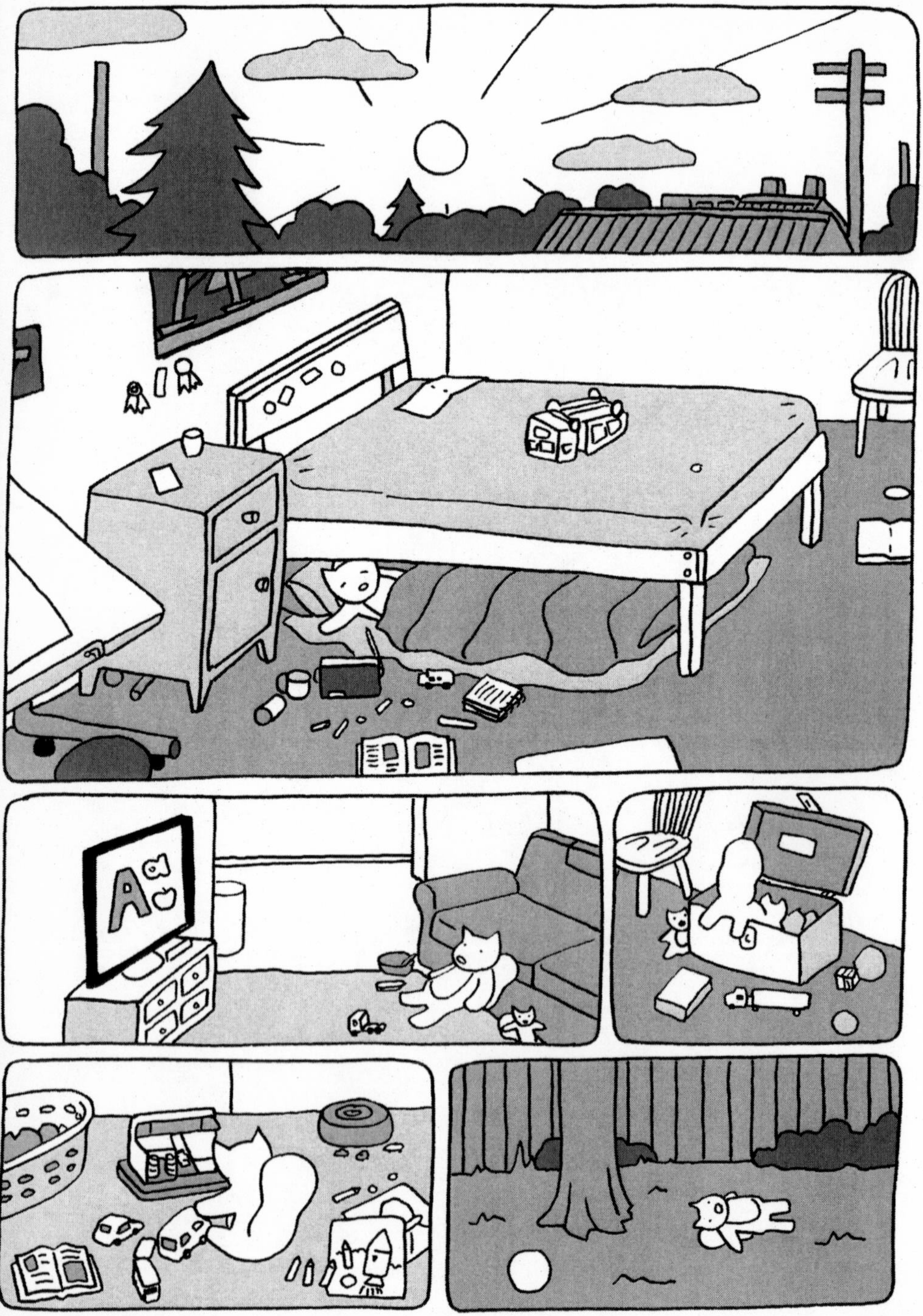

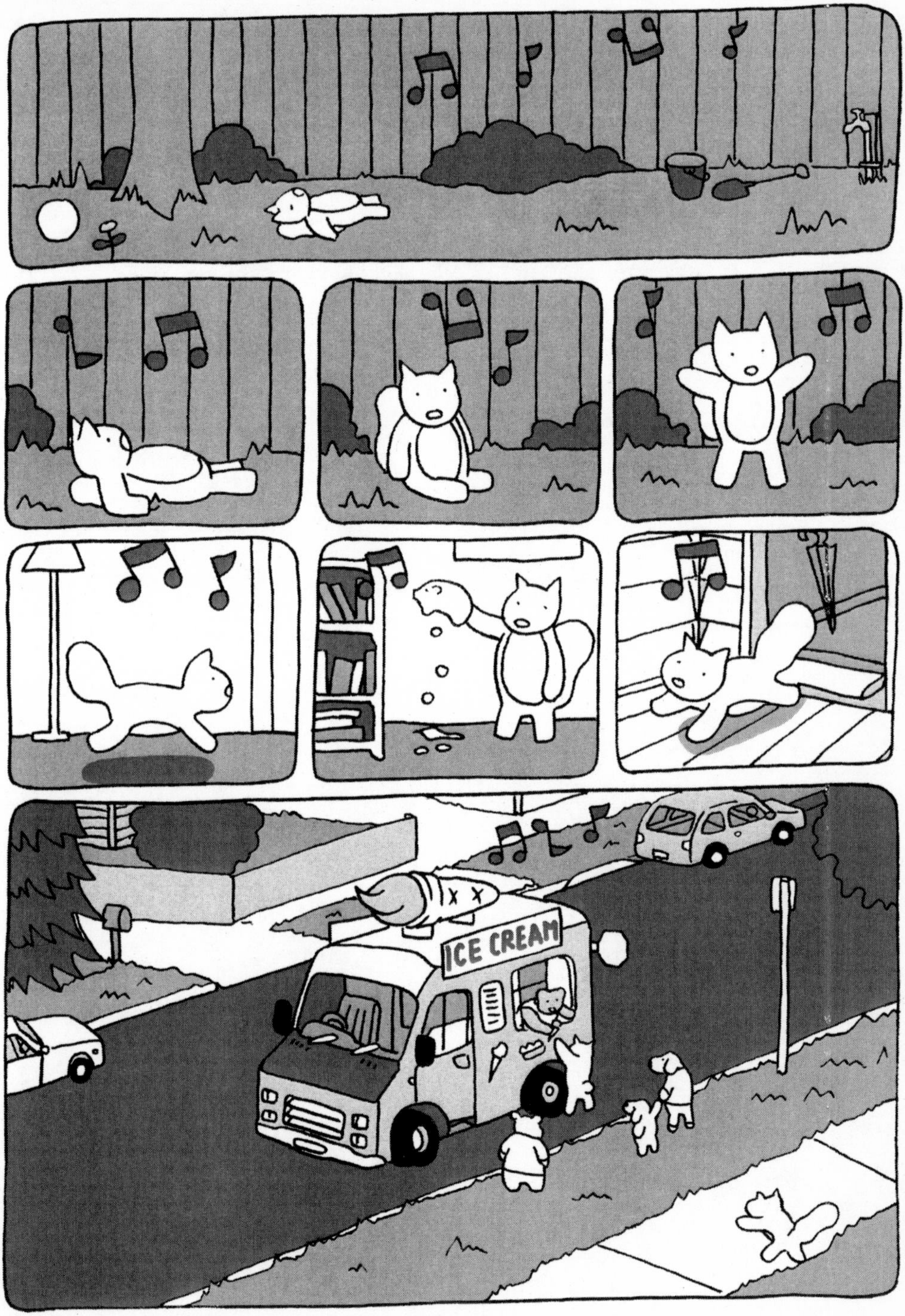
ICE CREAM

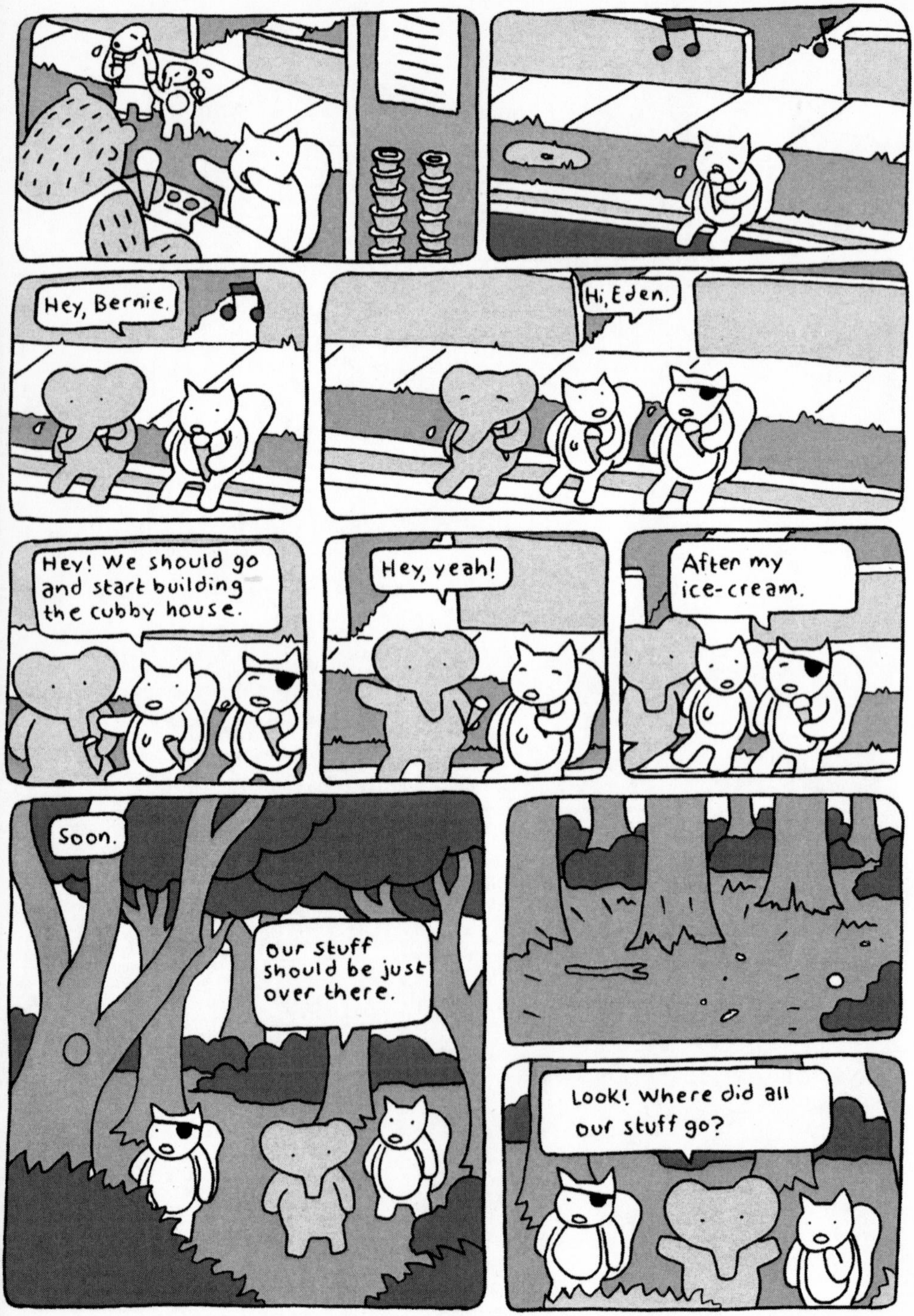

Hey, Bernie.
Hi, Eden.
Hey! We should go and start building the cubby house.
Hey, yeah!
After my ice-cream.
Soon.
Our stuff should be just over there.
Look! Where did all our stuff go?

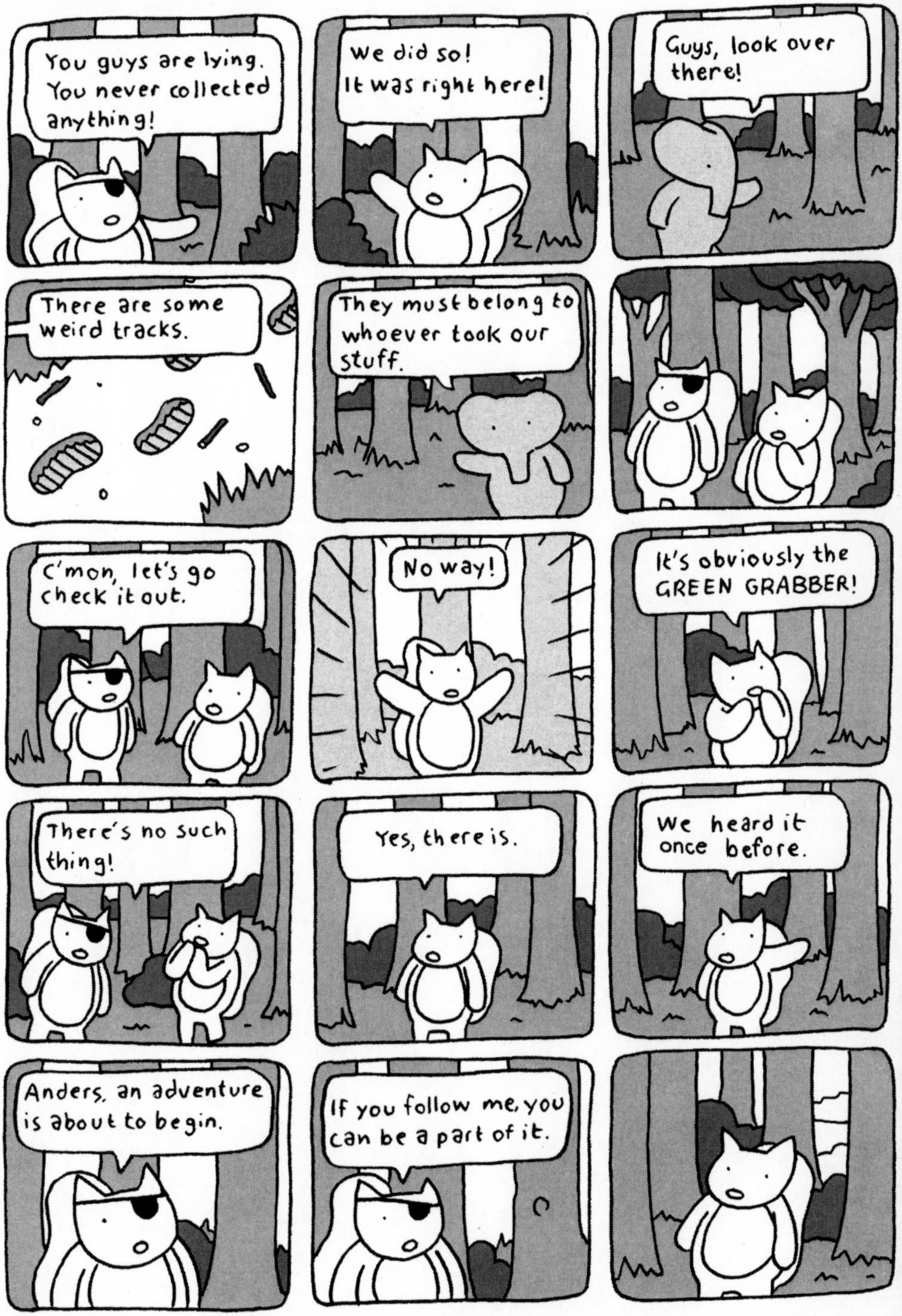
You guys are lying. You never collected anything!
We did so! It was right here!
Guys, look over there!
There are some weird tracks.
They must belong to whoever took our stuff.
C'mon, let's go check it out.
No way!
It's obviously the GREEN GRABBER!
There's no such thing!
Yes, there is.
We heard it once before.
Anders, an adventure is about to begin.
If you follow me, you can be a part of it.

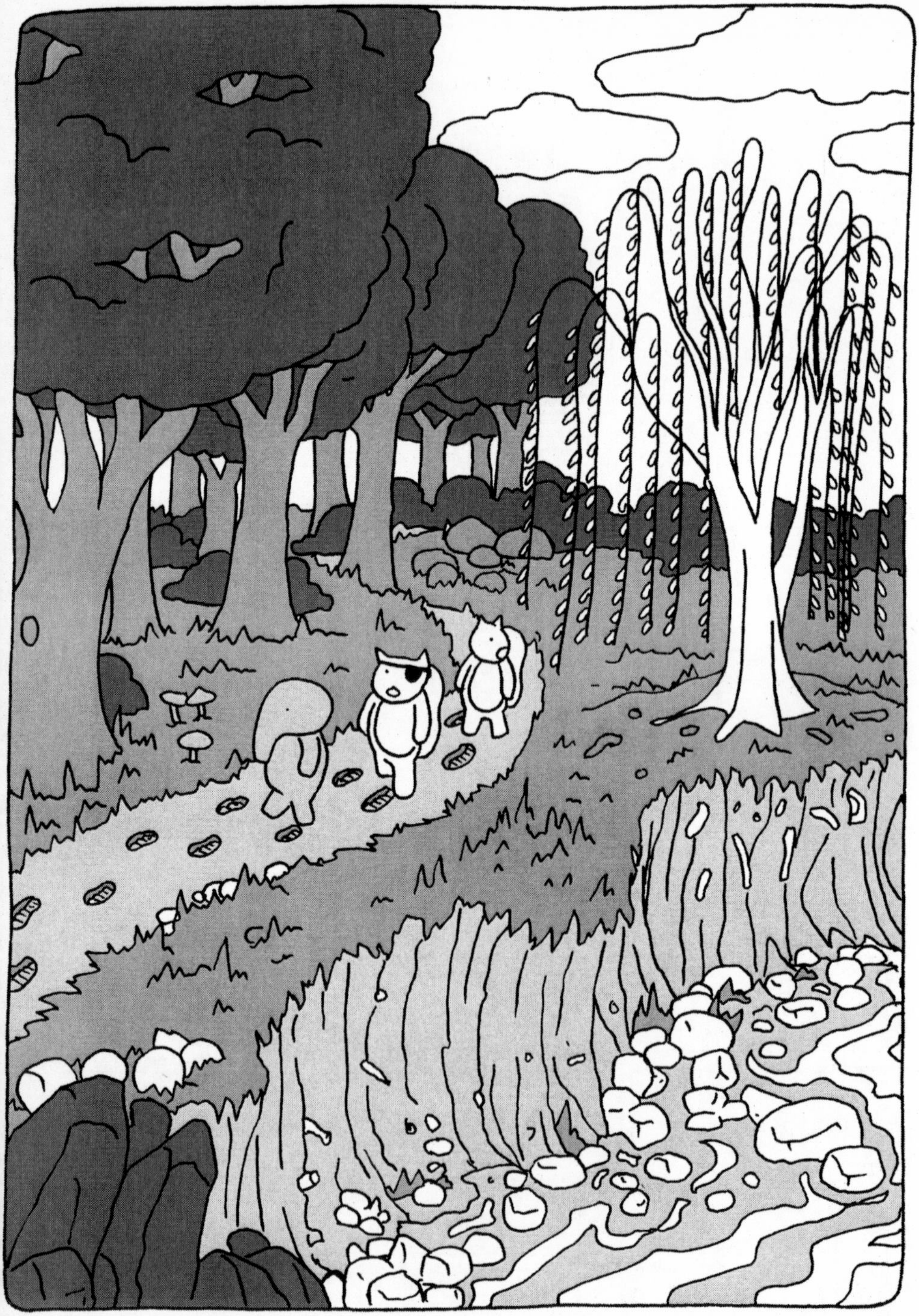

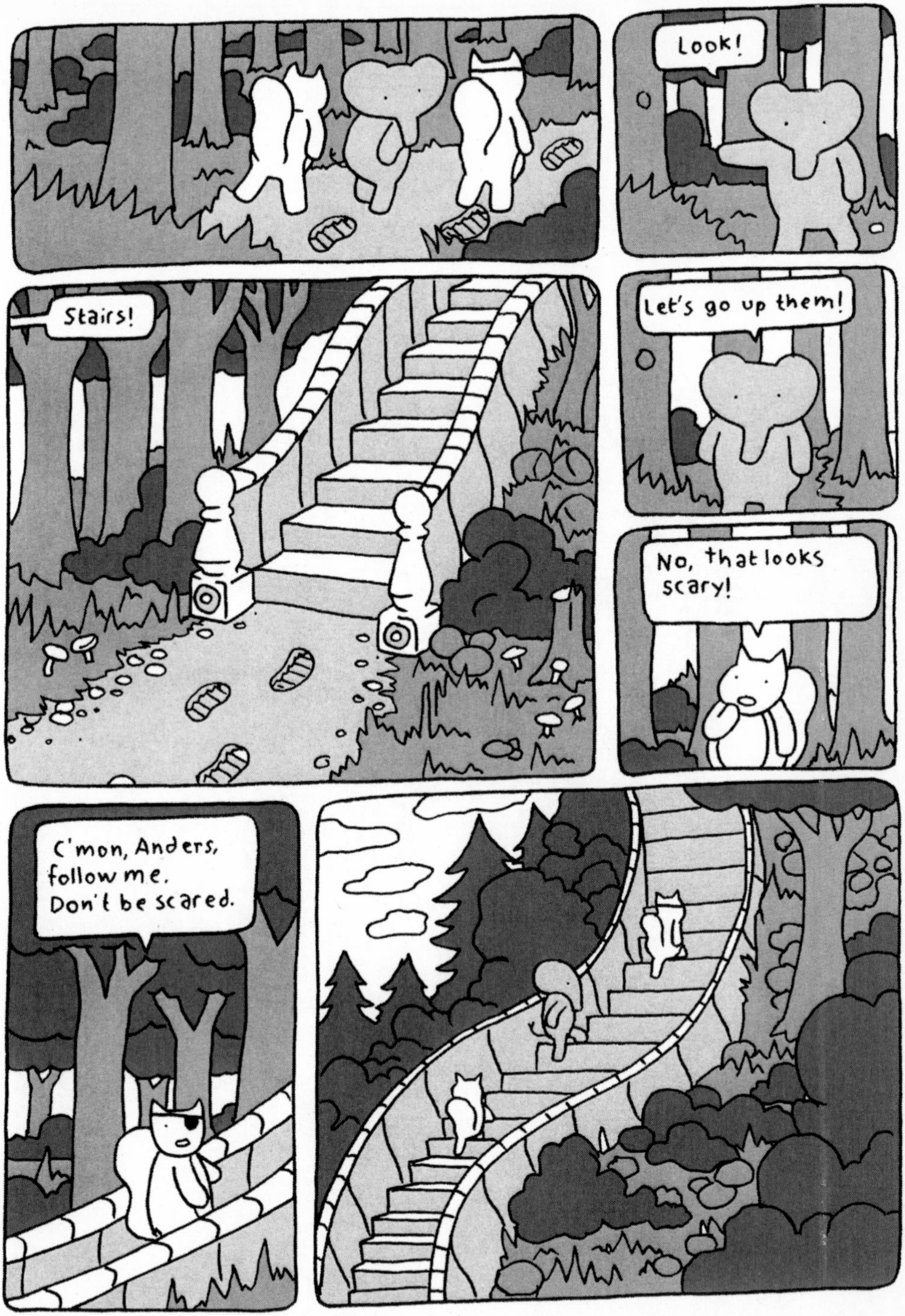
Look!
Stairs!
Let's go up them!
No, that looks scary!
C'mon, Anders, follow me. Don't be scared.

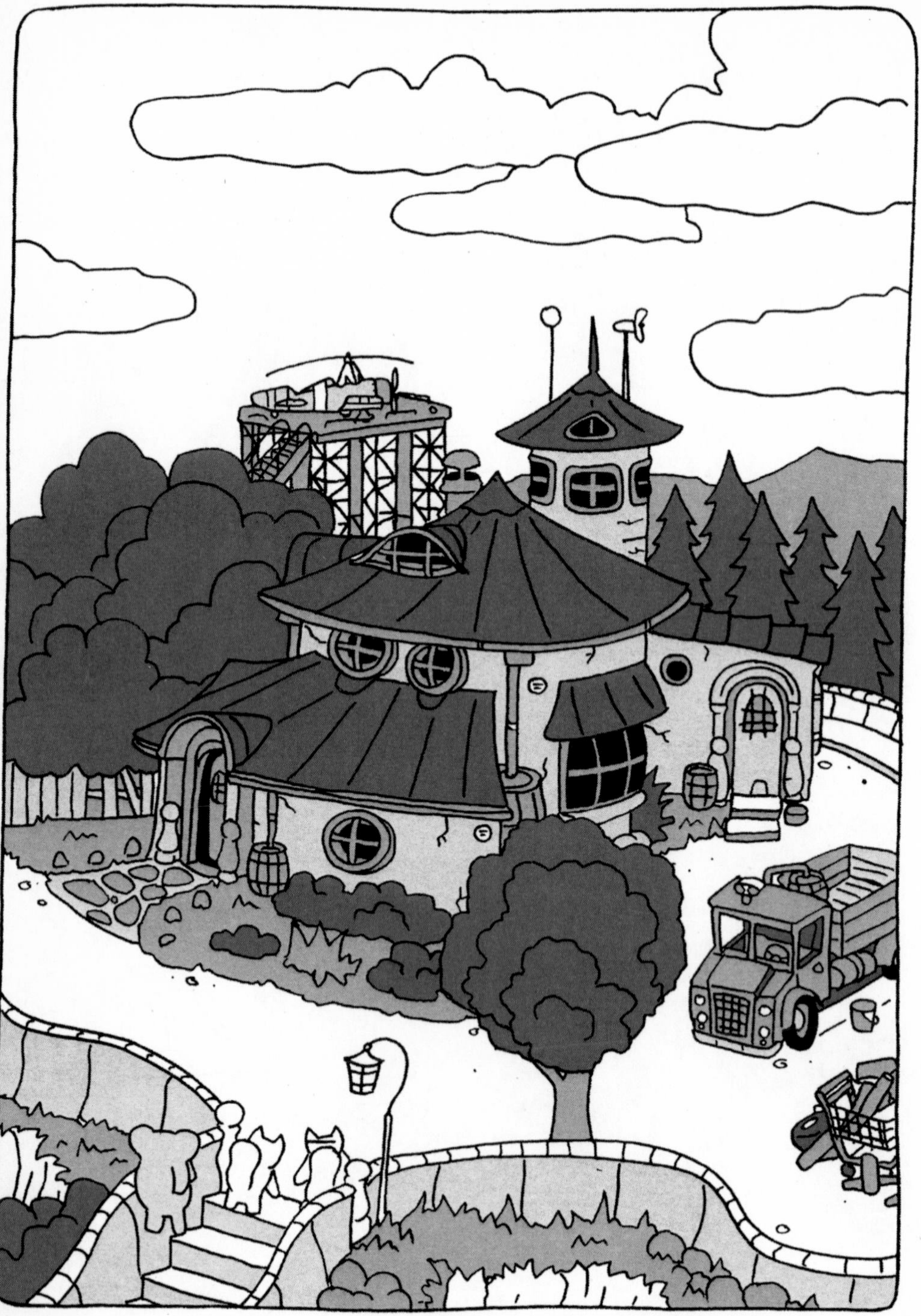

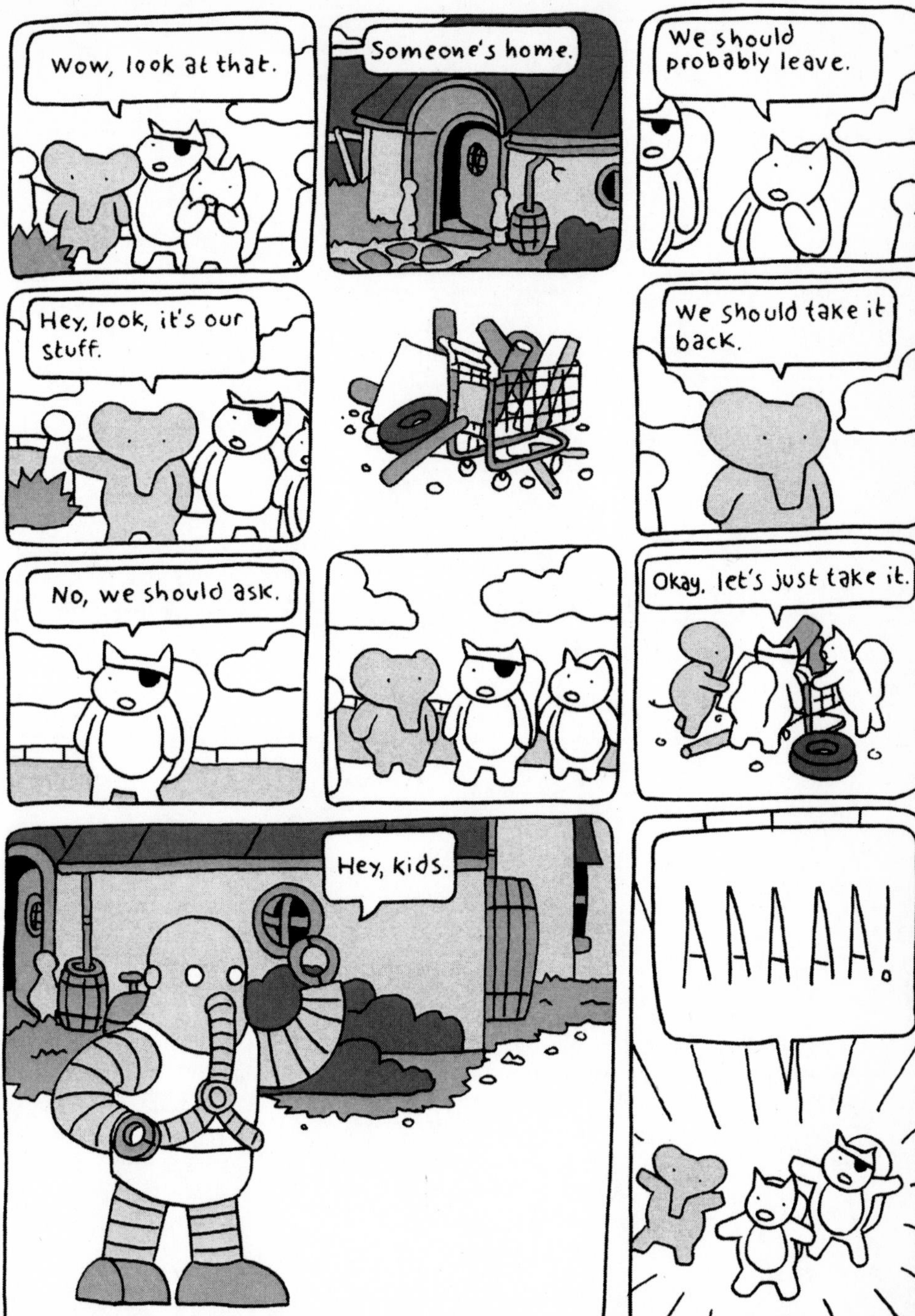
Wow, look at that.
Someone's home.
We should probably leave.
Hey, look, it's our stuff.
We should take it back.
No, we should ask.
Okay, let's just take it.
Hey, kids.
AAAAA!

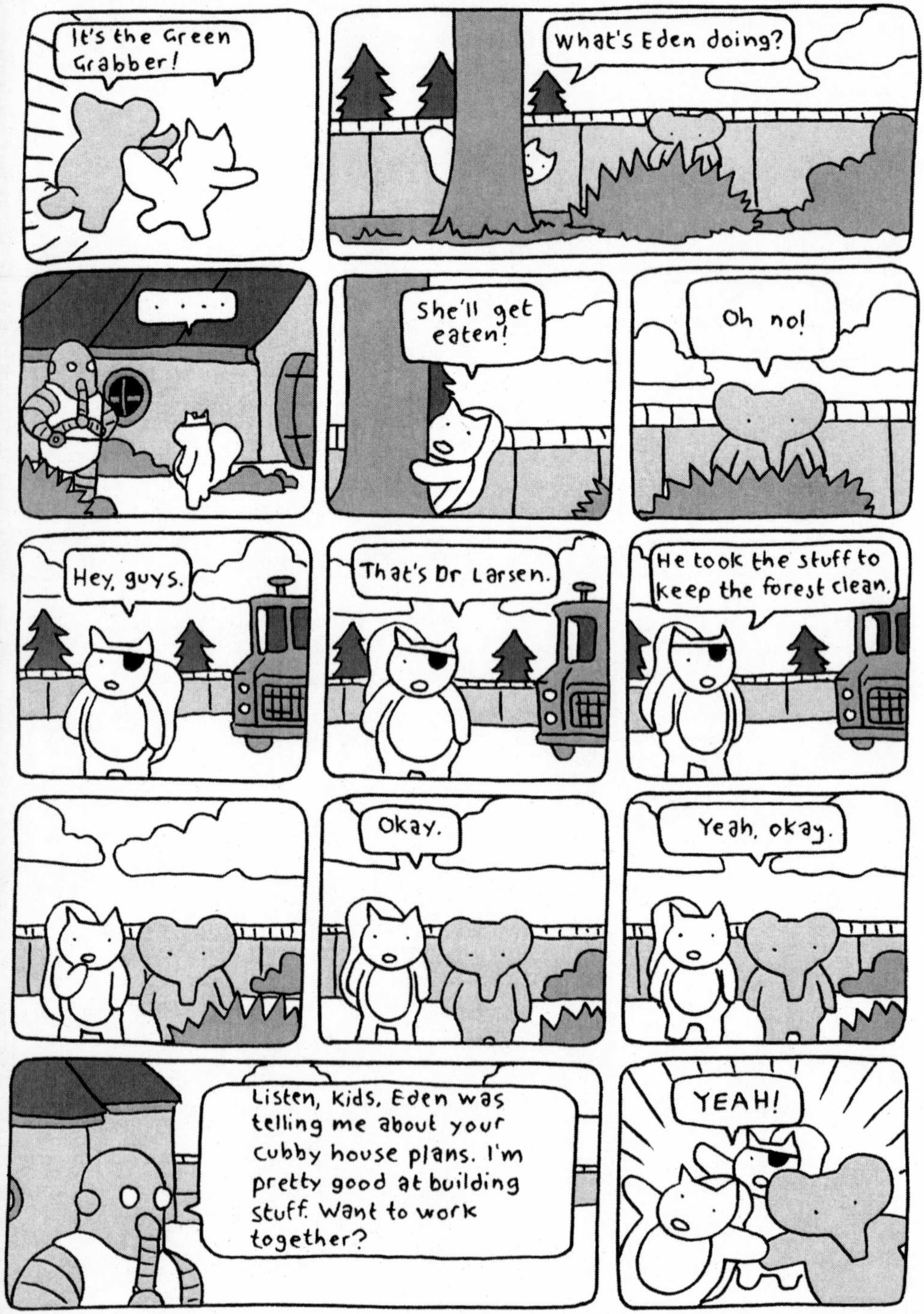
It's the Green Grabber!
What's Eden doing?
. . . .
She'll get eaten!
Oh no!
Hey, guys.
That's Dr Larsen.
He took the stuff to keep the forest clean.
Okay.
Yeah, okay.
Listen, kids, Eden was telling me about your cubby house plans. I'm pretty good at building stuff. Want to work together?
YEAH!

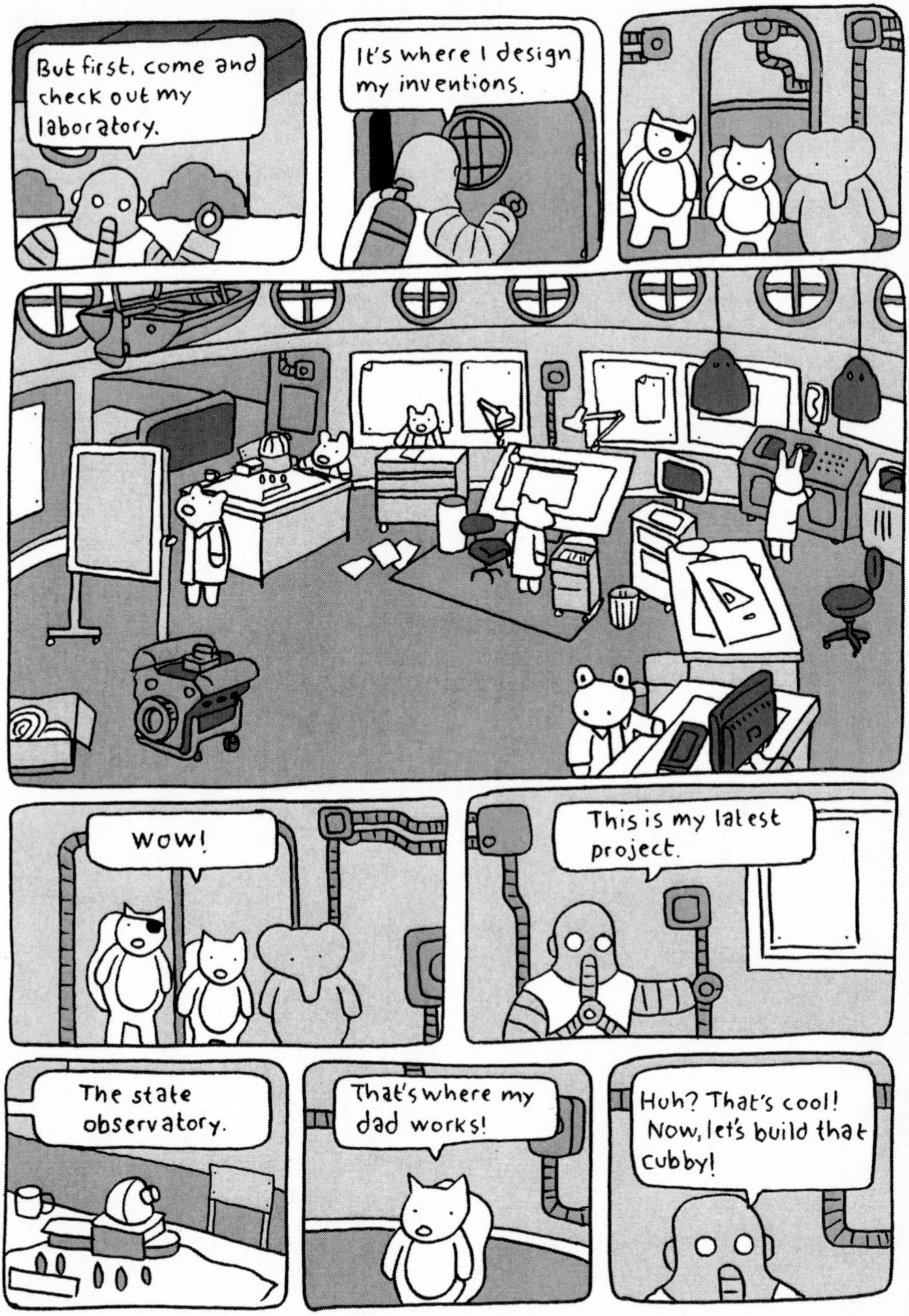
But first, come and check out my laboratory.
It's where I design my inventions.
WOW!
This is my latest project.
The state observatory.
That's where my dad works!
Huh? That's cool! Now, let's build that cubby!

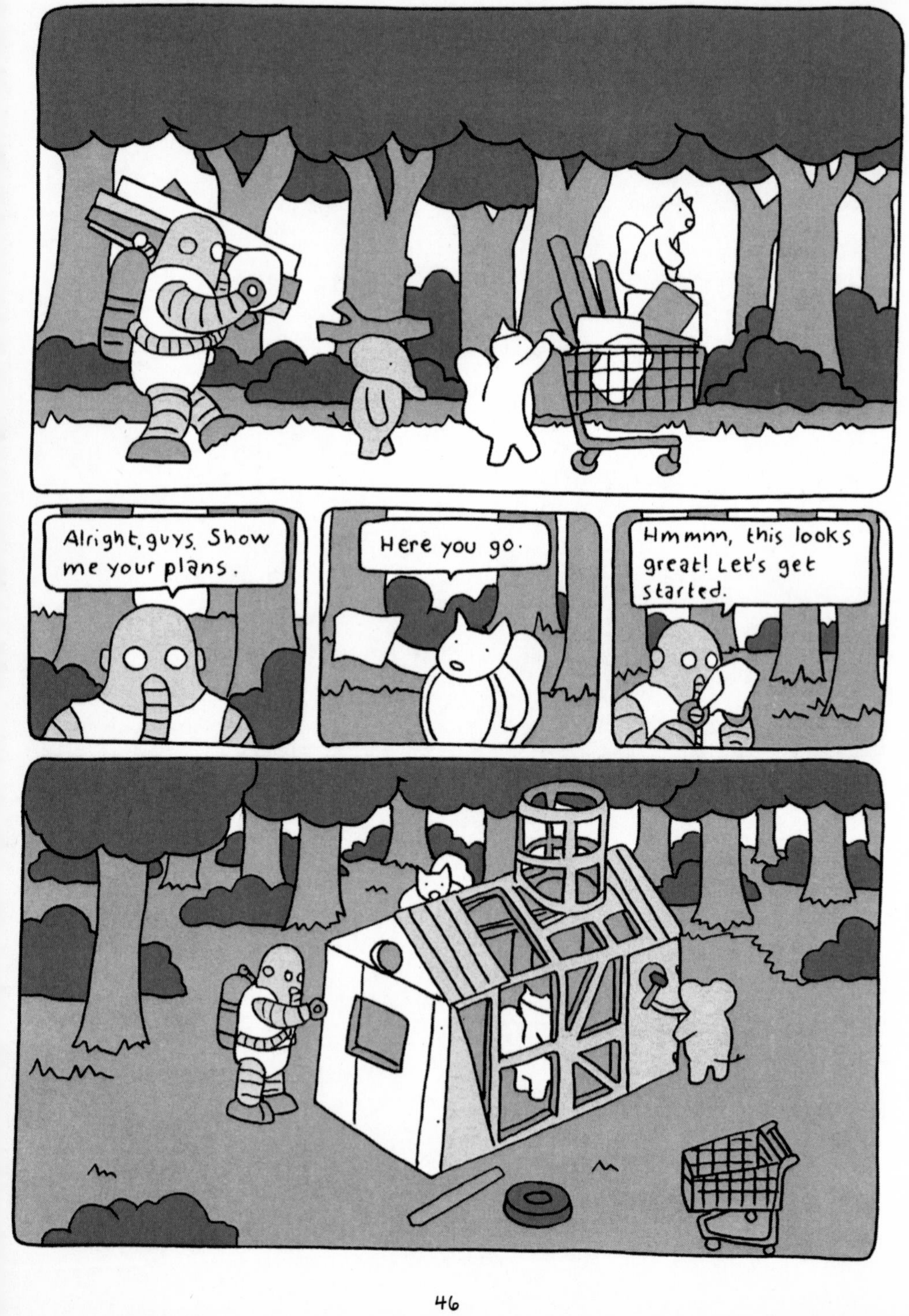
Alright, guys. Show me your plans.
Here you go.
Hmmnn, this looks great! Let's get started.

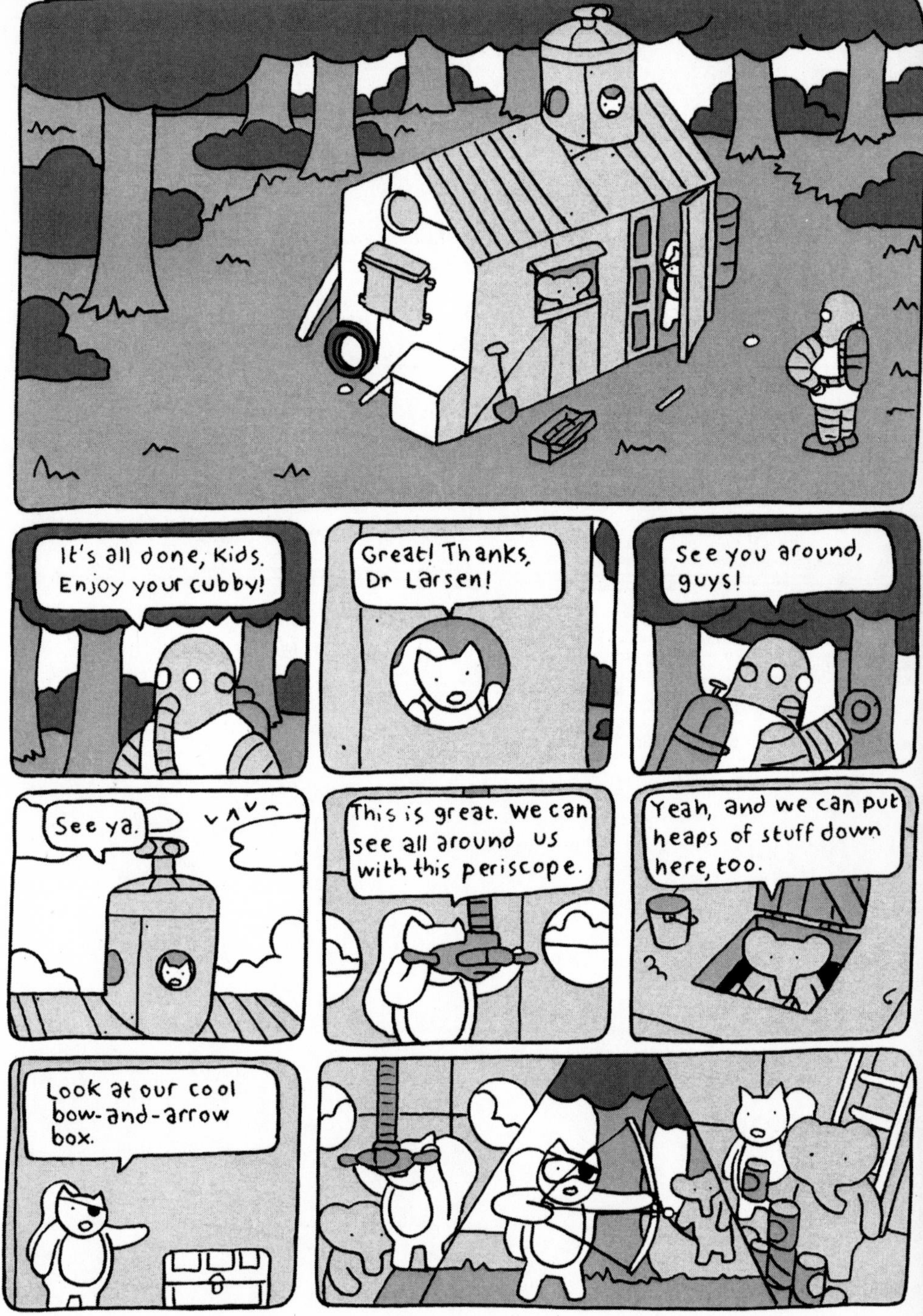
It's all done, Kids. Enjoy your cubby!
Great! Thanks, Dr Larsen!
See you around, guys!
See ya.
This is great. We can see all around us with this periscope.
Yeah, and we can put heaps of stuff down here, too.
Look at our cool bow-and-arrow box.

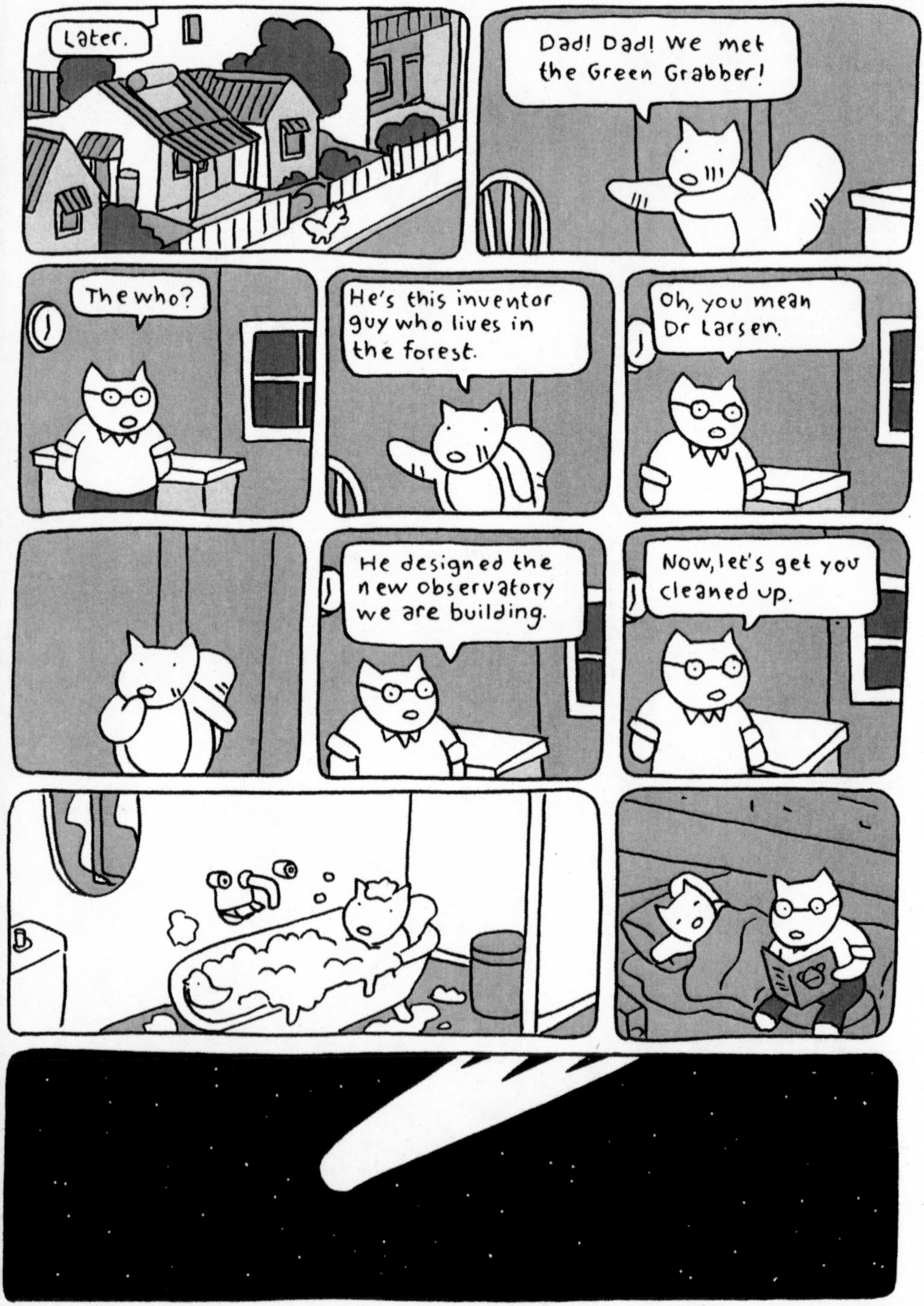
Later.
Dad! Dad! We met the Green Grabber!
The who?
He's this inventor guy who lives in the forest.
Oh, you mean Dr Larsen.
He designed the new observatory we are building.
Now, let's get you cleaned up.

Chapter 4

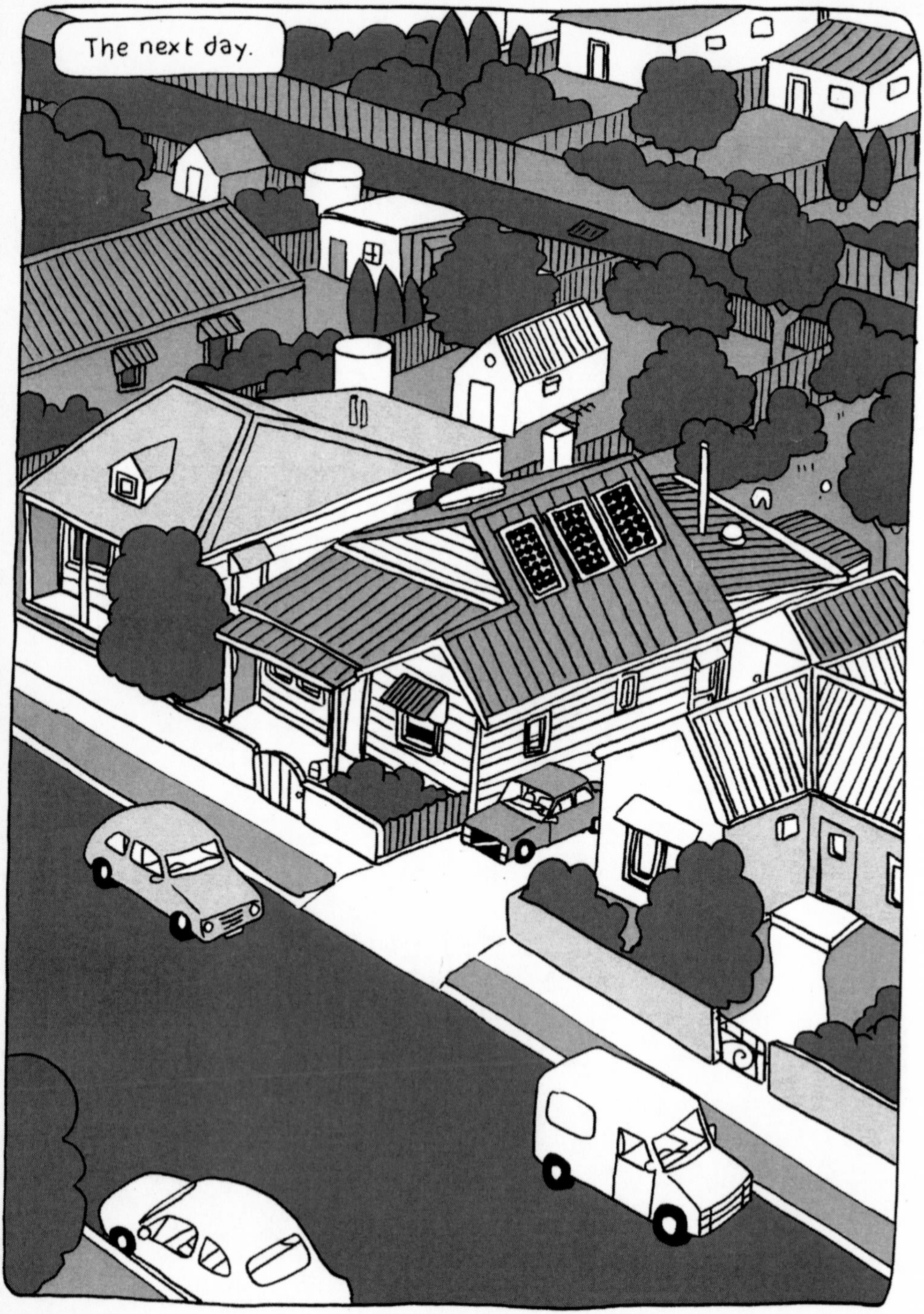
The next day.

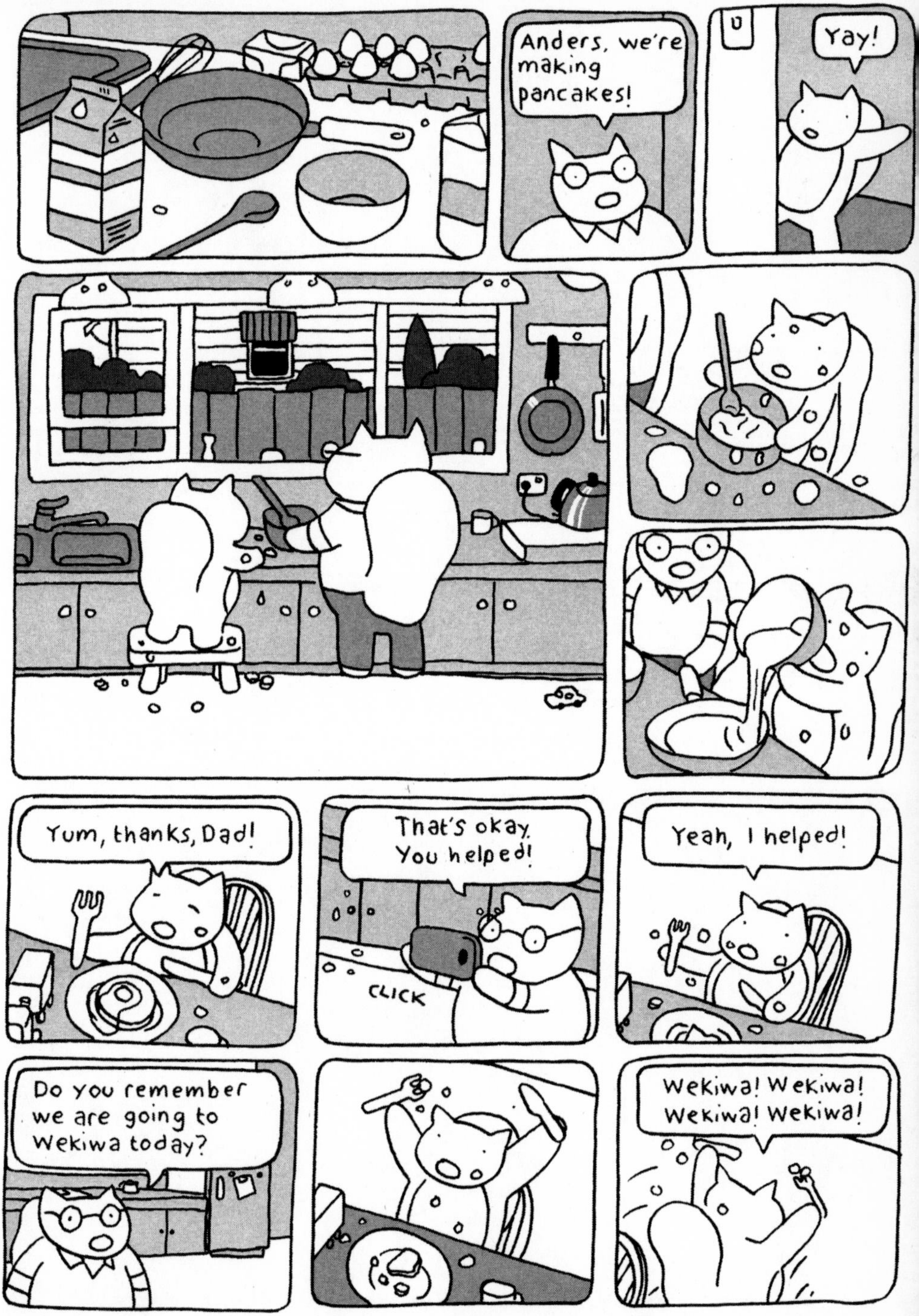
Anders, we're making pancakes!
Yay!
Yum, thanks, Dad!
That's okay. You helped!
CLICK
Yeah, I helped!
Do you remember we are going to Wekiwa today?
Wekiwa! Wekiwa! Wekiwa! Wekiwa!

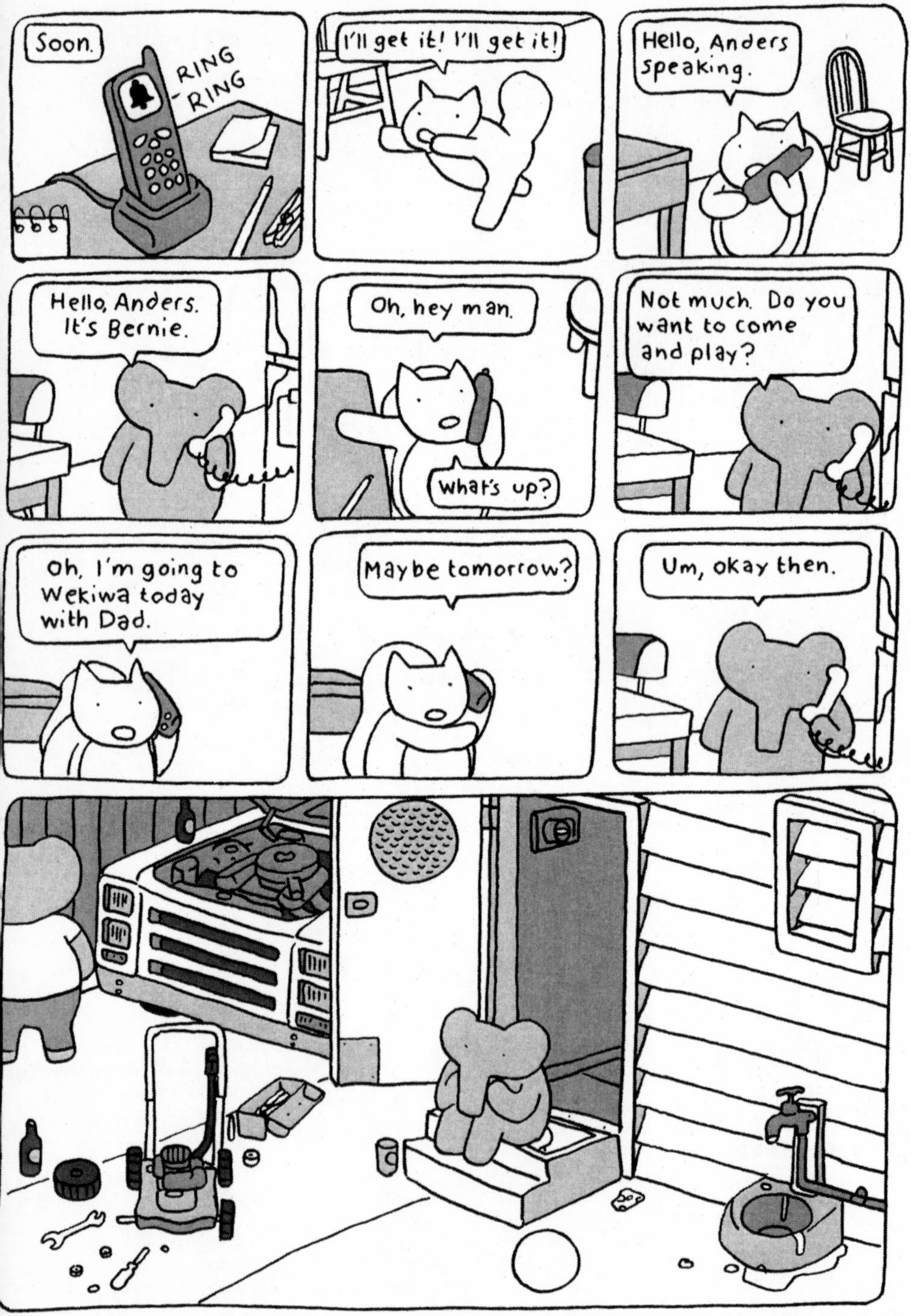
Soon.
RING RING
I'll get it! I'll get it!
Hello, Anders speaking.
Hello, Anders. It's Bernie.
Oh, hey man.
What's up?
Not much. Do you want to come and play?
Oh, I'm going to Wekiwa today with Dad.
Maybe tomorrow?
Um, okay then.

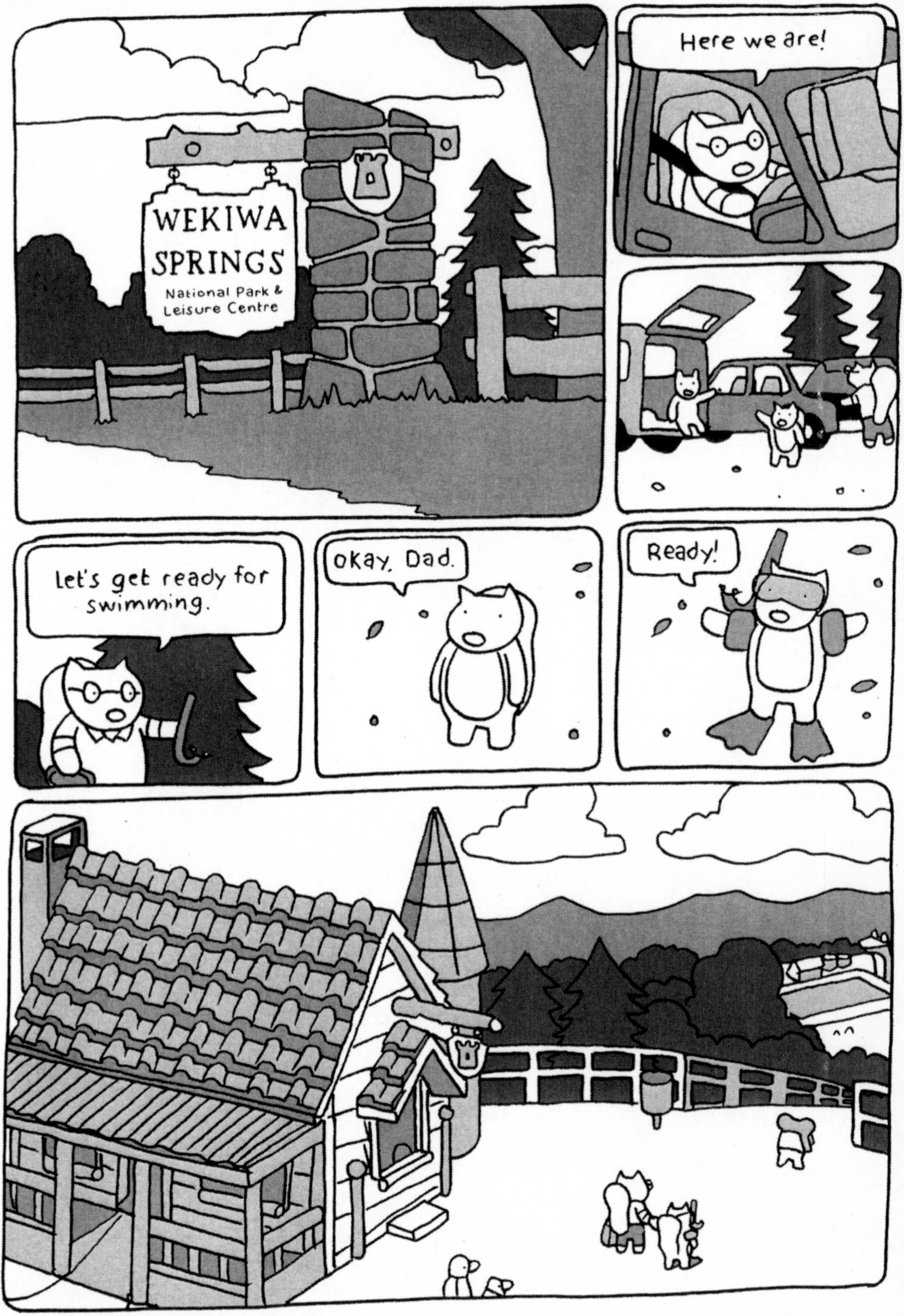
WEKIWA
SPRINGS
National Park &
Leisure Centre
Here we are!
let's get ready for swimming.
okay, Dad.
Ready!

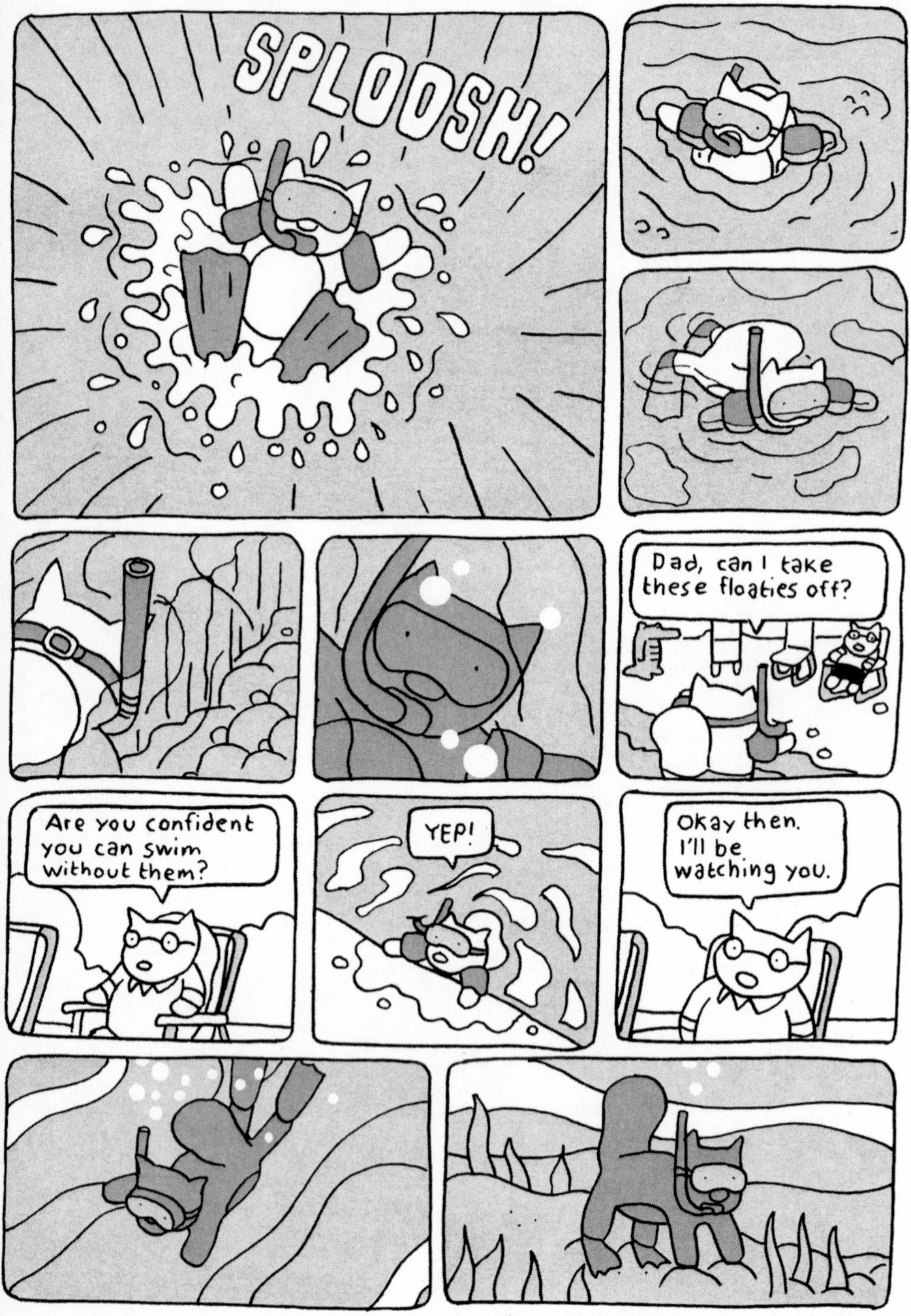
SPLOOSH!
Dad, can I take these floaties off?
Are you confident you can swim without them?
YEP!
Okay then. I'll be watching you.

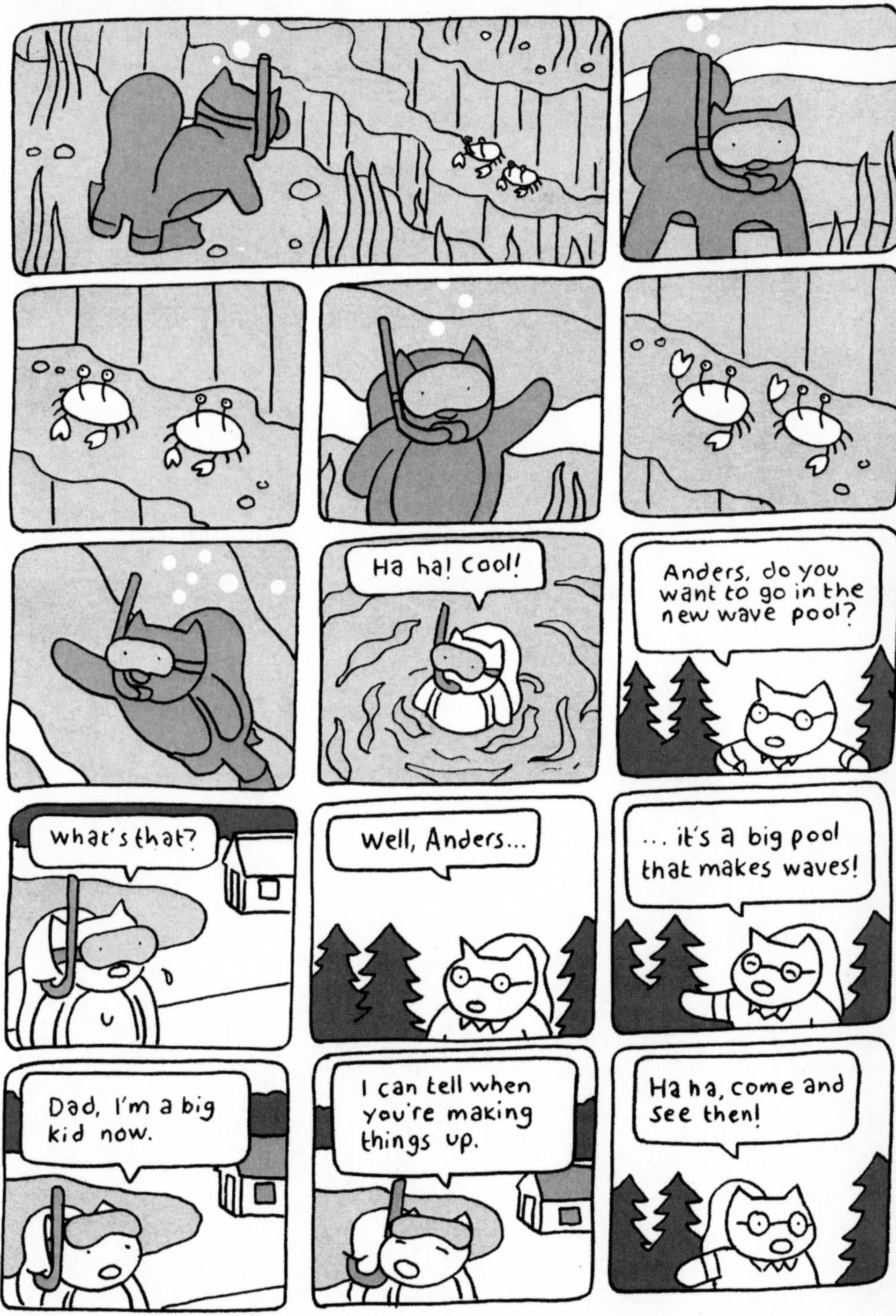
Ha ha! Cool!
Anders, do you want to go in the new wave pool?
What's that?
Well, Anders...
... it's a big pool that makes waves!
Dad, I'm a big kid now.
I can tell when you're making things up.
Ha ha, come and see then!

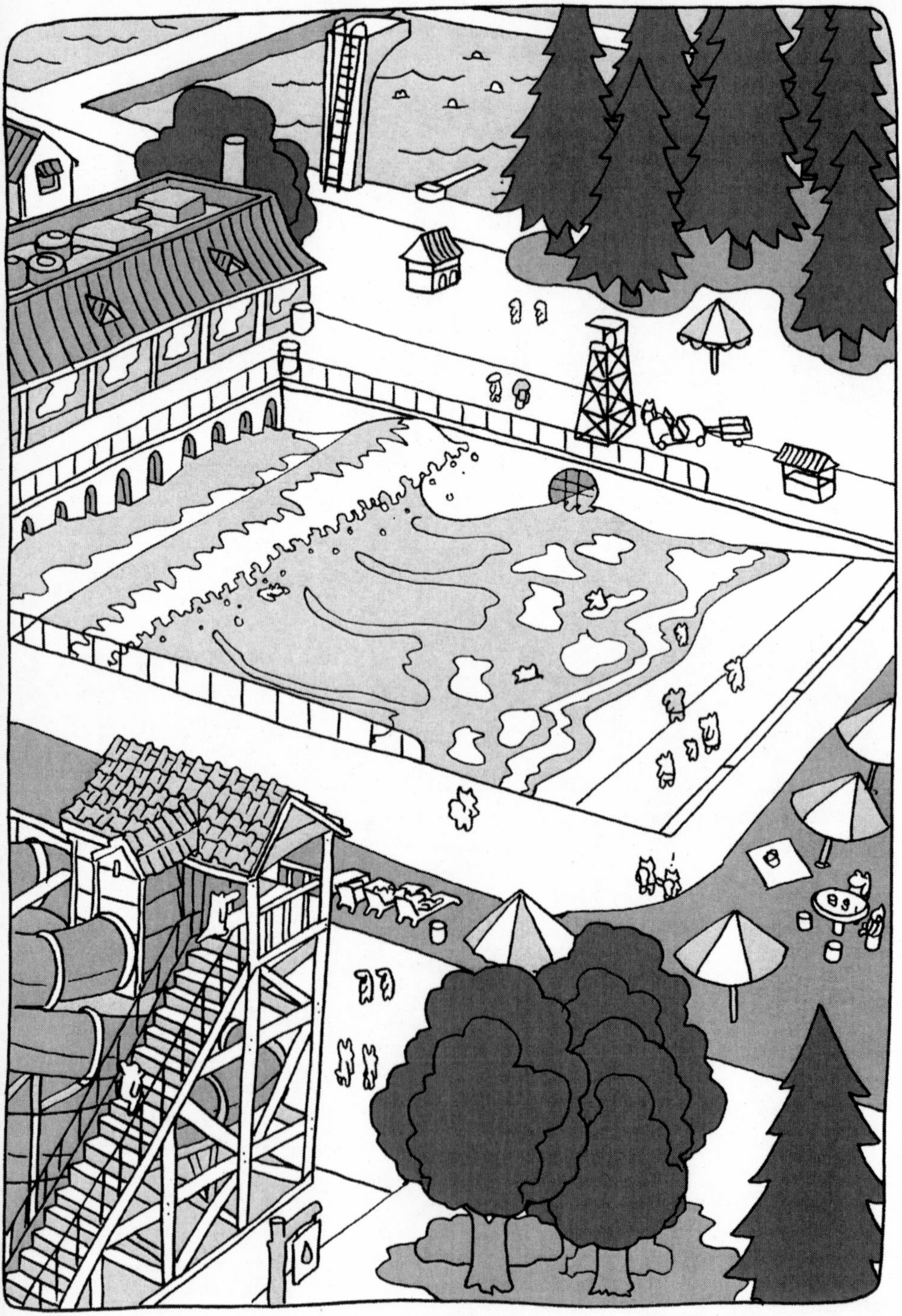

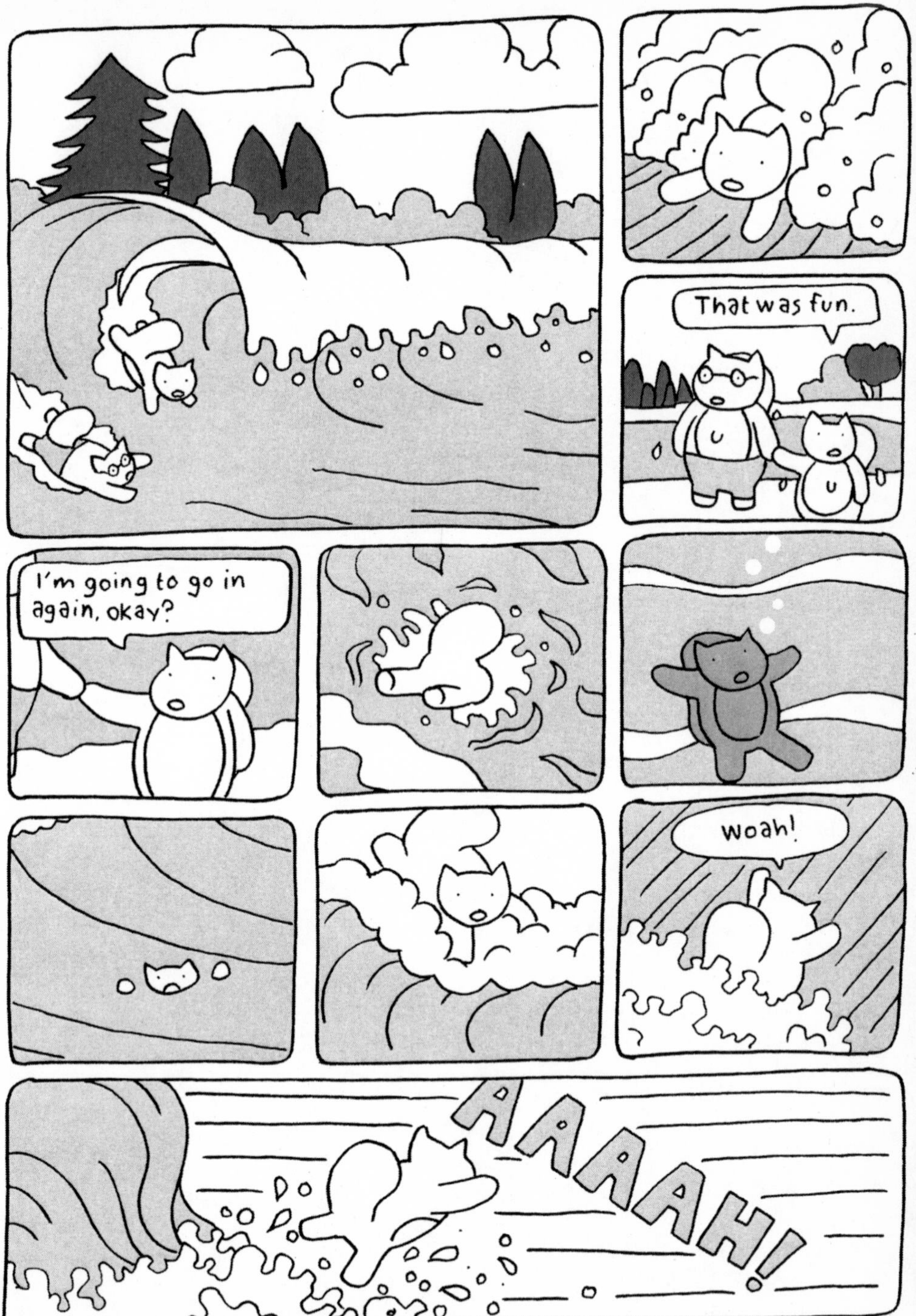

That was fun.
I'm going to go in again, okay?
woah!
AAAAAH!

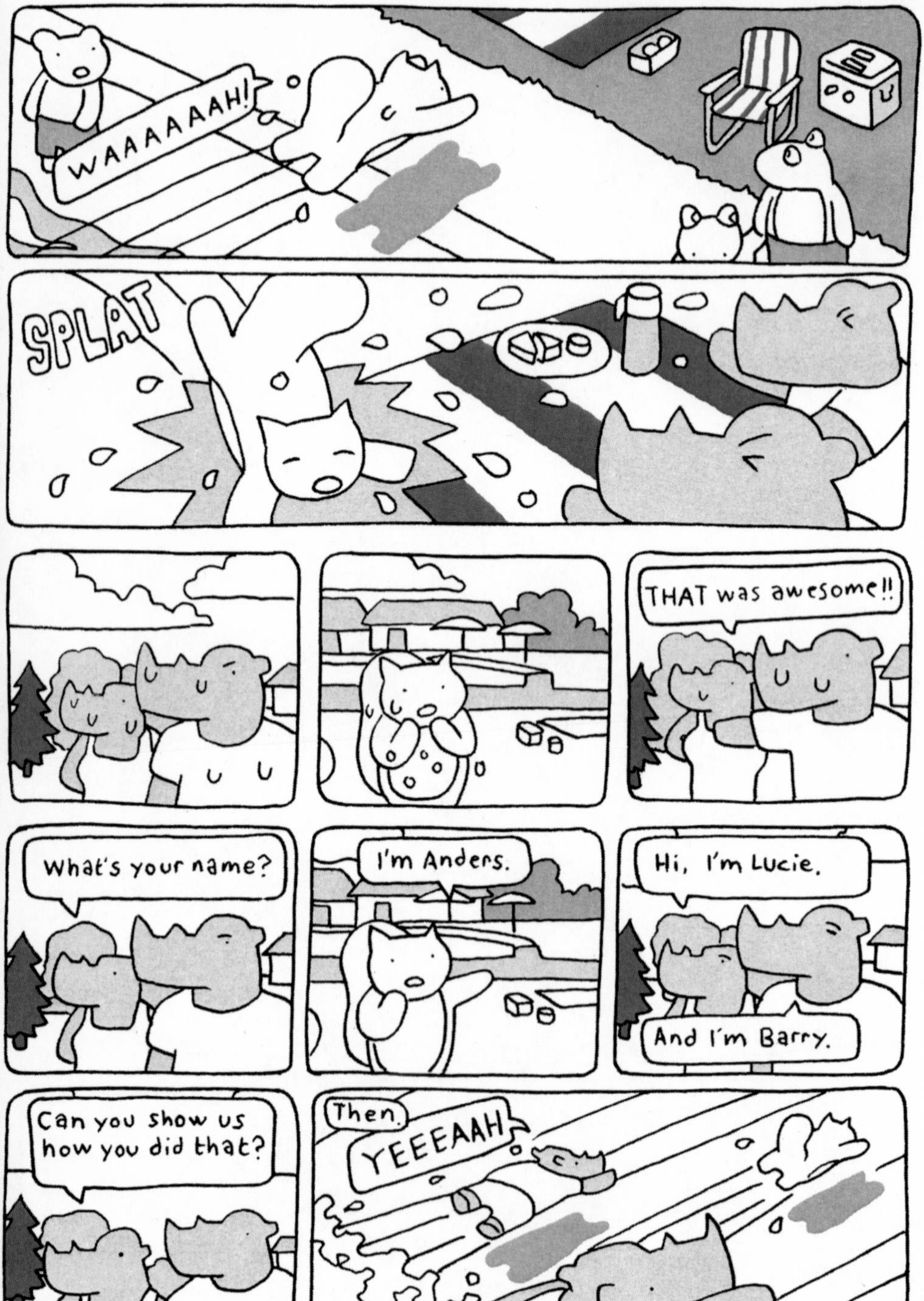
WAAAAAAH!
SPLAT
THAT was awesome!!
What's your name?
I'm Anders.
Hi, I'm Lucie.
And I'm Barry.
Can you show us how you did that?
Then.
YEEEAAH

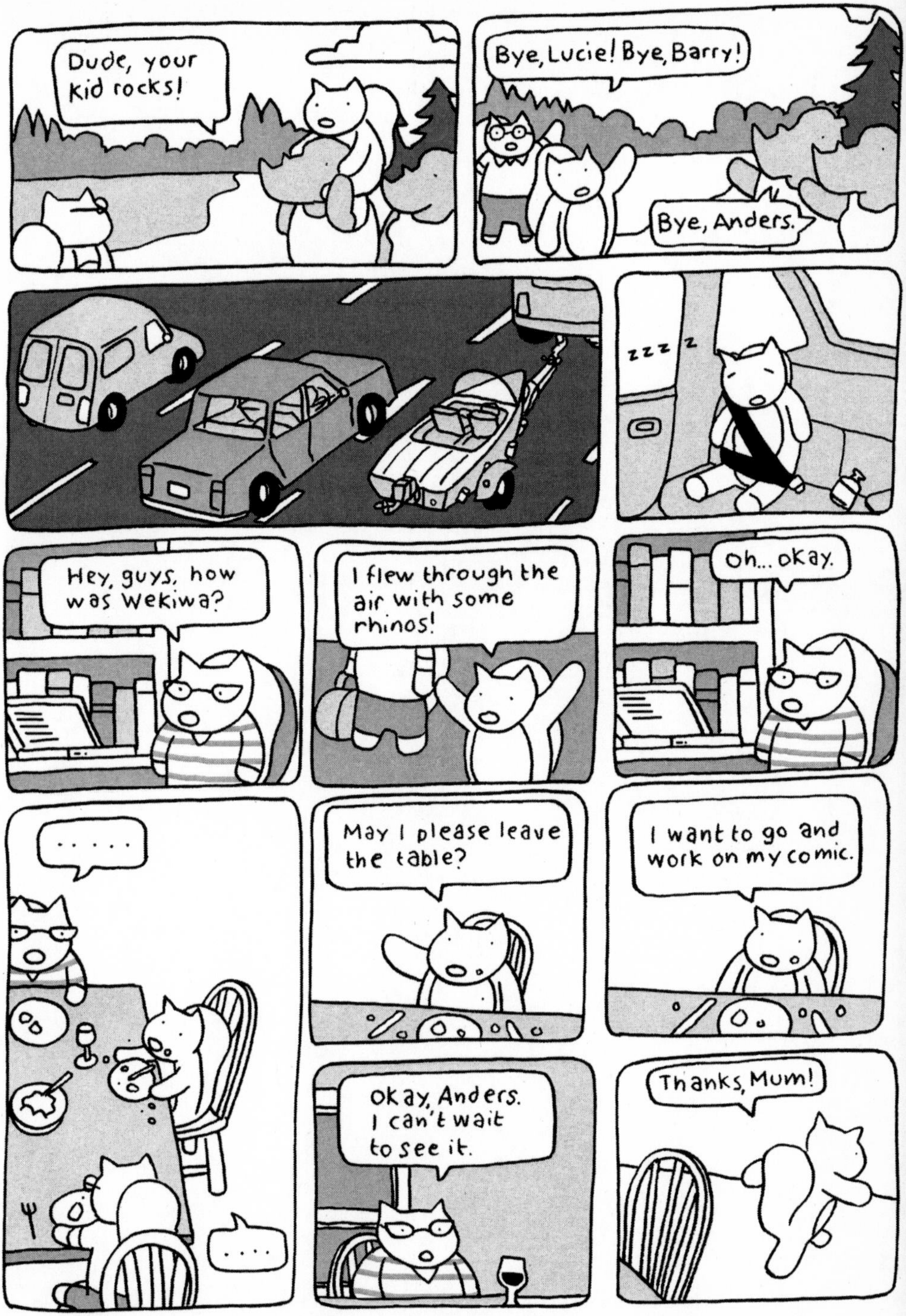
Dude, your kid rocks!
Bye, Lucie! Bye, Barry!
Bye, Anders.
z z z z
Hey, guys, how was Wekiwa?
I flew through the air with some rhinos!
Oh... okay.
. . . . .
. . . .
May I please leave the table?
I want to go and work on my comic.
Okay, Anders. I can't wait to see it.
Thanks, Mum!

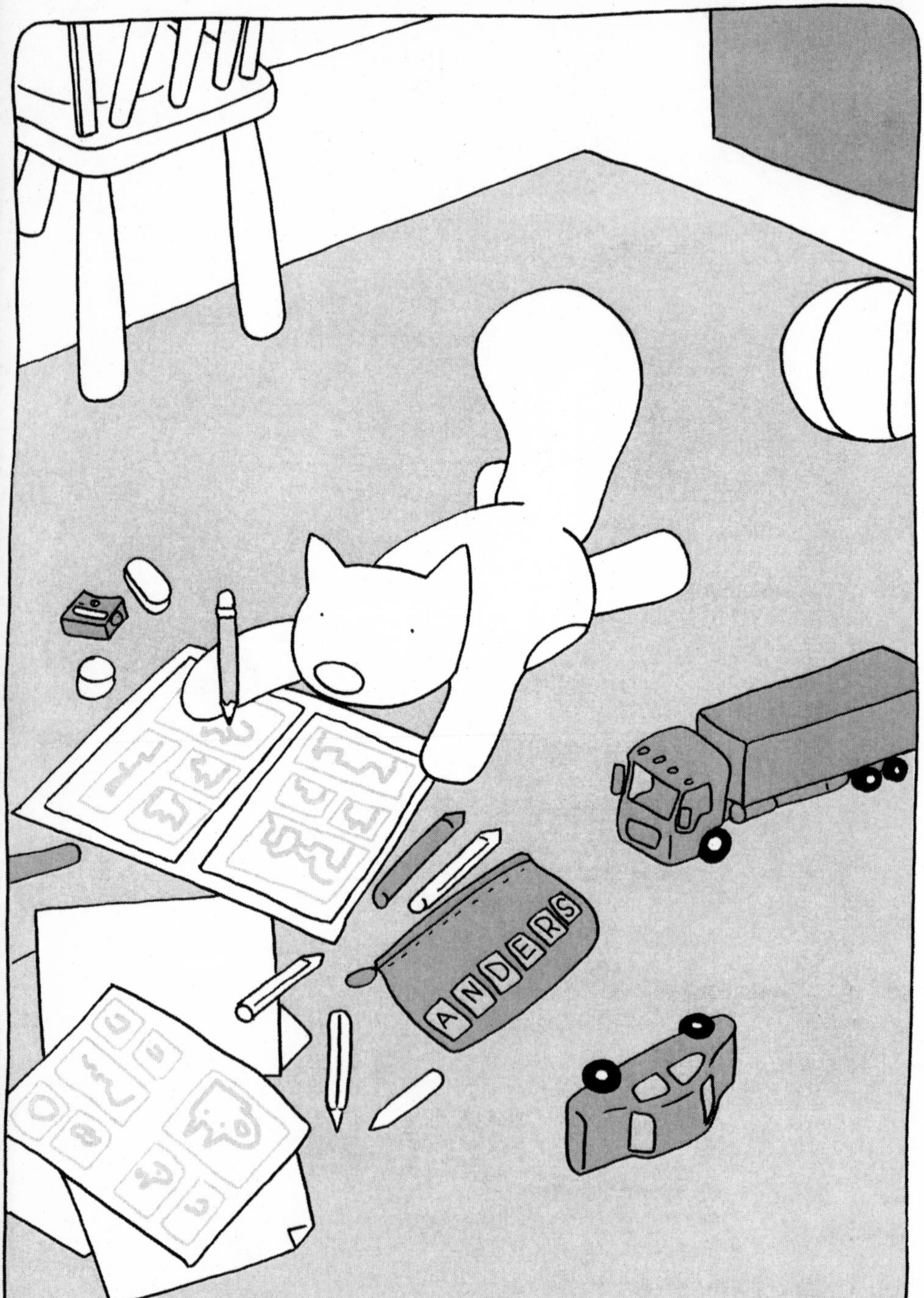
ANDERS

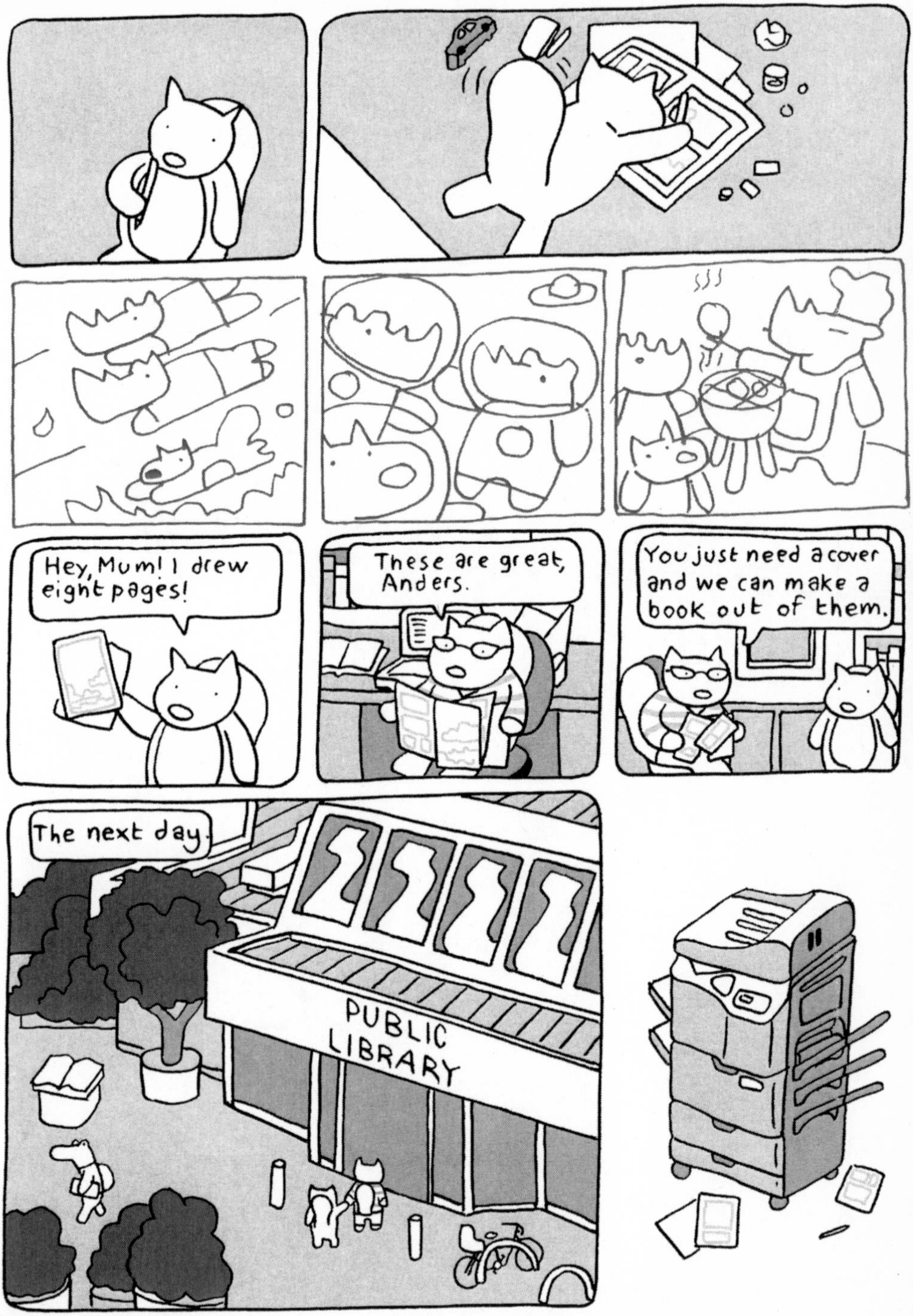
Hey, Mum! I drew eight pages!
These are great, Anders.
You just need a cover and we can make a book out of them.
The next day.
PUBLIC LIBRARY

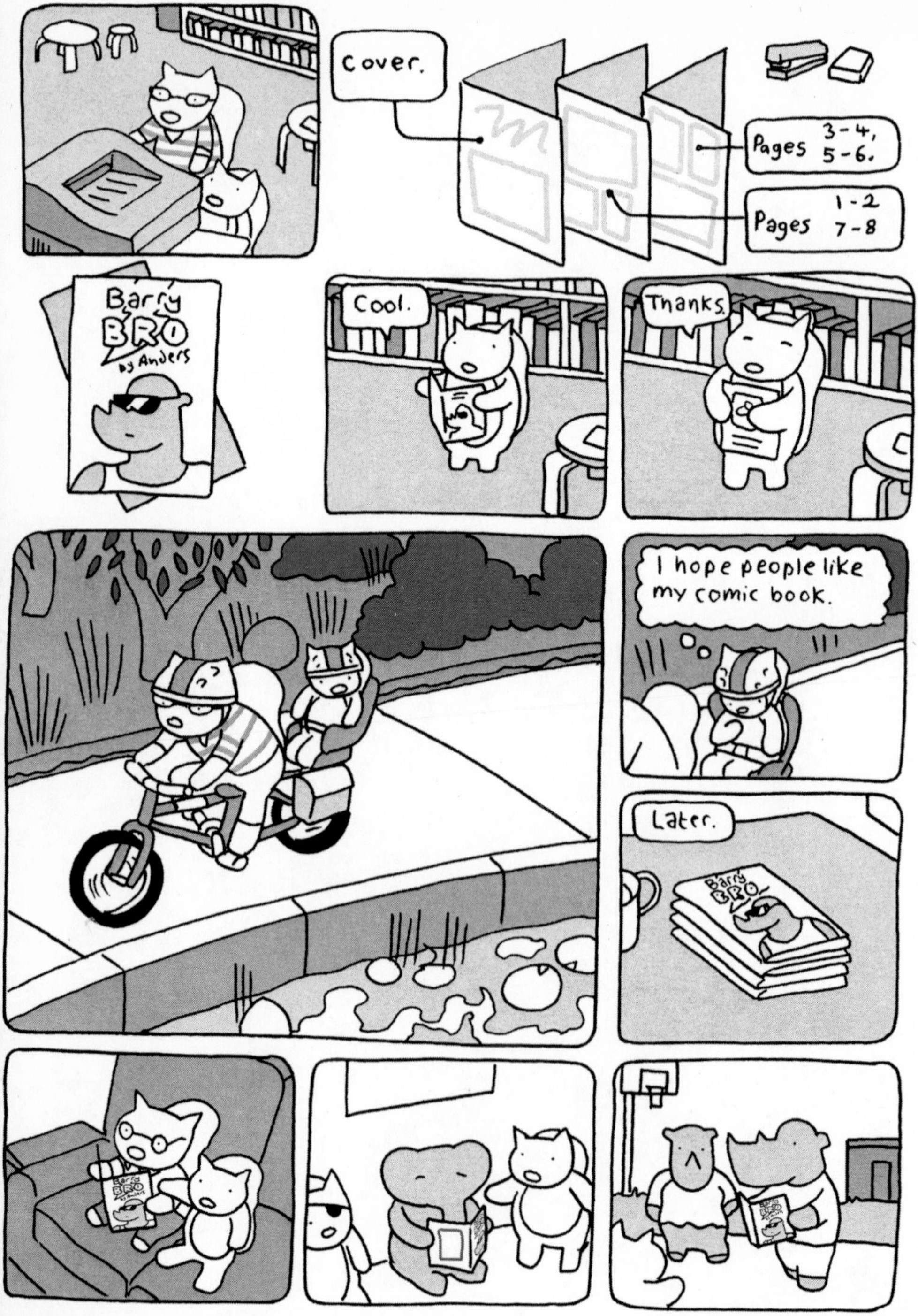
Cover.
Pages 3-4, 5-6.
Pages 1-2 7-8
Barry BRO by Anders
Cool.
Thanks.
I hope people like my comic book.
Later.

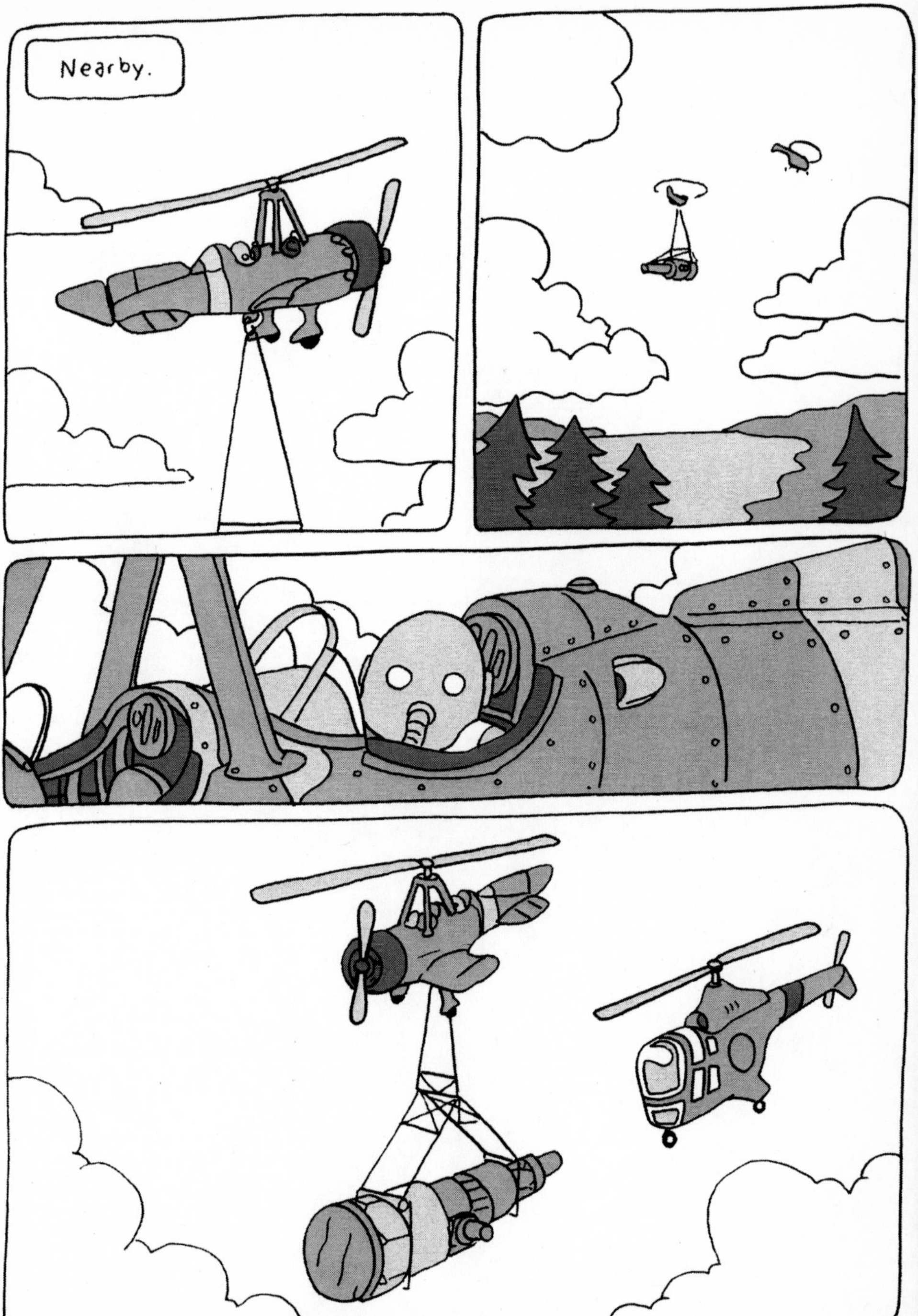
Nearby.

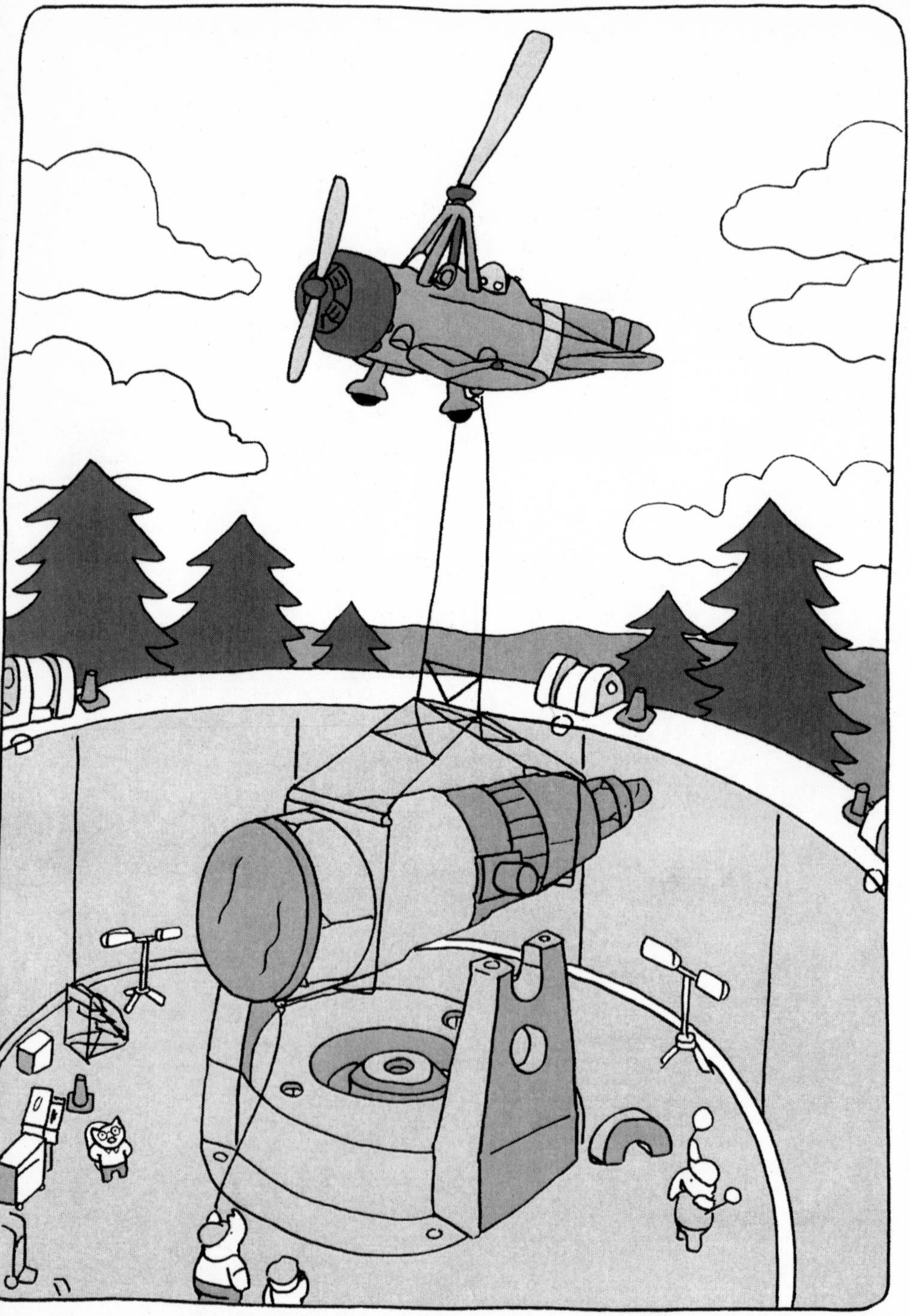

Chapter 5

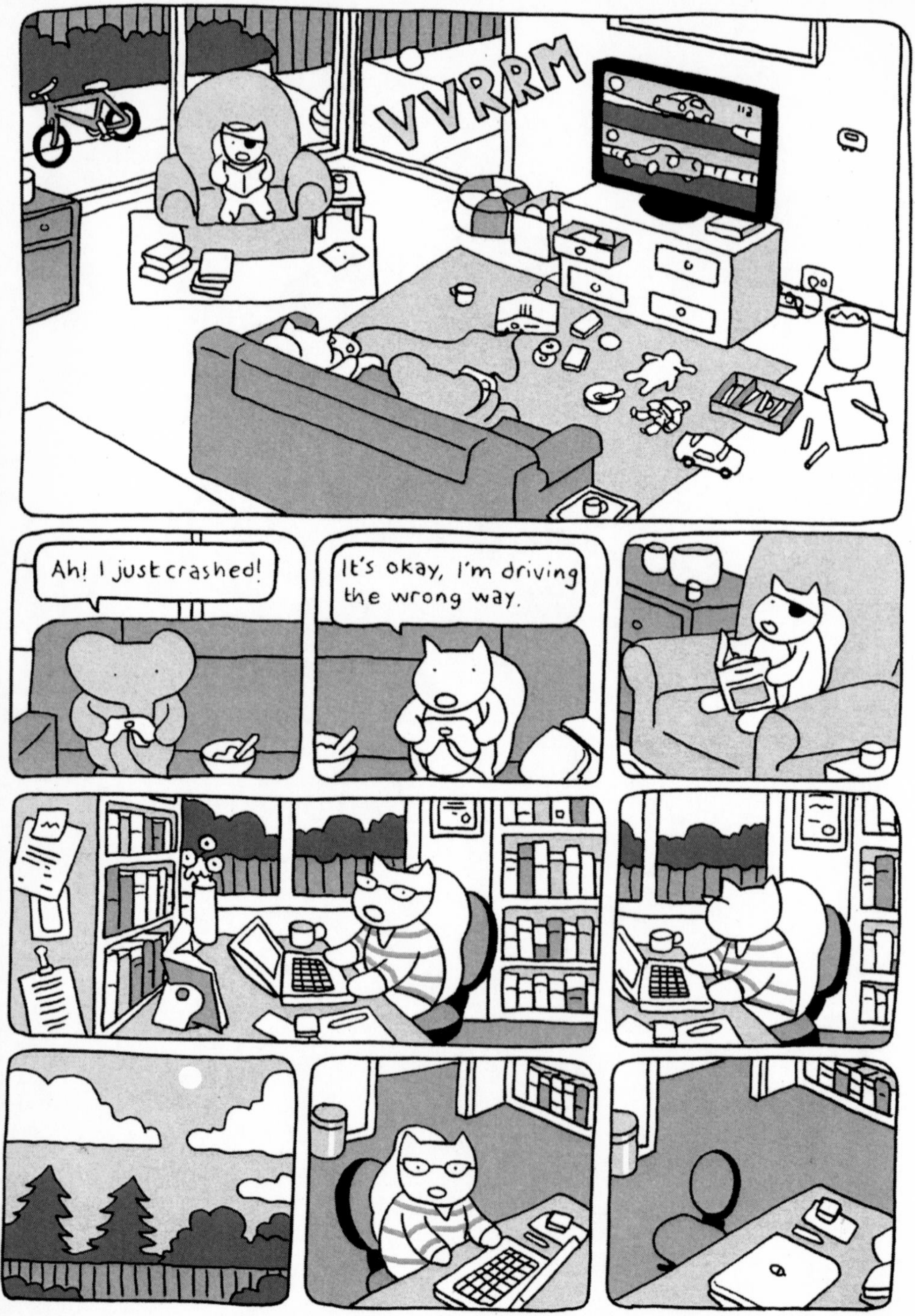
VVRRM
Ah! I just crashed!
It's okay, I'm driving the wrong way.

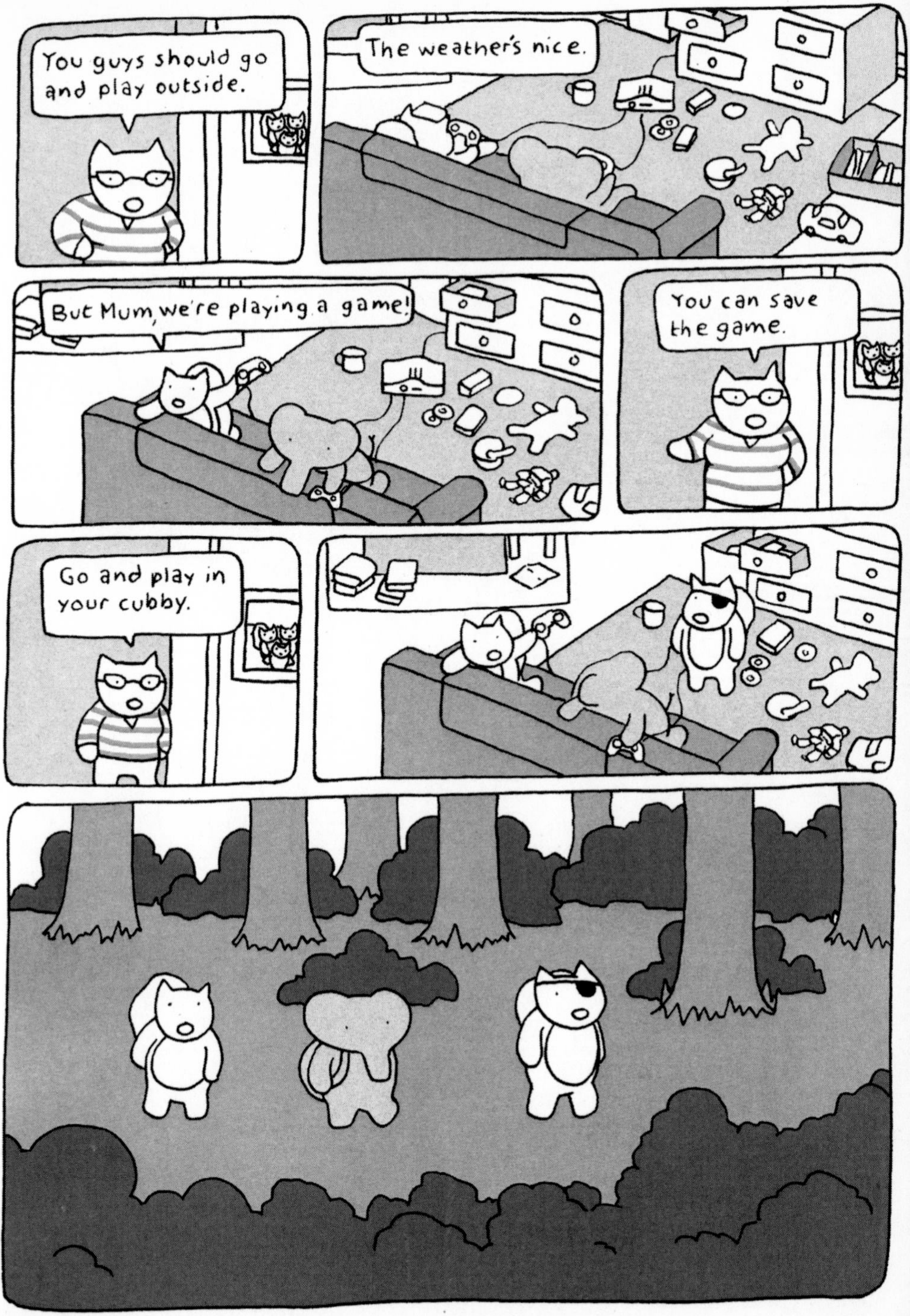
You guys should go and play outside.
The weather's nice.
But Mum, we're playing a game!
You can save the game.
Go and play in your cubby.

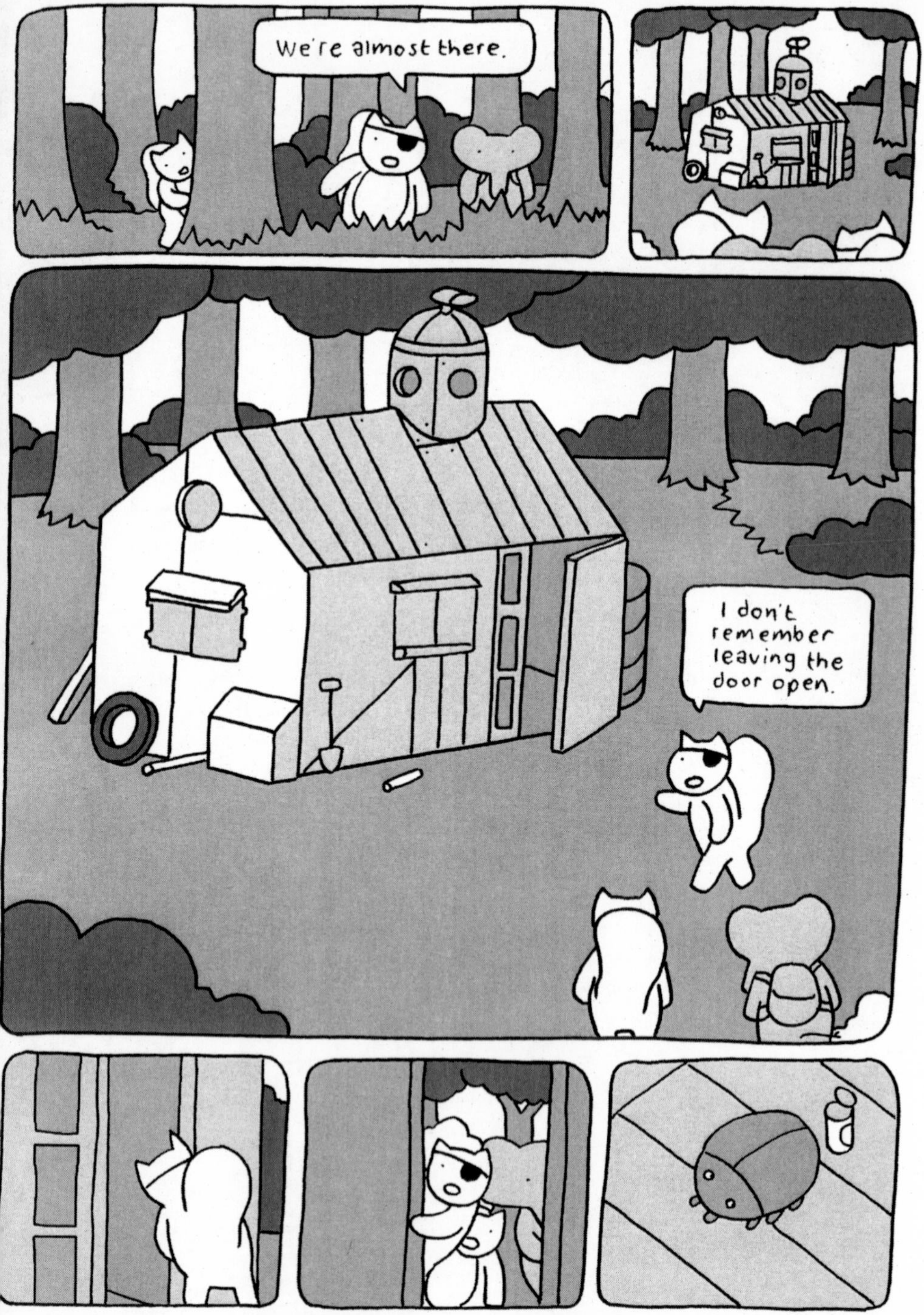
We're almost there.
I don't remember leaving the door open.

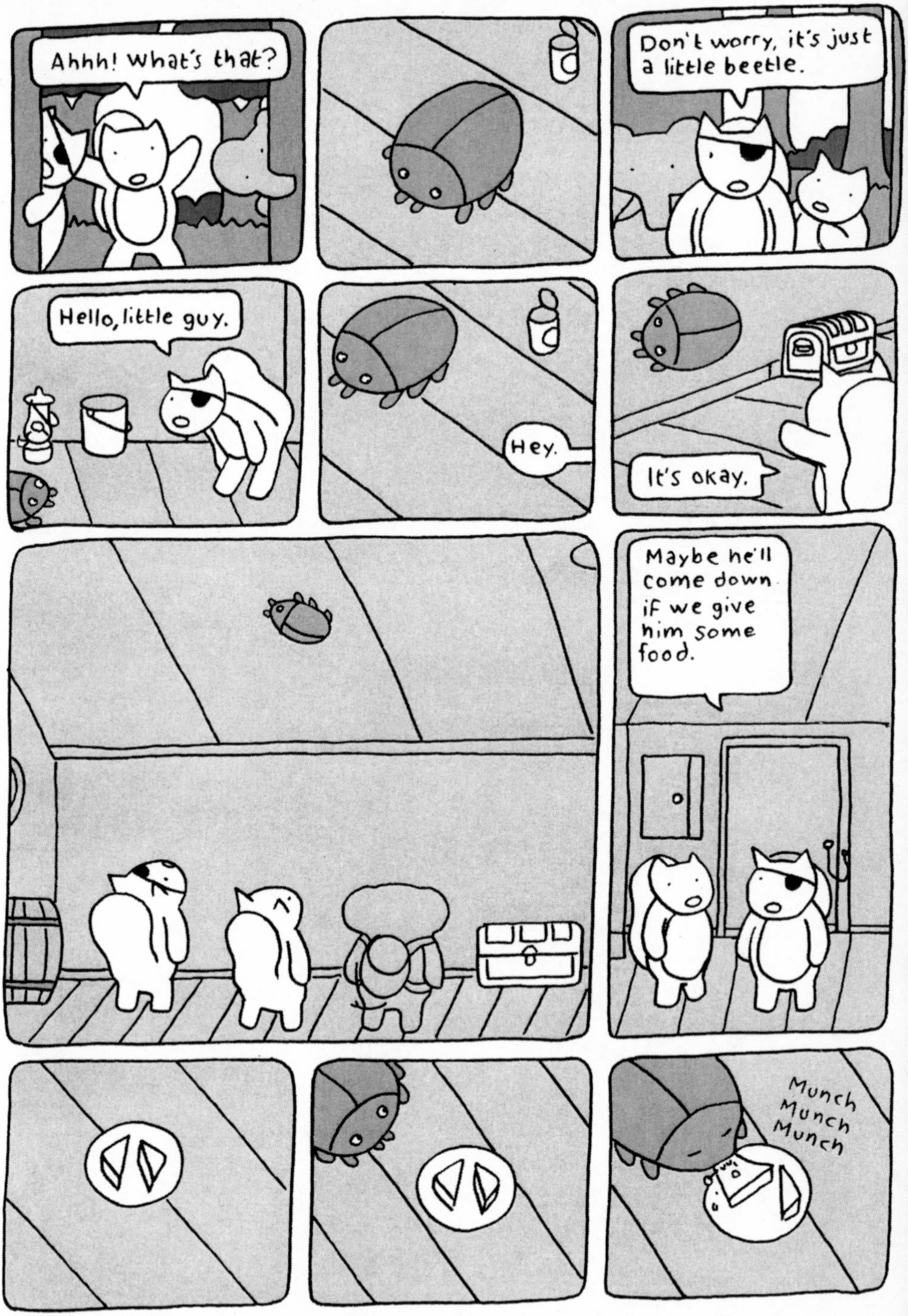
Ahhh! What's that?
Don't worry, it's just a little beetle.
Hello, little guy.
Hey.
It's okay.
Maybe he'll come down if we give him some food.
Munch
Munch
Munch

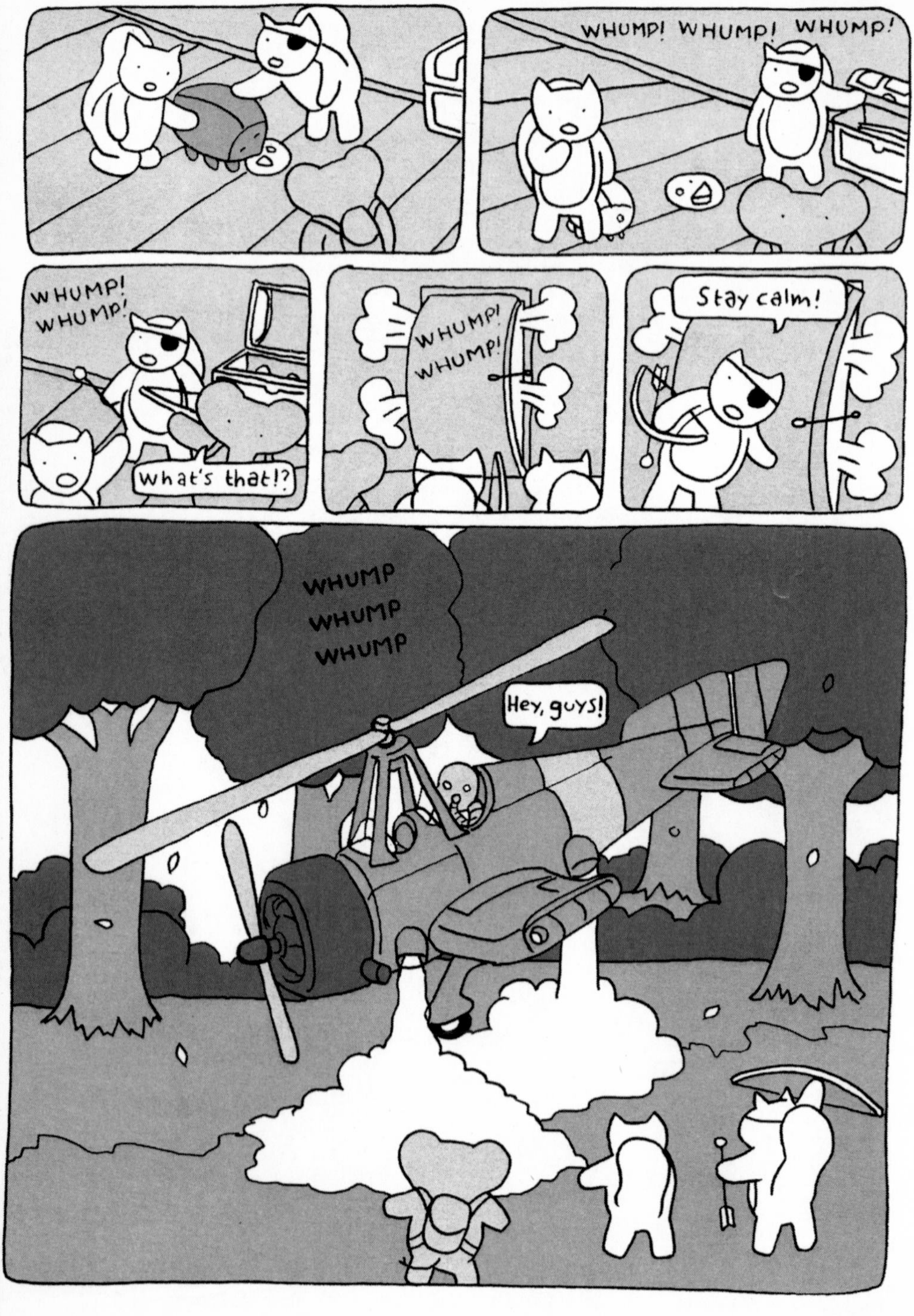
WHUMP! WHUMP! WHUMP!
WHUMP! WHUMP!
What's that!?
WHUMP! WHUMP!
Stay calm!
WHUMP
WHUMP
WHUMP
Hey, guys!

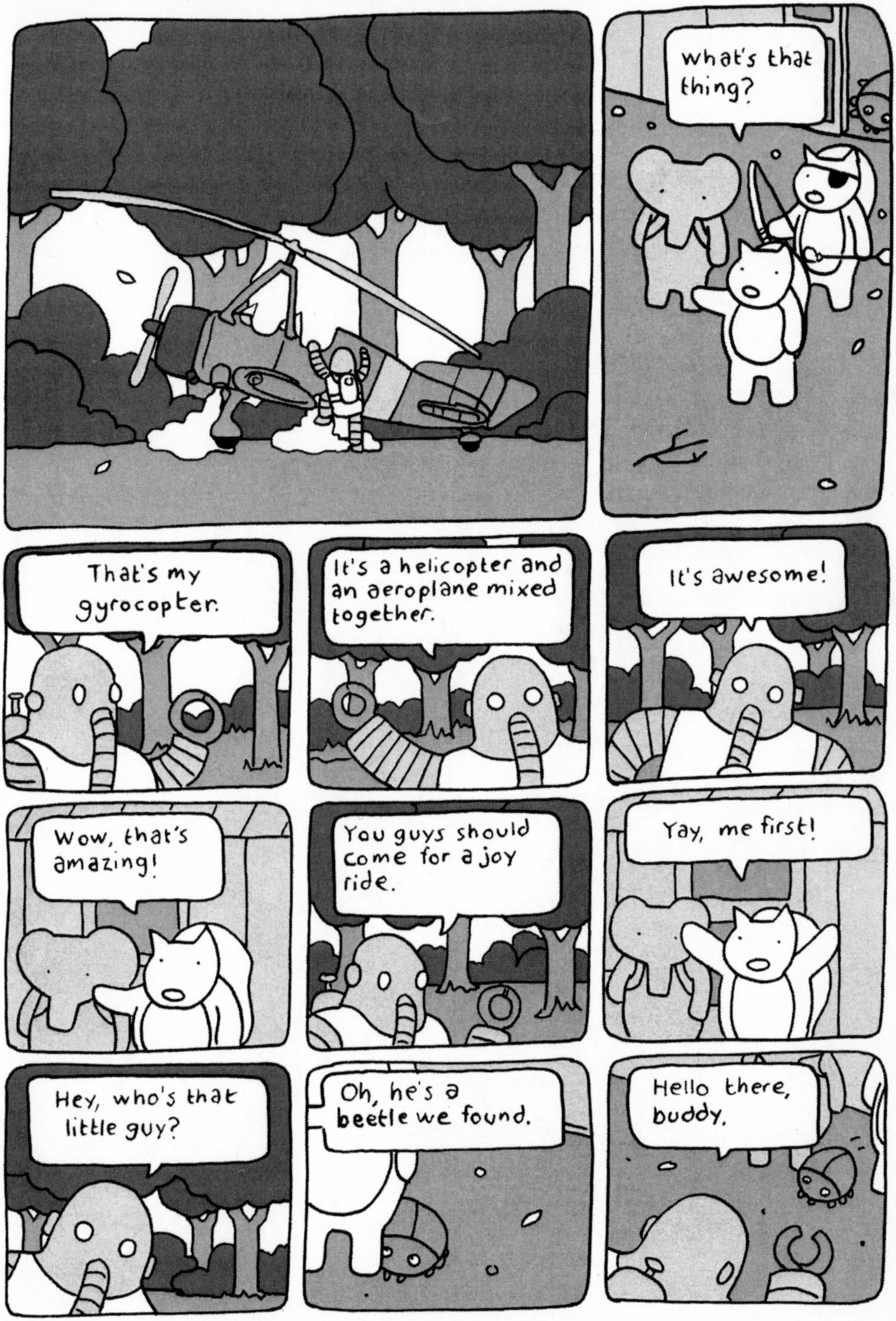
what's that thing?
That's my gyrocopter.
It's a helicopter and an aeroplane mixed together.
It's awesome!
Wow, that's amazing!
You guys should come for a joy ride.
Yay, me first!
Hey, who's that little guy?
Oh, he's a beetle we found.
Hello there, buddy.

SkiP

Looks like he needs help learning to fly.

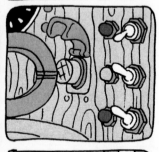

Let's take him up in the gyrocopter so he can see what it's like.

Then.

Contact!

Hold on!

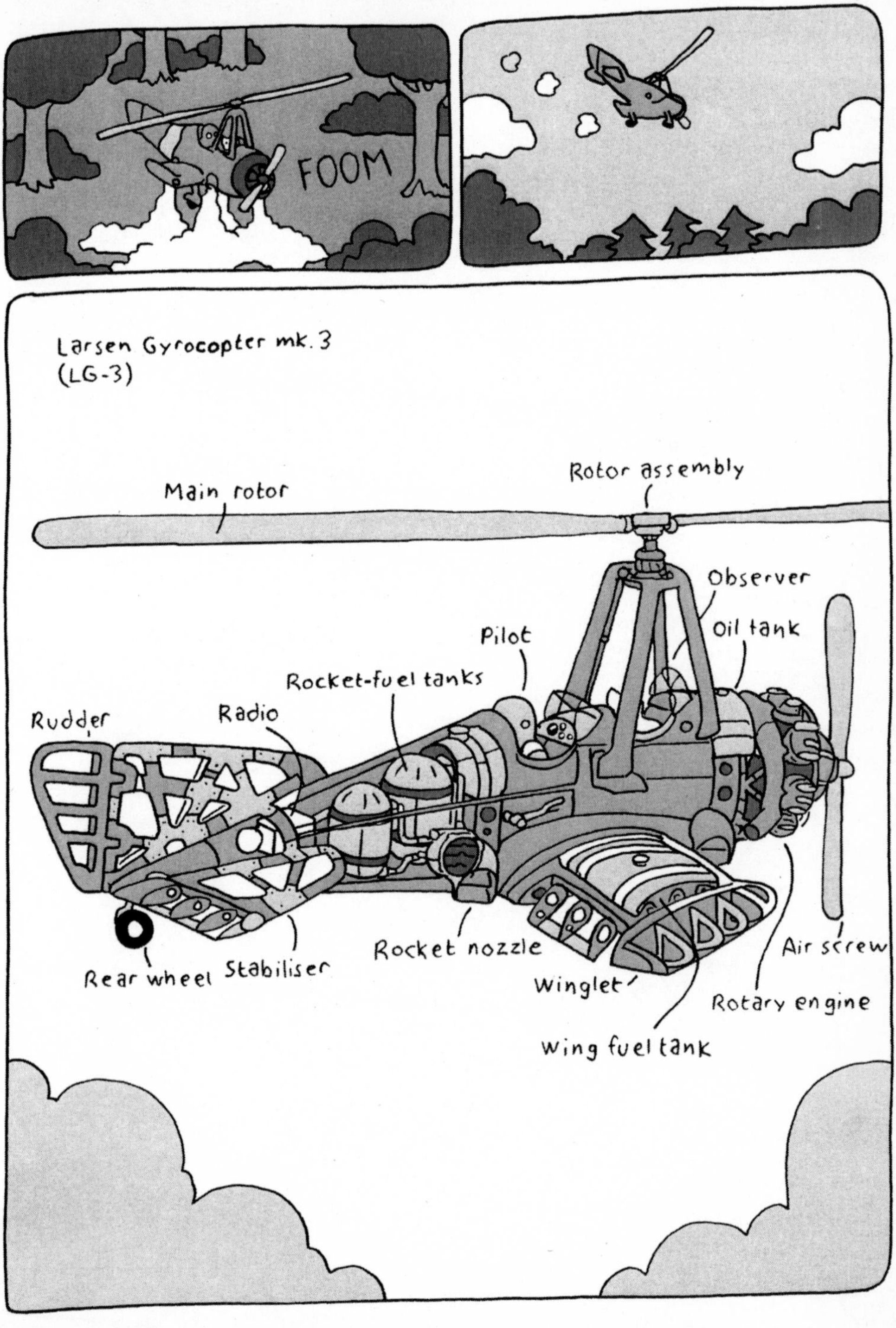
FOOM
Larsen Gyrocopter mk. 3
(LG-3)
Main rotor
Rotor assembly
Observer
Oil tank
Pilot
Rocket-fuel tanks
Rudder
Radio
Rear wheel
Stabiliser
Rocket nozzle
Winglet
Wing fuel tank
Rotary engine
Air screw

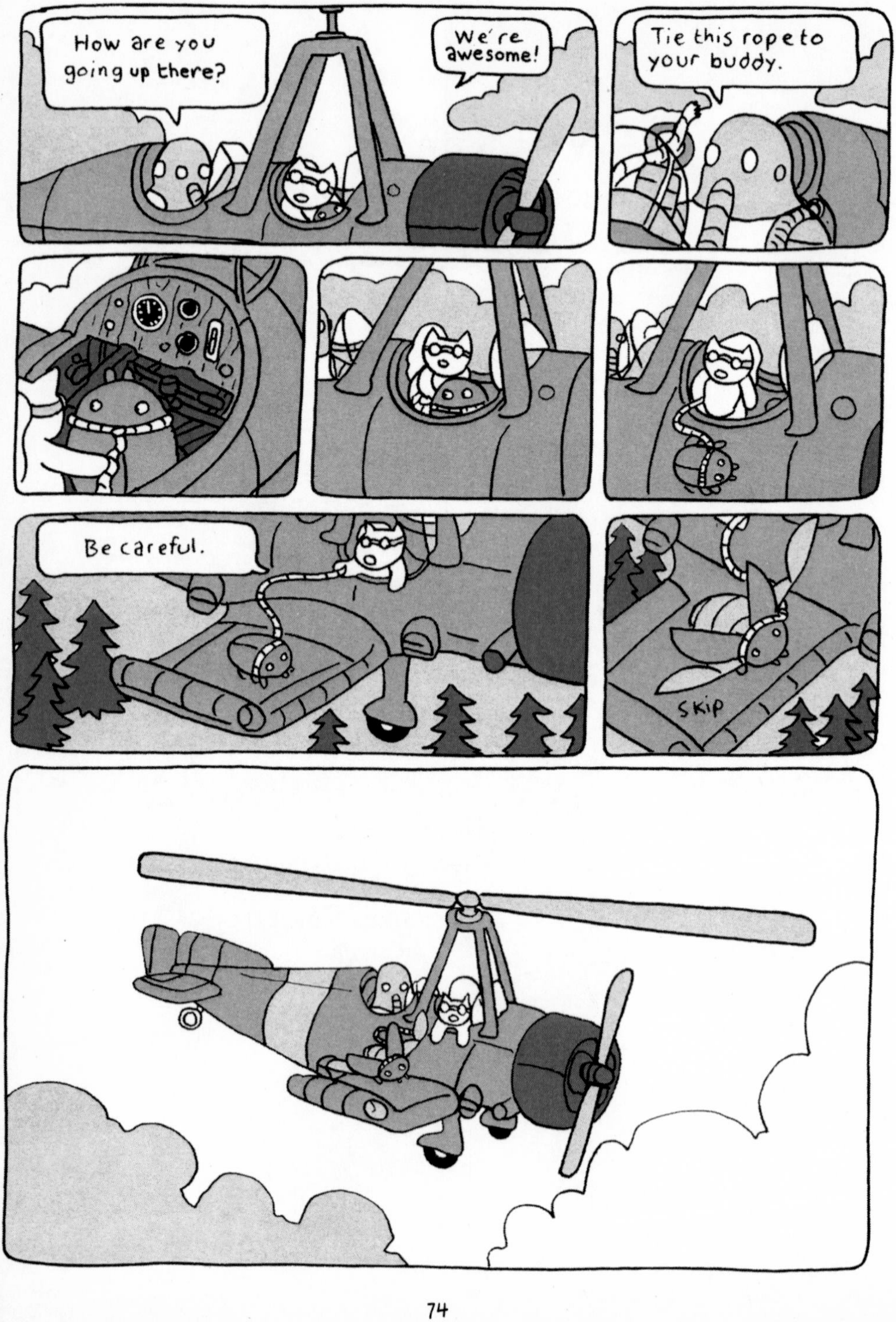
How are you going up there?
We're awesome!
Tie this rope to your buddy.
Be careful.
SKIP

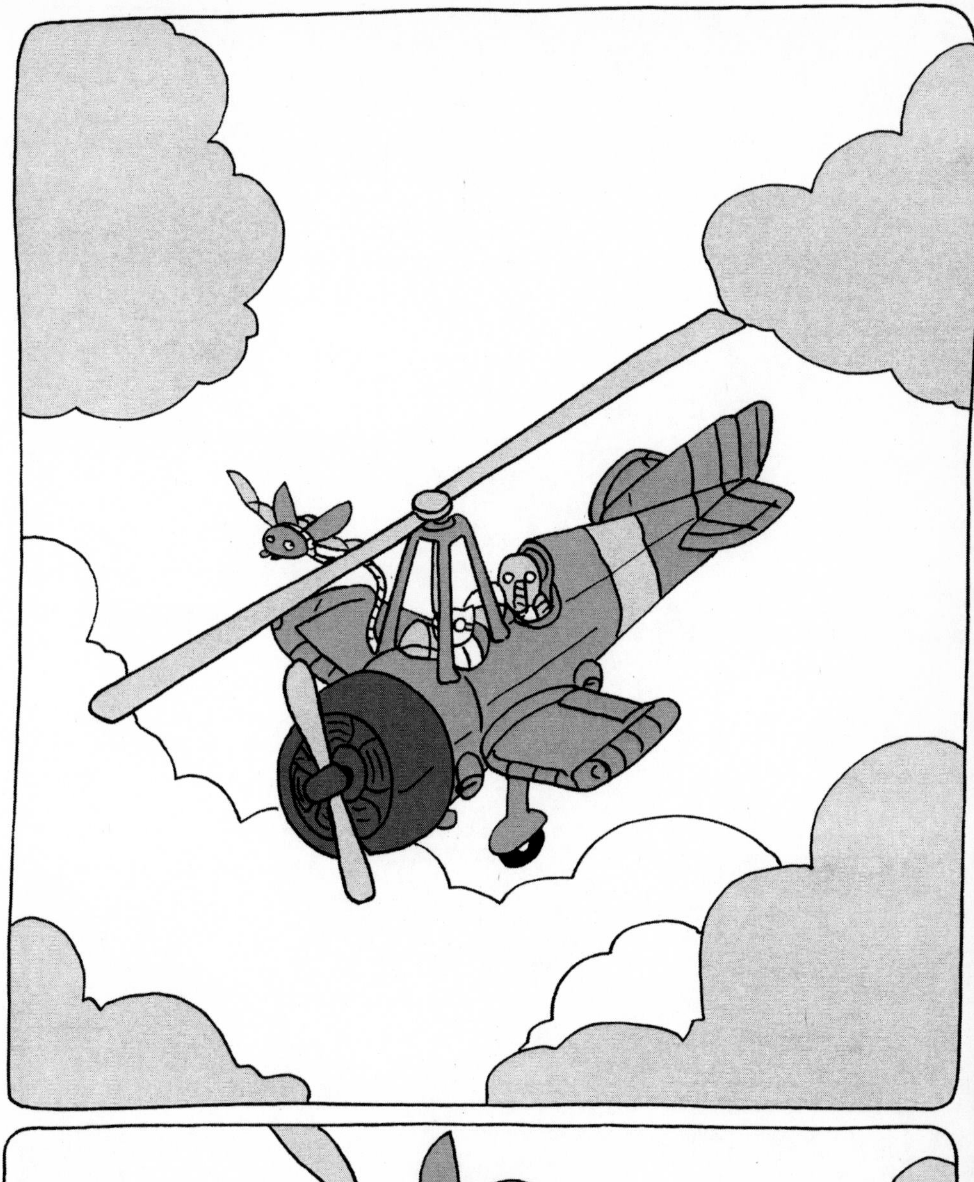
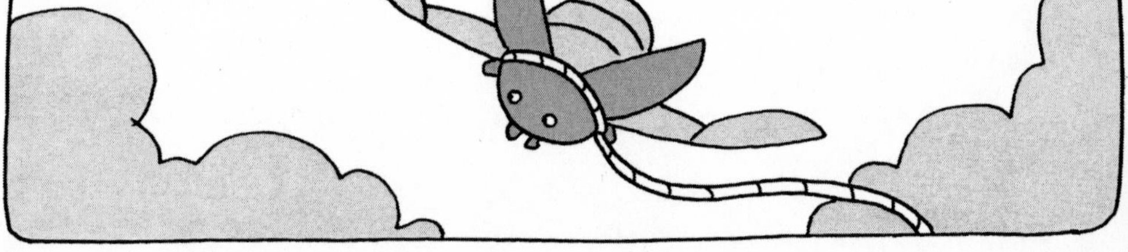

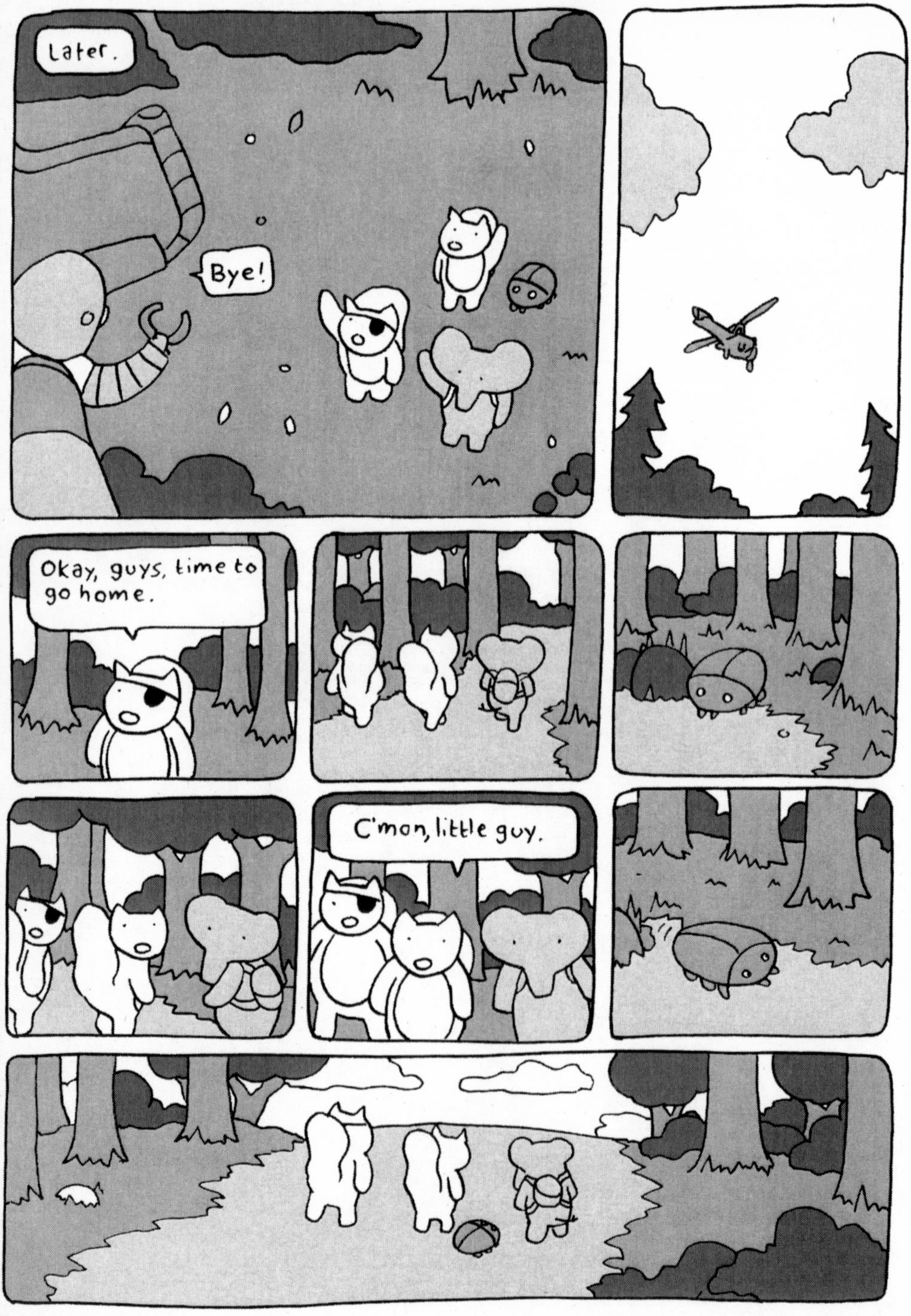
Later.
Bye!
Okay, guys, time to go home.
C'mon, little guy.

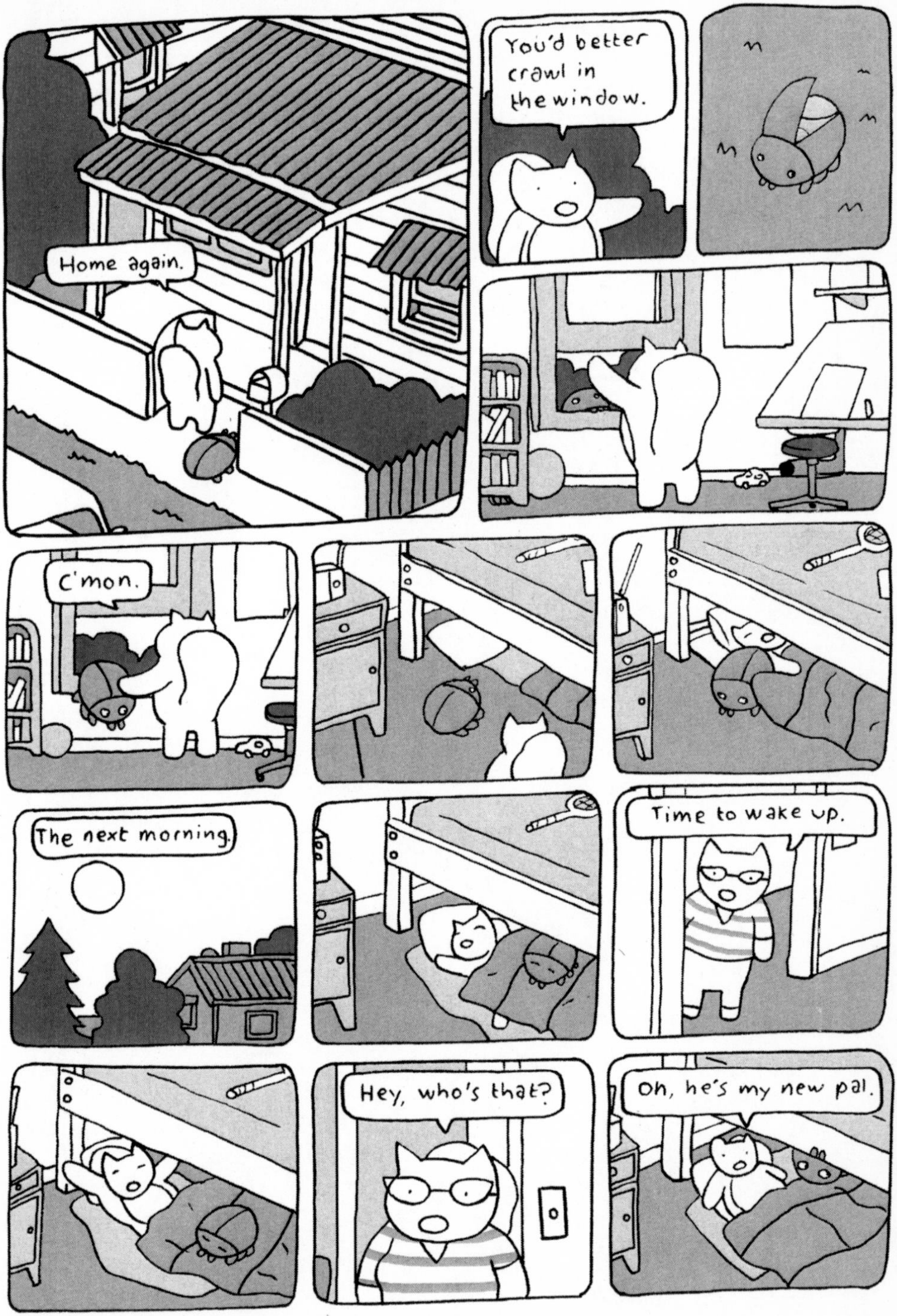
Home again.
You'd better crawl in the window.
C'mon.
The next morning.
Time to wake up.
Hey, who's that?
Oh, he's my new pal.

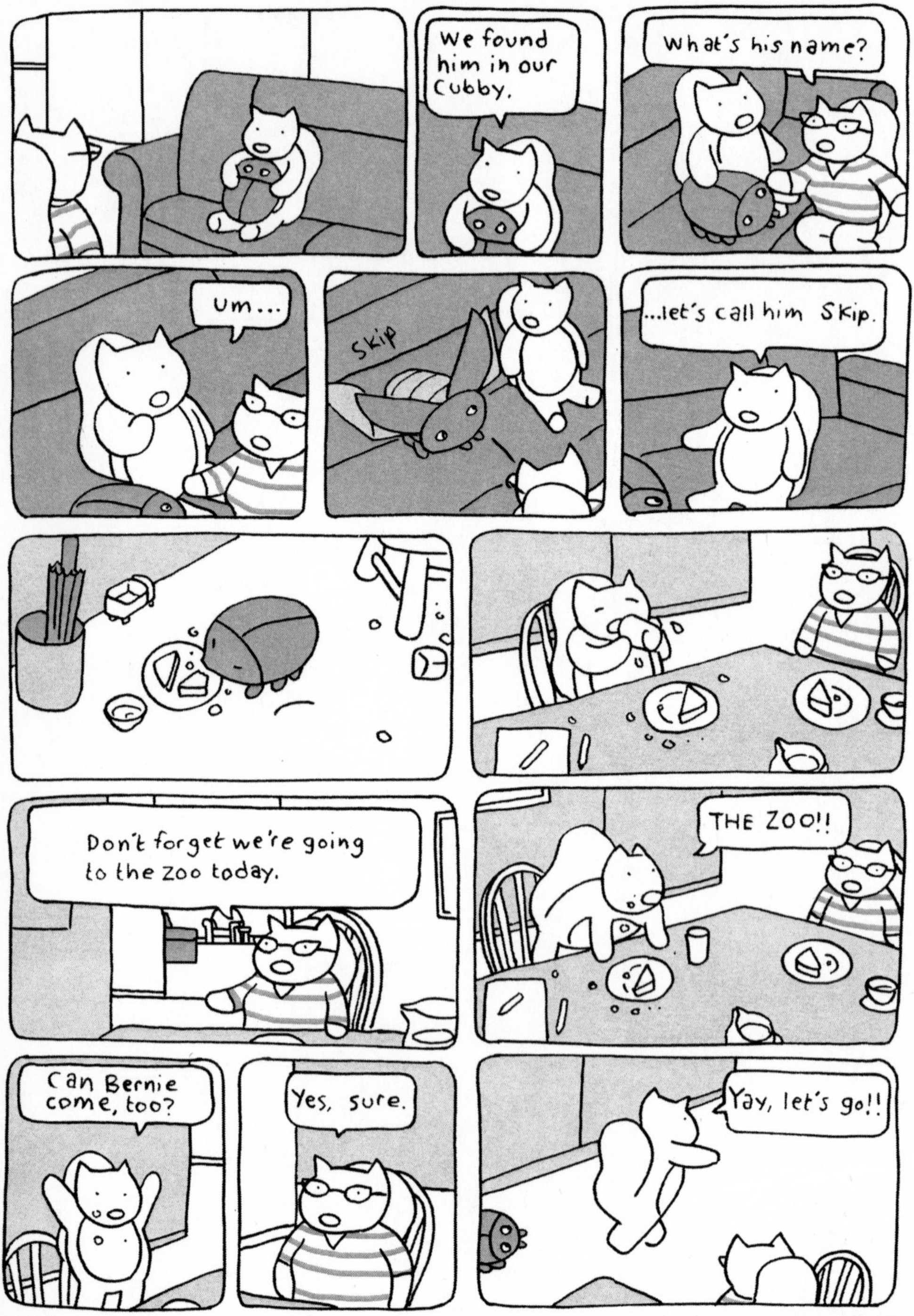
We found him in our Cubby.
What's his name?
Um...
Skip
...let's call him Skip.
Don't forget we're going to the zoo today.
THE ZOO!!
Can Bernie come, too?
Yes, sure.
Yay, let's go!!

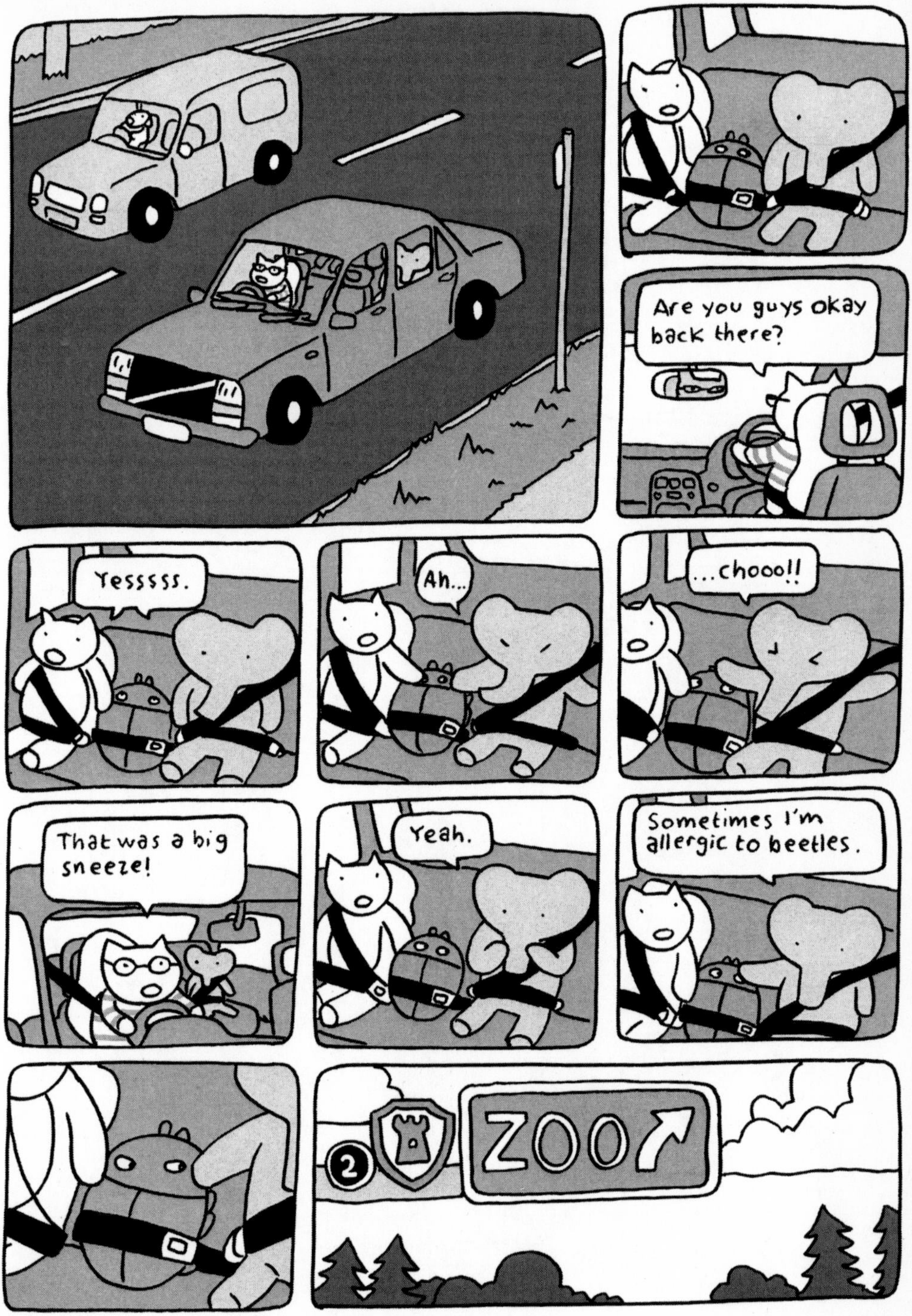
Are you guys okay back there?
Yesssss.
Ah...
...chooo!!
That was a big sneeze!
Yeah.
Sometimes I'm allergic to beetles.
ZOO
2

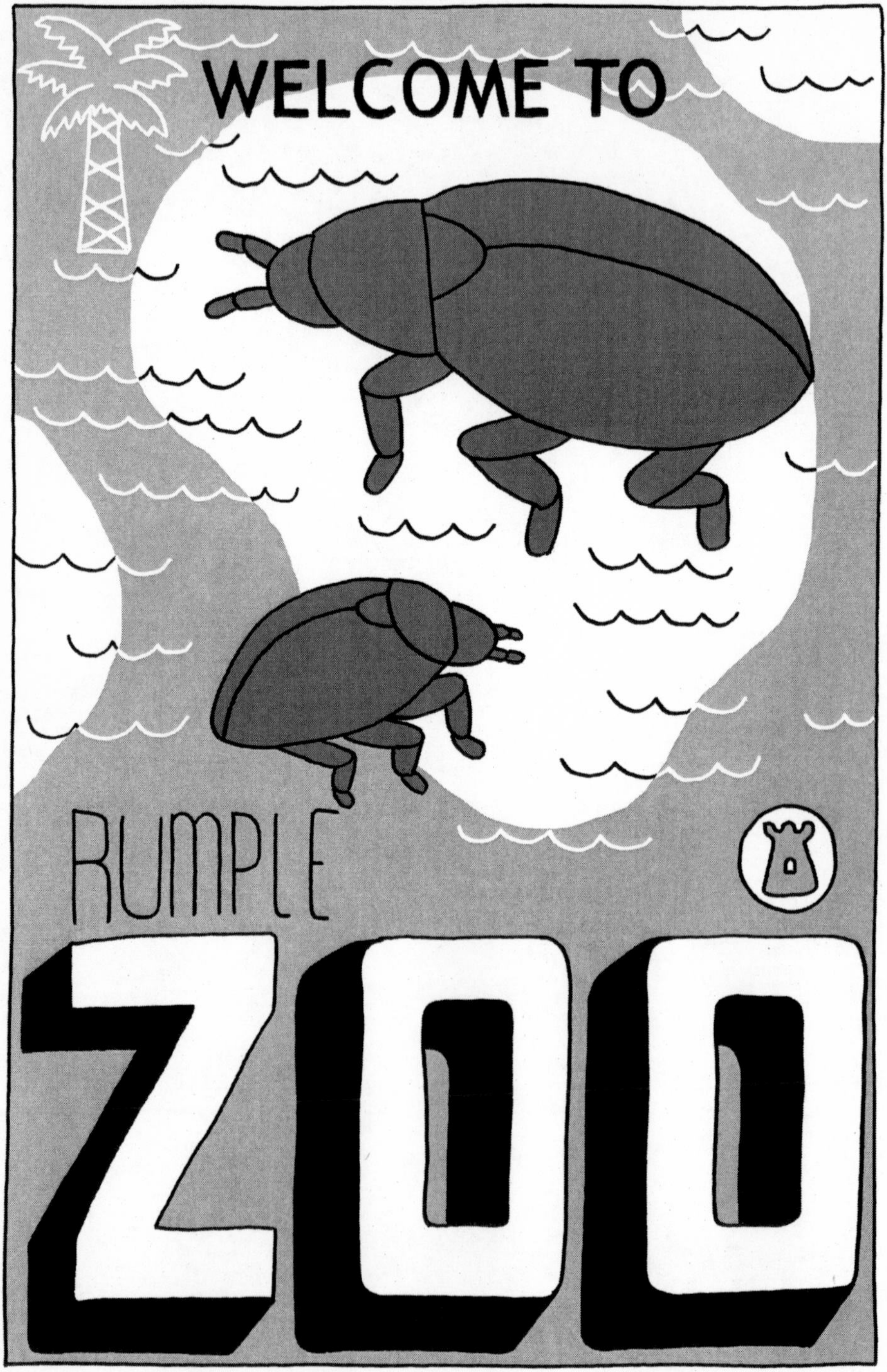
WELCOME TO
RUMPLE
ZOO

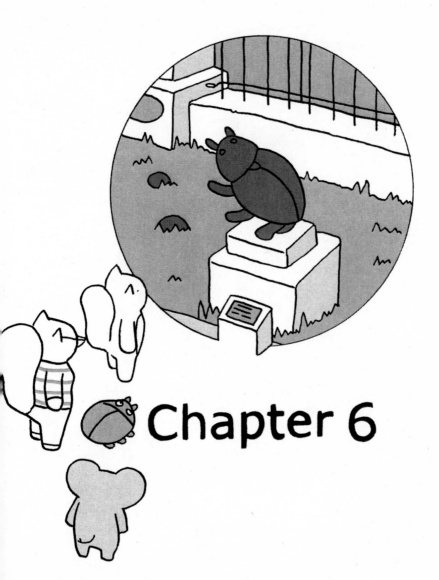

Chapter 6

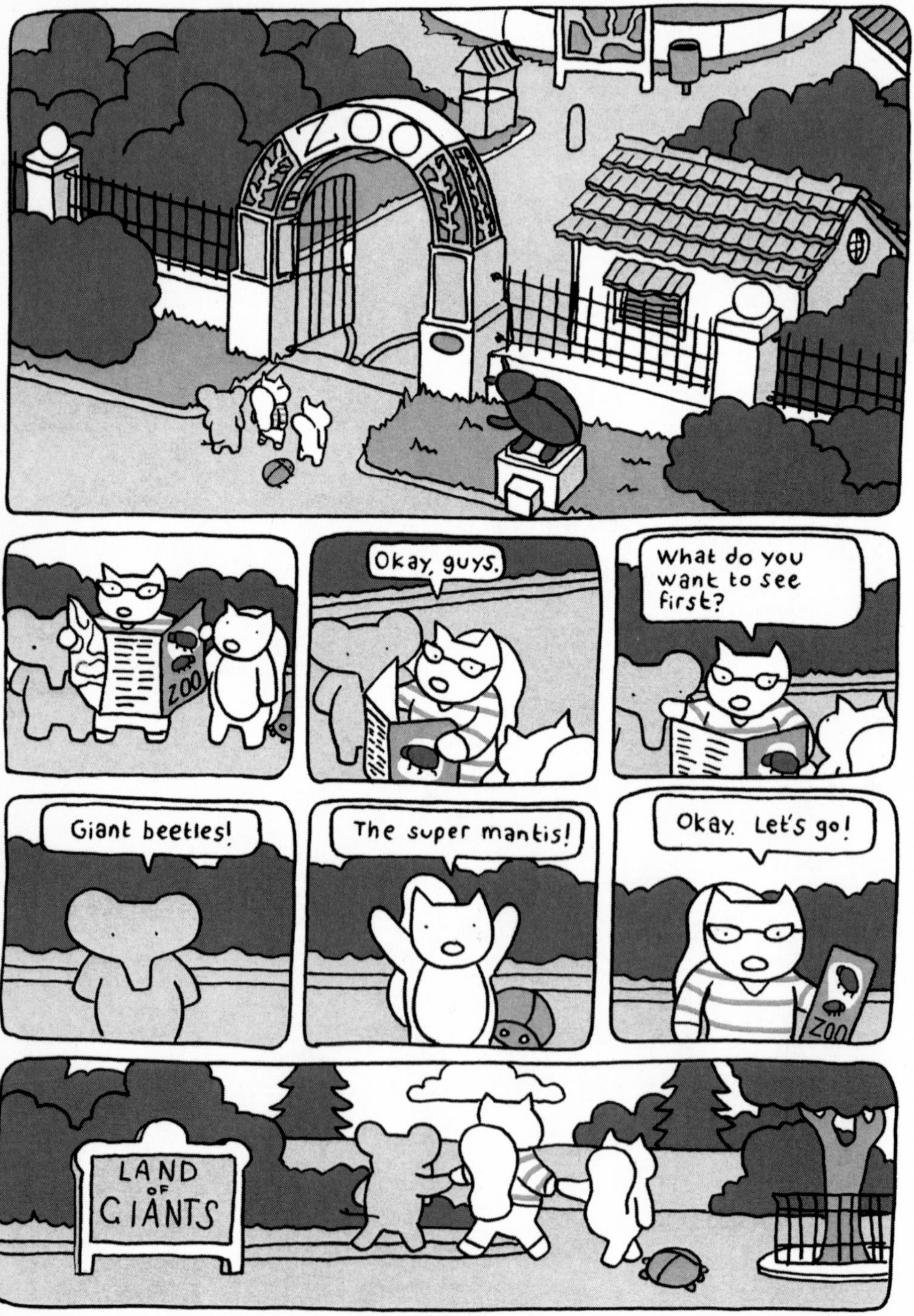
ZOO
ZOO
Okay, guys.
What do you want to see first?
Giant beetles!
The super mantis!
Okay. Let's go!
ZOO
LAND of GIANTS

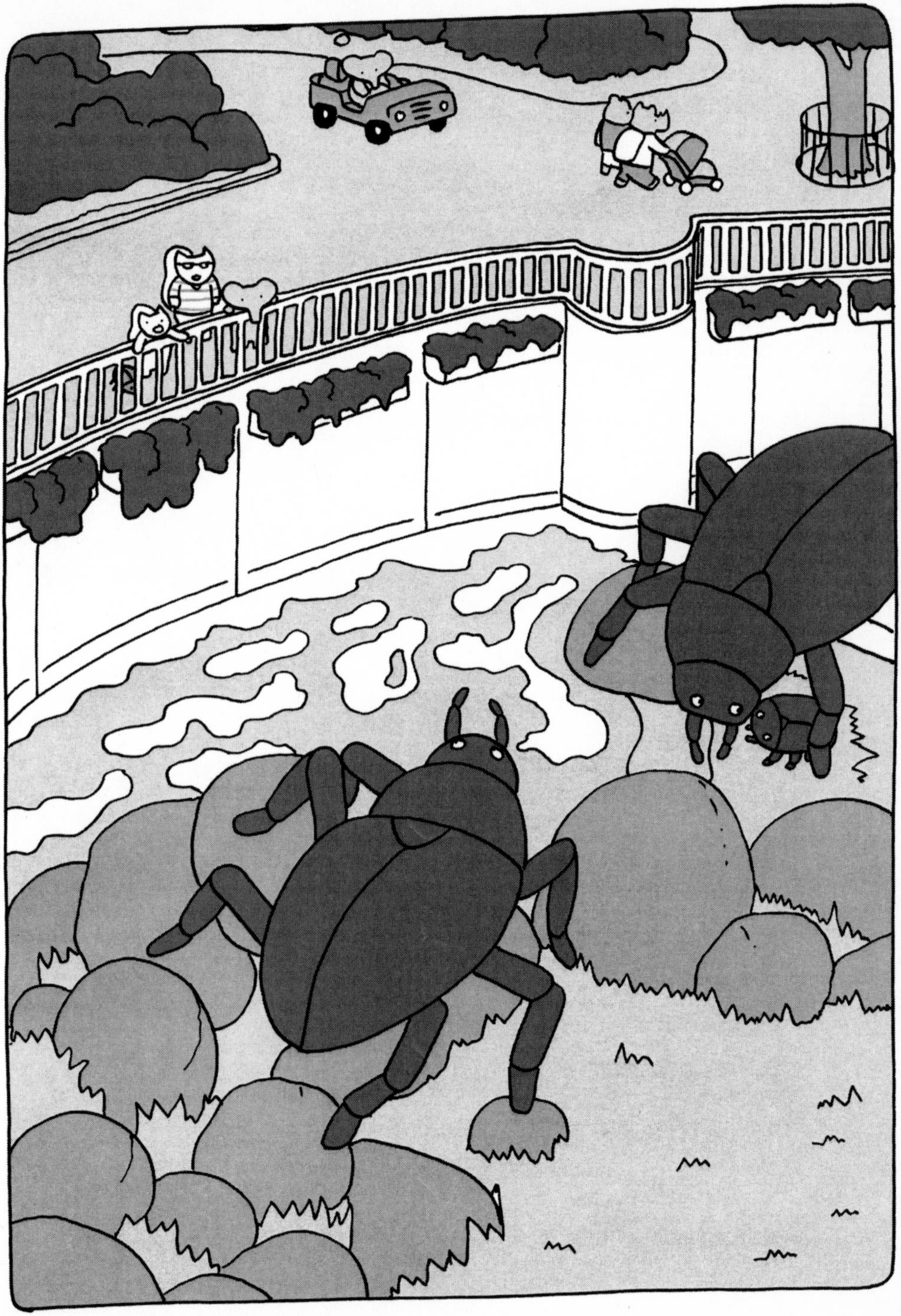

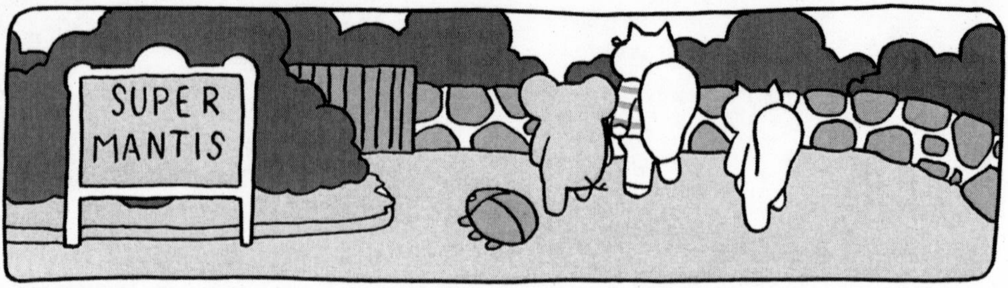
SUPER
MANTIS

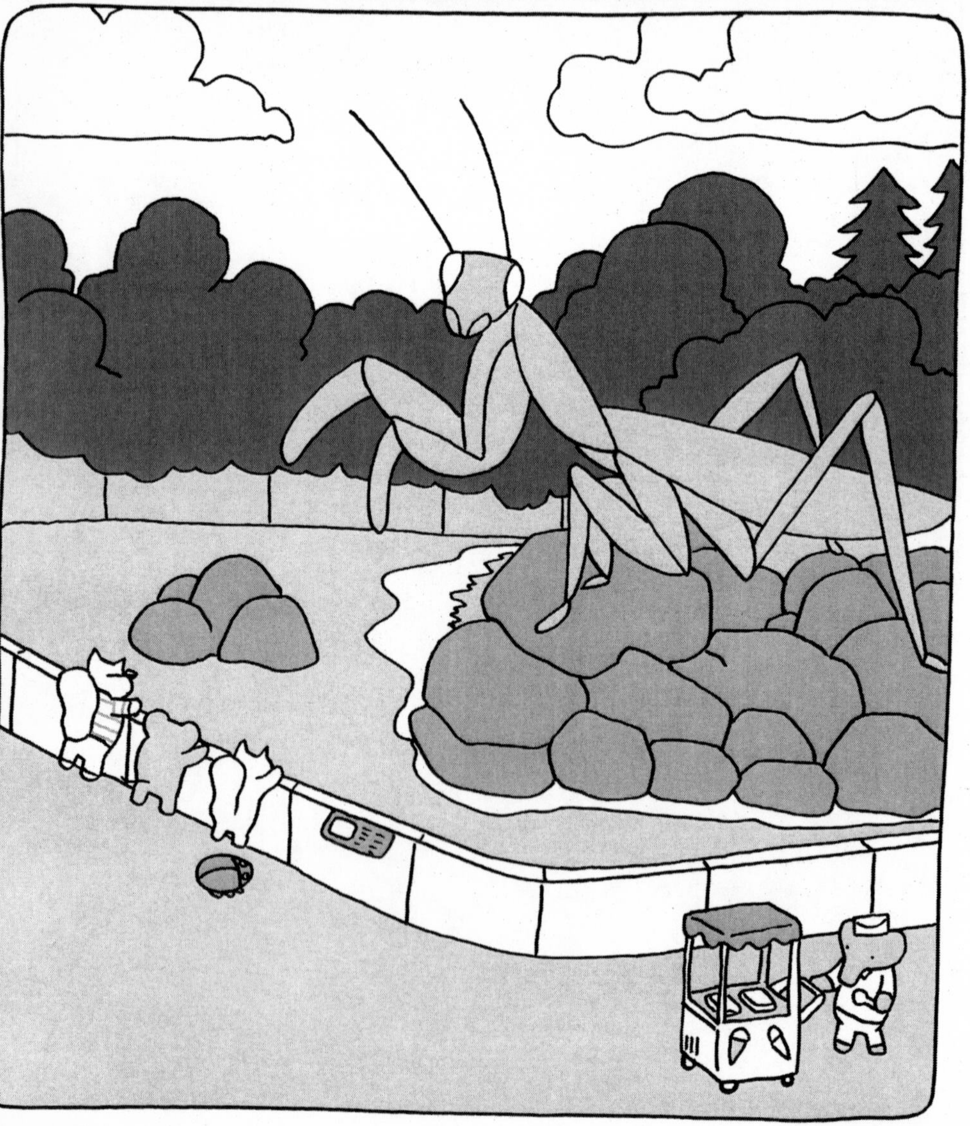

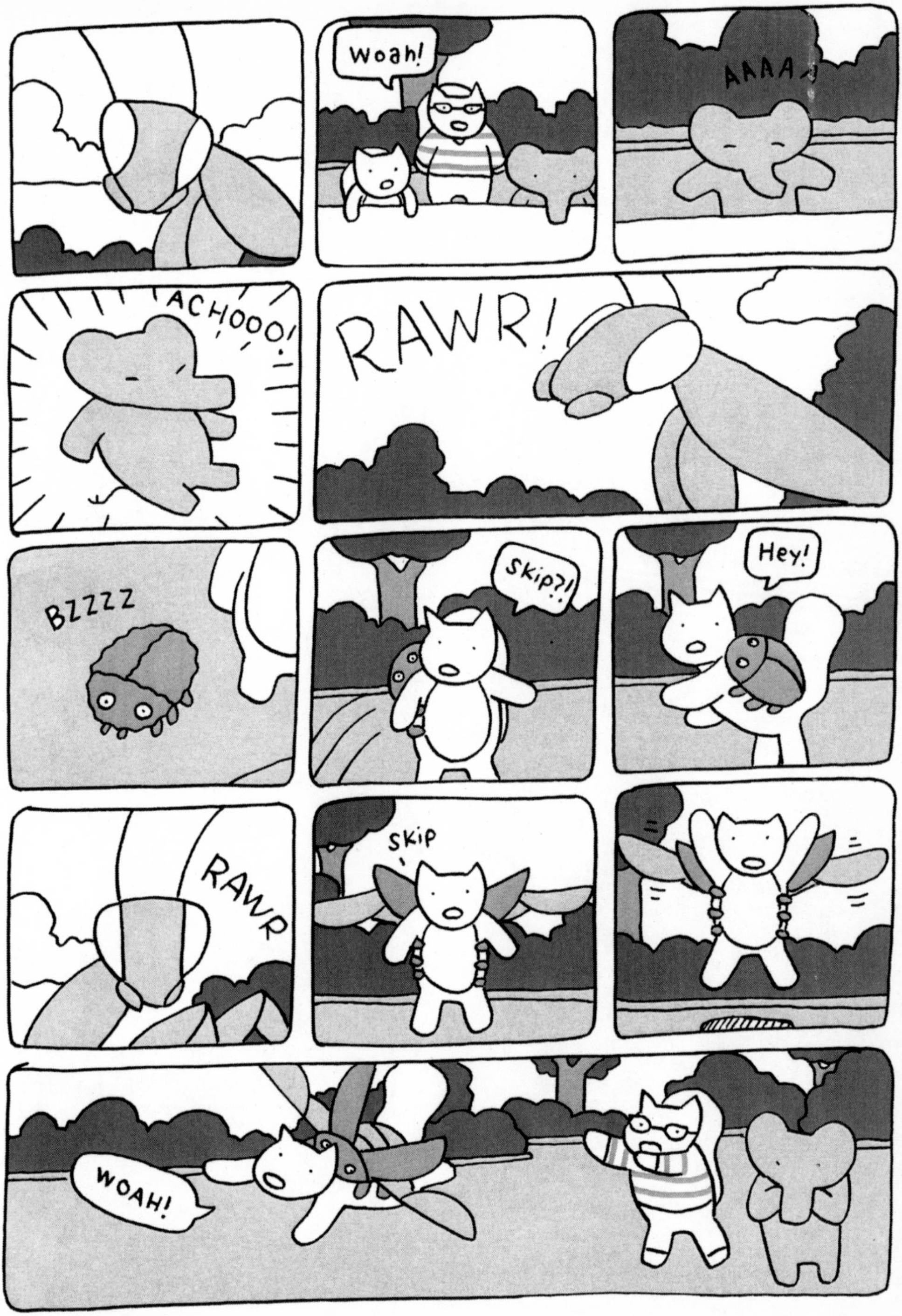
Woah!
AAAA
ACHOOO!
RAWR!
BZZZZ
Skip?!
Hey!
RAWR
SKIP
WOAH!

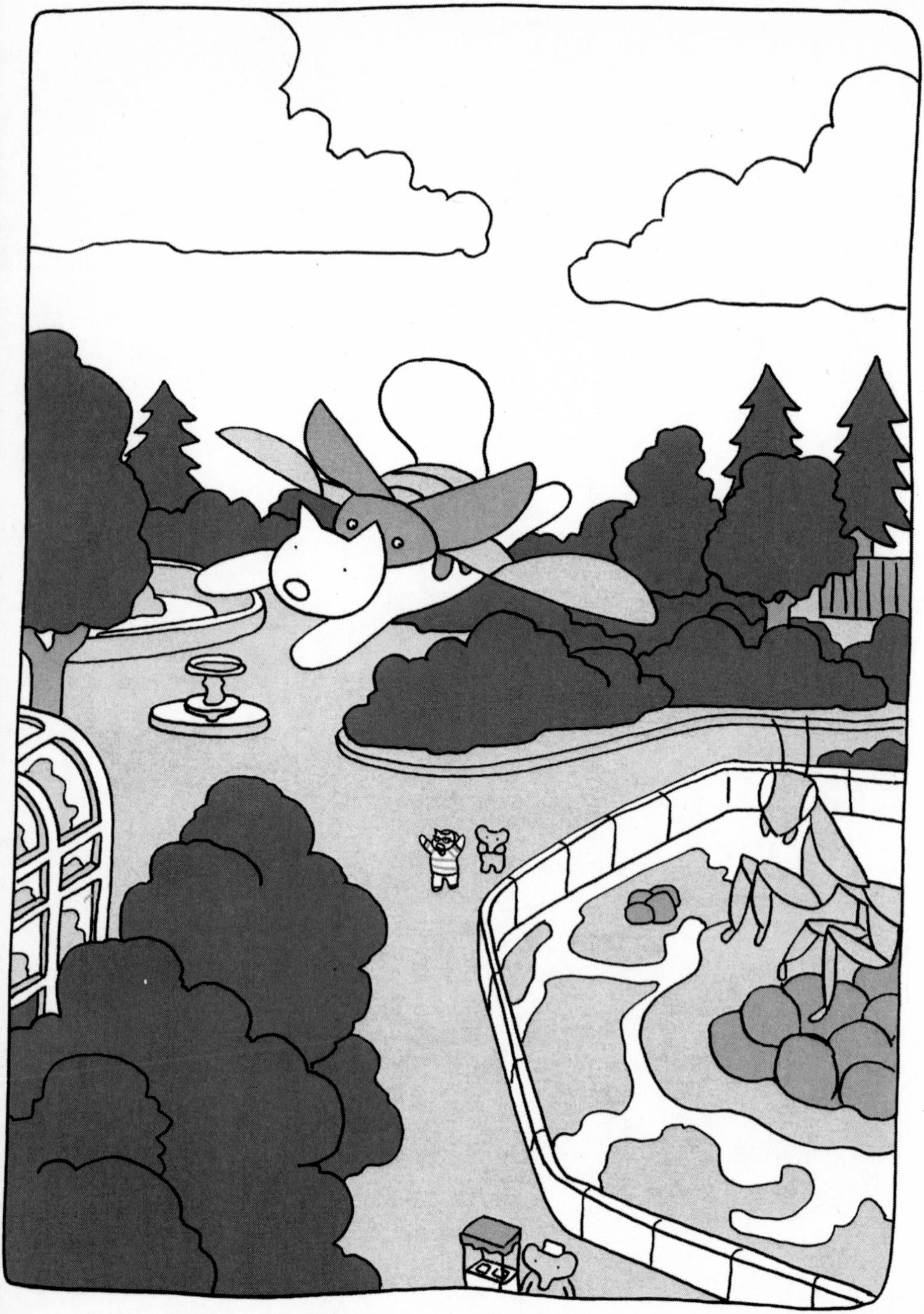

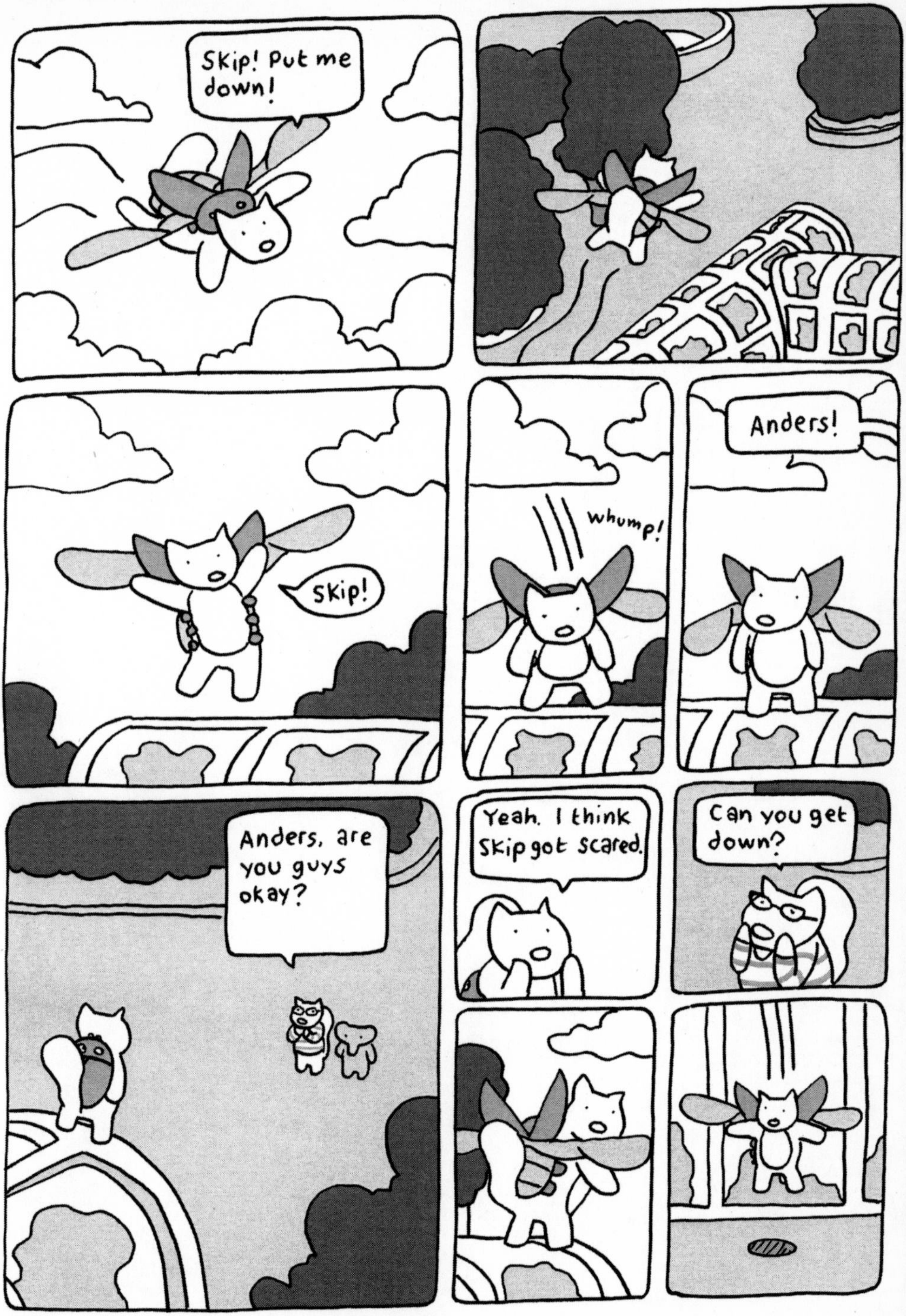
Skip! Put me down!
whump!
Skip!
Anders!
Anders, are you guys okay?
Yeah. I think Skip got scared.
Can you get down?

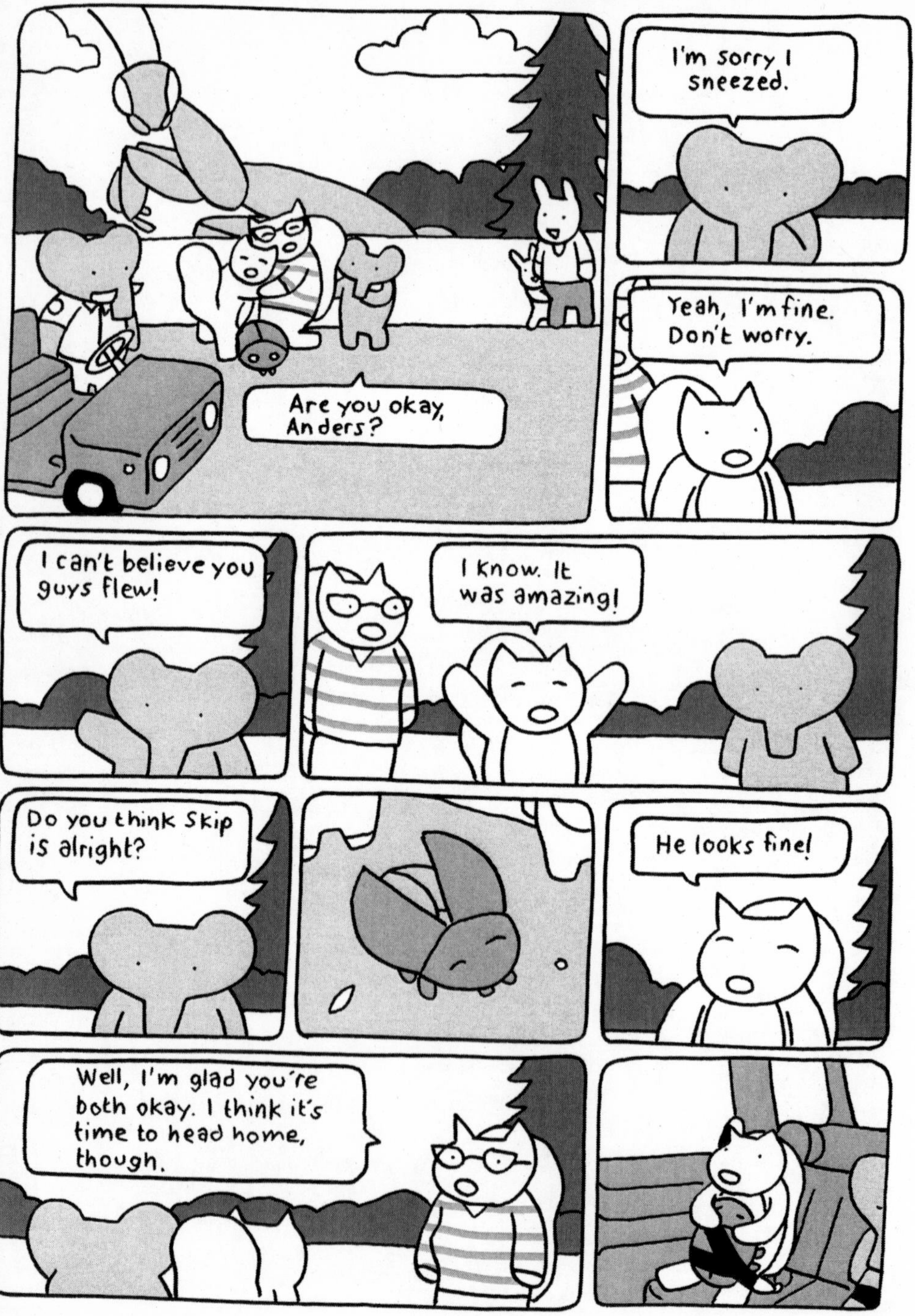
Are you okay, Anders?
I'm sorry I sneezed.
Yeah, I'm fine. Don't worry.
I can't believe you guys flew!
I know. It was amazing!
Do you think Skip is alright?
He looks fine!
Well, I'm glad you're both okay. I think it's time to head home, though.

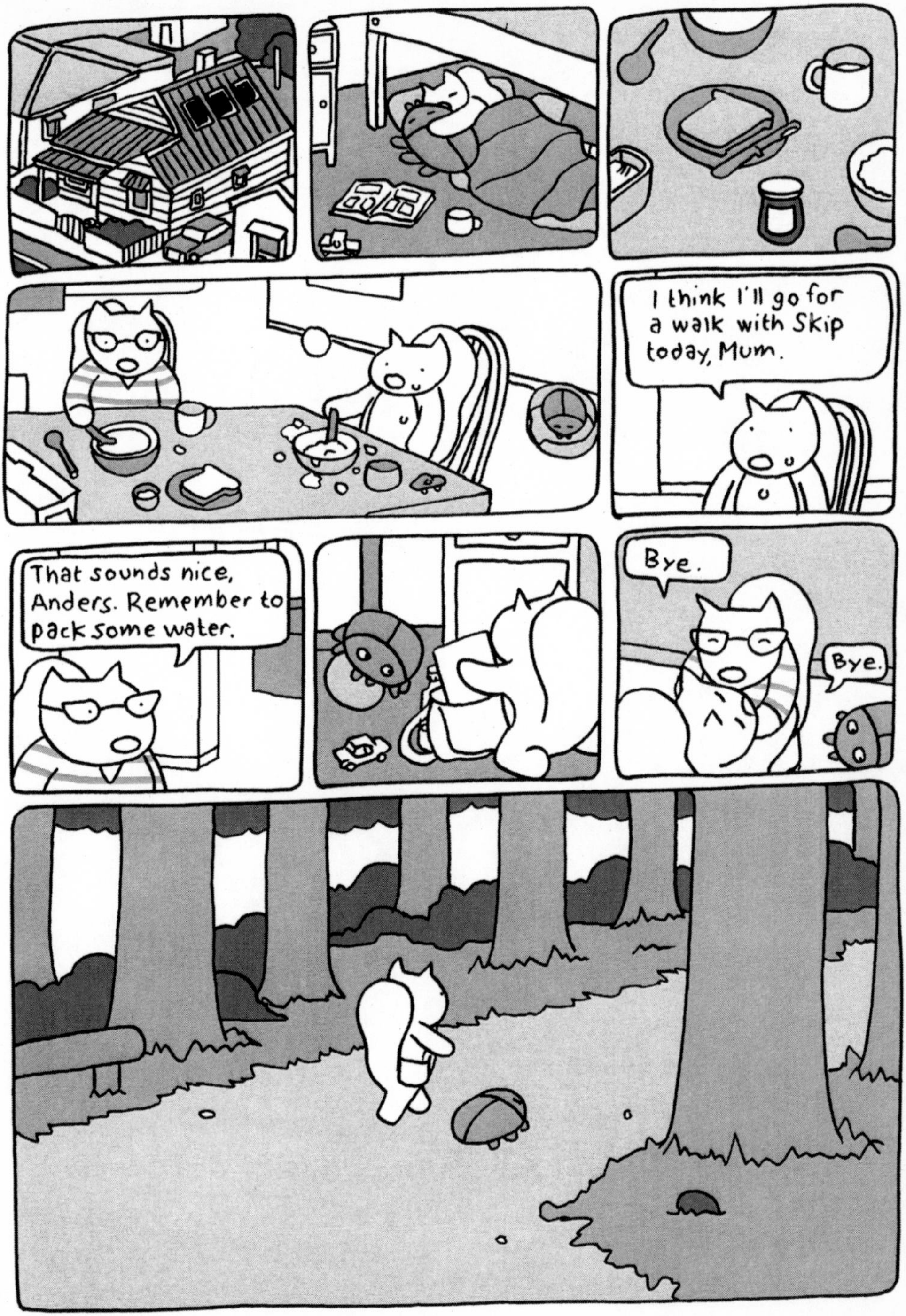
I think I'll go for a walk with Skip today, Mum.
That sounds nice, Anders. Remember to pack some water.
Bye.
Bye.

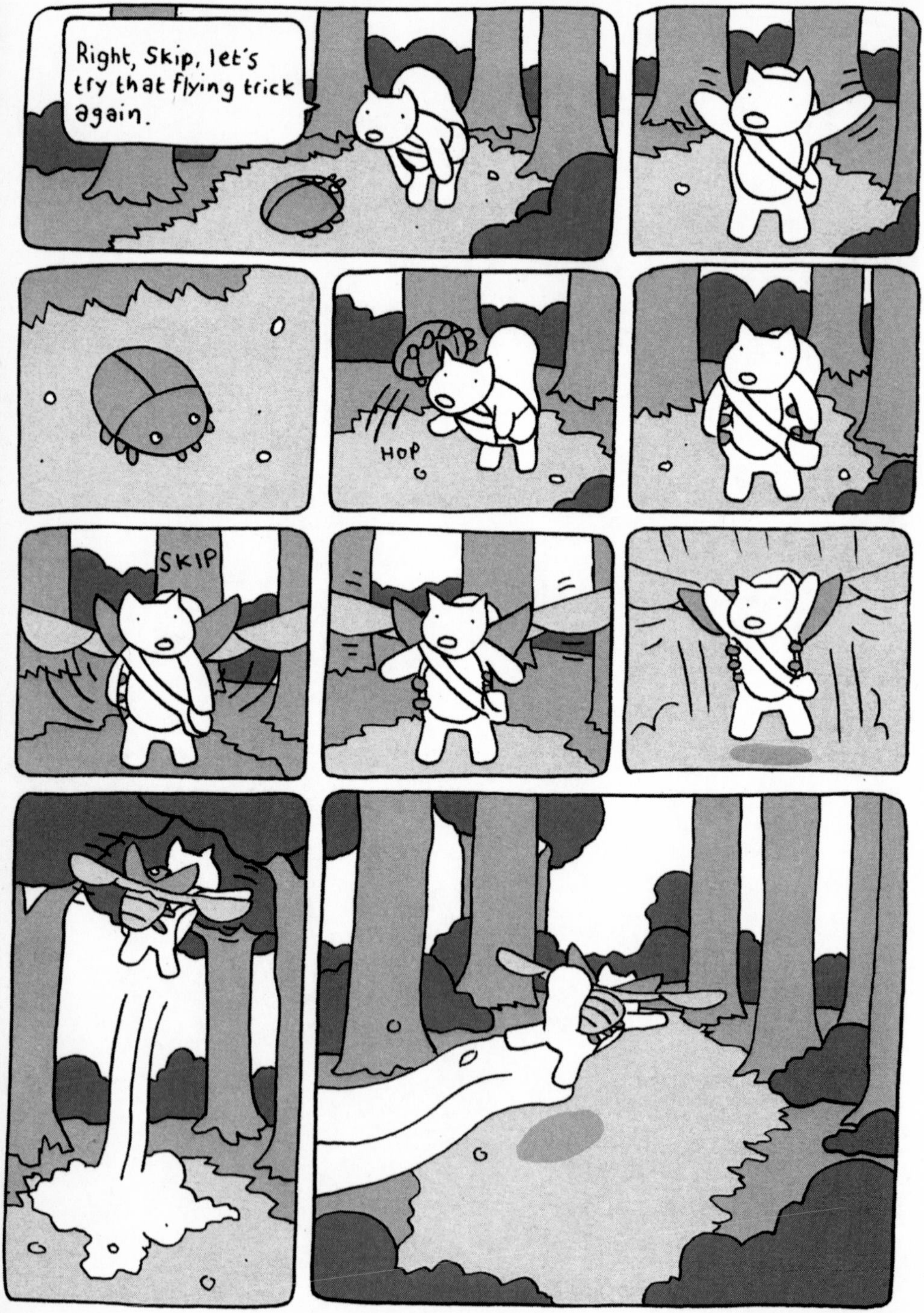
Right, Skip, let's try that flying trick again.
HOP
SKIP

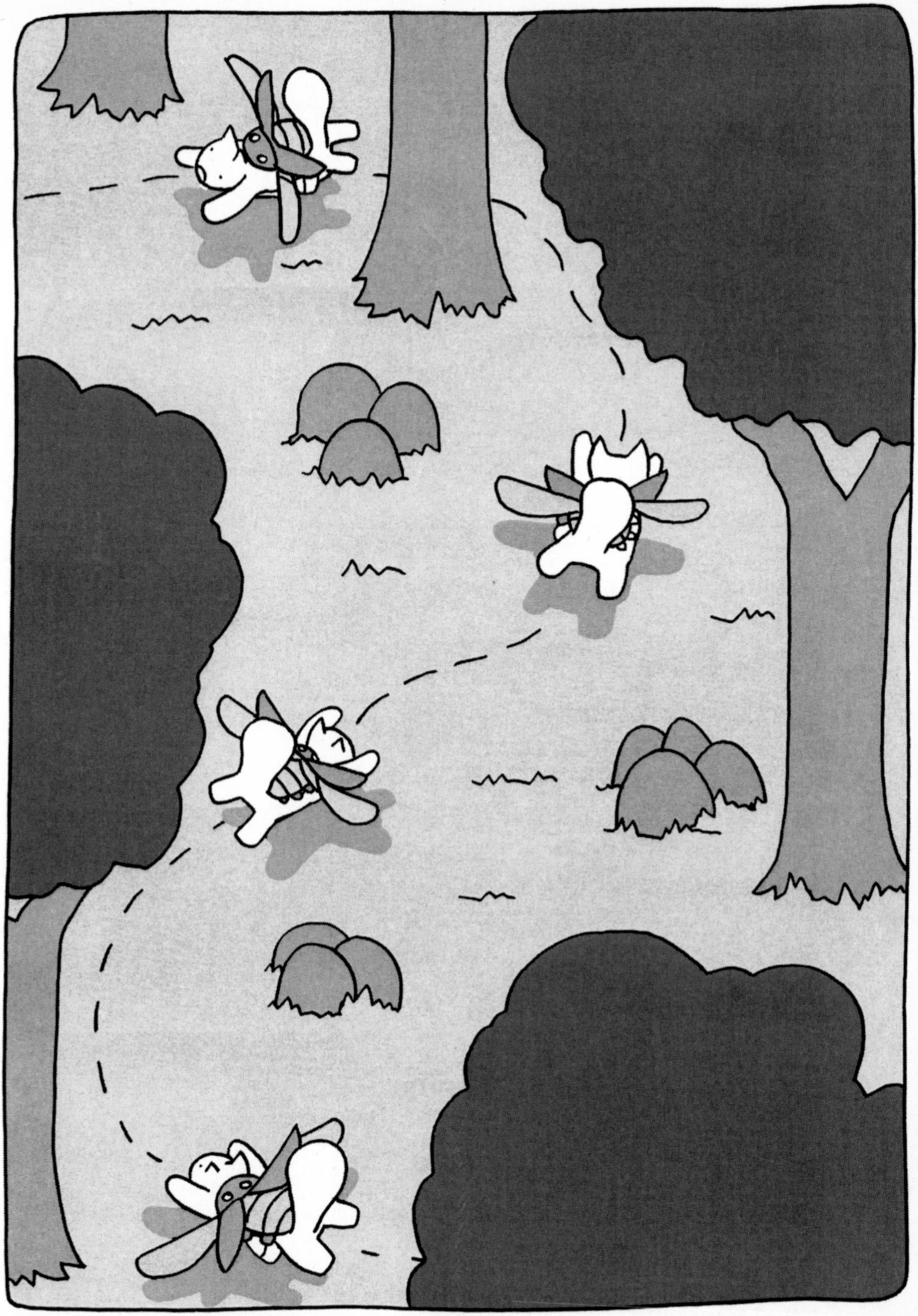

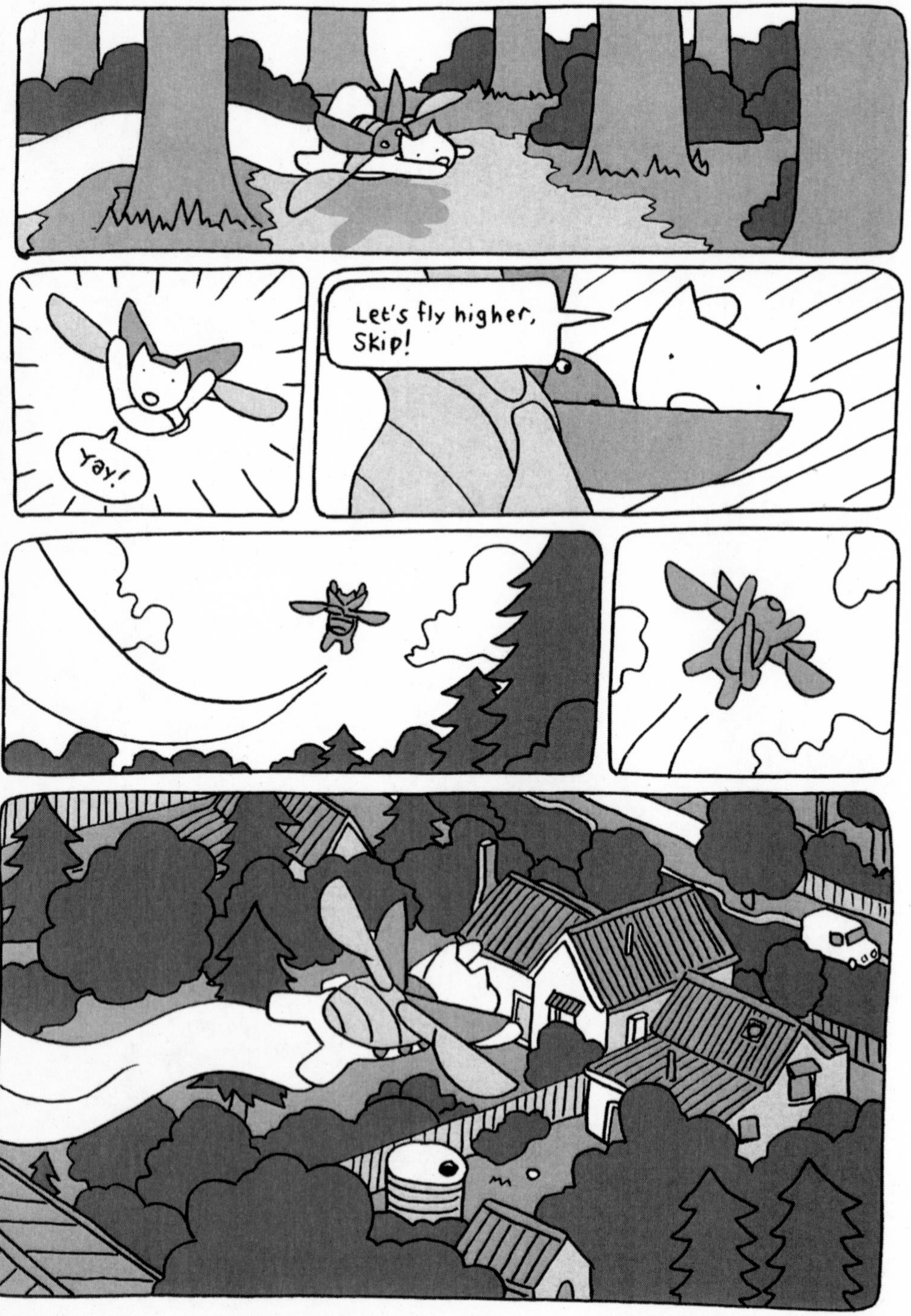
Yay!
Let's fly higher, Skip!

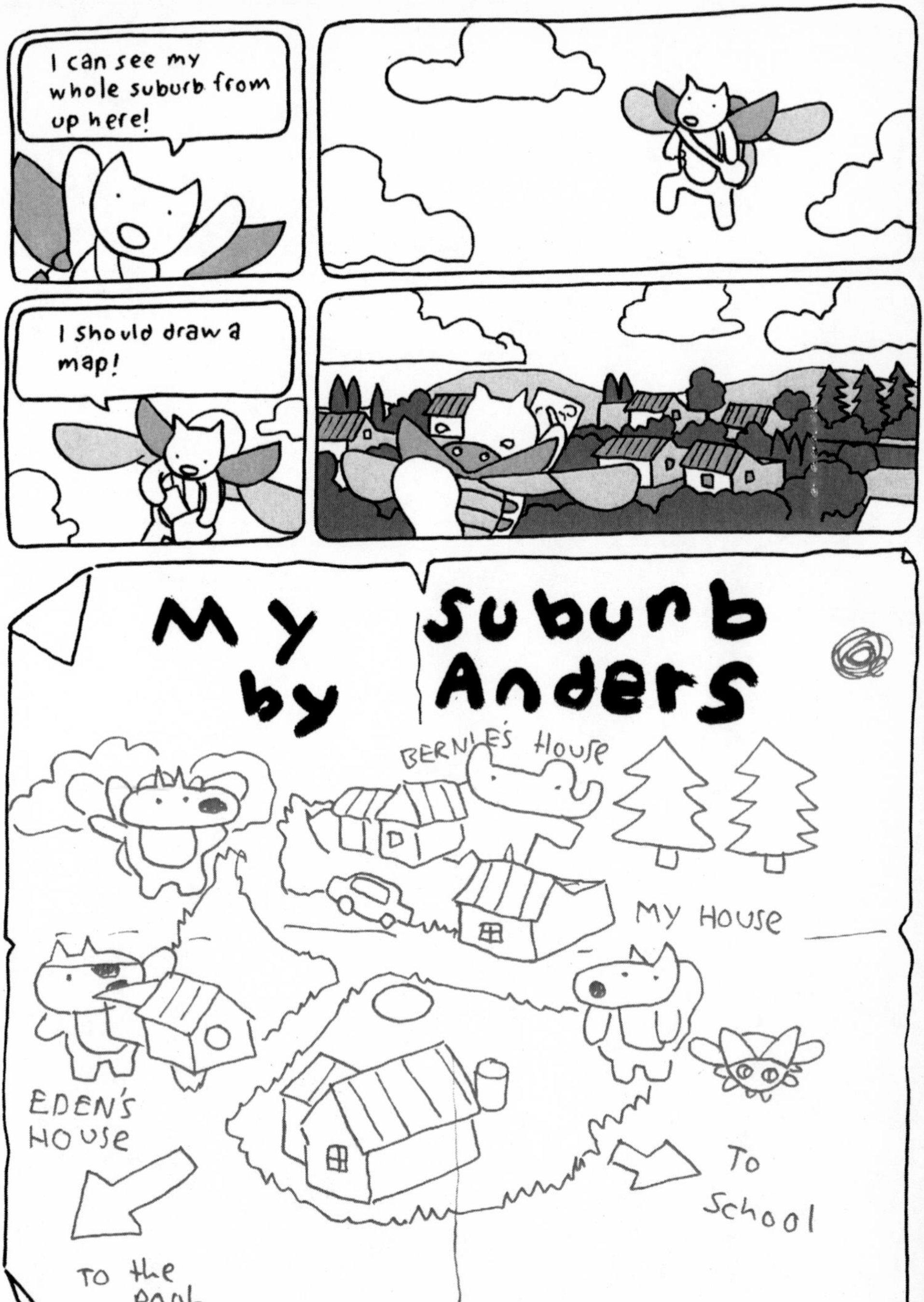
I can see my whole suburb from up here!
I should draw a map!
My Suburb by Anders
BERNIE'S HOUSE
MY HOUSE
EDEN'S HOUSE
TO the POOL
To School

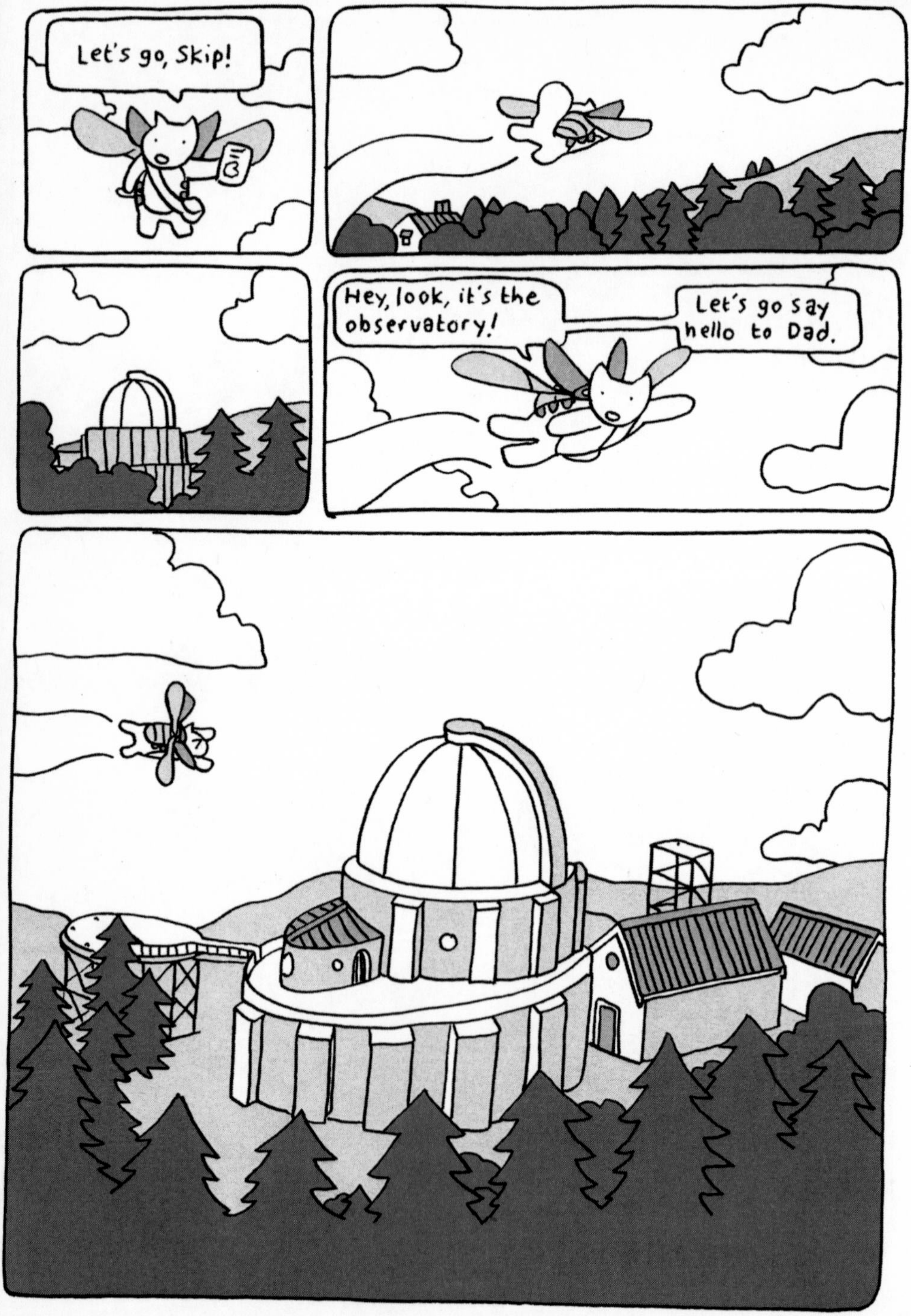
Let's go, Skip!
Hey, look, it's the observatory!
Let's go say hello to Dad.

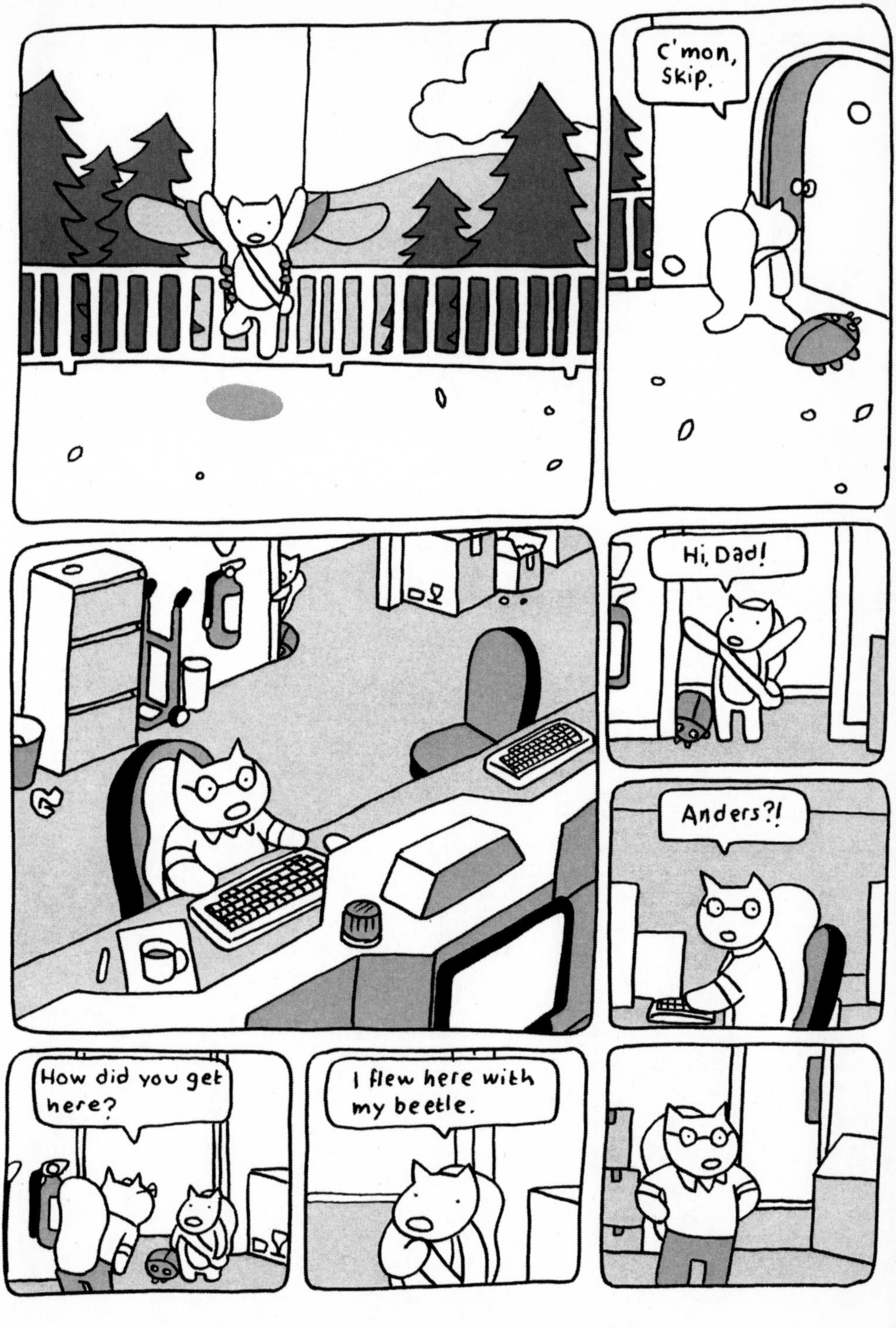
C'mon, Skip.
Hi, Dad!
Anders?!
How did you get here?
I flew here with my beetle.

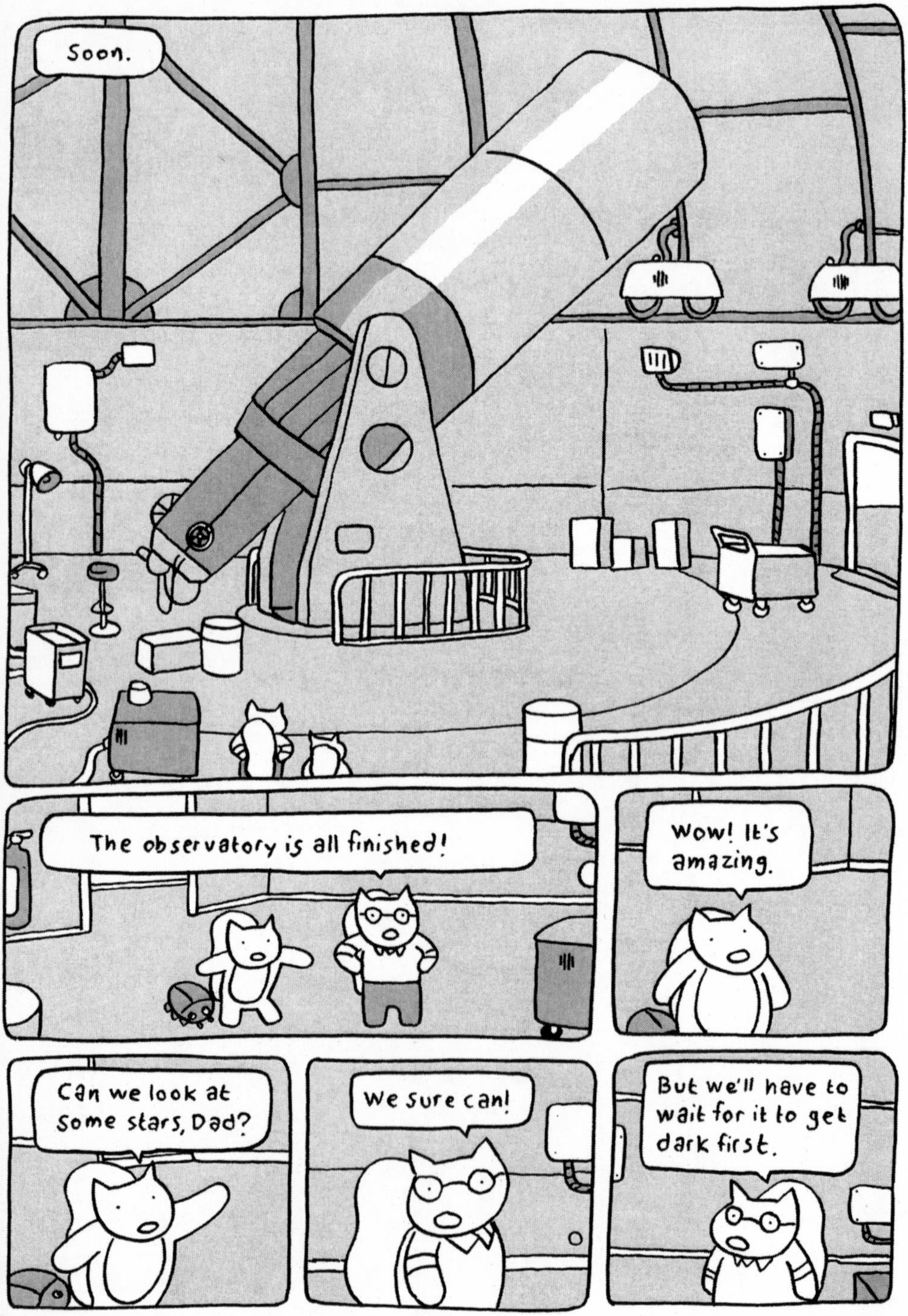
Soon.
The observatory is all finished!
Wow! It's amazing.
Can we look at some stars, Dad?
We sure can!
But we'll have to wait for it to get dark first.

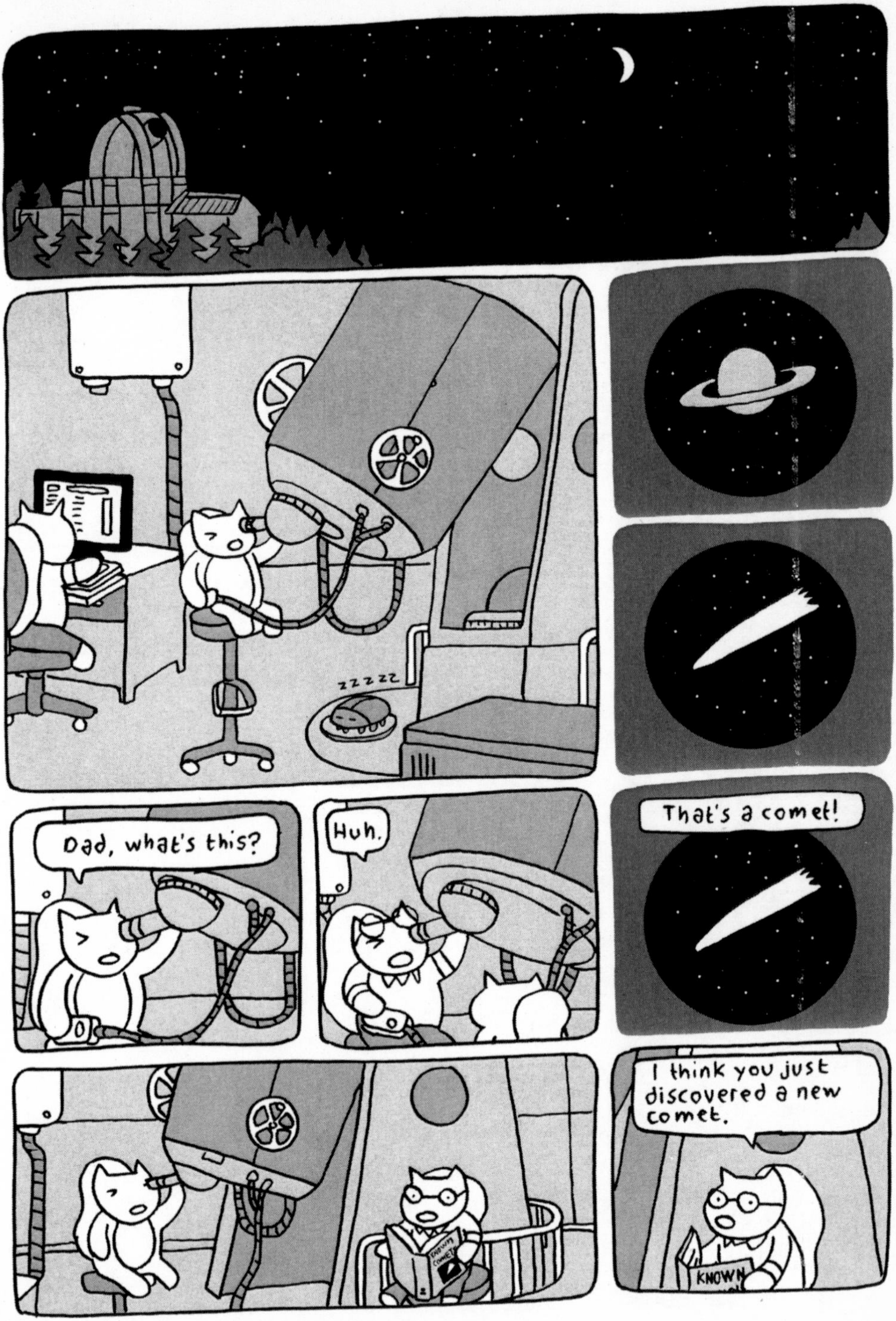
zzzzz
Dad, what's this?
Huh.
That's a comet!
I think you just discovered a new comet.
KNOWN

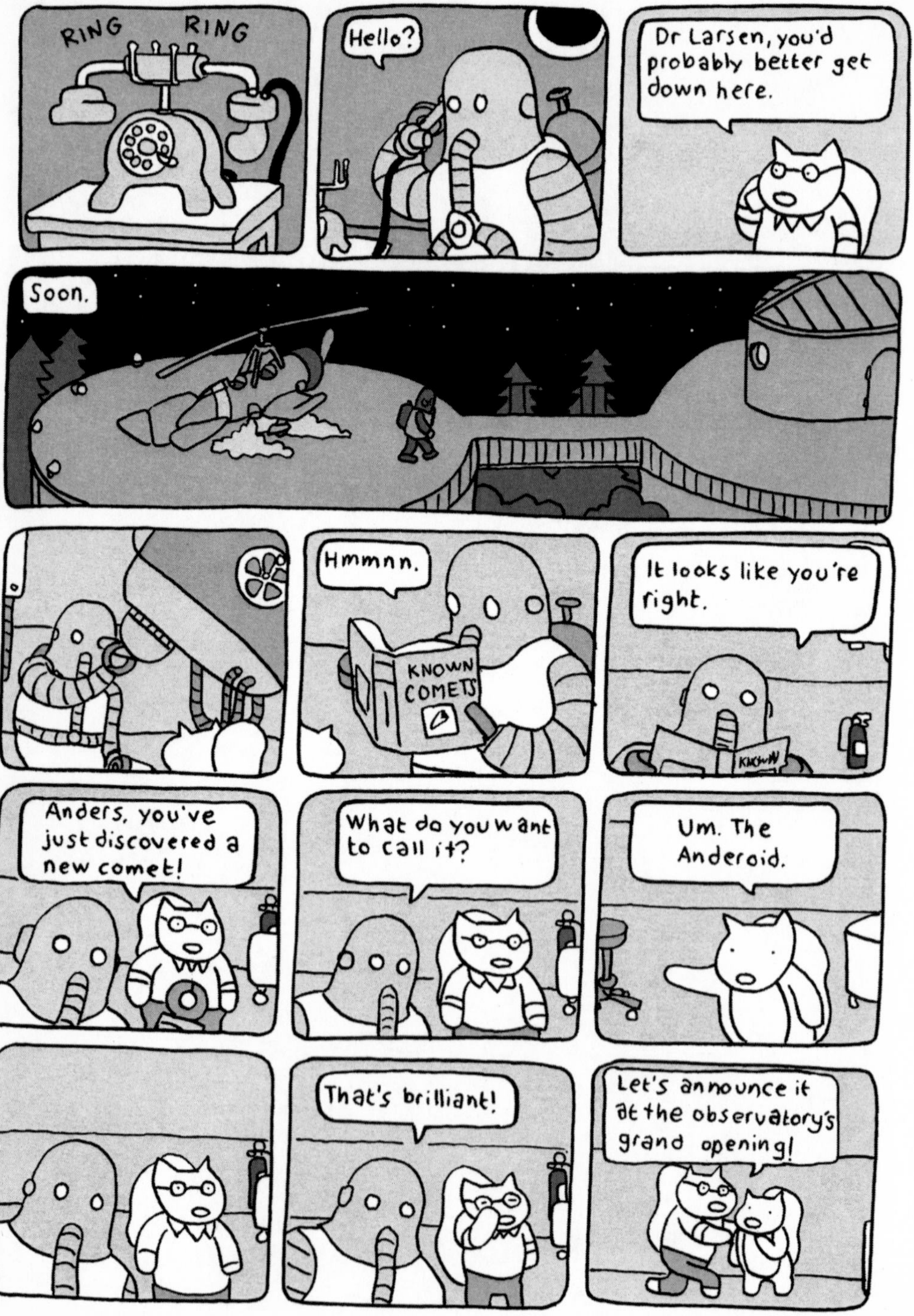
RING RING
Hello?
Dr Larsen, you'd probably better get down here.
Soon.
Hmmnn.
KNOWN COMETS
It looks like you're right.
Anders, you've just discovered a new comet!
What do you want to call it?
Um. The Anderoid.
That's brilliant!
Let's announce it at the observatory's grand opening!

Chapter 7

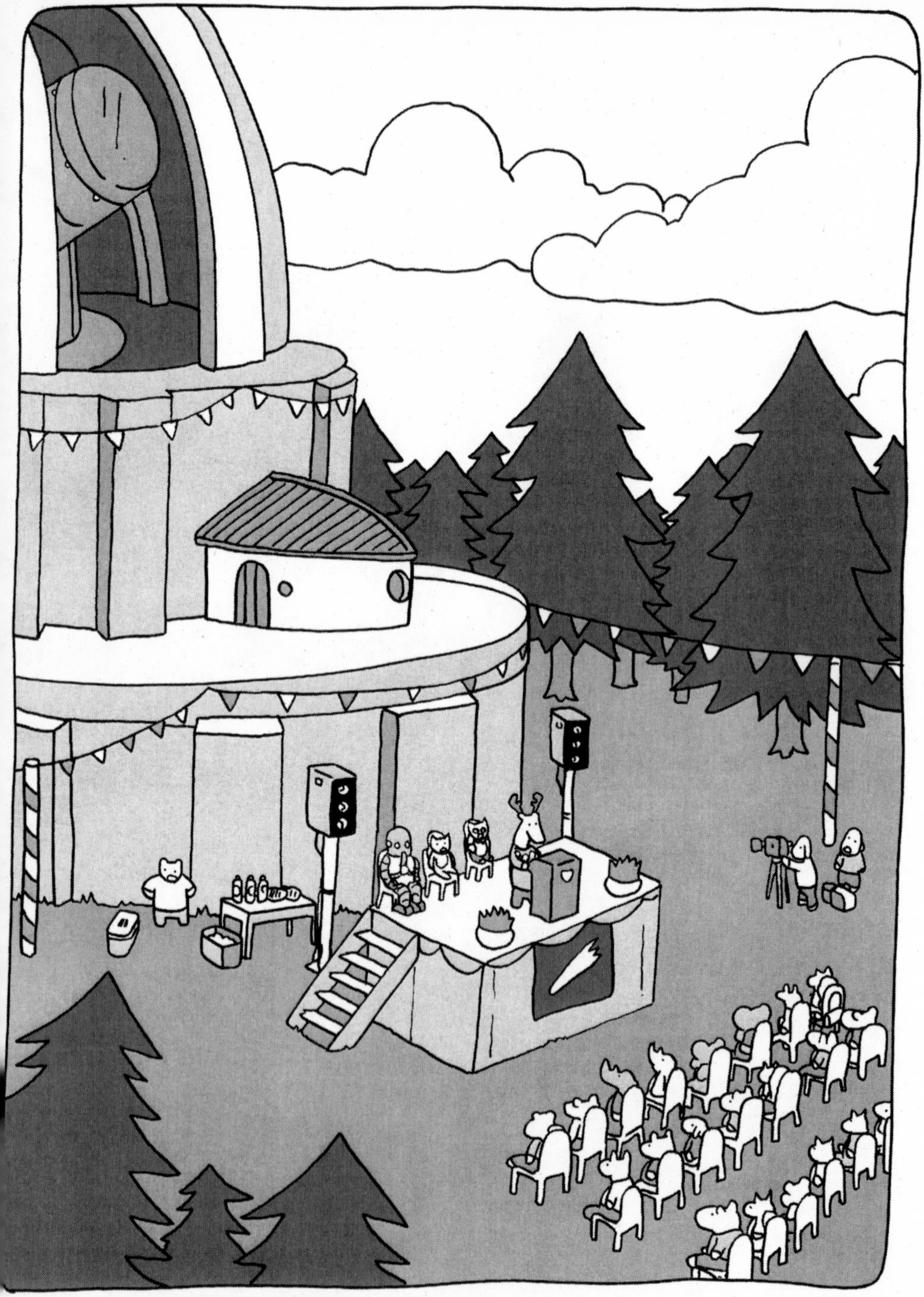

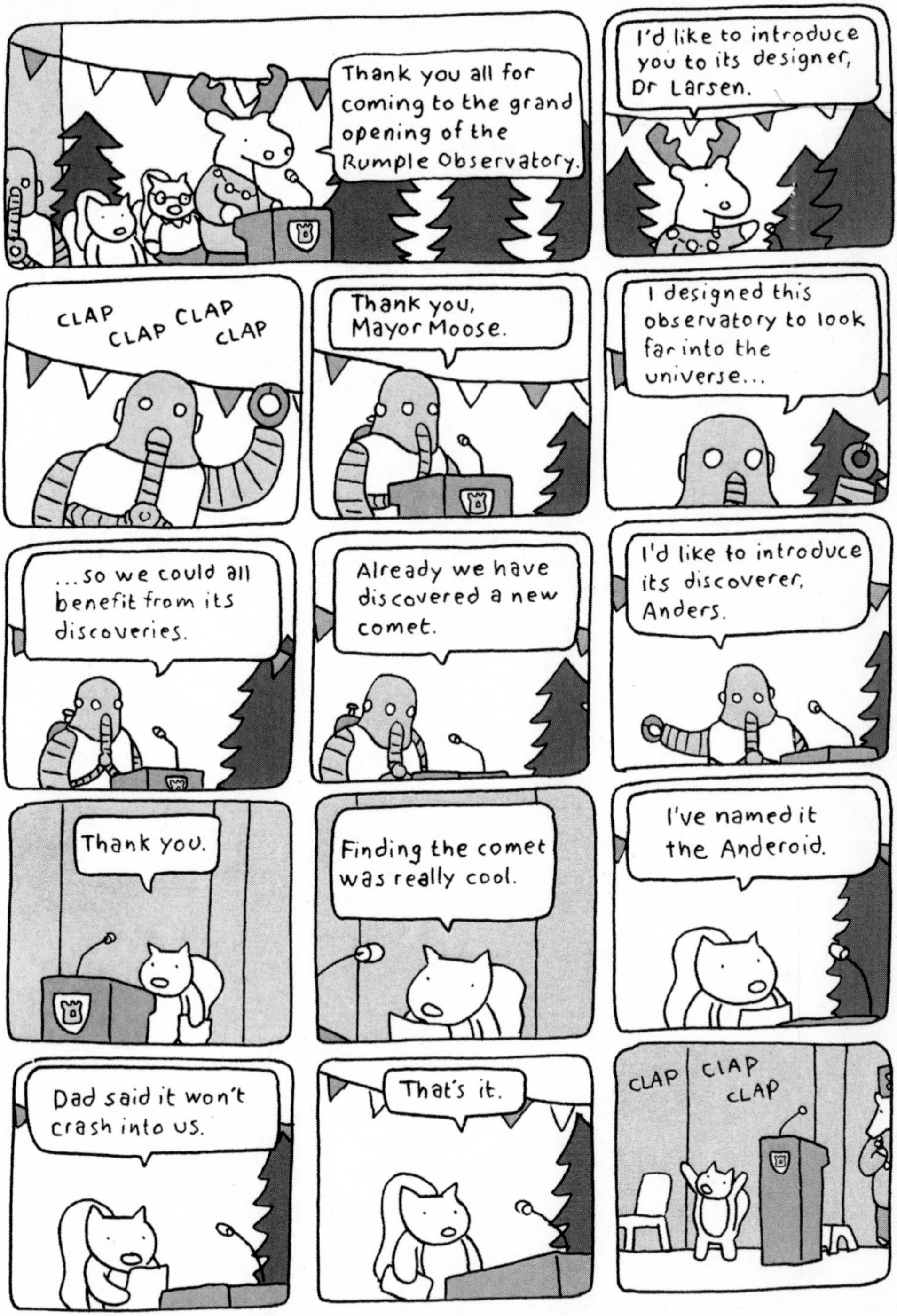
Thank you all for coming to the grand opening of the Rumple Observatory.
I'd like to introduce you to its designer, Dr Larsen.
CLAP CLAP CLAP CLAP
Thank you, Mayor Moose.
I designed this observatory to look far into the universe...
...so we could all benefit from its discoveries.
Already we have discovered a new comet.
I'd like to introduce its discoverer, Anders.
Thank you.
Finding the comet was really cool.
I've named it the Anderoid.
Dad said it won't crash into us.
That's it.
CLAP CLAP CLAP

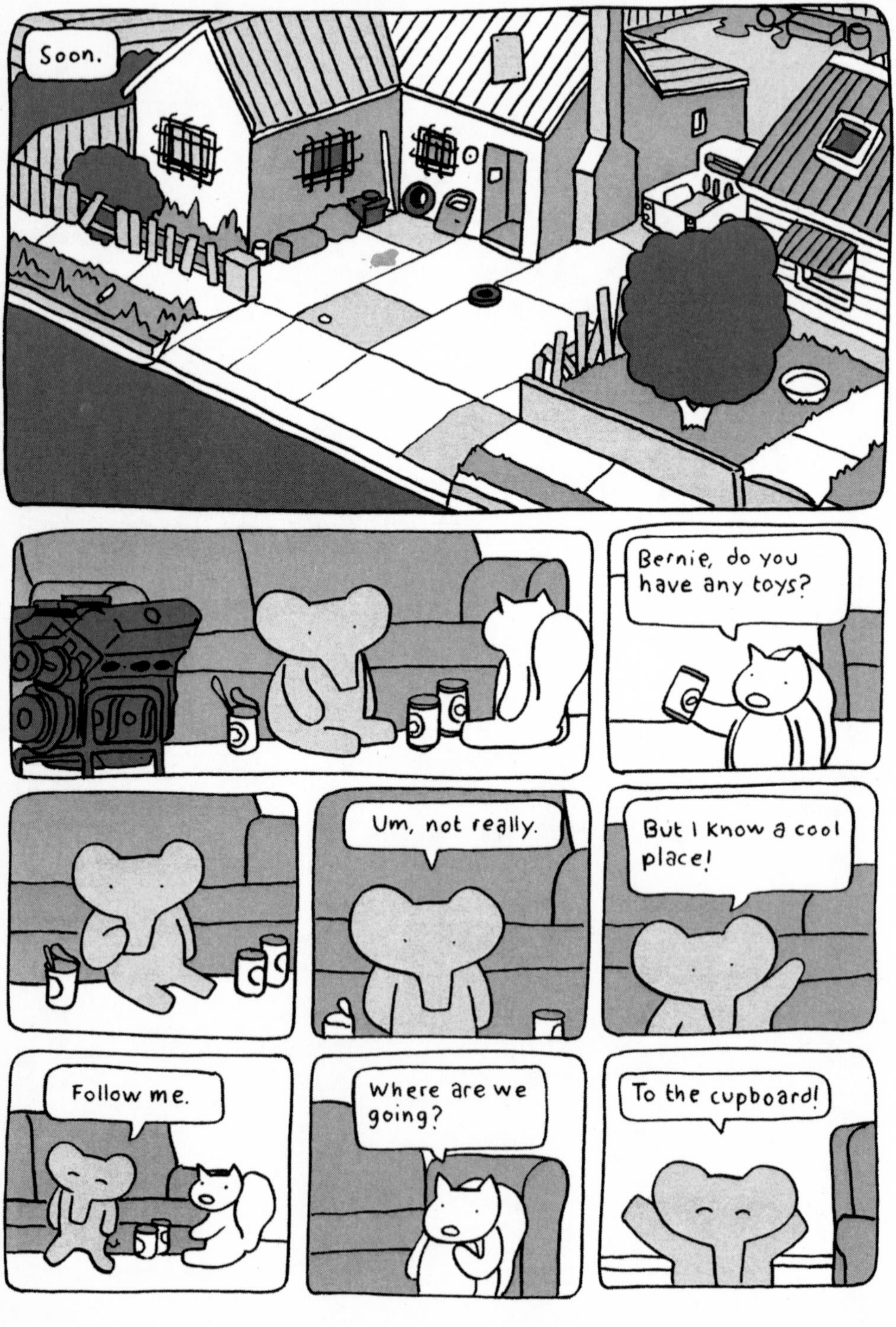
Soon.
Bernie, do you have any toys?
Um, not really.
But I know a cool place!
Follow me.
Where are we going?
To the cupboard!

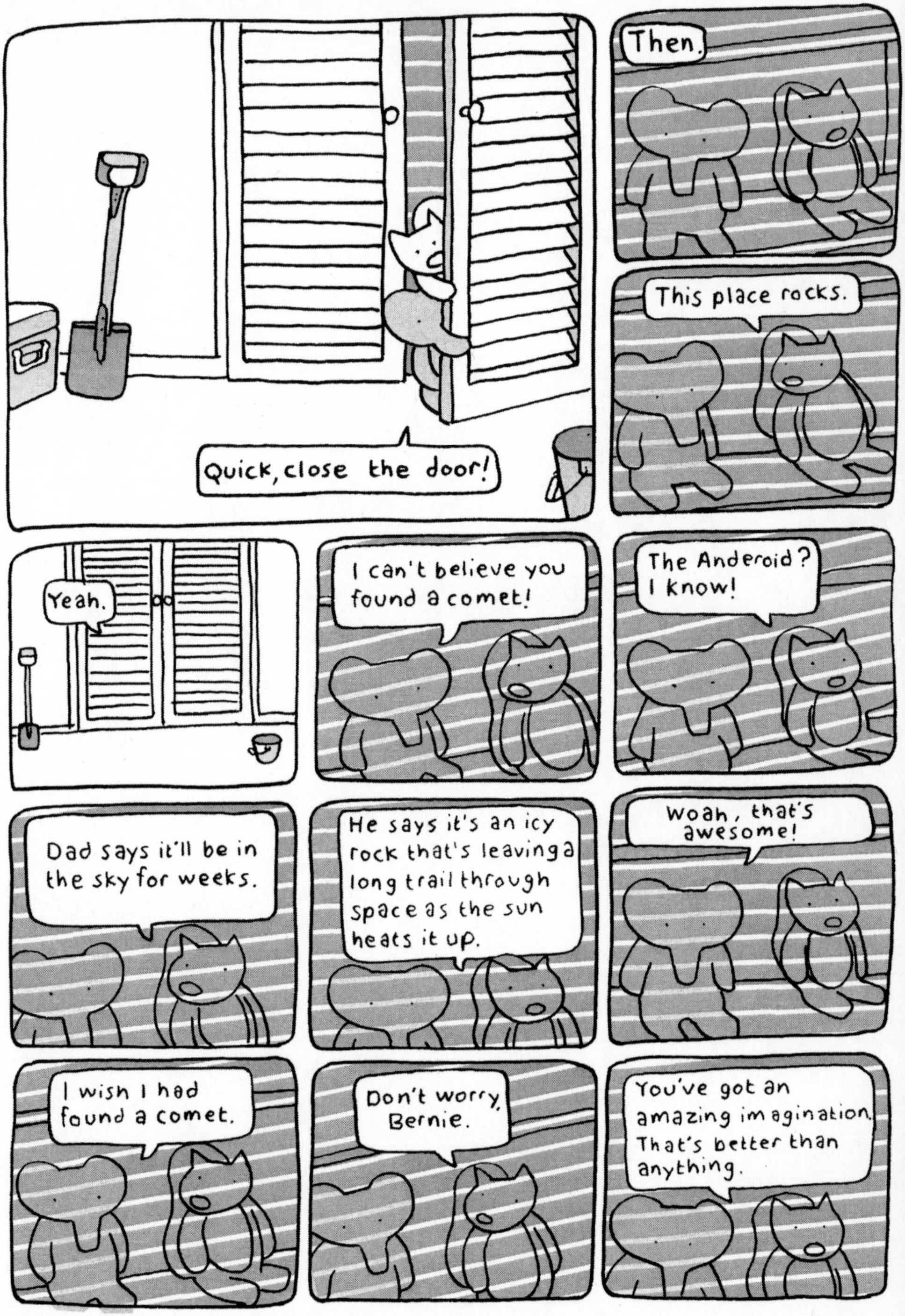
Quick, close the door!
Then.
This place rocks.
Yeah.
I can't believe you found a comet!
The Anderoid? I know!
Dad says it'll be in the sky for weeks.
He says it's an icy rock that's leaving a long trail through space as the sun heats it up.
Woah, that's awesome!
I wish I had found a comet.
Don't worry, Bernie.
You've got an amazing imagination. That's better than anything.

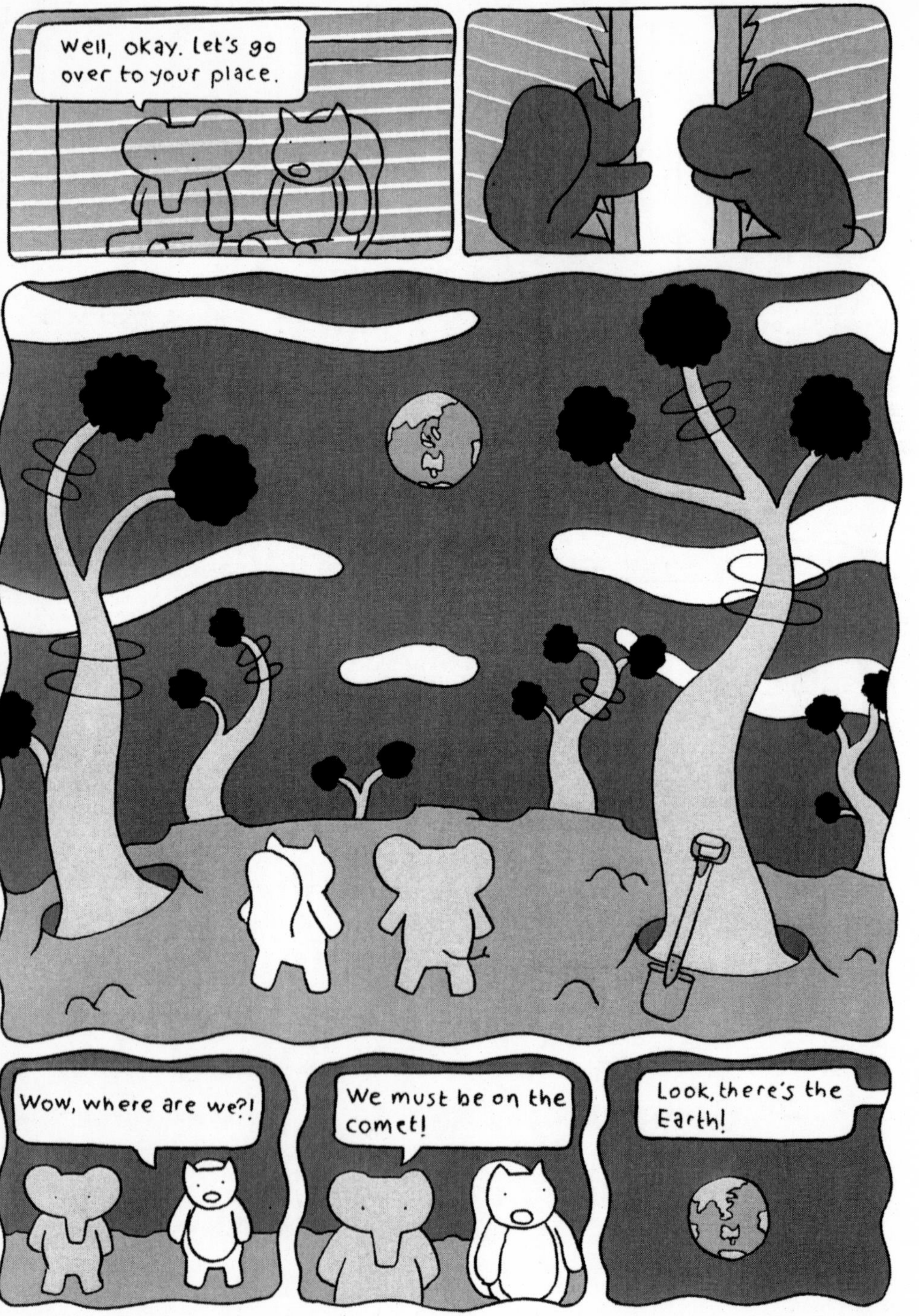
Well, okay. Let's go over to your place.
Wow, where are we?!
We must be on the comet!
Look, there's the Earth!

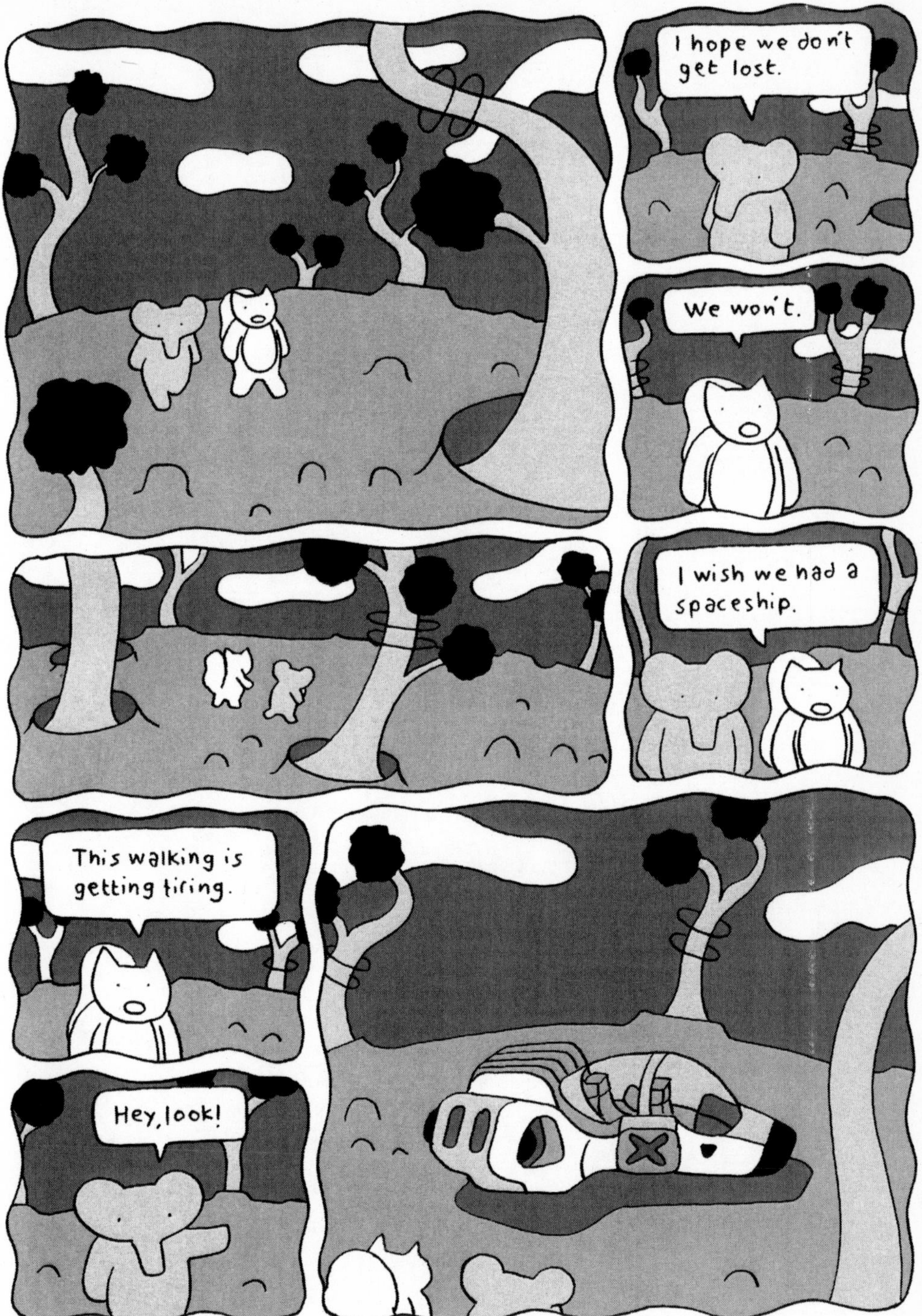
I hope we don't get lost.
We won't.
I wish we had a spaceship.
This walking is getting tiring.
Hey, look!

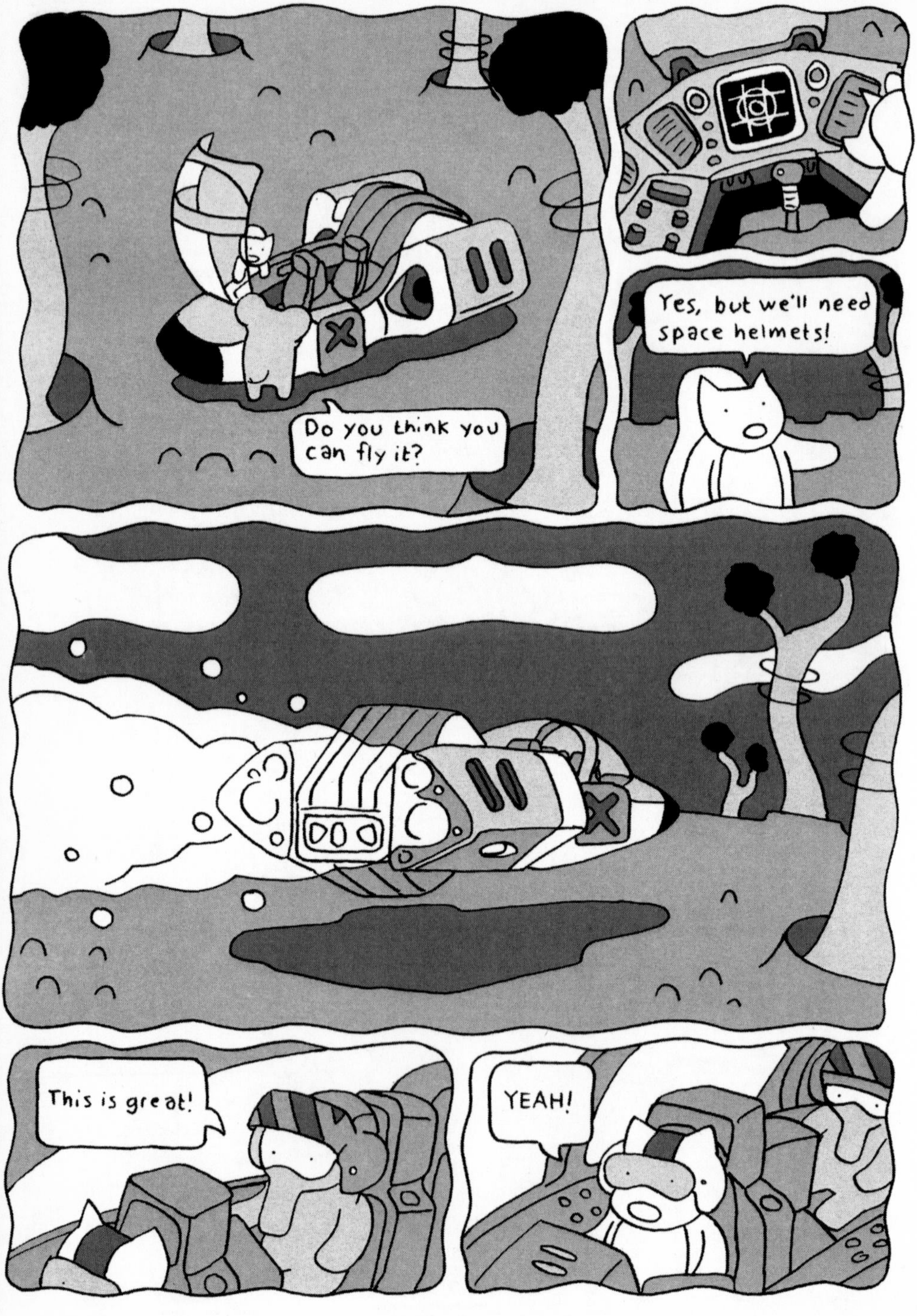
Do you think you can fly it?
Yes, but we'll need space helmets!
This is great!
YEAH!

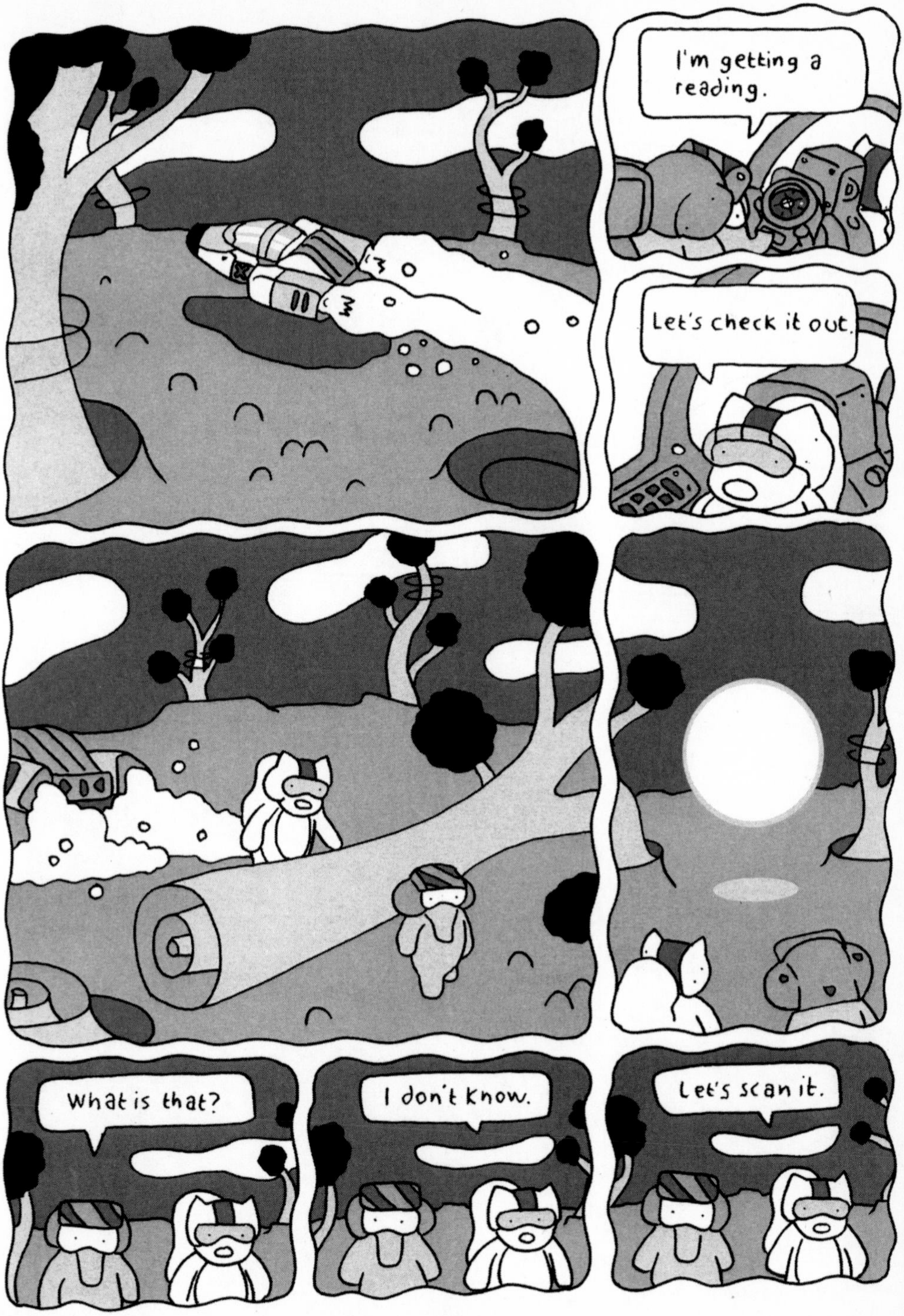
I'm getting a reading.
Let's check it out.
What is that?
I don't know.
Let's scan it.

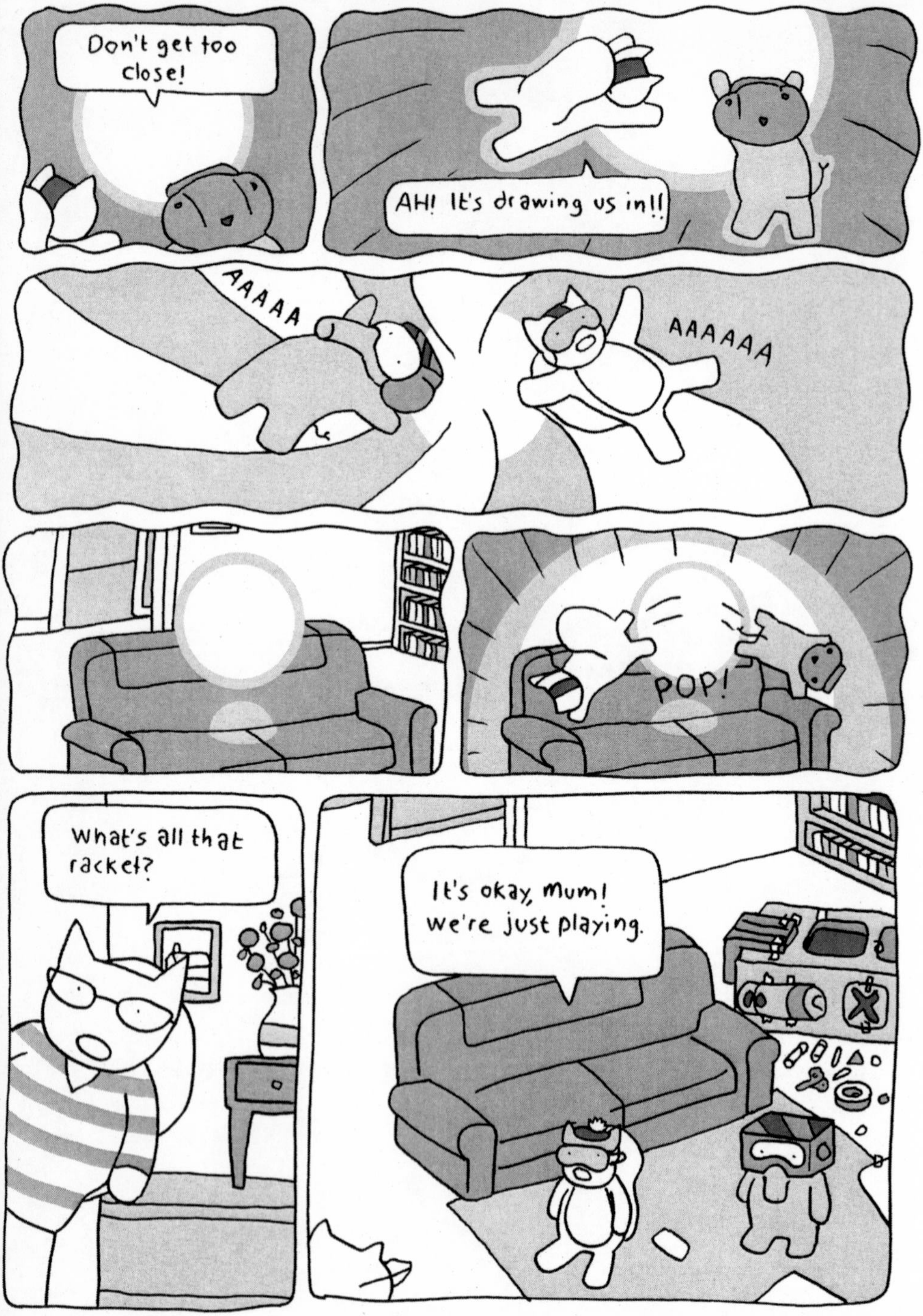

Don't get too close!
AH! It's drawing us in!!
AAAAA
AAAAAA
POP!
What's all that racket?
It's okay, mum! we're just playing.

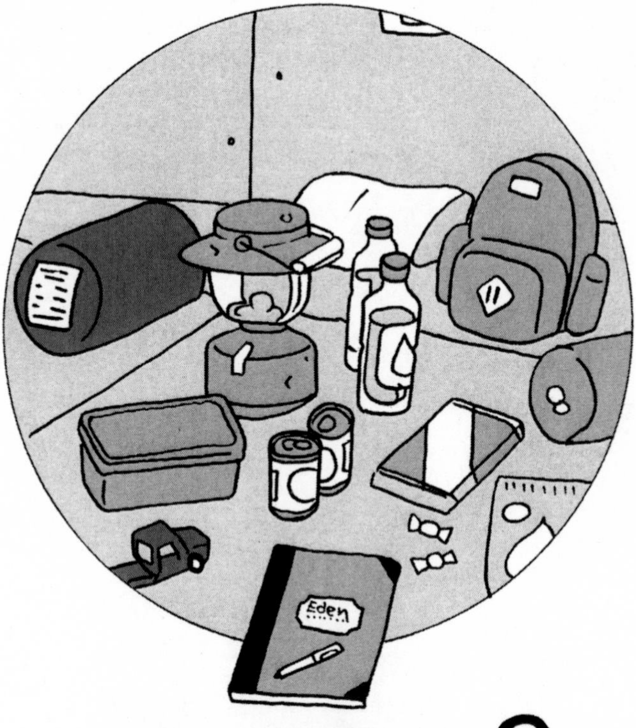
Eden

Chapter 8

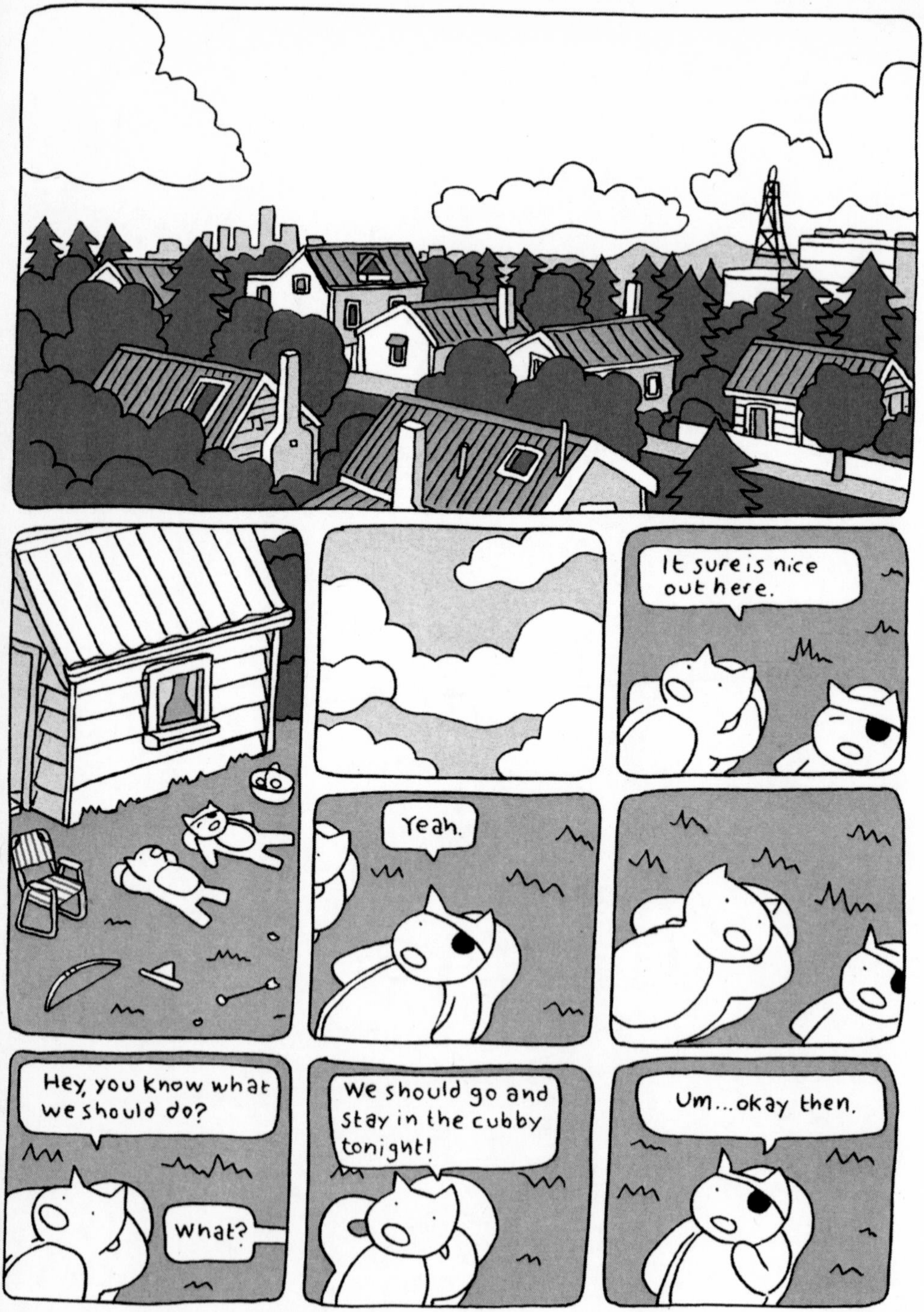

It sure is nice out here.
Yeah.
Hey, you know what we should do?
What?
We should go and stay in the cubby tonight!
Um...okay then.

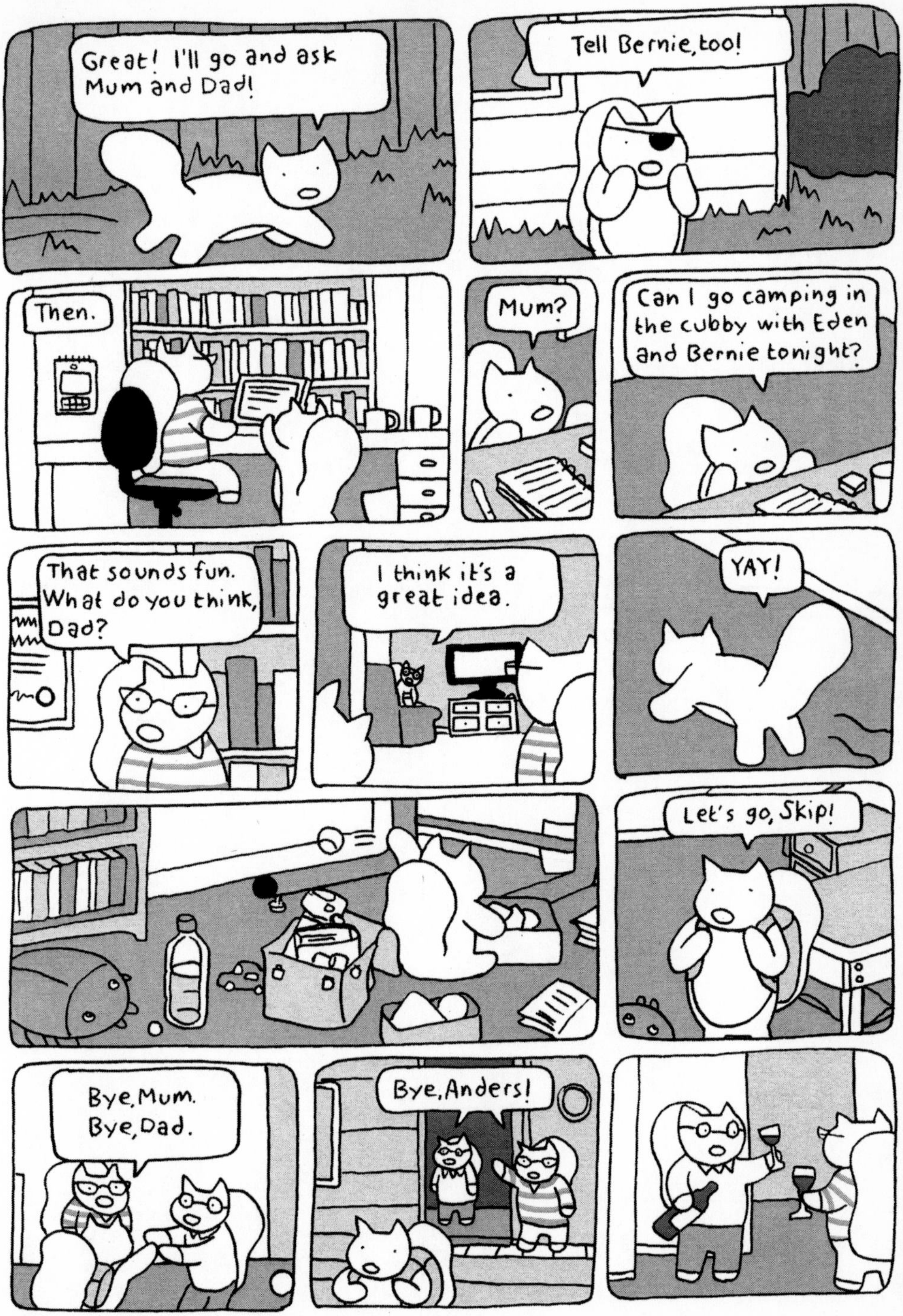
Great! I'll go and ask Mum and Dad!
Tell Bernie, too!
Then.
Mum?
Can I go camping in the cubby with Eden and Bernie tonight?
That sounds fun. What do you think, Dad?
I think it's a great idea.
YAY!
Let's go, Skip!
Bye, Mum. Bye, Dad.
Bye, Anders!

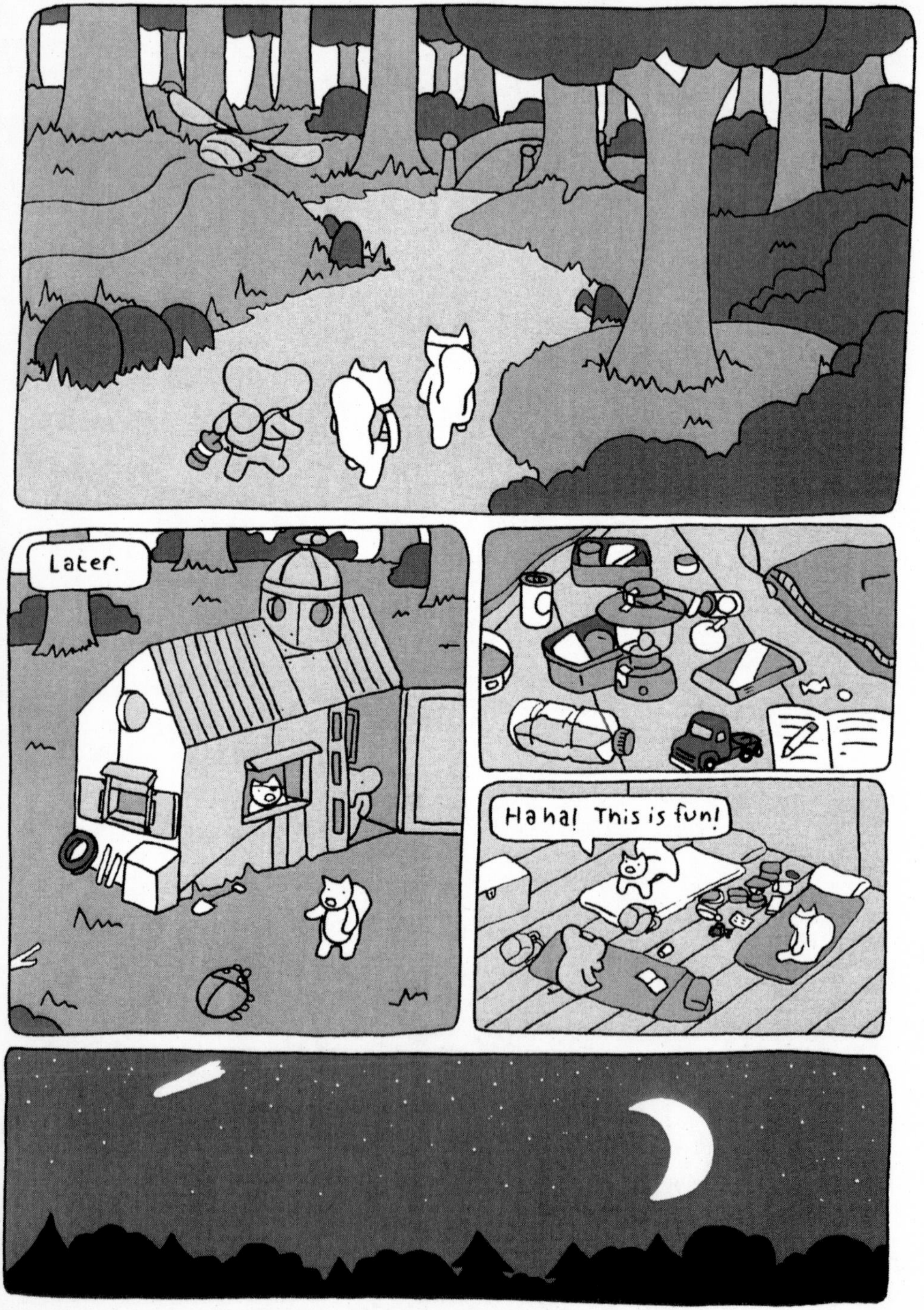
Later.
Ha ha! This is fun!

This cubby is the best thing ever!

I know, it's awesome.

I'd live here if I could.

Me, too.

I'd miss all my stuff.

So would I.

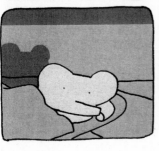

Guess what, guys?

What?

It's time for chocolate!

YESSS.

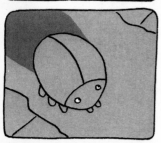

Have you guys heard of a bunyip?

A what?

A bunyip. It's a big monster that lives in the forest.

They say it eats kids and can smell chocolate from miles away.

Oh, be quiet, Bernie, that's not true!
They don't live around here, Eden.
Ah! Be quiet, you're making it worse.
POP
Bernie, turn the light back on!
I can't. The bulb must be broken.
Did anyone bring a torch?
NOOOOO.
Oh, I'm scared!
Don't worry, Eden.
munch! munch! munch!
Hey! Who's eating the chocolate?!
AAAAAHHH!

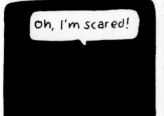

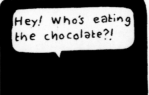

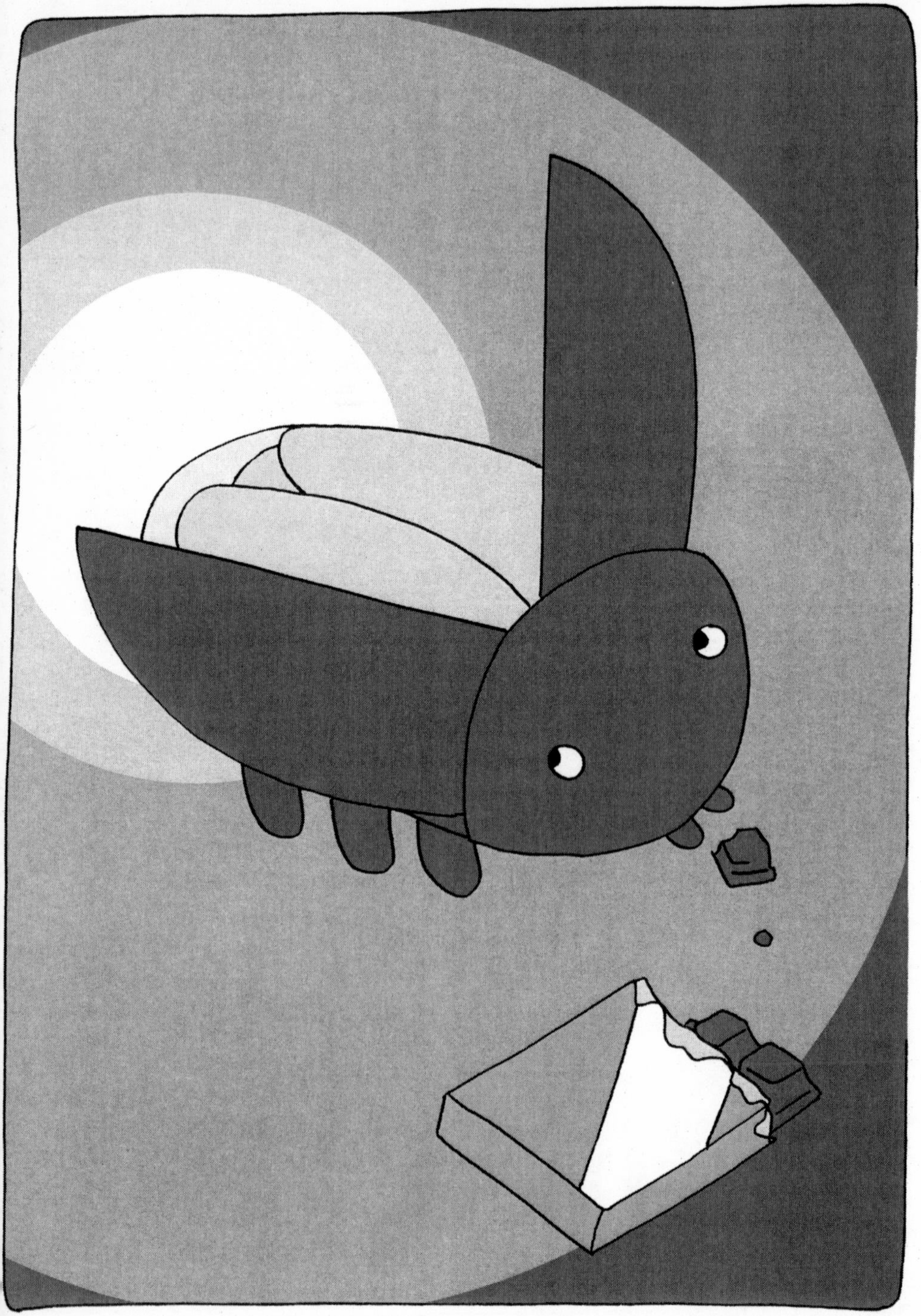

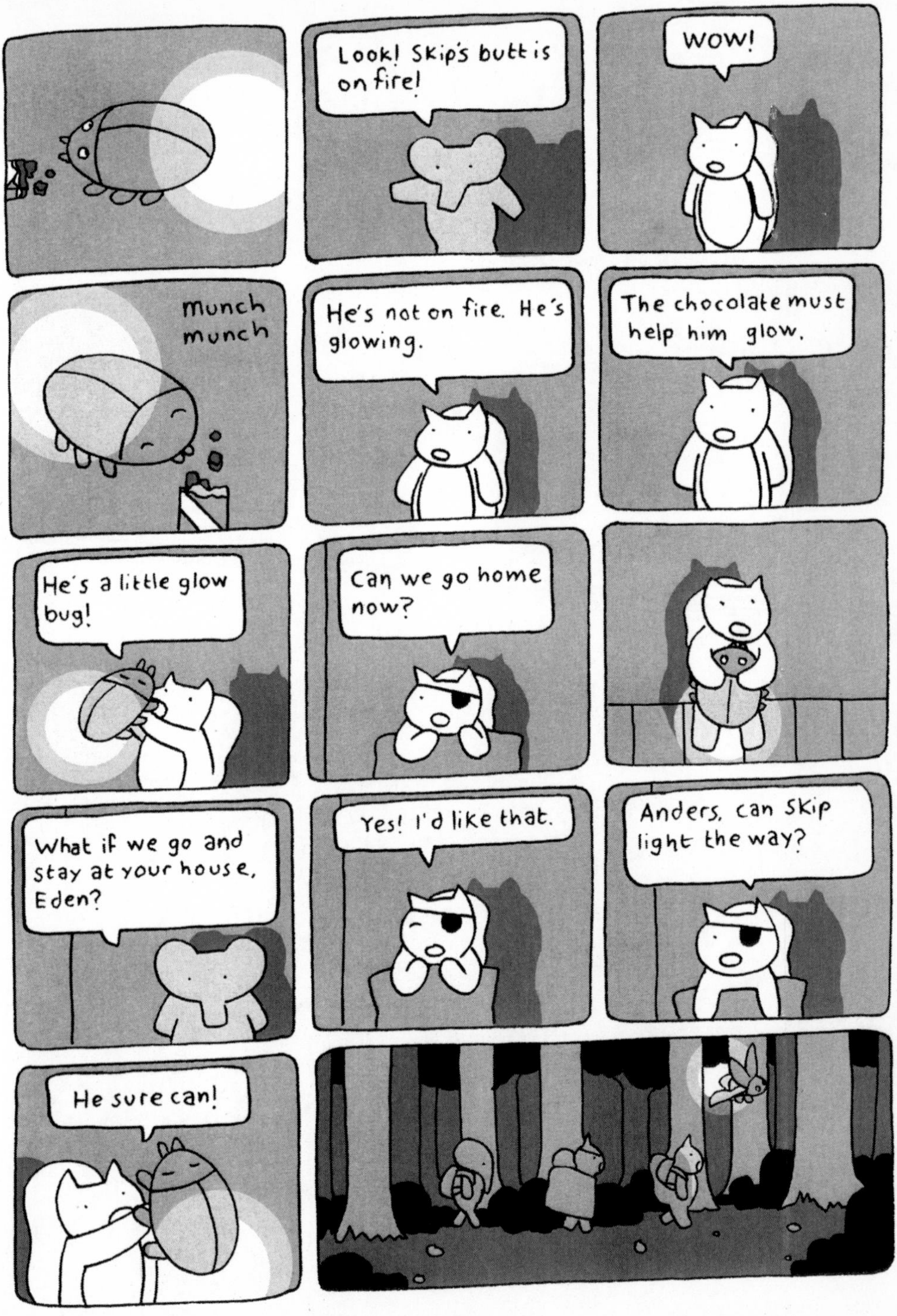
Look! Skip's butt is on fire!
WOW!
munch munch
He's not on fire. He's glowing.
The chocolate must help him glow.
He's a little glow bug!
Can we go home now?
What if we go and stay at your house, Eden?
Yes! I'd like that.
Anders, can Skip light the way?
He sure can!

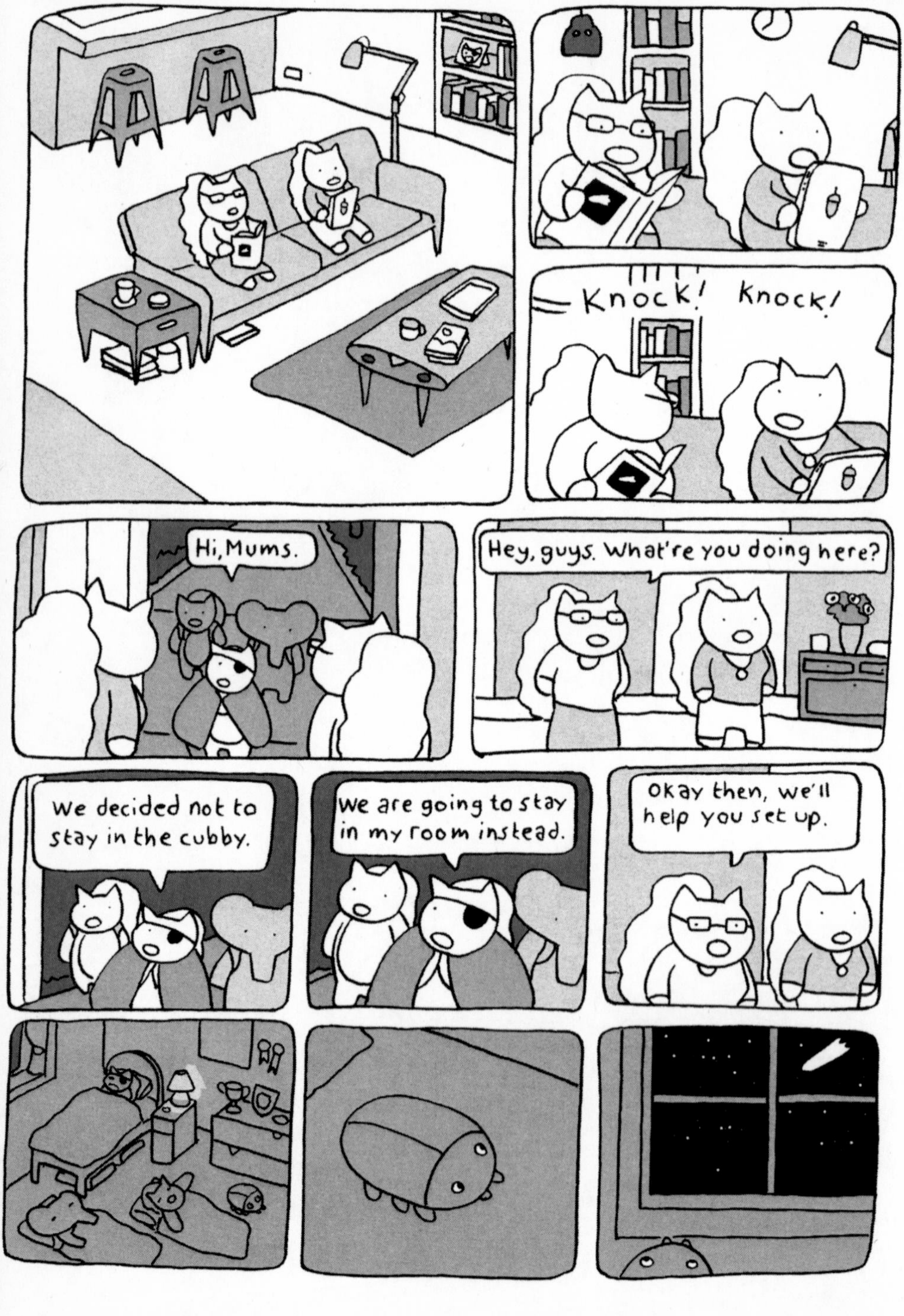
Knock! Knock!
Hi, Mums.
Hey, guys. What're you doing here?
We decided not to stay in the cubby.
We are going to stay in my room instead.
Okay then, we'll help you set up.

Chapter 9

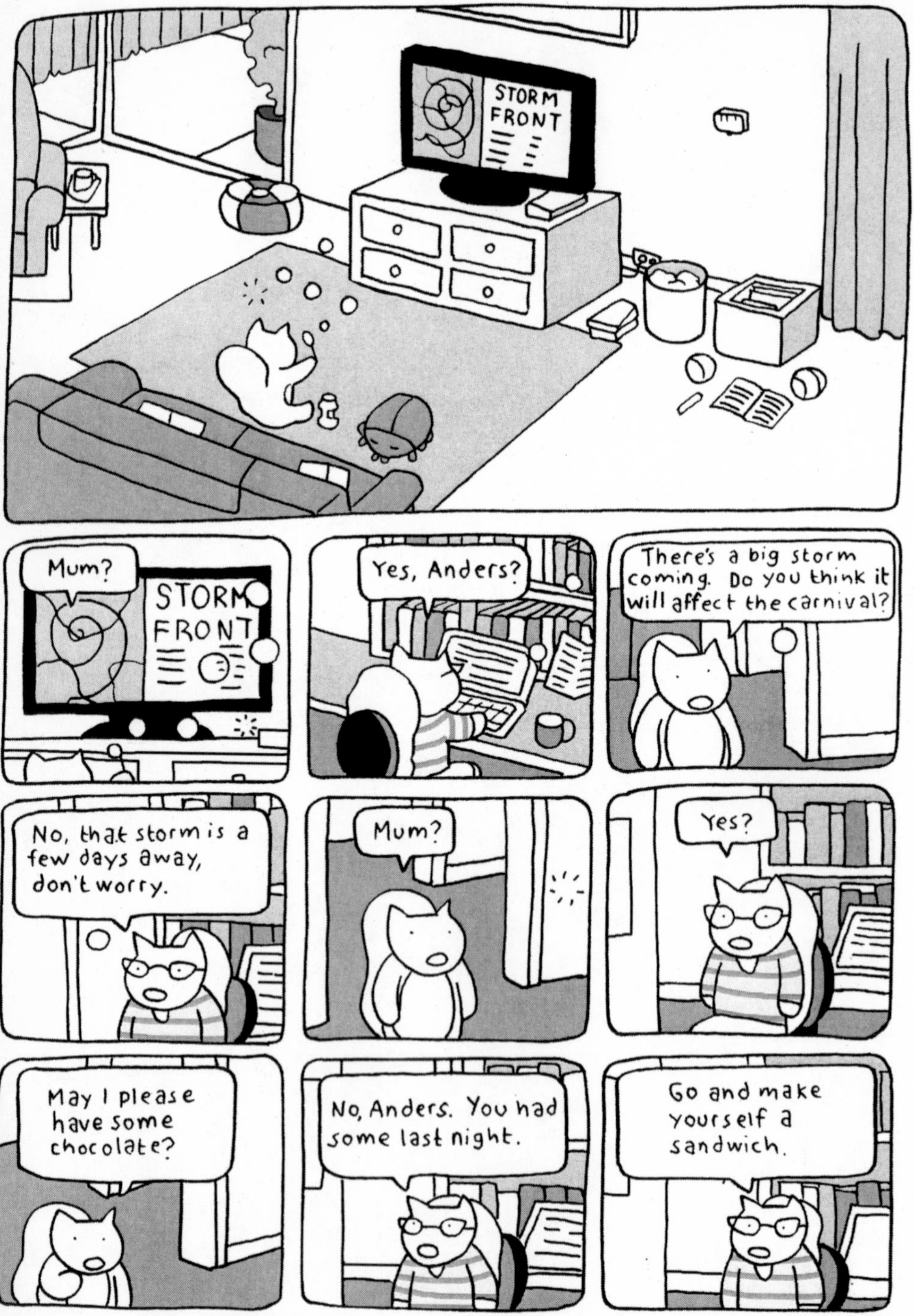
STORM FRONT
Mum?
STORM FRONT
Yes, Anders?
There's a big storm coming. Do you think it will affect the carnival?
No, that storm is a few days away, don't worry.
Mum?
Yes?
May I please have some chocolate?
No, Anders. You had some last night.
Go and make yourself a sandwich.

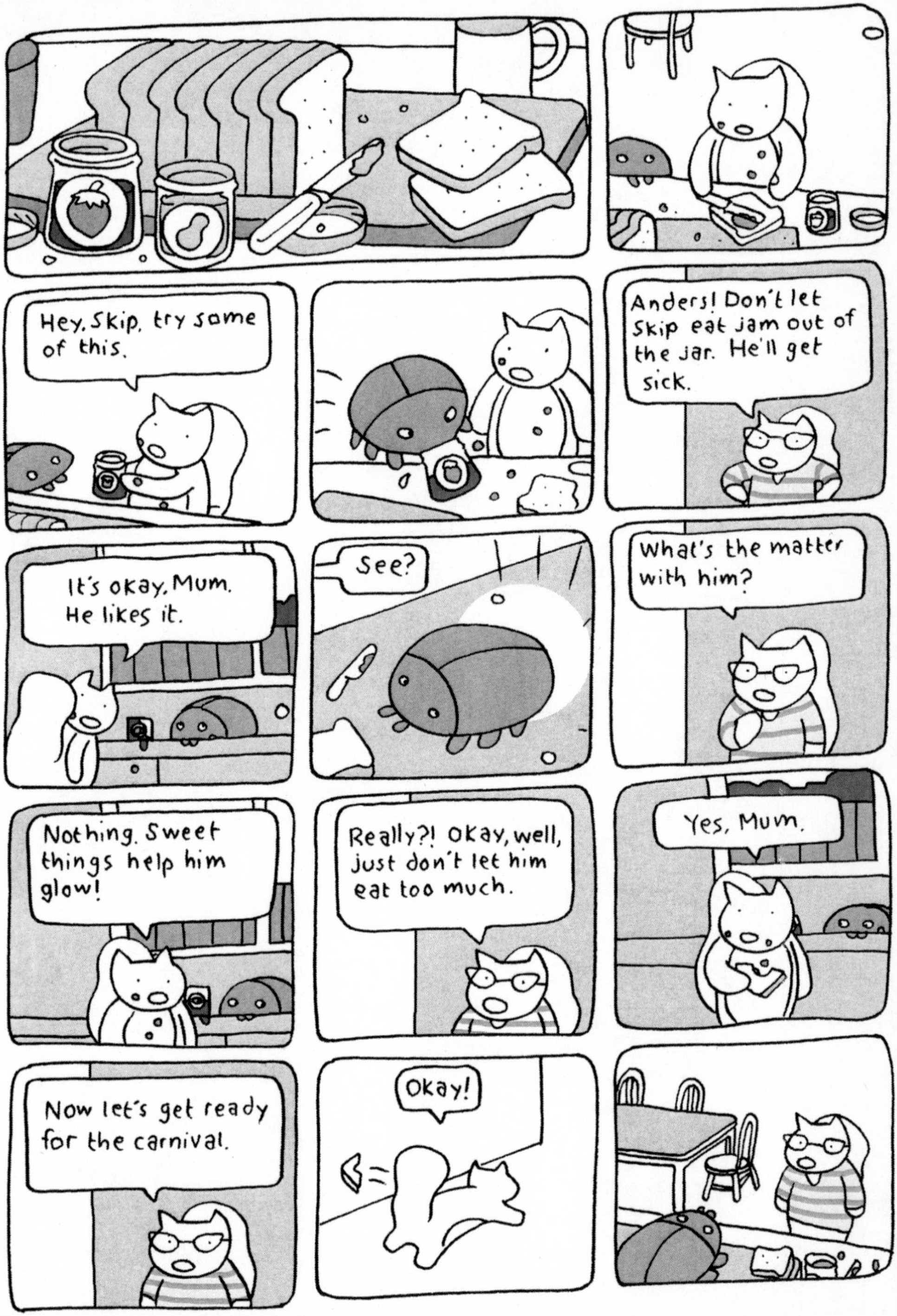

Hey, Skip, try some of this.
Anders! Don't let Skip eat jam out of the jar. He'll get sick.
It's okay, Mum. He likes it.
See?
What's the matter with him?
Nothing. Sweet things help him glow!
Really?! Okay, well, just don't let him eat too much.
Yes, Mum.
Now let's get ready for the carnival.
Okay!

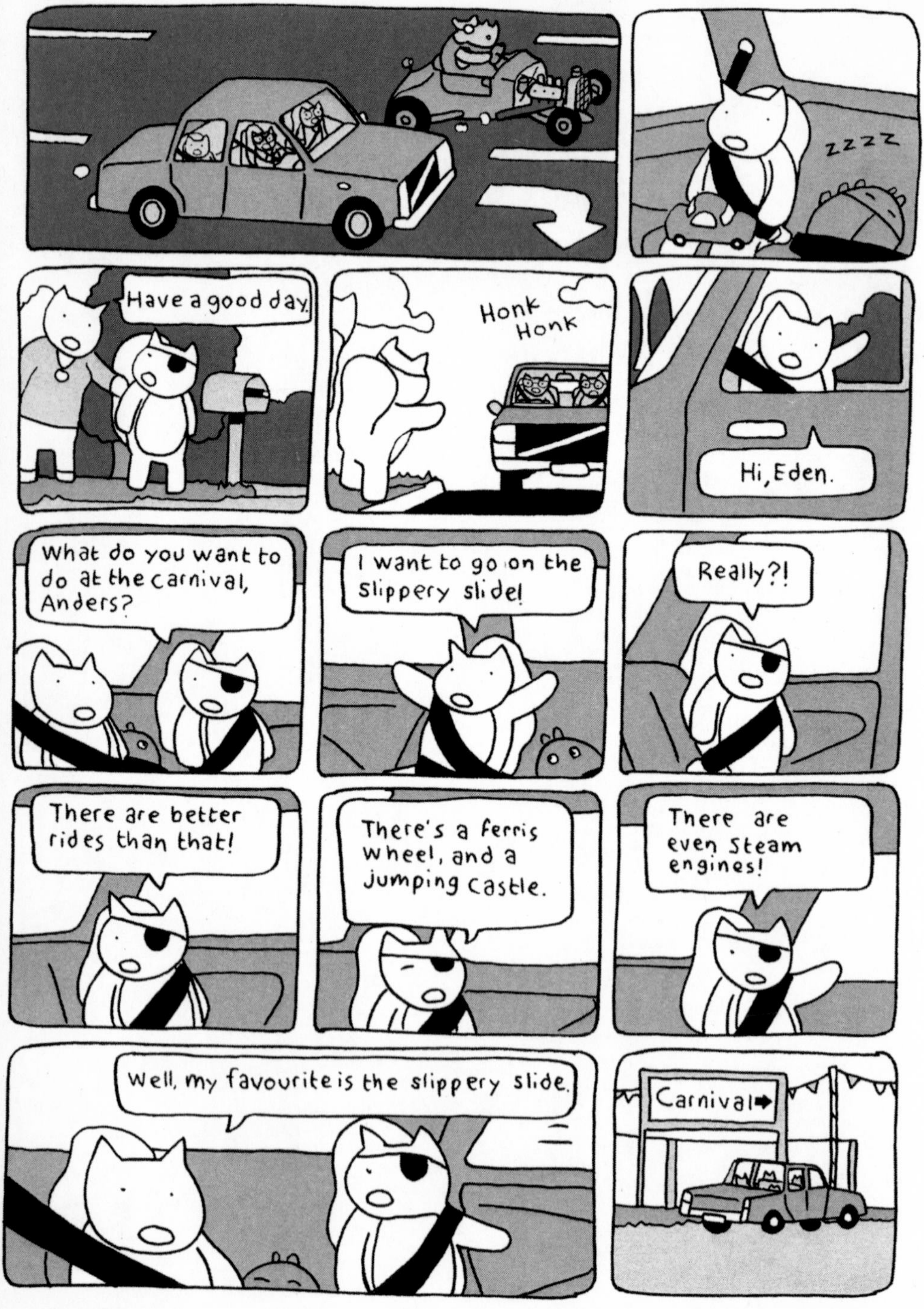
ZZZZ
Have a good day.
Honk
Honk
Hi, Eden.
What do you want to do at the carnival, Anders?
I want to go on the slippery slide!
Really?!
There are better rides than that!
There's a ferris wheel, and a jumping castle.
There are even steam engines!
Well, my favourite is the slippery slide.
Carnival

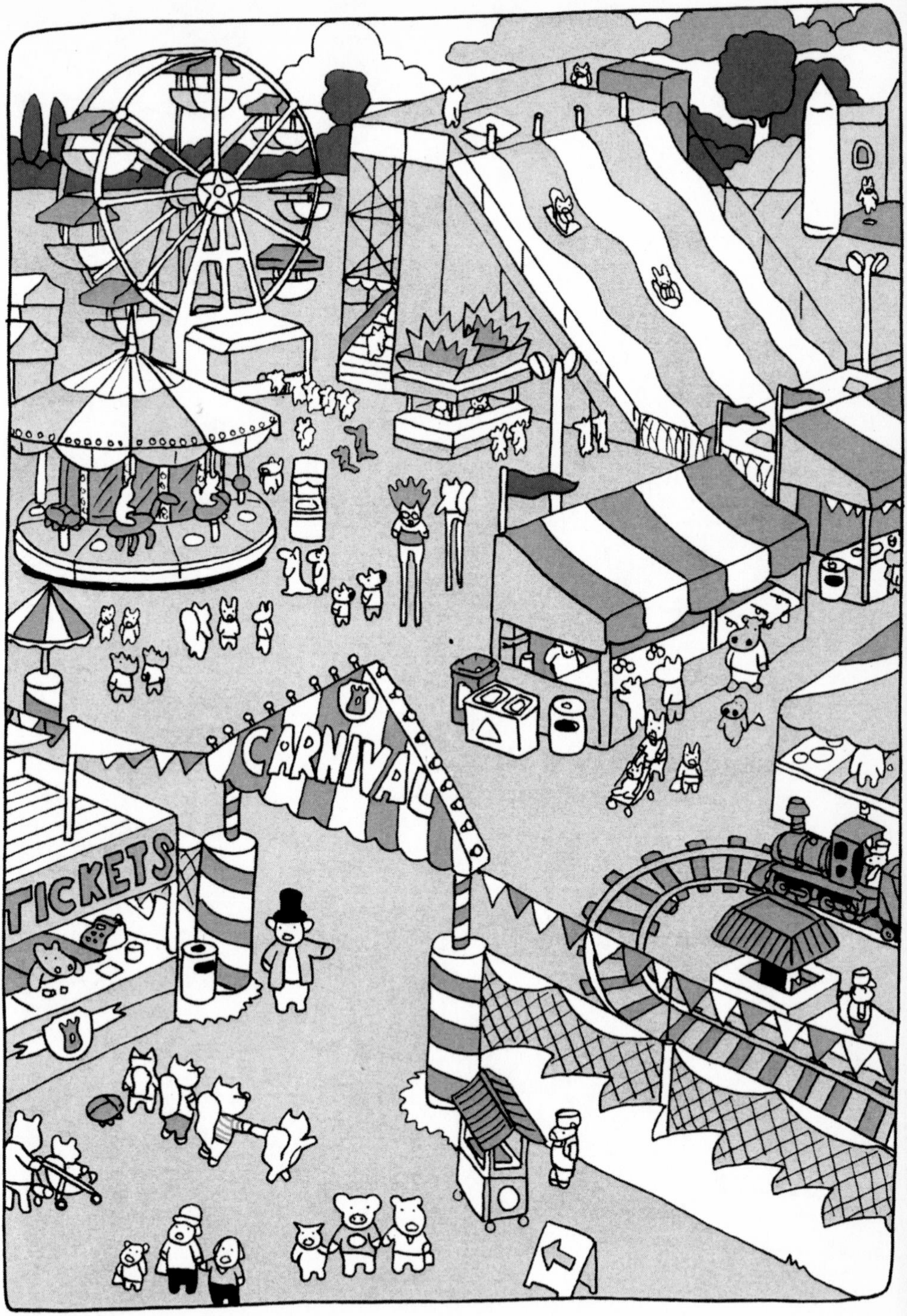
CARNIVAL
TICKETS

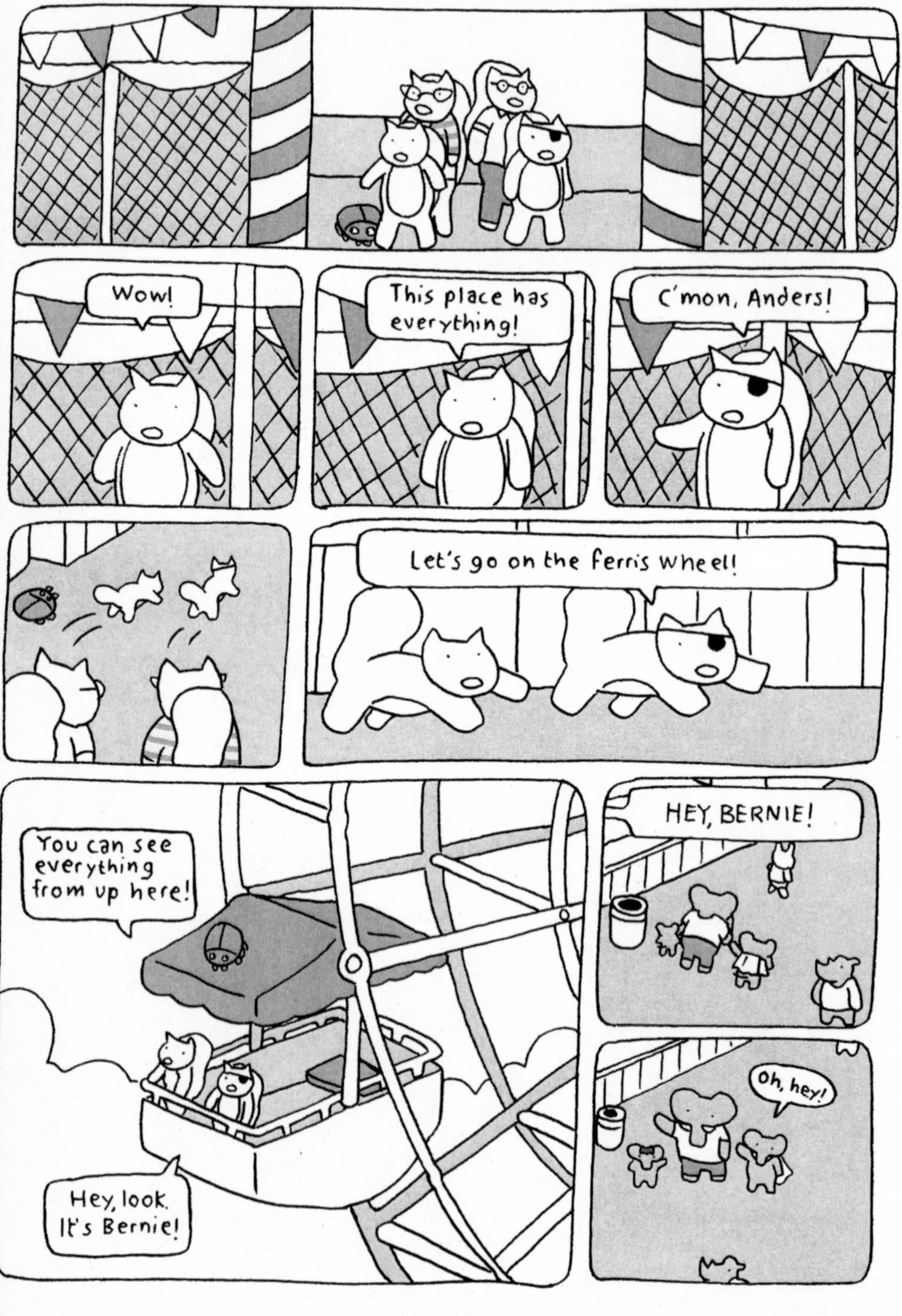
Wow!
This place has everything!
C'mon, Anders!
Let's go on the ferris wheel!
You can see everything from up here!
Hey, look. It's Bernie!
HEY, BERNIE!
Oh, hey!

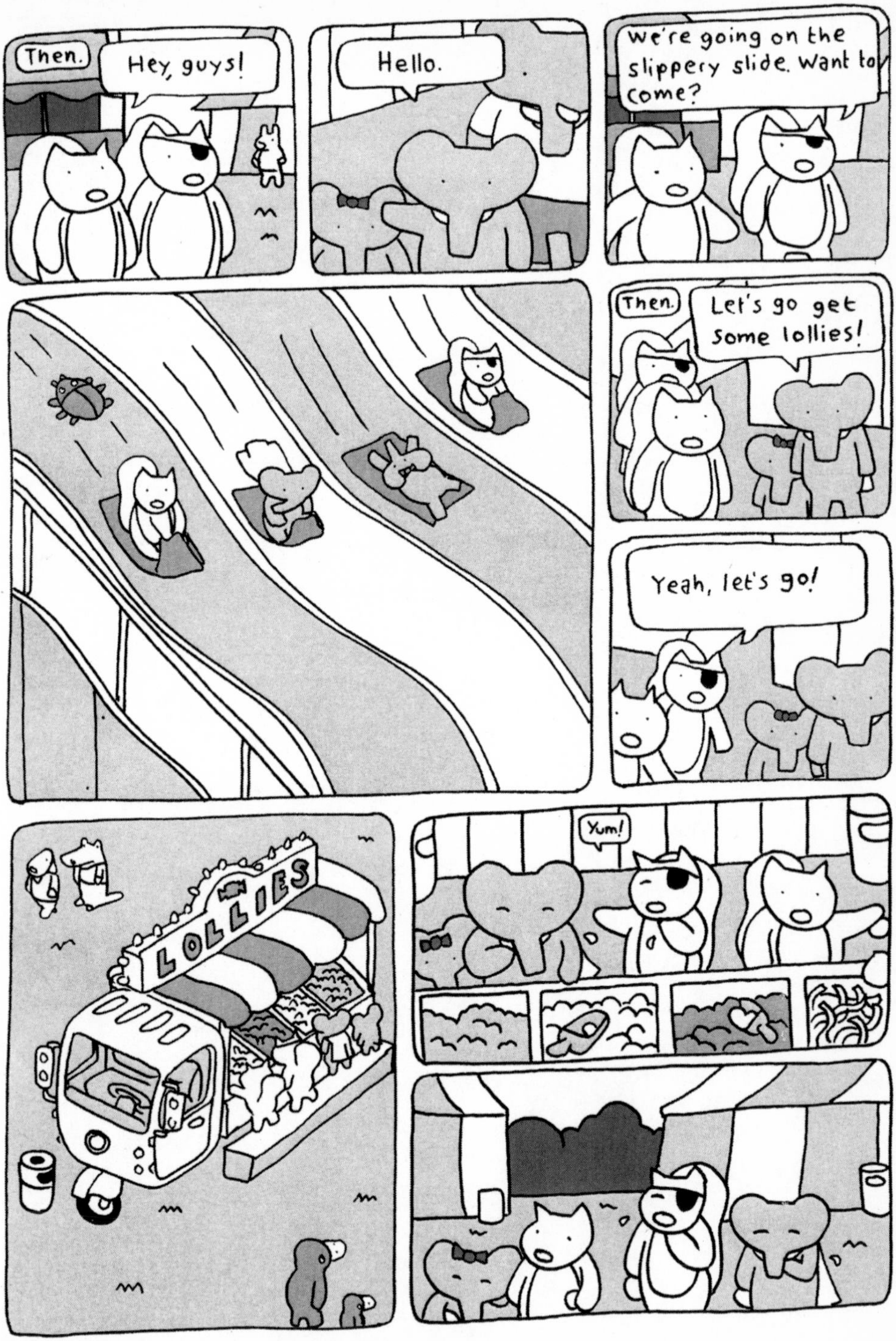
Then.
Hey, guys!
Hello.
We're going on the slippery slide. Want to come?
Then.
Let's go get some lollies!
Yeah, let's go!
LOLLIES
Yum!

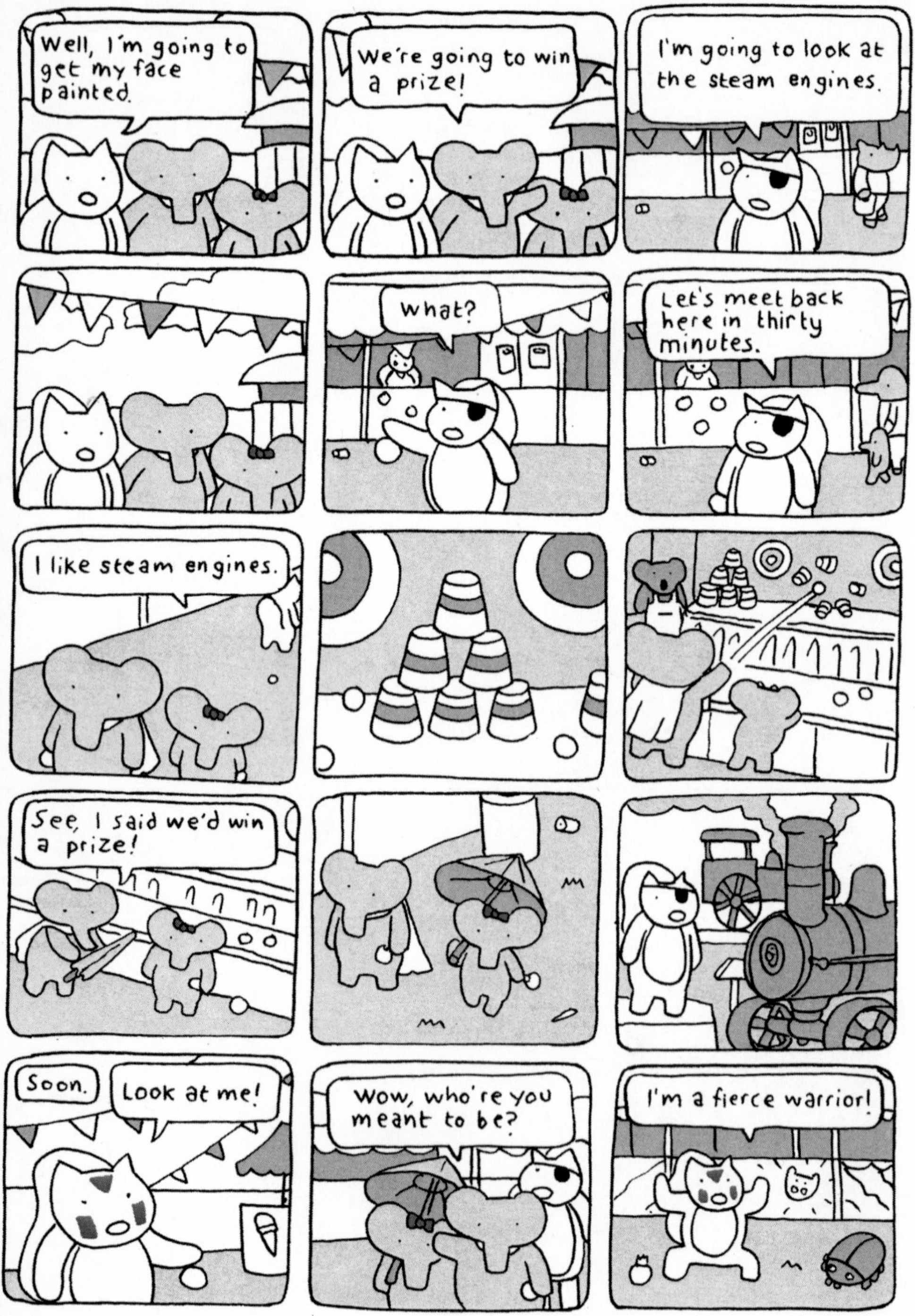
Well, I'm going to get my face painted.
We're going to win a prize!
I'm going to look at the steam engines.
What?
Let's meet back here in thirty minutes.
I like steam engines.
See, I said we'd win a prize!
Soon.
Look at me!
Wow, who're you meant to be?
I'm a fierce warrior!

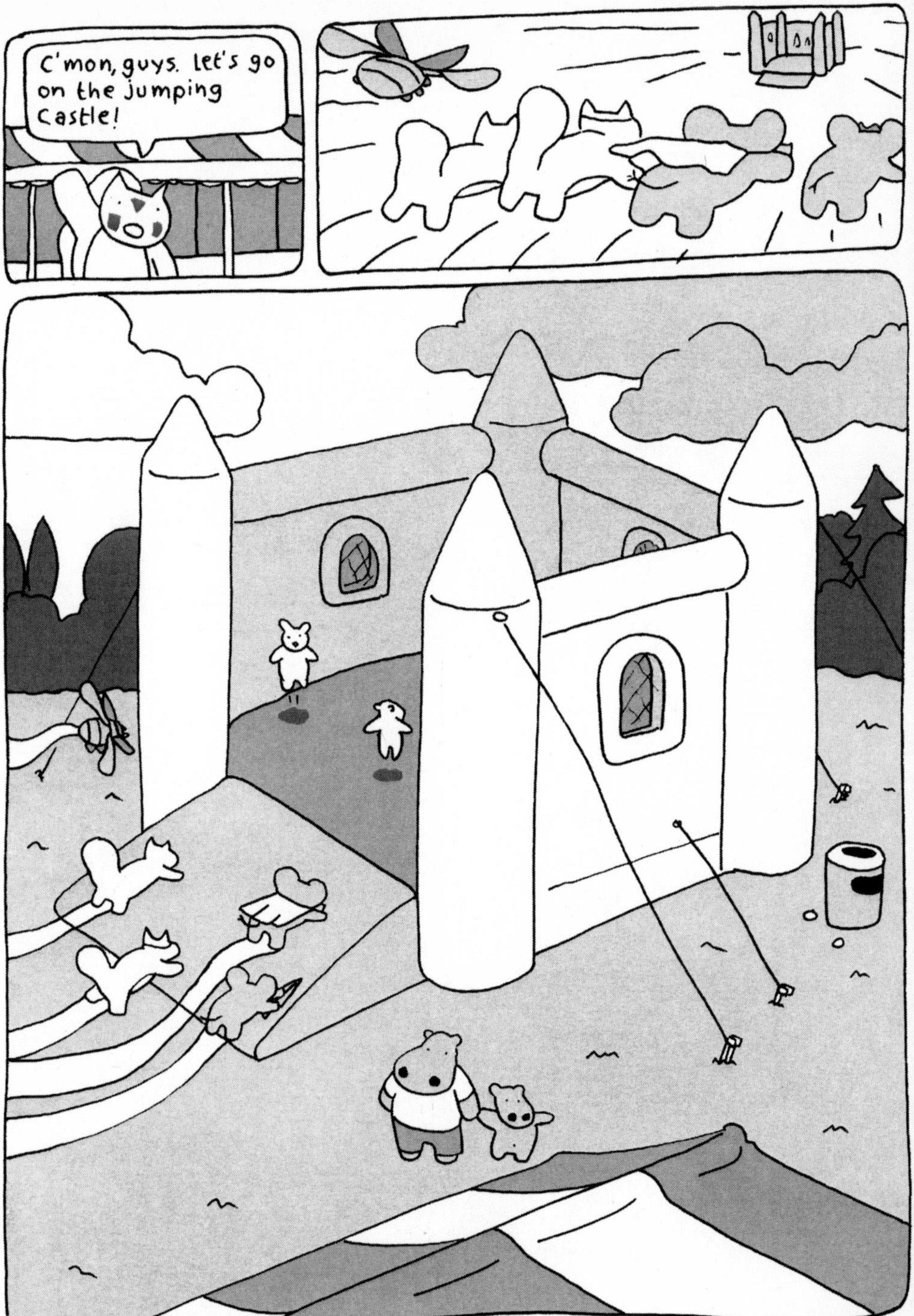
C'mon, guys. Let's go on the jumping castle!

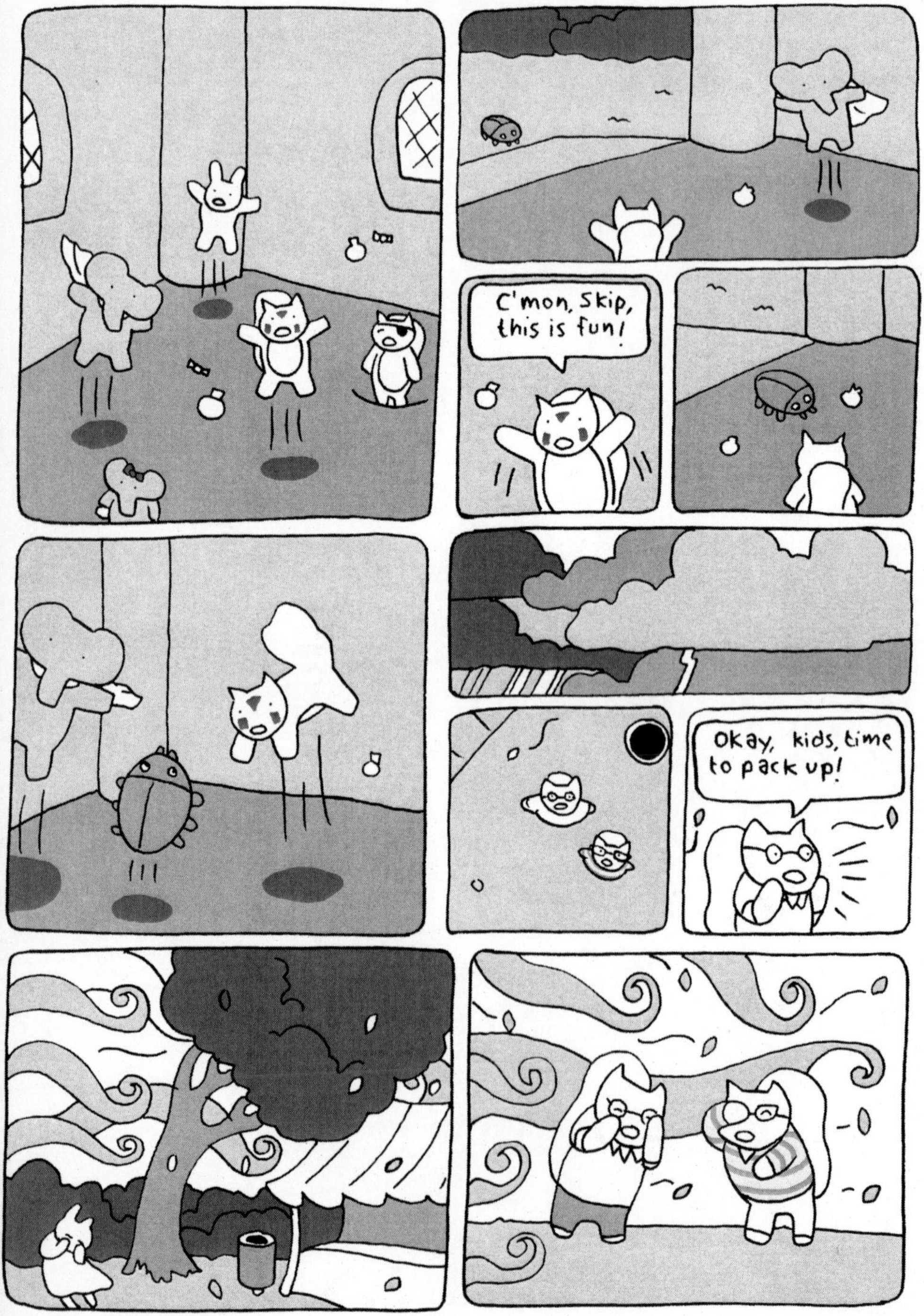
C'mon, Skip, this is fun!
Okay, kids, time to pack up!

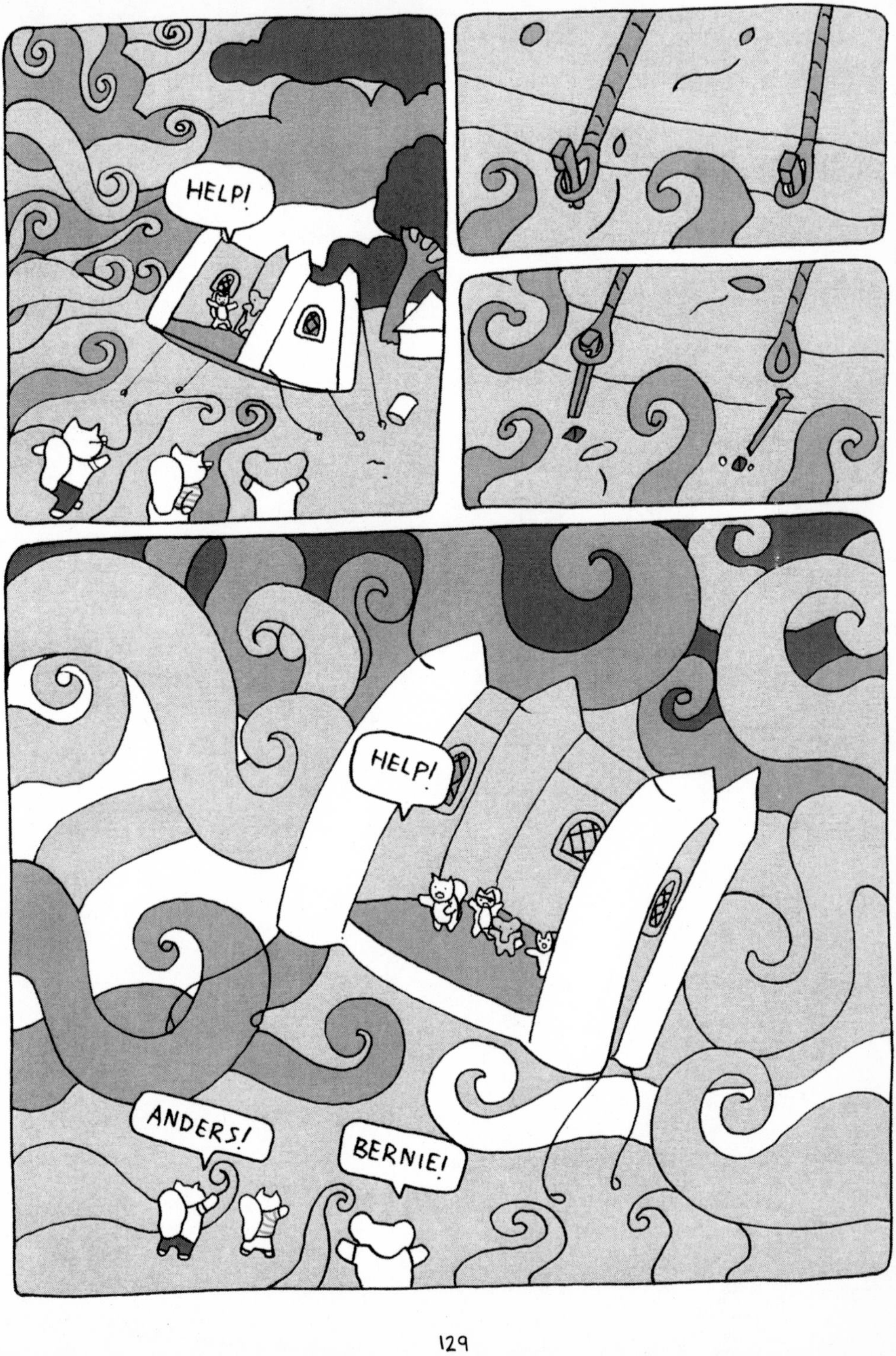
HELP!
HELP!
ANDERS!
BERNIE!

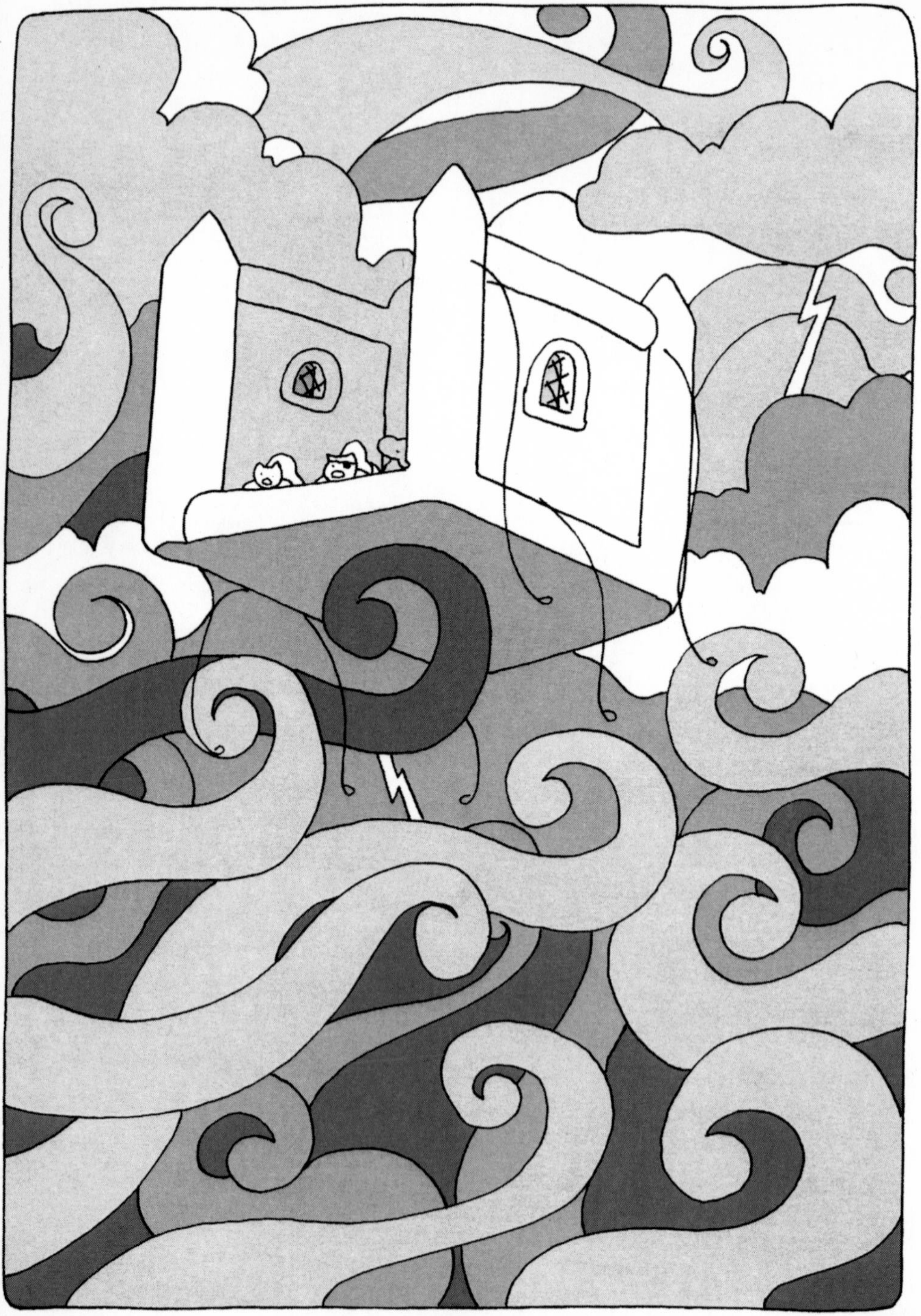

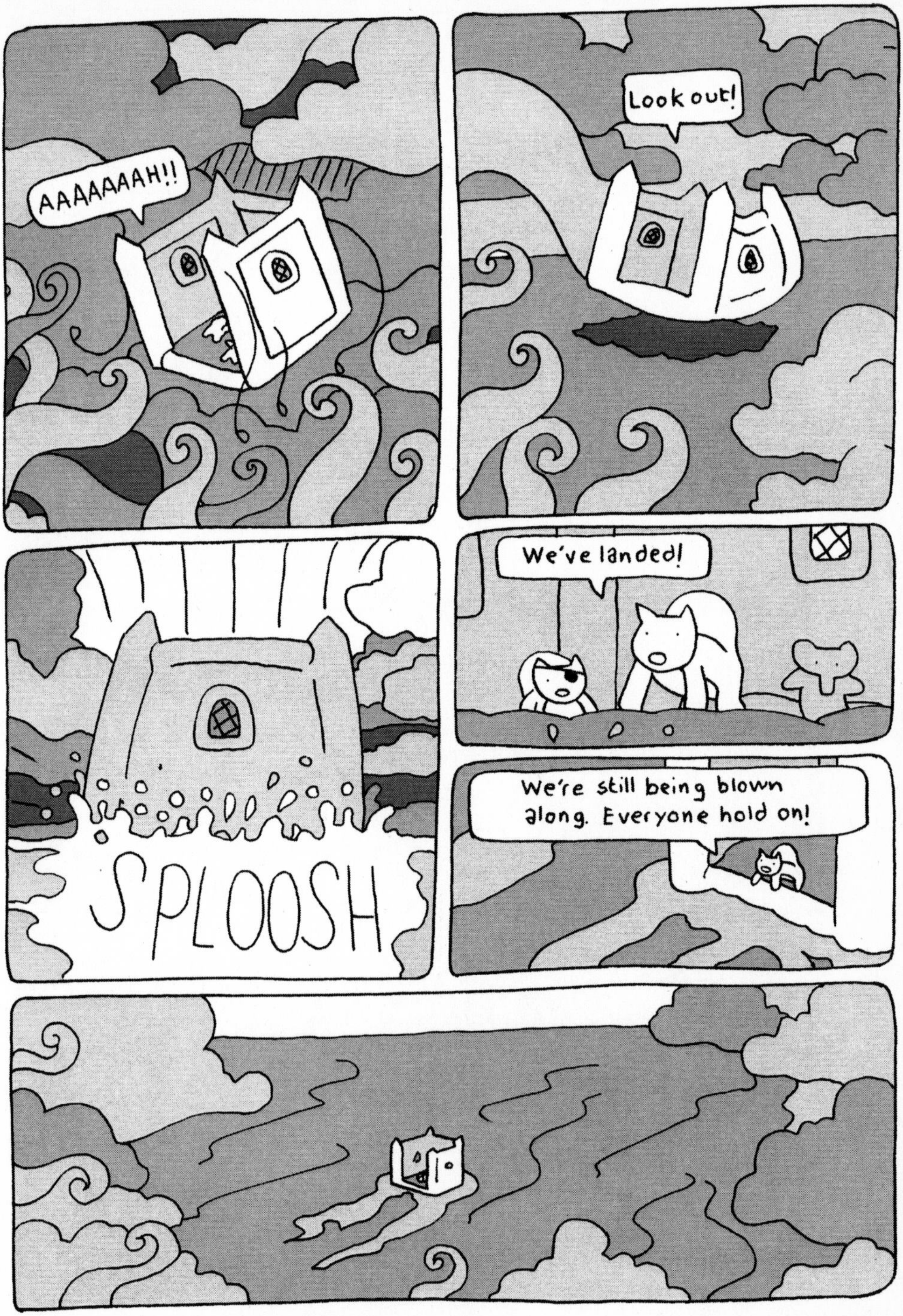

AAAAAAAH!!
Look out!
SPLOOSH
We've landed!
We're still being blown along. Everyone hold on!

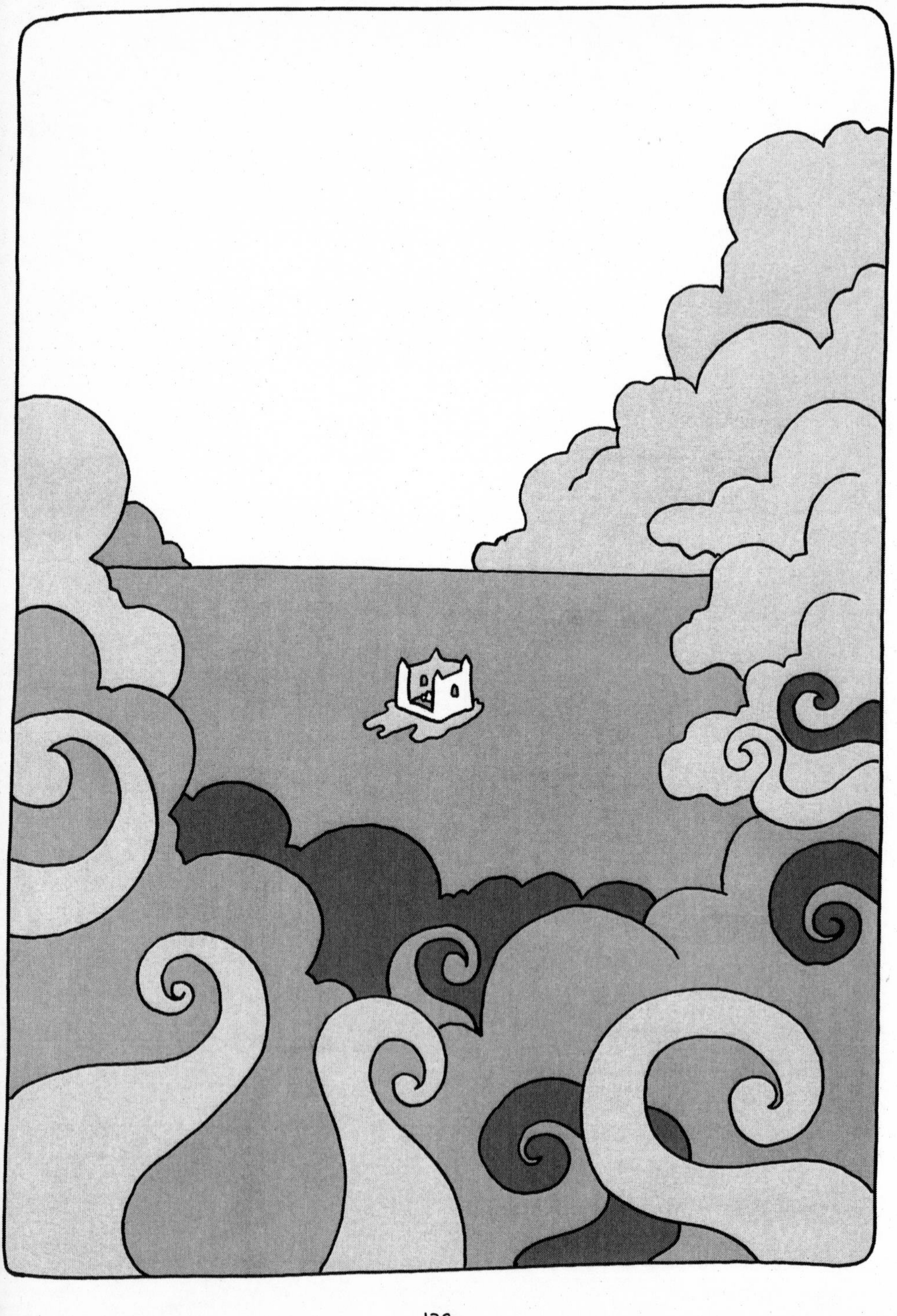

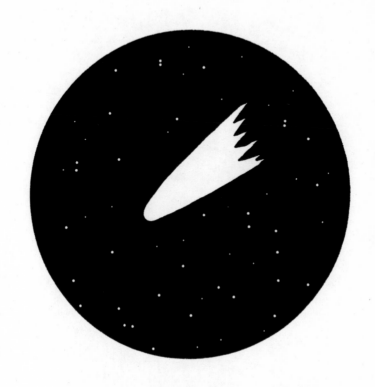

Chapter 10

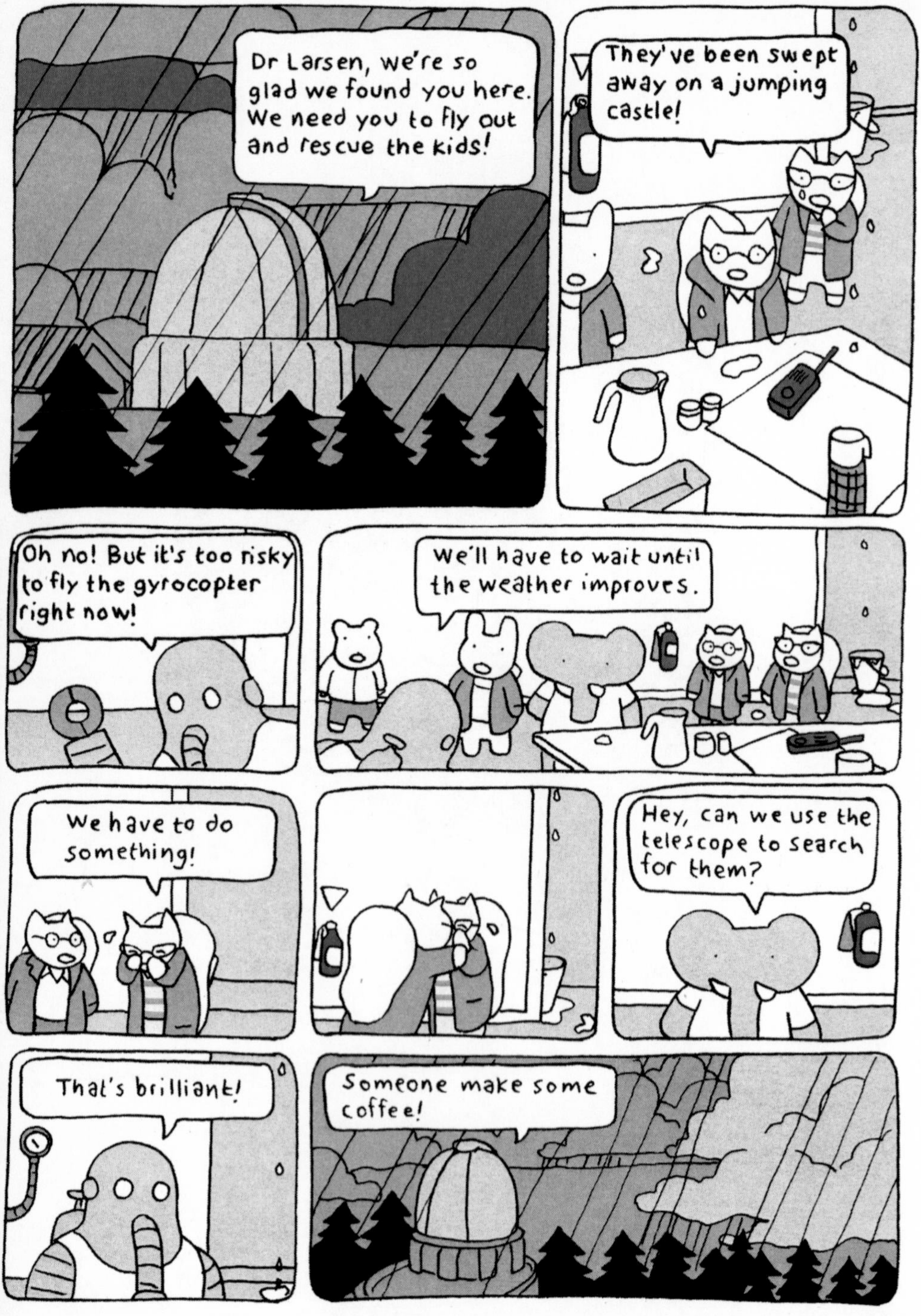
Dr Larsen, we're so glad we found you here. We need you to fly out and rescue the kids!
They've been swept away on a jumping castle!
Oh no! But it's too risky to fly the gyrocopter right now!
We'll have to wait until the weather improves.
We have to do something!
Hey, can we use the telescope to search for them?
That's brilliant!
Someone make some coffee!

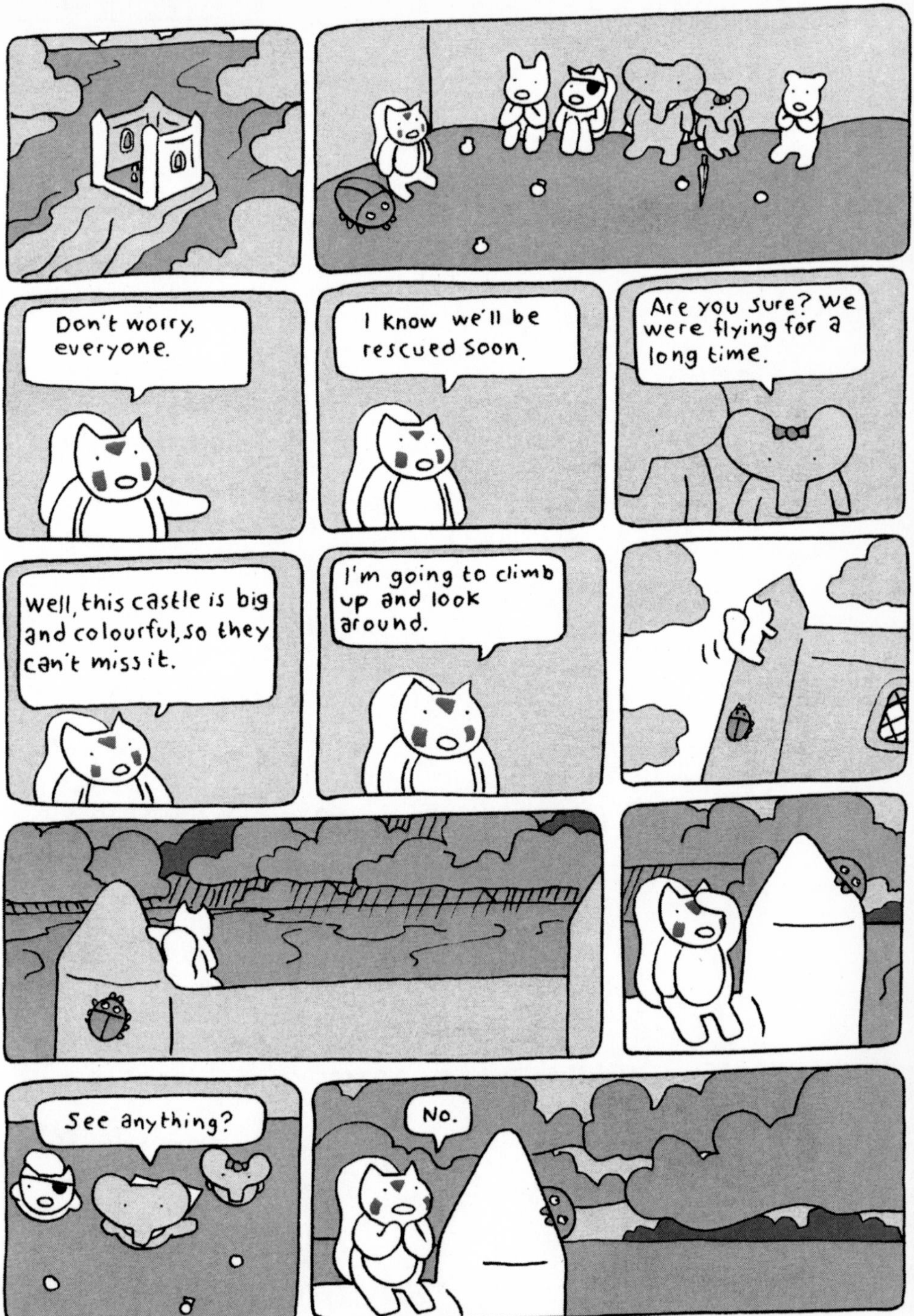
Don't worry, everyone.
I know we'll be rescued soon.
Are you sure? We were flying for a long time.
Well, this castle is big and colourful, so they can't miss it.
I'm going to climb up and look around.
See anything?
No.

Soon.

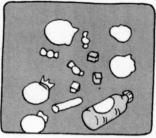

We should try to save these lollies.

We may be here for a while.

But I'm hungry.

Well, we can eat one or two.

Aren't you going to eat some, Anders?

I'm saving mine for Skip.

It will be dark soon.

Skip is cool.

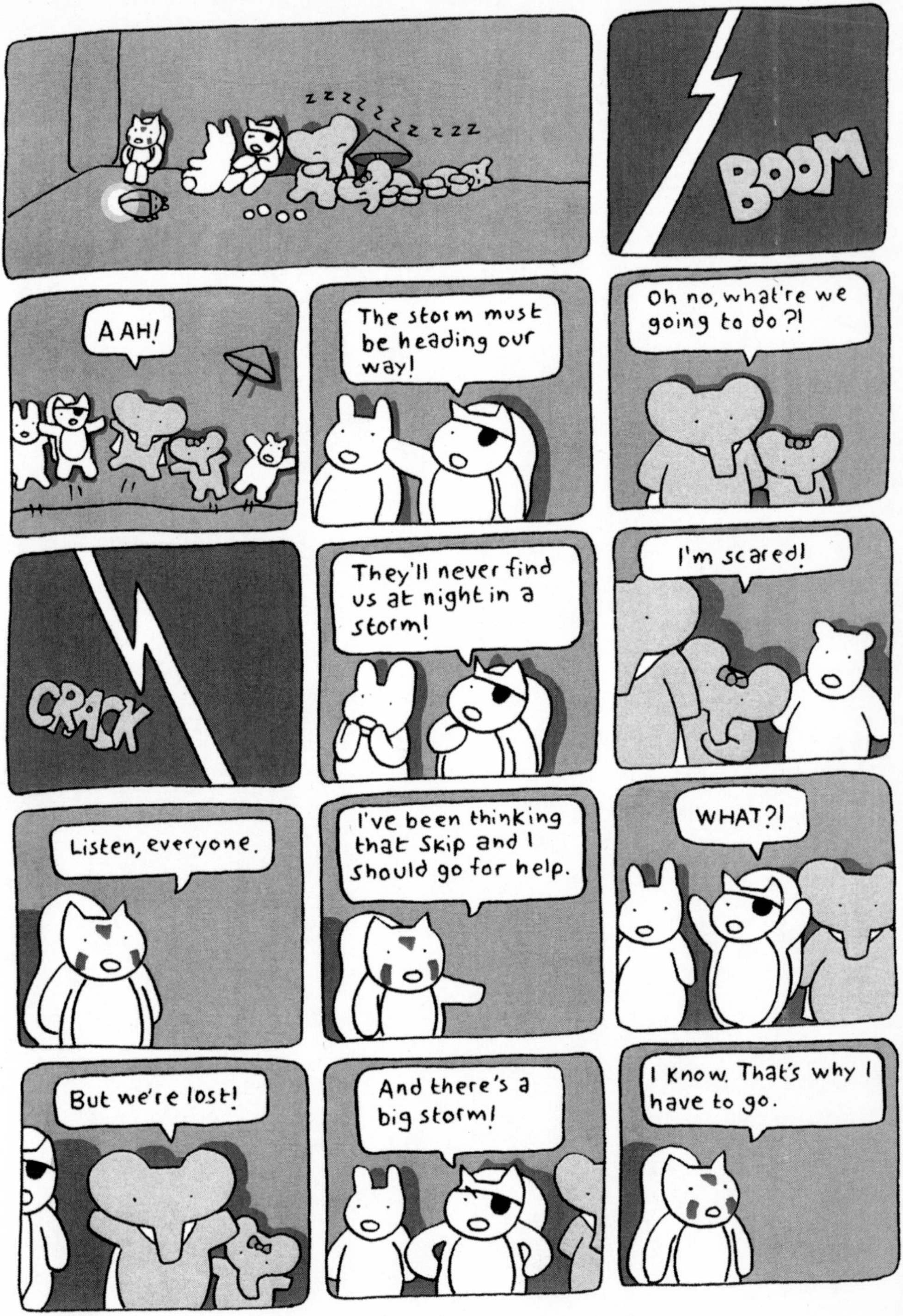
Z Z Z Z Z Z Z Z Z Z Z
BOOM
AAH!
The storm must be heading our way!
Oh no, what're we going to do?!
CRACK
They'll never find us at night in a storm!
I'm scared!
Listen, everyone.
I've been thinking that Skip and I should go for help.
WHAT?!
But we're lost!
And there's a big storm!
I know. That's why I have to go.

But it'll be dark without Skip.

I know.

And there's something else I have to ask.

I think Skip and I should take the rest of the lollies with us.

Why?!

To give Skip energy to fly and make light.

But we'll get hungry and it will be dark.

Anders is right. It's our best chance for rescue.

Let's vote on it. I vote to give the lollies to Anders so he can fly home.

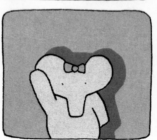

All those in favour raise your hand.

Okay, Anders, it's up to you and Skip.

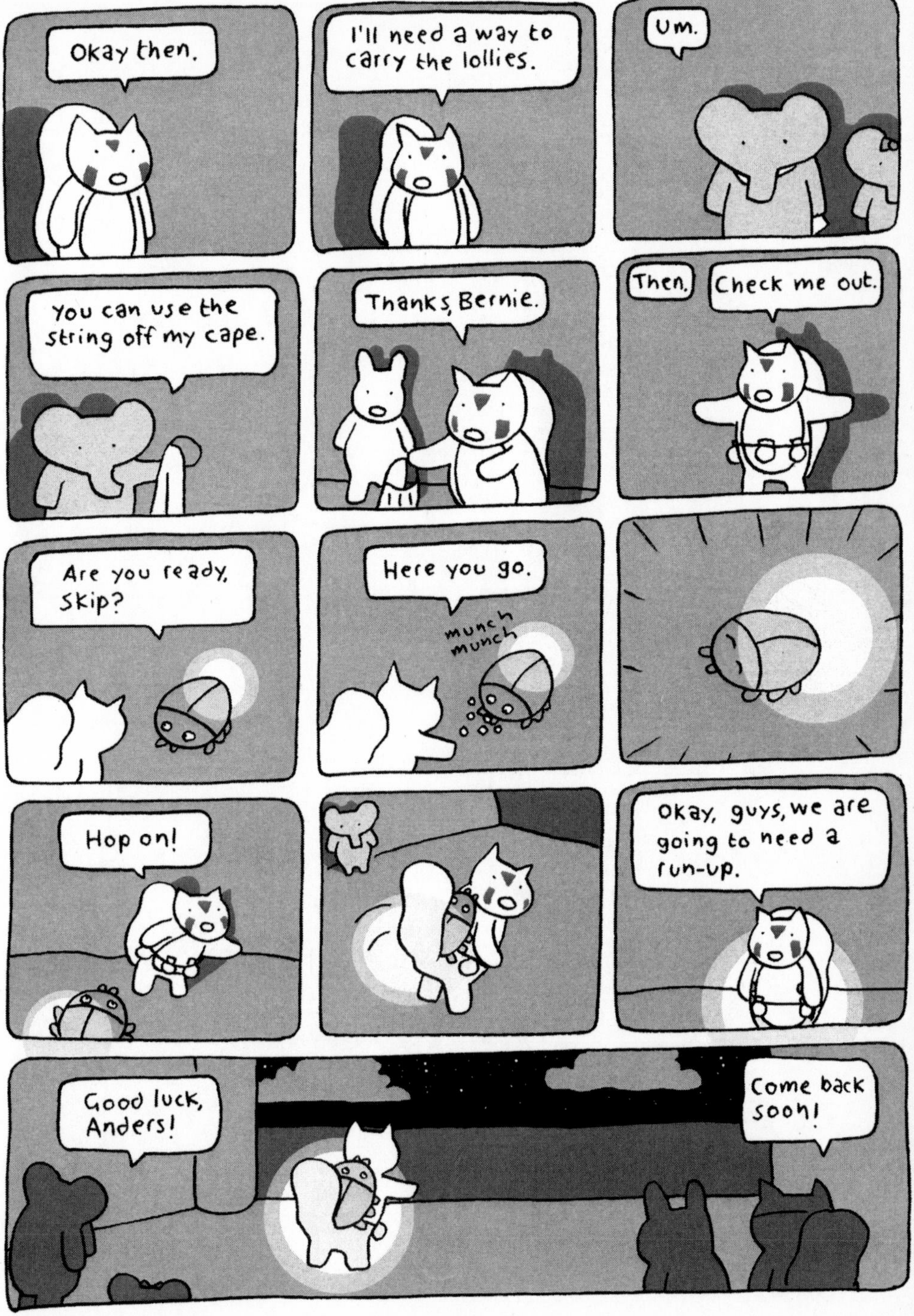
Okay then.
I'll need a way to carry the lollies.
Um.
You can use the string off my cape.
Thanks, Bernie.
Then.
Check me out.
Are you ready, Skip?
Here you go.
munch munch
Hop on!
Okay, guys, we are going to need a run-up.
Good luck, Anders!
Come back soon!

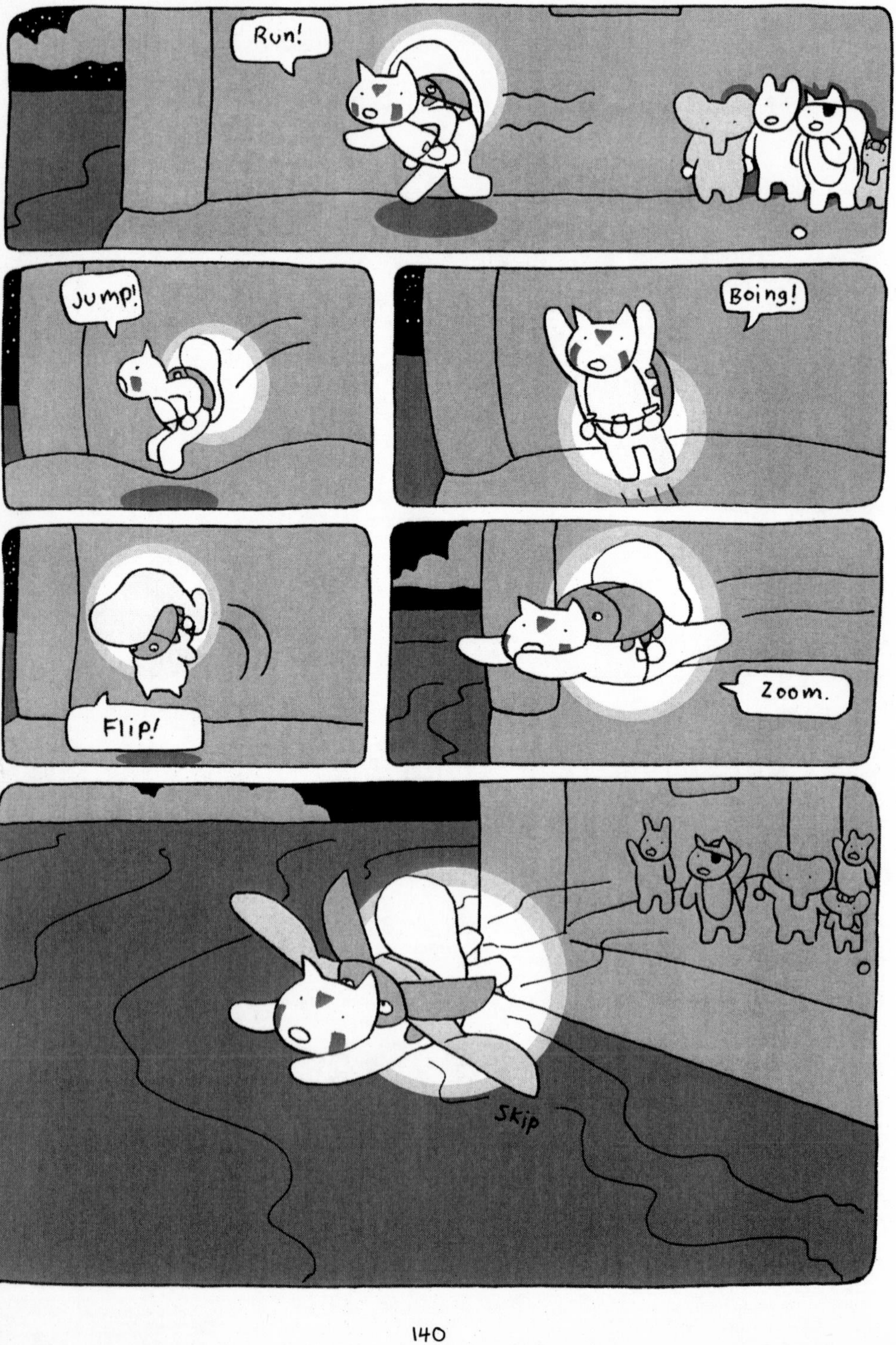
Run!
Jump!
Boing!
Flip!
Zoom.
Skip

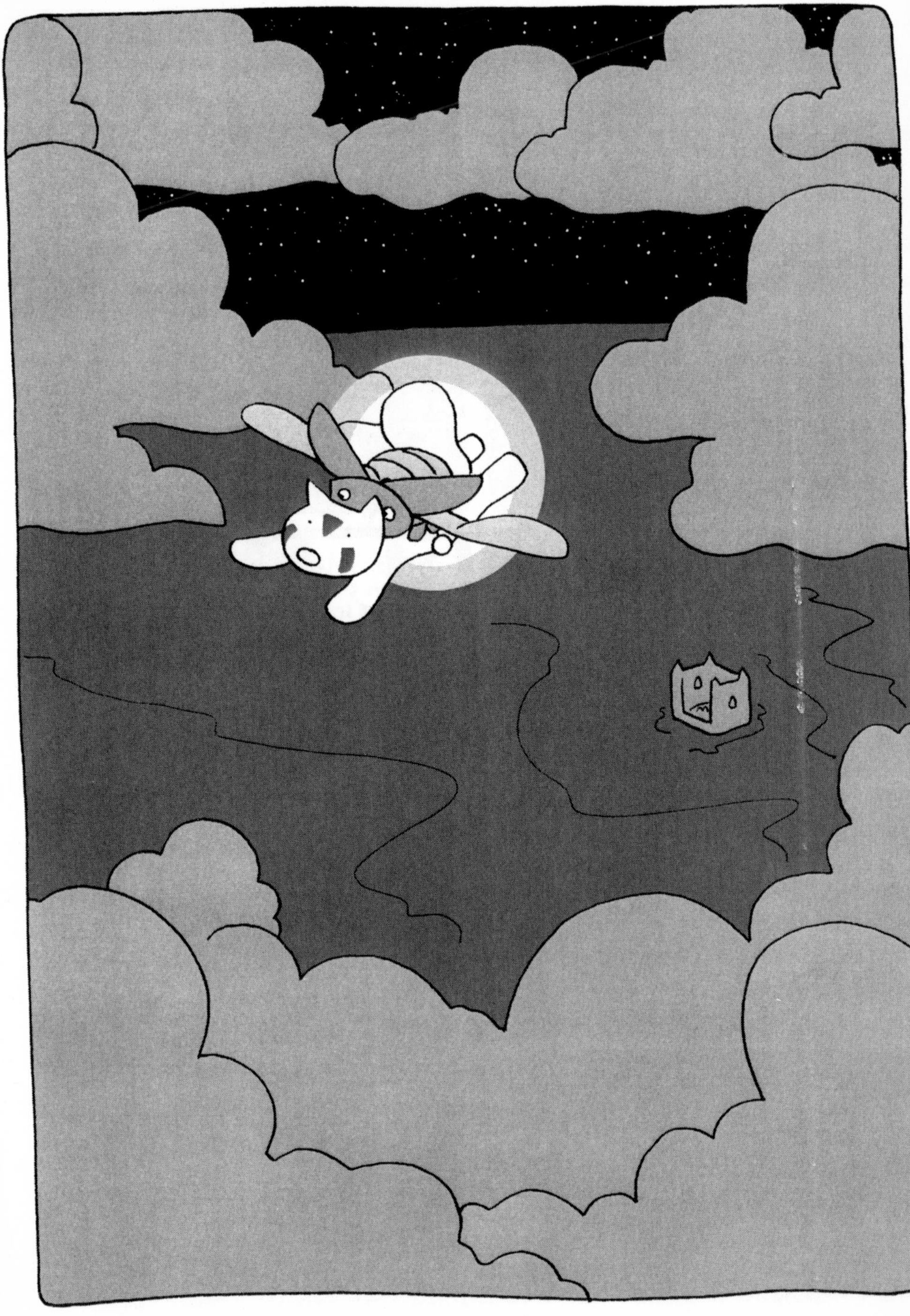

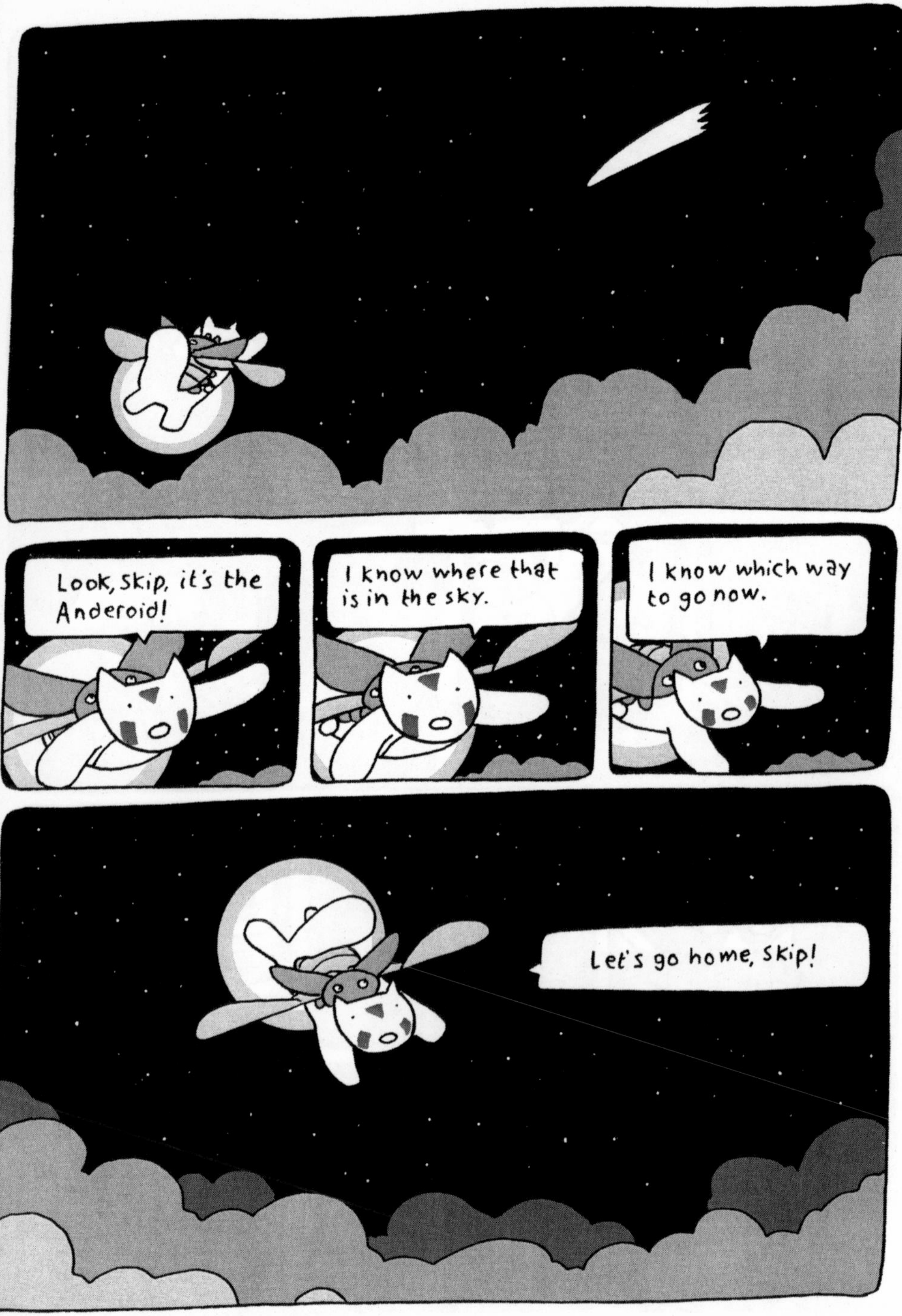
Look, Skip, it's the Anderoid!
I know where that is in the sky.
I know which way to go now.
Let's go home, Skip!

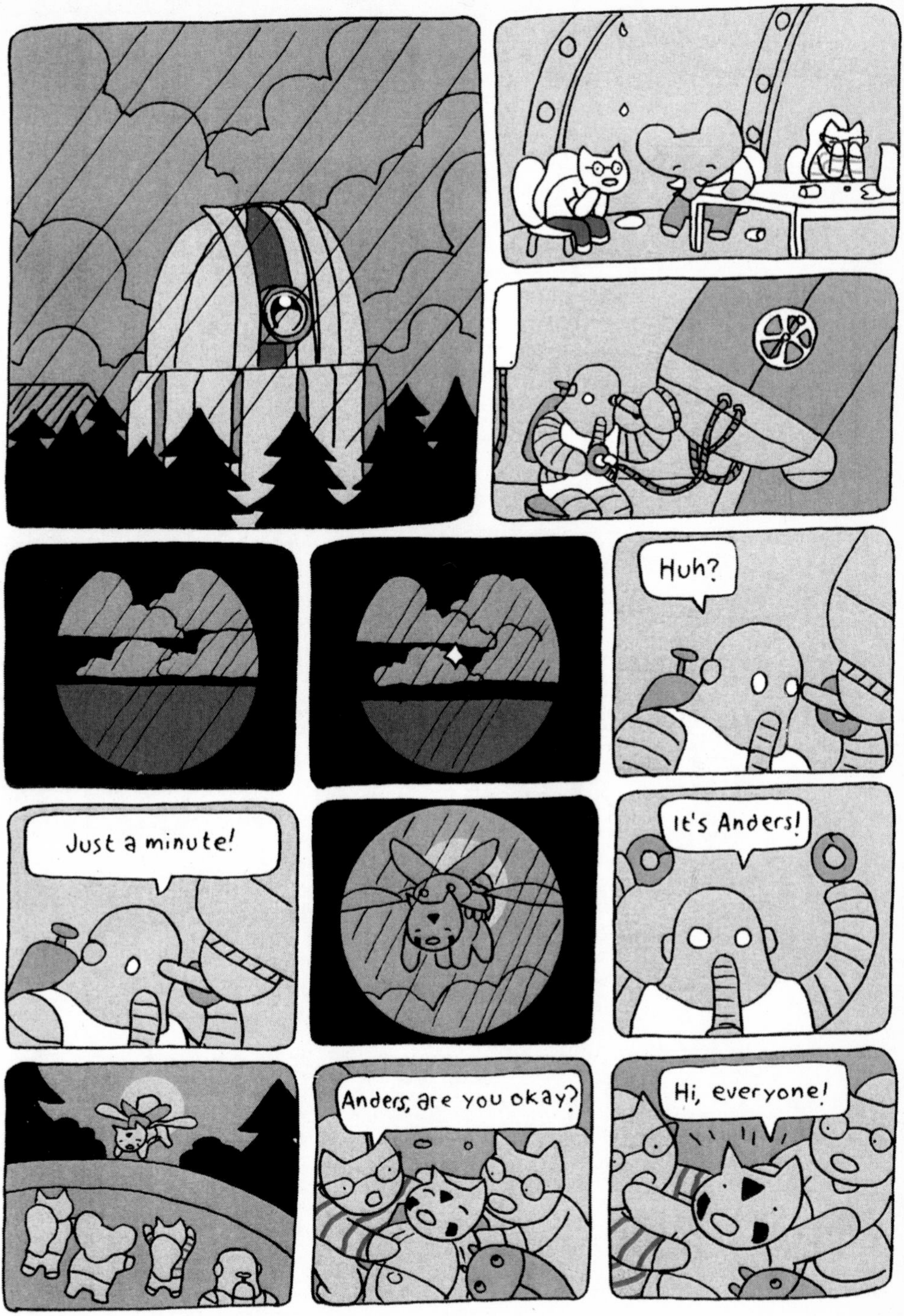
Huh?
Just a minute!
It's Anders!
Anders, are you okay?
Hi, everyone!

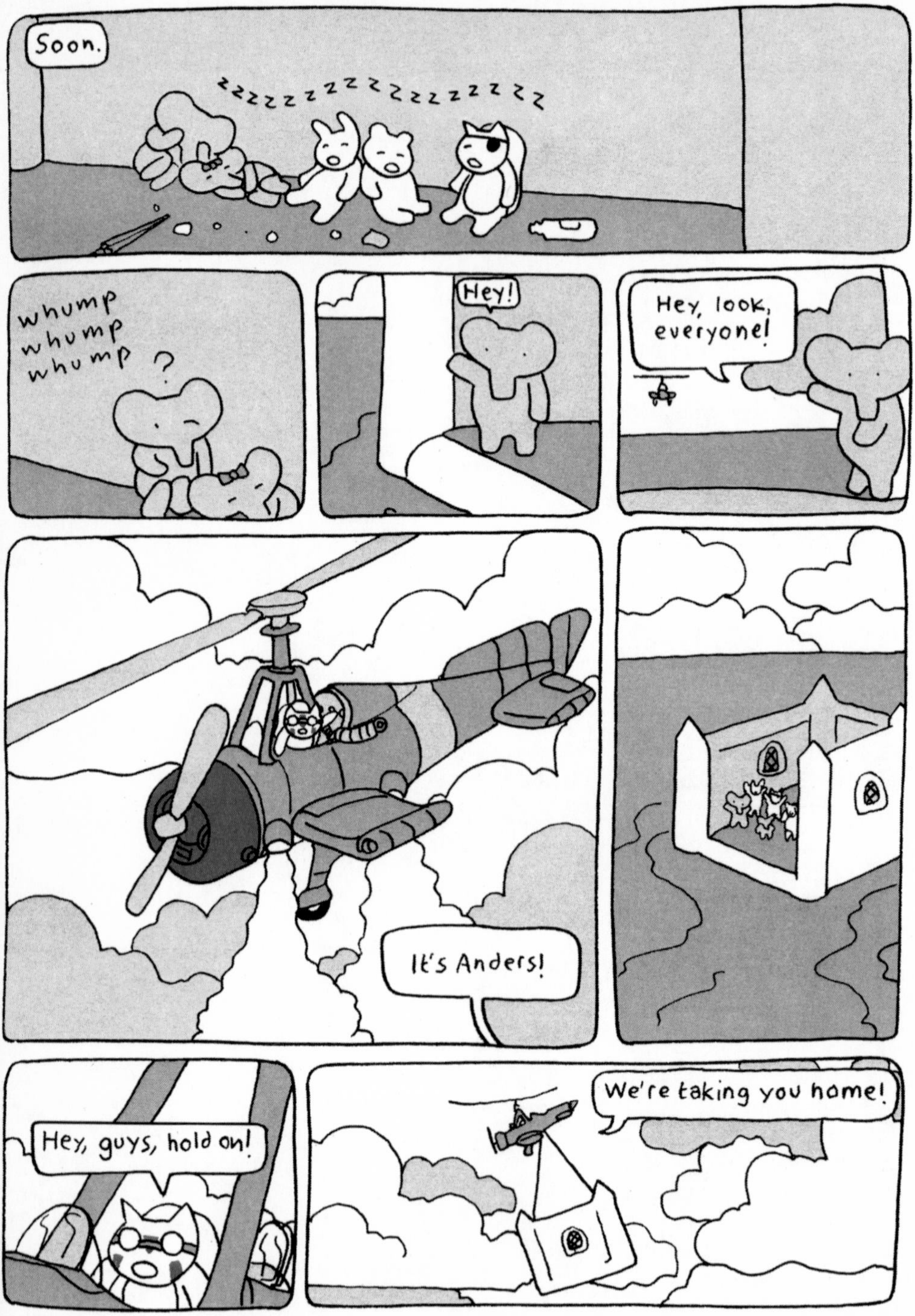
Soon.
zzzzzzzzzzzzzzzzz
whump
whump
whump
?
Hey!
Hey, look, everyone!
It's Anders!
Hey, guys, hold on!
We're taking you home!

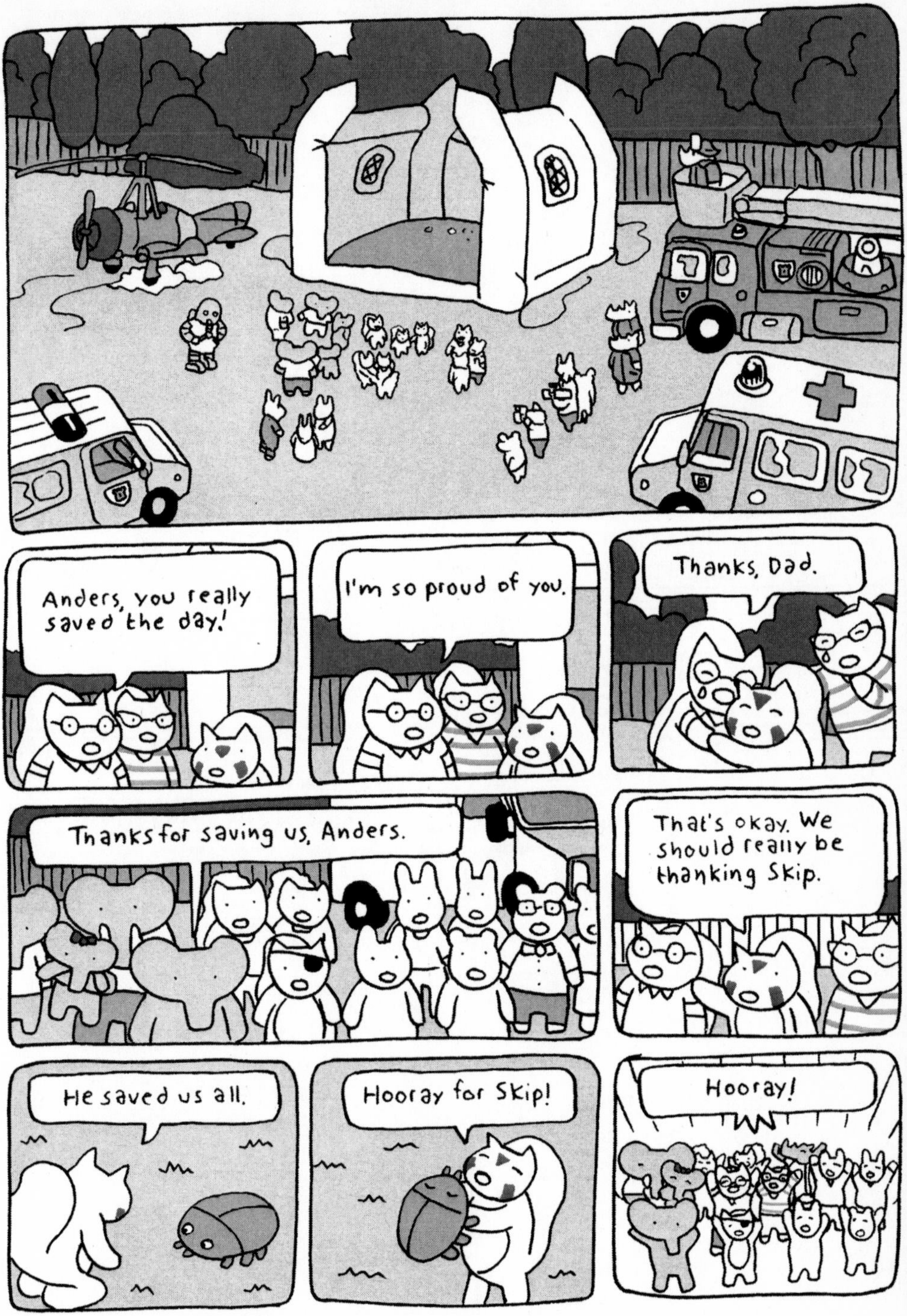
Anders, you really saved the day!
I'm so proud of you.
Thanks, Dad.
Thanks for saving us, Anders.
That's okay. We should really be thanking Skip.
He saved us all.
Hooray for Skip!
Hooray!

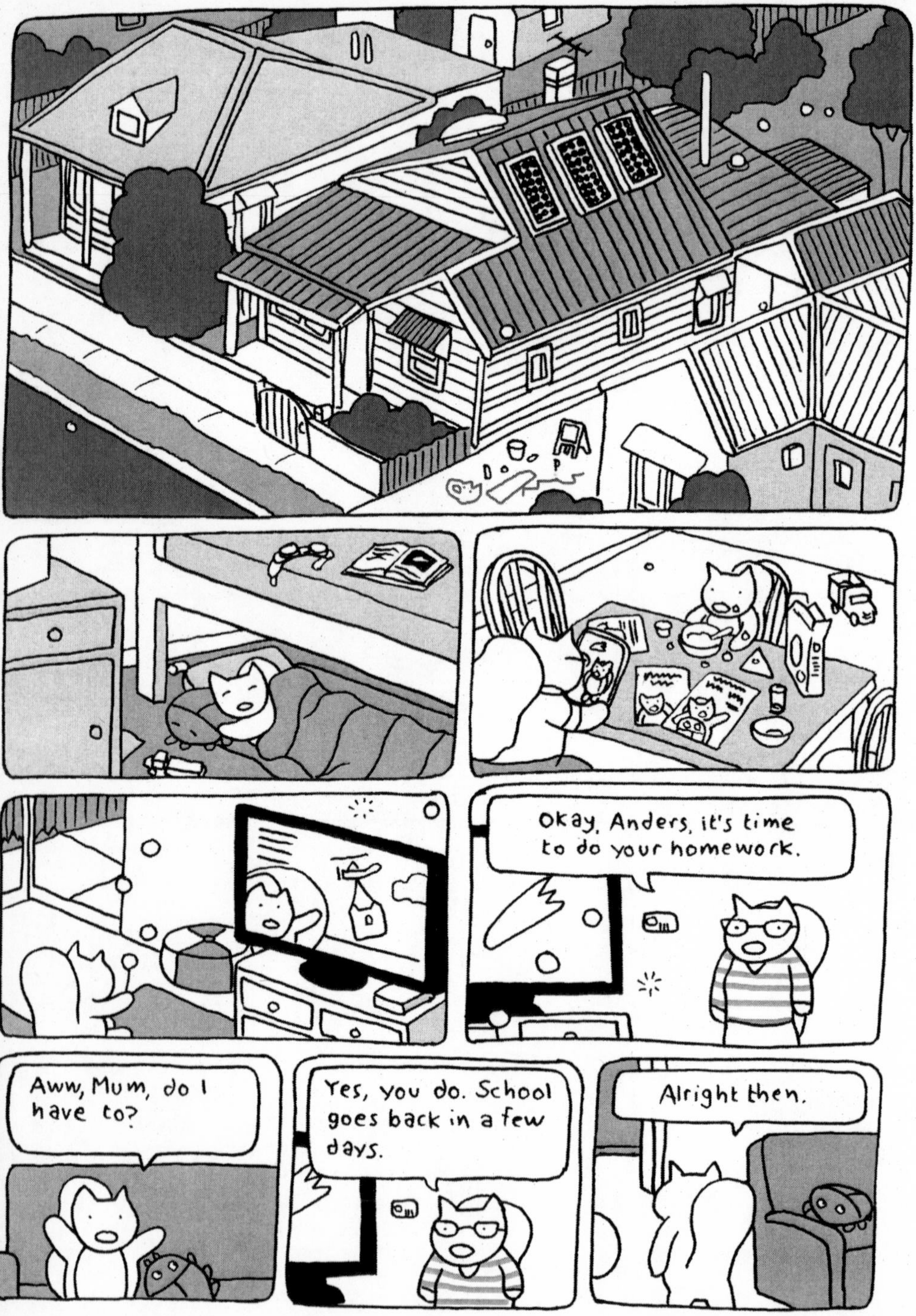
Okay, Anders, it's time to do your homework.
Aww, Mum, do I have to?
Yes, you do. School goes back in a few days.
Alright then.

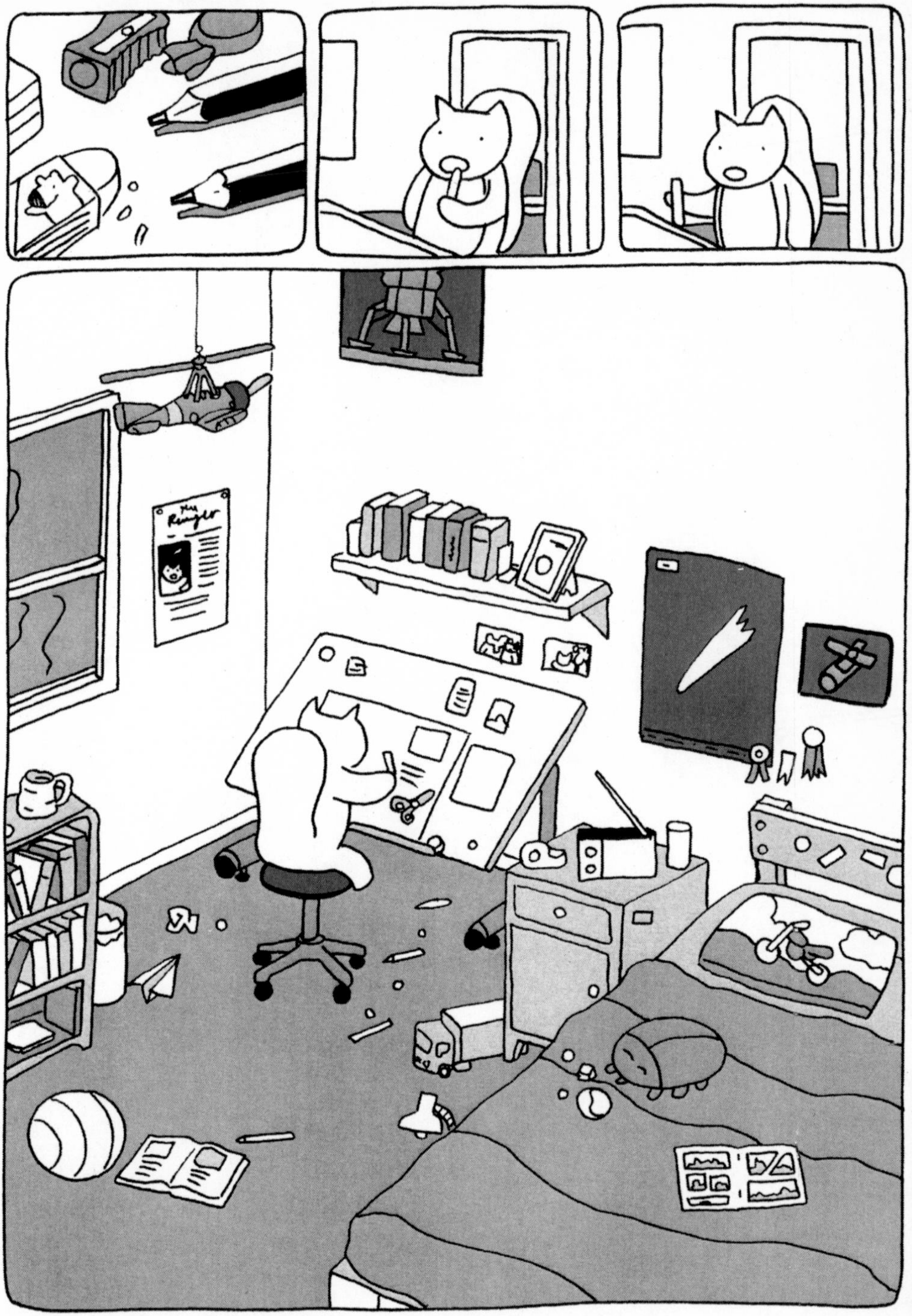

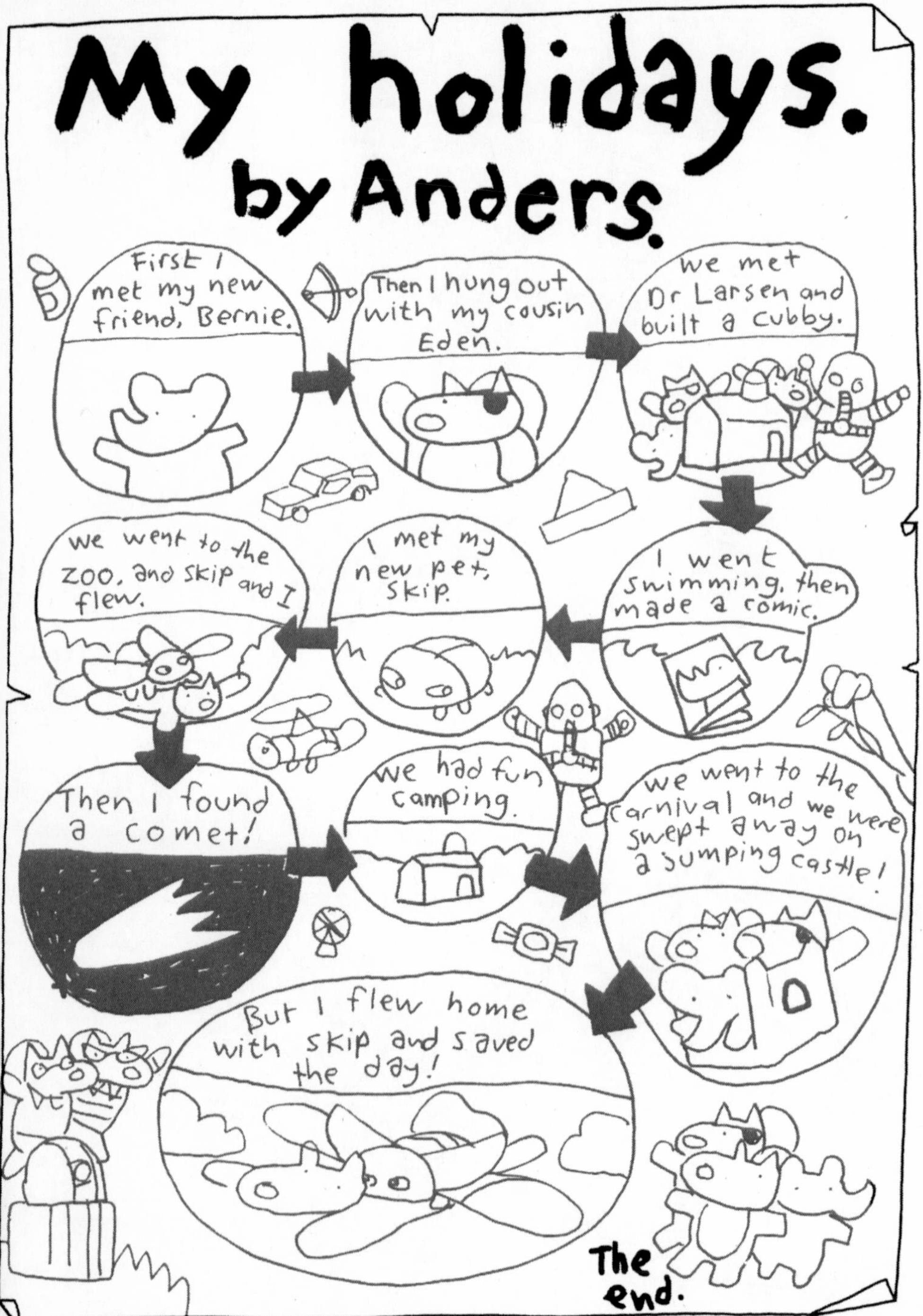
My holidays.
by Anders.
First I met my new friend, Bernie.
Then I hung out with my cousin Eden.
we met Dr Larsen and built a cubby.
I went swimming, then made a comic.
I met my new pet, Skip.
we went to the zoo, and Skip and I flew.
Then I found a comet!
we had fun camping.
we went to the carnival and we were swept away on a jumping castle!
But I flew home with Skip and saved the day!
The end.

Acknowledgements

I would like to thank the Australian Society
of Authors for their support, as well as the
Atlantic Centre for the Arts Residency Program,
particularly Dean Haspiel for his guidance.
Thanks to Rohan, Lucas and Charlotte.
I would also like to thank Erica Wagner, Elise Jones
and Sandra Nobes for their expertise and patience.

What is a
COMET?

A comet is a large icy ball of dirt and ice that zooms through space.

As it flies closer to the sun, it heats up.

This causes the comet to leave a trail of gas and dust behind it for thousands of kilometers.

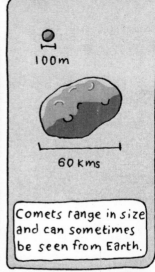

100m

60 kms

Comets range in size and can sometimes be seen from Earth.

Earth

Sun

As the comet flies through the solar system, the tail will turn away from the sun and grow longer.

There are over 5000 known comets, with more and more being discovered frequently.

Stay tuned for Anders' next adventure!

Gregory Mackay

About the Author

Gregory Mackay has been making comics since school.
He enjoys drawing and watercolour painting.
He likes drawing aeroplanes and machines,
as well as building models and painting pictures.
Anders and the Comet is his first book for children.